About

Rachael Thomas has al[...]
and is thrilled to be a M[...]
and works on a farm i[...]
glamour of a Mills &[...]
that makes slipping into her characters' worlds all the
more appealing. When she's not writing, or working
on the farm, she enjoys photography and visiting
historical castles and grand houses. Visit her at
rachaelthomas.co.uk.

Jennifer Hayward has been a fan of romance since
filching her sister's novels to escape her teenage angst.
Her career in journalism and PR, including years of
working alongside powerful, charismatic CEOs and
travelling the world, has provided perfect fodder for the
fast-paced, sexy stories she likes to write, always with
a touch of humour. A native of Canada's East Coast,
Jennifer lives in Toronto with her Viking husband and
young Viking-in-training.

USA TODAY bestselling author **Stefanie London** is a
voracious reader who has dreamed of being an author
her whole life. After sneaking several English-lit
subjects into her "very practical" business degree, she
got a job in corporate communications. But it wasn't
long before she turned to romance fiction. She recently
left her hometown of Melbourne to start a new
adventure in Toronto and now spends her days writing
contemporary romances with humour, heat and heart.

For more information on Stefanie and her books, check
out her website at stefanie-london.com or her Facebook
page at Facebook.com/stefanielondonauthor.

Postcards
COLLECTION

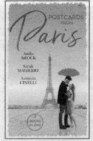

January 2019

February 2019

March 2019

April 2019

May 2019

June 2019

Postcards from New York

RACHAEL THOMAS

JENNIFER HAYWARD

STEFANIE LONDON

MILLS & BOON

First Published in Great Britain 2019
By Mills & Boon, an imprint of HarperCollins *Publishers*
1 London Bridge Street, London, SE1 9GF

POSTCARDS FROM NEW YORK © 2019 Harlequin Books S.A.

A Child Claimed by Gold © 2017 Rachael Thomas
A Debt Paid in the Marriage Bed © 2017 Jennifer Drogell
A Dangerously Sexy Secret © 2016 Stefanie Little

ISBN: 978-0-263-27568-1

0219

MIX
Paper from
responsible sources
FSC™ C007454

This book is produced from independently certified FSC™ paper to ensure responsible forest management.

For more information visit: www.harpercollins.co.uk/green

Printed and bound in Spain
by CPI, Barcelona

A CHILD CLAIMED
BY GOLD

RACHAEL THOMAS

CHAPTER ONE

NIKOLAI CUNNINGHAM BRACED himself against the icy-cold winds of the homeland he'd turned his back on as he waited for Emma Sanders to arrive on the next train. The heavy grey sky held the promise of more snow and matched his anger that a complete stranger had interfered in his life, bringing him back to Russia and a family he'd long ago disowned. He and his mother had left Vladimir for New York when he was ten years old and the shadow of the events preceding that day still clung to them, threatening to unravel everything.

The train rumbled into the station and he prepared himself for what he was certain would be the worst few days imaginable. His life was in New York, and returning to Vladimir had never been part of his plans. That was until his estranged grandmother had crept from the past, offering her family story to *World in Photographs*.

He'd also been contacted, no doubt because his grandmother had very graciously provided the name he now lived under, but he'd refused. At least, until he'd learnt his grandmother was more than ready to talk and expose everything he and his mother had fled from, probably putting the blame firmly at his mother's feet. In a bid to protect his mother from their painful past, and prevent his name being linked to the family name of Petrushov once more, he'd had no option but to return.

He stood back and watched the travellers climbing down from the train, scanning them quickly, trying to remember the image he'd seen of Miss Sanders on the Internet and match it to one of the disembarking passengers. Then he saw her, wrapped up against the cold in true Russian style, only her face visible between the *faux* fur hat and scarf. She looked about her nervously, clutching the handle of her small case in a gloved hand. She could have been Russian, she blended in so well, but her apprehension and uncertainty singled her out as a stranger to Vladimir.

Accepting he had to do this and face whatever came from it for his mother's sake, he pulled his coat collar tighter against the cold and walked towards her. She looked at him and he held her gaze as he strode along the platform, the determination to get this over with as fast as possible dominating all other thought.

'Miss Sanders.' He stopped in front of her, registering her height, which almost matched his, something he found strangely pleasing.

'Mr Petrushov?' Her voice was as clear and crisp as a frosty morning, but by contrast her eyes were a mossy green, reminding him of the depths of Russian forests in summer. Why was he noticing such details? She distracted him, knocked him off course, and only now he registered how she'd addressed him.

Nikolai's anger intensified. Beautiful or not, Miss Sanders obviously hadn't done her research well. It had been seventeen years since he'd abandoned the name Petrushov in favour of his stepfather's name, Cunningham.

'Nikolai Cunningham,' he corrected then, before any questions could be asked, continued, 'I trust you enjoyed your train journey from Moscow?'

'Sorry—and yes, I did, Mr Cunningham.' He saw her dark brows furrow in confusion, but refused to elaborate on why he, a Russian-born man, had a distinctly American surname. That was none of her business and he had every intention it would stay that way.

He looked down at the young woman, wrapped up against the cruel winds of winter, and although her alluring green eyes were a distraction he was unable to put aside his anger towards her. 'And you must be Miss Sanders from *World in Photographs*?' He added silently to himself, *the woman who wants to rip open my mother's past and delve into my childhood, no doubt in order to further her career.*

'Please, call me Emma,' she said and held out her gloved hand to him. He didn't take it but looked into the lustrous green of her eyes and wondered what colour her hair was beneath the fur of her hat. Her photo on the Internet hadn't done her any justice: she was stunning.

Irritation mingled with the anger. This was the last woman he wanted to stir his interests. Just being here in Vladimir meant she had the power to cause real hurt to his mother and he strongly suspected she didn't know yet just how much. It was up to him to ensure she never realised just how dramatic the true story of his family was.

He fully intended that she would be distracted by the undeniable beauty of a Russian winter and had already organised plenty of photo opportunities to keep her from the real story. A story that would destroy his mother and upend his world if it got out. All he had to do was prevent her meeting with the grandmother he hadn't seen since he was ten but he didn't yet know how to achieve that.

'We should get out of the wind,' he said firmly, trying to ignore the way the colour of her eyes reminded him of his childhood summers here in Vladimir. It was a place he hadn't thought of for a long time and certainly didn't want to think of now. 'I took the liberty of booking into the same hotel; that way, I can be of as much help to you as possible.'

His motives were much less honourable. All he intended to do was ensure she saw only what he wanted her to see and certainly not what he feared his grandmother wanted to share with her—a family torn apart by deceit.

'Thank you.' She smiled up at him and satisfaction made him return the smile. He was already winning her round. Just a few more days of this nonsense and he could head back to New York and put all this behind him. 'That's very thoughtful of you.'

'The hotel has a very comfortable lounge where I suggest we go over just what you need for your article.'

She believed he was being thoughtful. What would she say if she knew he was determined to hide all he could, despite his grandmother's attempt to ruin the family name? That was another matter he had to deal with and one thing was for certain: Miss Emma Sanders wouldn't be a witness to that particular showdown.

'That would be a good idea.' She laughed softly and, although the scarf around her face hid her lips and she drew her shoulders up against the cold, from the way her eyes sparkled he could imagine she was smiling at him. The image stirred sensations which contrasted wildly with the anger and irritation he'd been harbouring since discovering that his grandmother had agreed to be interviewed for the magazine.

'Allow me,' he said and reached for her luggage, pleased it was a small case and her photography bag. This meant she didn't have any intentions to make her stay any longer than the three days *World in Photographs* had requested from him and his family.

His family. That was a joke.

'Thank you.' This time, as she pulled her scarf a little lower with gloved hands, he could see she was smiling. It also had an unexpected effect on him. The idea of kissing those lips flashed through his mind, sending a trail of blazing lust hurtling through him. That train of thought would achieve nothing and he grimly pushed it away. This was not a time to allow lust to reign and certainly not with this woman.

'This way, Miss Sanders,' he said purposefully, ignoring her invitation to use her first name, and walked briskly away without ensuring she was following, heading for the hotel he'd booked into. He'd purposefully chosen the same hotel as the interfering Miss Sanders, enabling him to ensure she didn't meddle in the dark, hidden past of his family. Had that been the right decision?

Now that he'd met Emma Sanders he knew he'd be able to charm and distract her, making sure she learnt only the romantic ideals about his family story she was no doubt searching for. The only problem was that he suspected he himself was in danger of falling victim to her charms and distractions.

'I expect you are used to this cold, but it's a shock for me,' she said as they stepped inside, out of the wind. The warmth of the hotel, set out as if a village of cosy log cabins, gave it an intimate and even romantic feel that would no doubt help his cause. Very soon he'd have Miss Emma Sanders believing he was more than pleased to talk about his family history.

'My home is in New York, Miss Sanders.'

'Oh,' she said, pulling off her hat as they entered the lounge area of the main part of the hotel, the heat of the log fire a welcome relief from outside. 'I'm sorry; I assumed you lived here with your grandmother.'

He watched as she removed her scarf, revealing long, straight hair the colour of sable, and for a brief moment he forgot himself, forgot that this woman had the power to hurt his mother and expose him for what he really was, as that earlier trail of lust streaked through him again. Mentally he shook himself. He might have a history of brief and hot affairs with women, but this was one woman he could not want.

'Never assume anything, Miss Sanders.' Angered by his reaction at seeing beneath the layers of dark fur she wore, as if born to Russian winters, he fought to keep his tone neutral. She was a beautiful woman, and his body's reaction to her meant that his voice was anything but neutral and much harsher than it should have been.

She looked up at him, a question in her eyes, her slender dark brows furrowed into a frown of confusion. 'Life has taught me that, Mr Petrushov.'

'Cunningham,' he corrected her again, but something in the way she said those words and the look of haunted fear which had rushed across her beautiful face as she'd spoken nudged at his conscience. He shouldn't be so hard, so aggressive. Not if he wanted to steer her away from the truth of his family. Maybe playing to the attraction sizzling between them would be the way to create that distraction?

He wondered what she meant as he picked up on the inference that life hadn't been easy for her. He resisted the urge to ask, not wanting to draw her into a conversation that may turn back on him. Over the years he'd become adept at providing just enough information about himself to satisfy people, but never enough for them to know the full facts.

'Then we already understand one another.' He pulled off his coat and hat, hung them up then took hers from her, his fingers unexpectedly brushing against hers. A jolt of heat surged through him and, as she pulled her hand back, she looked up at him, her green eyes wide and startled. Her full lips, slicked with gloss, parted and he had an almost uncontrollable urge to lower his head and kiss her. Not a gentle brushing of lips but a hard, demanding kiss. The kind of kiss which led to fierce and passionate sex.

What the hell was he thinking?

She stepped back away from him as a flush of colour covered her pale face and her eyes darkened to resemble the deepest ocean. She'd felt it too, of that there was no doubt. If she had been any other woman, he wouldn't have thought twice about acting on the attraction. But she wasn't any other woman. She could tear open his past, threatening not just his mother's happiness but his reputation. He wouldn't allow it to happen—not at any cost.

'Yes, yes, we do. We—we understand each other

perfectly.' She stumbled over her words and he stifled a smile of satisfaction. Maybe the attraction could be used to ensure she didn't find out just who he really was. If a touch and a brief moment of sexual chemistry could disarm her, that would be a pleasant way to distract her from digging around too much into his family's past.

Emma hated the way she could hardly form a sentence as Nikolai Cunningham all but scrutinised her. He had muddled her mind and sent her insides into turmoil from the moment they'd met. It was as if a spark of recognition had reached out from him, inexplicably drawing her closer.

She thought of Richard, the man she'd always wished could be more than just a friend, and compared him to this powerful specimen of masculinity. Richard was attractive but safe, but this man was undeniably handsome and oozed a lethal kind of sex appeal. She shivered as something arced between them. He held her gaze and she knew she had to remember he was also the man who held the key to her successfully completing this assignment and securing a long-term contract with *World in Photographs*.

What happened over the next few days could launch her career as a photographer. More importantly, it would provide a regular income, which was badly needed if she was to stand any chance at all of supporting her younger sister Jess as she embarked on a lifetime dream of becoming a ballerina. They'd both had so many knockbacks in life, going from foster home to foster home, that she wanted her younger sister to do what made her happy. And she was good at it—talented, in fact. After the things they'd experienced together, they both deserved happiness, and if Jess was happy then so was she.

The tall, dark-haired man who'd just sent a frisson of awareness zipping around her had been distinctly cold towards her initially, more so than the icy winds. Something had inexplicably changed in the last few moments. He'd looked at her differently, making heat surge through her in a way she'd never known before, and she wasn't sure she was able to deal with it. Thoughts of Richard had never done that to her.

'I shall accompany you to the meeting with Marya Petrushov, who is my grandmother, but first I will take you to several locations you can use for the photographs you require.' Something about the tone of his voice made it clear that to ask for more than this right now would be inadvisable, especially the way he'd said his grandmother's name. She immediately sensed unresolved issues and wondered how often he saw his grandmother with so many miles between them.

Throwing caution to the wind and quelling her curiosity for now, she looked directly at him, her chin lifted slightly, and clearly set out her terms. 'I not only need photographs of locations, Mr Petrushov, but of you and your grandmother—along with any other family members.'

Her brief was to step inside the life of the Russian family which had made its wealth only decades ago and see just how it lived. If she didn't deliver on that brief, she'd never get her contract, which would mean she'd have no way of funding Jess in one of Russia's elite ballet schools. The fact that this meeting was taking place in a town only a night-train-ride away from where Jess had a much-coveted place at a world famous ballet school was a good sign and she'd believed it couldn't go wrong, that it was meant to be.

Now, looking at Nikolai as he laid down his own rules about the interview, she had serious doubts it would ever go right. He dominated the entire room they'd walked into; even though the residents' lounge was large and spacious, he had taken command of every bit of that space. He was undoubtedly in control.

He also intimidated her, not that she would ever let him know that. It wouldn't do to let a man who was obviously used to being in charge see subservience. No, she would stand her ground. She sensed she would have to be as strong as him if she wanted to get what the brief dictated.

'There are no other family members, Miss Sanders.' He made his way towards a group of comfortable chairs around the warmth of the fire and she followed, determined he wasn't going to put her off so easily. She only had a week here in Russia and she wanted to see Jess before flying back to London.

He gestured to her to sit and then took the chair next to hers, his long legs suddenly emphasised as he sat. Nerves filled her and the way he watched her unsettled her more than she'd ever known. She wished she knew what he was thinking, but those dark eyes of his were unreadable.

'A photo of you and your grandmother...' She hadn't even finished her suggestion when he leant forward, bringing them close to one another in an intimate kind of way. It was too close and her words faltered into nothing.

'No.' That one word silenced any suggestions she

had, the anger in it reverberating around the room like a rogue firework. Then, as if he realised how hard and unyielding that sounded, he sat back and offered an explanation. 'I have not seen my grandmother for many years, so a loving family photo will not be possible, Miss Sanders.'

This wasn't going well. With each passing second, her dream of easily pulling together the article and then slipping away to Perm to see Jess for a few days was rapidly disintegrating. The wild and untamed look in his eyes as he regarded her suspiciously left her in no doubt that he meant what he said.

'Look, Mr Petrushov—sorry, Cunningham.' Now, to make matters worse, she'd called him by his family name again and, judging by the tightness of his jaw, that was not something which would endear her to him. She pressed on, not sure this whole situation could get any worse. 'I don't know what your problem is with me, but I am here to do a job. Your grandmother agreed with *World in Photographs* to be interviewed and photographed for the magazine and my job is to ensure that happens.'

She glared up at him, hoping to match his dominance with her determination, and wondered why she'd ever agreed to take on the interview role when photography was her field. The answer to that was her commitment to allowing her sister to follow her dreams.

He looked at her, his gaze slowly searching her face, lingering just a little too long on her lips. Tension crackled in the air around them and she was totally unaware of anything except the two of them. Mentally she shook herself free of it. Now was not a good time to become attracted to a man, and certainly not this man.

All through her teenage years she'd steadfastly held on to to a vow never to succumb to the temptation of a man. She'd managed that until she'd met Richard, a fellow photographer and the first man to pay her any kind of attention. She'd hoped their friendship would turn into something more, but two years down the line nothing had changed, and she watched in disillusion from the sidelines as he dated other women.

'And it is my duty to ensure my family isn't upset by your intrusion into our life, Miss Sanders.' He spoke slowly, his dark eyes hard and glittering, a very clear warning laced into every word. How could she be intruding when the old lady had agreed to be interviewed?

'I have no wish to upset anyone.' She looked up at him, into those midnight-black eyes, and knew she couldn't fight fire with fire. Her life with her mother, before she and Jess had been put into care, had taught her that. If she tried to match his strength and determination, she'd never get this assignment done. She lowered her gaze and looked down at her hands before looking back up from beneath her lashes. 'I apologise. Can we start again?'

The request completely stunned Nikolai. Moments ago she'd been brimming with fire. Passionate indignation had burned in her eyes, making his fight not to give in to the temptation to kiss her almost impossible. Now within seconds she'd become soft and compliant. Such a drastic changed filled him with suspicion. She was playing games with him.

'You want to go back into the cold and shake hands?'

He couldn't resist teasing her and was rewarded with a light flush of pink to her cheeks.

'No.' She laughed softly and her smile made her eyes shine, as if the sun was breaking through the forest and bouncing off fresh, green, spring leaves. 'I think we should start again with our conversation. Let's have a hot drink and discuss how we can both help each other out.'

Now he really was surprised. She was up to something, trying to manipulate the situation round to what she wanted. It was what the woman he should have married had always done and he'd been fool enough to let her—until he'd ended the charade that had been their engagement. She'd only wanted him for what he could provide for her.

'I don't think there is anything you can offer that will help me, Miss Sanders, but we will have a drink, and I will tell you how the next few days are going to work.'

Before she could say anything else, he signalled to a member of staff and ordered tea—something he wouldn't have requested in New York but, being back in Russia, his childhood memories were resurfacing in an unsettling way. Until he saw the flicker of interest in her eyes, he hadn't registered he'd used the first language he'd spoken as a child before his world had been torn apart by the pain of his mother's secret.

A secret that now haunted him. It was the same secret he suspected his grandmother wanted to unleash in the article and, just like her son, his cruel father, she was spiteful enough to manipulate him back to Russia to witness it all.

'Please, call me Emma,' she said, leaning back in

the chair opposite him, her jeans, tight around long, shapely legs, snagging his attention, filling his mind with thoughts he had no right to be thinking. 'And may I call you Nikolai?'

'Nikolai, yes,' he replied sharply. He had wanted to change his name to Nik when he'd left Russia as a young child—it had been his way of distancing himself from his father's family—but his mother had begged him to keep Nikolai, telling him she'd chosen the name because it was a family name and that he should keep some of his Russian roots.

'I get the distinct impression that you are not at all willing for me to talk to your grandmother, Nikolai— and yet it was her who approached *World in Photographs*, which makes me think there is something you don't want told.'

'How very shrewd.' And he'd thought he was going to turn on the charm and make her bend to his will. It seemed he'd greatly underestimated this woman. Her act of innocent shyness was exactly that. An act. Just like his ex, she was able to be whatever was necessary to get what she wanted.

'Perhaps we can come to some sort of agreement, one that will give me enough information to complete my job and afford your family enough privacy.' She sat back in her chair and looked at him, her dark brows raised in a silent show of triumph. If that was what she thought she'd achieved, he'd let her think that— for now.

'On one condition.' He picked up his tea, took a sip then met her gaze. He looked into her eyes and for the briefest of moments thought he'd seen anxiety. No, more than that—fear.

'And what is that condition?'

'That you tell me why this job is so important to you. Why come all the way from London to Vladimir for the ramblings of an old woman?' He had no idea if his grandmother rambled; he hadn't seen her for almost twenty-three years. It had been the day of his father's funeral and as a bemused ten-year-old he'd had no idea what was going on. No idea why his grandmother had turned him and his mother out. It was only six years later he'd learnt the disturbing truth and had vowed to do all he could to protect his mother from any further pain. A vow he fully intended to keep now.

'I took the job because it was a way of coming to Russia. It was as if fate was giving me the perfect opportunity. My sister, Jess, has a place at Perm Ballet School and once I've got what I need I'm going to spend a few days with her.' Her lovely green eyes filled with genuine excitement and that familiar pang of injustice almost stifled him. She'd had a happy childhood, had formed bonds with her sister, but his had been far from that thanks to one brutal act by his father, a man he had no wish to acknowledge as such.

'Your sister is here? In Russia?' This was the last thing he'd expected to discover and certainly hadn't turned up when he'd had Emma Sanders's background checked out. She had debts and she was far from well-known in the field of photography. Other than that, he'd found nothing of any significance. Nothing he could manipulate to make this situation work for him.

'Yes, ballet is her dream, and I intend to see that she can follow it.' Her face lit up and pride filled her voice and he saw an entirely different woman from the one he'd met outside just a short while ago. 'She's only sixteen and taking this job means I will be able to see her sooner than we'd planned, even if it's just a few days before I head back to London.'

At least now he could understand why she'd taken the job. Initially his suspicious mind had come to conclusions that weren't even there. She simply hadn't enough money to fly to Russia and see her sister so had taken the job. He did, however, still have doubts as to his grandmother's motives for instigating it all. Just what was she hoping to achieve? But, worse than that, how far was Emma prepared to go in order to impress *World in Photographs* in an attempt to launch her career?

'Then we can help one another, Emma. I can take you to places linked with my family's past where you can take as many photographs as you desire.' He paused, unsure why he'd used that word. Was it because of the way her body distracted him, making him want her? Colour heightened her cheeks again, making her appear shy and innocent, and he wondered if she understood the underlying sexual tension which was definitely building between them.

'And can I meet your grandmother? Ask her a few questions?' Her voice had become a little husky and she bit down on her lower lip, an action he wouldn't read into. Not if he wanted to stay in control of this nonsense and thwart his grandmother's attempt at stirring up trouble once more.

'Yes, but first we'll go to the places that are linked to my family. I have already made the arrangements for tomorrow.'

She looked happy, as if he'd just handed her a free pass. 'In that case, I will look forward to spending a few days with you.'

The irritating thing was, he also found himself looking forward to being with her. The very woman he'd wanted to despise on sight and he was undeniably attracted to her.

CHAPTER TWO

THE NEXT MORNING Emma was full of excitement and it wasn't just that, after a shaky start, this assignment, thanks to Nikolai's plans, would be done quickly and she could head off to meet Jess. She was taken aback to realise she was also excited to see Nikolai Cunningham again. After yesterday afternoon in his company, she was convinced he couldn't be as severe as he'd first appeared when she'd stepped off the train. Then he'd created such a formidable picture of power and command and she'd wished she'd been able to photograph him as he'd stood there, glaring at her.

It unnerved her to admit the excitement hadn't dissipated after they'd met and he'd shown her to his car. If anything it had increased and she had no idea why. After wasting several years worshipping Richard from afar and not being noticed, she didn't want to fall for the charms of another man—especially one as unattainable as Nikolai Cunningham.

'Where are we going now?' The large black car seemed to have glided silently through the white landscape and she'd wished many times she could stop and take photographs. Not for the magazine, but for herself. Her creative mind was working overtime and she saw images as if through the lens all over the place.

'To the place I knew as home until I was ten years old. It's just on the outskirts of Vladimir.' He looked straight ahead as he drove, his profile set into firm, determined lines. She had the distinct impression it was the last place he wanted to go and wondered at his motives for taking her there. He didn't strike her as a compliant man. Far from it.

'And who lives there now? Your grandmother?' she couldn't help but ask. The brief for the assignment and the need to be professional, to get the job done and leave on time, pushed to the forefront of her mind. She had to get this right, had to put the spin on it the magazine wanted, but everything she'd seen or been told so far was in total contrast to what she was supposed to portray. This wasn't a happy-ever-after story, unless you counted the global success of Nikolai's banking business that he'd created to complement his stepfather's exclusive real-estate business.

His silence deepened and she turned her attention to the road ahead. Moments later the car turned off onto a snow-covered lane that had no tracks on it at all, no hint that anyone had gone that way recently. Was the house empty?

Nikolai spoke harshly, in what she assumed was Russian, and most definitely sounded like a curse. She looked from him to the crumbling façade ahead of what must have once been a great house. It had rounded towers, some with turrets and others with pointed roofs, which reached into the grey sky above. The black holes, where once windows of assorted sizes had looked out over the flat landscape, seemed like watchful eyes.

Emma's heart went out to Nikolai as she pieced together the small amount she knew about him. None of it made sense, but it was obvious he hadn't expected this empty shell. She'd planned to take photographs of the place he'd grown up in, maybe even convince him to be in one, but now none of that felt right.

He got out of the car, seemingly unaware of her presence, and for a moment she sat and watched him. Then the photographer in her made that impossible for long. The image of his solitary figure, dressed in dark clothes, standing and looking at the neglected building, stark against the white landscape, was too much of a temptation. She had to take the photo.

Quietly, so as not to disturb him, she got out of the car, her camera in hand. The snow crunched under her boots as she moved a little closer. Seconds later she began taking photos. He remained oblivious to the clicks of the lens and as she looked back through the images she knew she wouldn't be using them for the article. These told a story of pain and loss and they were for her alone.

'This is where my family lived before my father died.' He didn't turn to speak to her, as if doing so would give away his emotions. Was he afraid of appearing weak? His tone had an icy edge to it, but she waited for him to continue. 'This is the first time I've seen it since I was a ten-year-old boy. My mother and I left for a new life in New York after that.'

'That must have been hard.' She moved instinctively towards him, but the cold glare in his eyes as he finally turned to face her warned against it. She just wanted him to know that she understood what it felt like to be displaced in life, not to know who you really were. Just like her and Jess, he'd been pushed from one adult to another and had known great sadness.

'Hard?' Nikolai could barely control his anger—not just at this woman, who was bringing all he'd thought he'd forgotten about his childhood back out for inspection, but also at his grandmother for instigating it. 'I don't think you could possibly know.'

He thought she'd say something, defend herself, but instead she shrugged, walked back to the car and took out her camera bag. He watched as she set up her tripod and again started to take photos of the old house. The camera clicked and, each time he heard it, it was as if it was opening yet another memory.

'Do you have any happy memories of this place?' She looked at him. Against the white snow and grey sky she looked stunning and he allowed this to distract him from the past. He didn't want to go there, not for anyone.

It was too late. A sense of terror crept over him as he saw himself, a young boy of eight, hiding beneath the antique table his father had been so proud to buy with his new-found wealth. He'd gone there seeing it as a place of safety, sure his father's temper wouldn't hurt his latest prized possession. He'd been wrong, very wrong. As his mother had begged and pleaded for his father to leave him alone, he'd been dragged out from beneath the table and lifted off his feet. He'd wriggled like mad, kicking and squealing, desperate to get away, yet knowing if he did his father would turn his attention to his mother. It was him or her and, in a bid to save her from at least one beating, he'd snarled words of hatred at his father. After that he couldn't remember what had happened.

He didn't want to.

He pushed the memories back. Analysing them wouldn't help anyone now, least of all himself.

'Not here, no,' he replied sternly and walked over to Emma, who was looking over her shoulder as she viewed the images she'd taken. The house didn't look so insidious on the screen of the camera, as if viewing it through the lens had defused the terrible memories of living there with his mother and father.

Emma's scent drifted up through the crisp air to meet him and he closed his eyes as summer flowers triggered happier memories. 'I was happiest in the summer, when we visited my mother's family.'

Why had he said that? Inwardly he berated himself for giving her information she could act on. At the thought of the country home his mother's parents had kept, he realised it was the perfect place to take her. He could hire a troika and sit back and watch as the romance of Russia unfolded. What woman wouldn't resist such a romantic story? It would be just what he needed to charm her away from the dark secrets he had to keep hidden away.

'Where was that? Close by?' Her interest was caught and she looked up at him, smiling and looking happier than he'd seen her since she'd arrived on the train. Then she looked vulnerable—beautiful and vulnerable.

'It is, yes.' He could hardly answer her as the attraction wound itself round him, drawing him ever closer to her.

'Can we go there?' she asked tentatively, her genuine smile and soft blush doing untold things to him. Why, he didn't know. He much preferred his women to be bold, dramatic and experienced at mutually benefi-

cial affairs. Instinctively he knew Emma was not like
that at all. She was the sort of woman who'd planned
out a happy-ever-after, even as a small child. Definitely not for him.

'We will go tomorrow,' he said, stepping back from
the temptation of this woman.

The next morning, as instructed by Nikolai, Emma
waited, wearing her warmest clothes and even more excited than yesterday. Somehow they had drawn closer
with each passing hour yesterday and, even though
he didn't talk to her about the past and let her into his
thoughts, he had shown her many wonderful places
and she already had lots of images.

She also realised she liked him—perhaps a little too
much. If she was honest, she was attracted to him in a
way she hadn't known before, not even with Richard.

'Ready?' he said as he met her in the hotel reception.

Like a child about to be shown a Christmas tree,
she couldn't stem the excitement and smiled up at him.
He was clean shaven this morning, and as wrapped up
as she was, but that didn't stop the pulse of attraction
leaping between them. The only difference was this
time his smile reached his eyes and they smouldered
at her, making her pulse rate soar.

'Yes; are we going to the house you told me about
yesterday?'

'We are, yes. The house I spent summers at with
my mother and her parents.'

She wanted to ask if his father had gone there too,
but didn't dare risk spoiling the softer mood he was
in. She sensed his father was the cause of the sudden
change in his mood yesterday at his childhood home,

but didn't have the courage to ask. Instead she focused her attention on what was happening now. 'Is it far?'

'No, a short car ride, then something special,' he said and to her surprise took her hand and led her into the street to the same big, black car he'd driven the previous day. Her heart fluttered as she fought to control the powerful surge of attraction rushing through her; she'd never felt anything like it before.

Then the something special Nikolai had teased her with turned out to be a ride across the snow in a sleigh, pulled by three proud horses, and Emma was totally blown away by the whole experience—and by the enforced close proximity of Nikolai as they sat snuggled under a heavy throw. 'This is amazing. I can use it in the article.'

'It's called a troika; racing them is a tradition from over one hundred years ago that's enjoying a resurgence.' She could barely focus on what he was saying as his thigh pressed hard against hers and even through all their layers of clothes her skin felt scorched.

After a little while the troika driver slowed to a halt, the horses snorting into the cold air, and Emma looked at Nikolai. Again something fizzed between them, but this time he held her gaze, looking intently into her eyes just the way she would have envisaged a lover doing. 'Thank you,' she whispered softly, her breath hanging briefly in the air, mingling with his in the most intimate way, and making her blush.

'The pleasure is all mine, Emma.' The fact that he'd used her name didn't go unnoticed and a shimmer of pleasure rushed over her, making her shudder, but it wasn't from the cold. 'Are you cold?'

'No, not at all,' she said, shyness creeping over her,

and she lowered her gaze, concentrating on the throw which covered their legs, locking them into the small space together.

With a gloved hand, Nikolai lifted her chin, forcing her to look at him once more, and what she saw in the inky black depths of his eyes was as terrifying as it was exciting. 'You are very beautiful, Emma.'

She swallowed hard, unable to move away from him, trapped with her legs all but welded to his beneath the cover. 'You shouldn't say things like that.'

Was that really her voice? She had no idea she could sound so husky and so trembling at the same time. Deep within her, silly, romantic notions she always shunned sprang to life. Did he really find her attractive? Would he want to kiss her and, if he did, what would it be like?

'It's the truth.'

Her heart was thumping in her chest and she was sure he must hear it. Her breathing had become more rapid, and so had his, if their white, misty breath was anything to go by. She searched his face for any hint of teasing, any sign that he was toying with her. She didn't have any experience with men, but she knew well enough from friends how they could make a woman lose all sense of self, something Richard had never done to her.

There was nothing, not a single trace of him teasing her, and she knew she was in danger of slipping under the spell that the magic of the moment was weaving around them. If they had been in a hotel lounge, talking in front of an open fire as they had done the afternoon she arrived, would he be saying these things to her?

'I didn't come here to become mixed up with a man.'

Even as her body yearned for the unknown, her mind kept to the practical issue of keeping her feet firmly on the ground.

'Do we have to get "mixed up", as you so nicely put it?' His voice was deep and laden with a hidden agenda.

She looked away, across the vast, white expanse of the snowy landscape, and asked herself the same question. If she took the kiss she was sure he wanted to give, would that change anything between them? No, because it couldn't. She had a job to do and then it would be time to move on with her life.

She'd waited in the hope that Richard would move their friendship to something more intimate and now she wondered if that had been wrong. Or was it just Richard who was wrong?

'No, I guess we don't.' She hoped she sounded as though she knew what she was doing, as if she'd been in this very situation many times before. The reality was very different. She'd never had a man look at her with such fierce desire in his eyes, never wanted to feel his lips claim hers.

He responded by moving closer and brushing his lips over hers very gently and suddenly she wasn't cold any more as heat scorched through her. She moved her lips against his, a soft sigh of pleasure slipping from her, only to be caught by him. What was happening to her?

A jolt threw her away from him and she dragged in a long, cold breath as the restless horses shifted in their harnesses. The driver spoke to Nikolai and she blushed, burying her face deeper in her scarf to hide her embarrassment. What was happening to her?

'The driver says snow is on the way and suggests we

see what is necessary and head back.' Nikolai hadn't intended to kiss her like that; he'd just wanted to make her feel special, to give her the fairy-tale ride through the snow to a beautiful location. He'd wanted all that to distract her—at least, he had, until he'd tasted her lips, felt them welcoming him and encouraging him to take more.

'Yes, yes, of course.' She sounded flustered as she took her camera out of its protective case. 'I'll just take a few frames and then you can tell me about it on the way back. I'd rather be in the warm when the snow arrives.'

He pushed back the image of that warmth being his bed and forced himself to focus on the task at hand. He had to distract her from the truth of his family history by showing her the façade they had lived behind.

'This,' he said as he helped her from the troika, 'Is where my mother and I spent each summer until we left Russia. In the summer, though, it was much greener and warmer than now.'

He hadn't thought of those summer days for such a long time, consigning them to the past he wanted to forget, but now, as he began to talk to Emma, it wasn't nearly as hard to look back on them as he'd always feared.

'And this was your mother's family home?' she asked as she lined up the shot and took a photo of the one place he'd been happy as a child.

'It was, but I never saw it like this, all covered in snow. It was always summer when we visited and I'd run with the dogs in the orchard, enjoying the freedom.'

It hadn't been just the freedom of running free in the summer sun, it had been the freedom from the terror of his father: from not having to hide when his filthy temper struck; of not having to worry about his mother as his father's voice rose to aggressive shouts. It had been freedom from pain—for both of them. He'd realised much later on that his mother's parents must have known what was going on and it had been their way of offering sanctuary. He just couldn't understand why his mother hadn't taken it permanently.

'And is your grandmother here to talk to us now?' Hope was shining in her voice. She thought he meant the grandmother who had started this whole nonsense off.

'No, they passed away before my father. Marya Petrushov is my father's mother. The one who contacted *World in Photographs*. She lives in Vladimir.'

'So we can see her?'

She turned her attention to packing away the camera, obviously happy with the photos she'd taken, and he was glad she couldn't see his face—because right now he was sure it must be contorted with rage and contempt for the woman who had done nothing to help him or his mother. Instead she'd preferred to make excuses for her son and for that he could never forgive her.

'Tomorrow. But right now we should return to the hotel.'

Just as he couldn't put off returning to the hotel because of the impending snow, he knew he couldn't put off meeting his grandmother again any longer. Maybe facing her for the first time would be easier with someone else at his side. It might also be the worst possible decision he'd ever made.

CHAPTER THREE

NIKOLAI LOOKED OUT of the window of the hotel bar as darkness descended. The snow was falling ever harder and he couldn't help but feel relieved. At this rate they wouldn't be able to get to his grandmother's home before Emma had to return to London. He'd almost given away the secret himself when he'd taken her to his childhood home; but at least she now had something for her story, and he could relax, maybe even enjoy the evening with her.

'It's snowing really hard.' Emma's voice, soft and gentle, held a hint of anxiety as she joined him in the hotel bar.

'That is normal for these parts,' he said as she sat down, unable to drag his eyes from her. She wore a black dress which moulded to every curve of her body, but when she removed her jacket, exposing her shoulders and slender arms, that spark of attraction he'd been trying to ignore roared forward, more persistent in its need for satisfaction.

She sat down opposite him in the comfortable chairs of the lounge area and crossed her legs, affording him a tantalising view of her lower leg, now deliciously on display, and the black high heels she wore only reinforced his need to feel those legs around him. Was she doing it on purpose? Was she trying to distract him?

'Thank you,' she said firmly and he looked at her face, liking the extra make-up she wore. It accentuated the green of her eyes and he wondered how they would look filled with passion and desire. 'For what you have shown me, I mean. It can't have been easy seeing your childhood home in ruins.'

The sincerity in her voice made him curious about her childhood and he remembered what she'd said within those first moments of meeting him: *life has taught me that, Mr Petrushov.* Had life been equally unkind to her?

'What of your family home?' he asked, instantly recognising the way she tensed and the tightening of her jaw. He wasn't the only one with secrets which still hung over him.

'A family home isn't something I was lucky enough to have. My sister and I were put into care when we were young.' She looked away from him; he watched her swallow down her pain and had to fight hard against the urge to go to her and offer comfort—sure it wouldn't be comfort for long.

'I didn't intend to upset you.' He leant forward in the chair and her perfume weaved itself around him, increasing the desire for her which pumped around his body. Desire he couldn't act on, not if he wanted to keep this whole situation free of complications.

'Maybe it's only fair, after what you endured yesterday. It must have been heart-breaking, seeing your family home like that.' She turned to look at him and suddenly they were very close. He held her gaze, looking into those green eyes and seeing an array of emotions swirling within them. He watched her lips move as she spoke again. 'I feel responsible for that.'

She looked down again at her hands clasped in her lap. For a moment he followed her gaze and then something he'd never experienced before pushed him on. He needed to touch her so he reached out and with his thumb and finger lifted her chin, forcing her to look at him.

The spark of attraction that had been between them from the moment she had got off the train mutated into desire as her gaze locked with his. It arced between them, pulling them together. He pressed the pad of his thumb along her bottom lip and he knew he'd already crossed the line, already passed the point of no return. All he could hope for now was that she would stop this madness from going further. She didn't. She stayed still, her eyes wide and beautiful, and when his fingers caressed her soft skin again her eyes fluttered closed, long lashes spreading out over her pale skin.

Did she have any idea what she was doing to him?

'Maybe we should eat.' Her voice was husky as she looked back up at him, her eyes full of desire. Food was the last thing he wanted, but he couldn't give in to the hot surge of lust racing through him, not when he'd decided this woman was off limits; he'd always prized himself on control.

As she closed her eyes slowly, her lips parting slightly, he wondered how the hell he was supposed to hang on to any sense of decency. She was so alluring, so tempting. When she opened her eyes again the mossy green was swirling with the same lust-filled desire which coursed wildly through his veins and he knew it was too late. There was only one way this heated attraction could be calmed now.

'It is not food I hunger for.' He leant even closer, still holding her chin, and pressed his lips briefly against hers, leaving her in no doubt what it was he hungered for. Was he insane? He'd gone past caring. Somewhere in the recess of his mind he knew this was so wrong, but the thought of kissing her, making her his, was so very right.

Emma could hardly breathe. The message in Nikolai's eyes was so very clear she couldn't miss it. He wanted her. She had no idea how she knew that, having done nothing more than kiss a man. But on a primal level that she'd never known existed within her she recognised the hunger in those inky-black eyes.

Hunger for her.

After years of believing she was unattractive to men, this powerful, dominating man wanted her. Worse than that—she wanted him too. She wanted to taste his kiss and feel his arms around her. She was so far from home, and everything she'd hoped this trip would bring looked in doubt, but right now none of that mattered. Only the searing hot attraction between them mattered. Only the promise of being desired for the woman she was.

What was it her last foster mother had always said? *Live for the moment.* She let the advice swirl in her mind, pushing back the cruel words her father had taunted her with the one and only time she'd met him.

She looked again at Nikolai, at the intensity in his eyes. She'd never done that before, never taken the lead with a man, even though she'd always hoped she and

Richard could be something. Now she knew why. What she felt for him was purely friendship, whereas what she felt for Nikolai, and had done since the moment they'd met, was far more intense. She had no choice but to live for the moment. If she kissed him, allowed herself to step into the sanctuary of his strong arms, would that be living for the moment?

'Neither am I.' Her whisper was so soft she wondered if she'd actually said anything, but the slight rise of his brows and the deepening intensity in his eyes told her she had—and he'd understood.

In answer he lowered his head and covered her lips with his, moving them gently until hers parted, allowing him to deepen the kiss. Heat exploded through her and she knew this was far more than a kiss; this was a prelude to something she'd never done before. He deepened the kiss again, setting light to her whole body. They couldn't do this here. Anyone could see them.

She pulled back, alarmed at how her heart raced, thumping in her chest like a horse galloping across the finishing line. Except this wasn't the end. This was only the beginning. Empowered by that knowledge and the need to let go of restraint and become a real woman, one who knew desire and passion, she smiled at him. 'Let's go upstairs.'

He looked down at her, his eyes searching hers, and she hoped he wouldn't be able to tell how inexperienced she was. A man like this must have had many lovers and the last thing he'd want would be a shy virgin. Although she couldn't change the fact that she'd never done more than kiss a man lightly on the lips, she could stop herself from being shy. All she needed to do was let go and live for the moment.

'It can't be anything more than this night,' he said as he took her hand. 'I don't want a relationship and commitment. I'm not looking for love and happiness. I want to know you understand that, Emma.'

'Love and happiness,' she said, a little too sharply, if his hardening expression was any gauge. 'It doesn't exist, Nikolai. I'm not a fool. In just three days we will go our separate ways and it will be as if this night never happened.'

Where had all that come from? Had passion muddled her mind? She was actually asking to spend the night with him, just one night and nothing more. She who'd told herself she would wait for her Prince Charming, although deep down she knew he didn't exist. Her childhood might have been hard, but it had grounded her expectations of life. She knew true love didn't exist—or, if it did, it never lasted once passion had subsided.

He said nothing. Instead he took her hand in his and led her away from the hotel lounge. Her hand was small in his as she glanced down at it, but she didn't pull back. Her step didn't falter. She was emboldened by the fizz of powerful desire humming in her body, the freedom to be a very different woman and a chance to erase the ever-present doubt her father had planted within her by denying she existed.

As they walked along the corridors of the chalet-style building she wondered if anyone else could tell that she was on fire at the thought of what she was about to do. But there wasn't anyone around and finally he stopped outside his room. She leant against the wall, needing the support of something solid as her knees weakened just from the intensity in his eyes.

'Are you sure this is what you want?' His voice broke as desire turned it into a very sexy whisper. He touched his hand to her face, brushing his fingers down her cheek, but she kept her gaze firmly on him.

Did he think she was playing games? She'd never been as sure of anything in her life. Whatever had ignited between them during those first moments they had met was destined to end like this. There could be no other outcome. Even she knew that and this was exactly what she wanted.

'Yes.' The word came out as a husky whisper and boldly she placed the palms of her hands on his chest, relishing the strength beneath his shirt and cashmere sweater.

His arms wrapped around her, pulling her against him, and a startled gasp slipped from her as she felt the hardness of him pressing intimately against her, awakening her further. To hide her embarrassment she slipped her hands around his neck, her fingers sliding into the dark hair at his collar.

His mouth claimed hers in a demanding kiss, one which stoked the fire he'd lit, sending it roaring higher until she knew it would totally consume her. The dark stubble on his face burned her skin with pleasure. His tongue slid into her mouth, tasting her, teasing her. She matched his kiss, demanding as much from him as he did from her. Whatever this was, she intended to make the most of it. Just for one night she would give in to her own needs and do exactly what she wanted. For one night she was going to put herself first, believe in herself, believe that at least someone cared, someone wanted her.

His hands cupped her bottom, pulling her tighter

against him. His breathing had become as ragged as hers and she plunged her fingers deep into his hair, kissing him harder still. When he broke the kiss she gasped and let her head fall back, her carefully pinned-up hair beginning to fall apart—just as she was.

He kissed down her neck and she arched herself harder against him. She gasped as he kissed lower still over the swell of her breast and right along the neckline of her dress. It wasn't enough. She wanted more, much more.

'Take me to your bed.' Horrified and excited that she'd been bold enough to say what she felt, what she wanted, she laughed. Who was this woman?

'That is exactly what I intend to do, Emma Sanders. You can be sure of that.' Instead of letting her go and opening the door of his room, he kissed her again, one hand holding her back as the other slid up her side and to her breast.

Pleasure exploded around her as his fingers teased her hardened nipple through the fabric of her dress. She couldn't take much more of this. As if he read her thoughts, he pulled back and let her go. She stood and watched as he unlocked the room and pushed the door open. Was she really doing this? Was she really about to step into this man's room and give herself to him?

Embarrassment rushed over her again, but she hid it with boldness, walking towards him with a suggestive smile on her lips. Tonight she wasn't Emma Sanders, responsible for everyone else, she was just a woman drowning in desire. With a gentleness which surprised her after the kiss that had bruised her lips, he took her hand and led her into the room. Quietly he clicked the door shut and they were left in almost darkness, the

only light coming from outside, creeping in through
the blinds in beams of whiteness.

Nikolai looked at Emma, not wanting to turn the lights
on, but wanting to see how beautiful she was. In one
minute she seemed bold and seductive and then, as if a
switch had been flicked, she looked innocent and shy.
He had no idea which was the real Emma, but either
way she was full of passion and desire. More importantly she shared his views. Love and happiness were
only for the select few and they were not destined to
be two of those.

'You are very beautiful,' he said as he moved towards her. Those expressive green eyes widened,
pushing the desire within him higher still. He'd never
wanted a woman as much as he wanted her and for
that very reason he intended to savour every moment.
Was it because she didn't threaten him by hinting at
beyond the here and now, looking for more than just
one night? Or was it because they had both known
pain and hardship in their lives? Either way, he wasn't
going to rush one minute of their night together, not
when it was all they had.

'Nikolai…' She breathed his name, a hint of a question lingering in her whisper.

'Now is not for talking,' he said gently, pulling her
to him. 'It's for pleasure like this.'

Before she could say anything else, he kissed her,
resisting the urge to deepen the kiss and demand so
much more. Savour the moment. Those words played
in his mind as her lips parted beneath his, her tongue
tentatively entwining with his.

With practised ease, his fingers found the zip at the

back of her dress and pulled it slowly down her back as she deepened the kiss. He pulled back from her, needing a moment to gather his control again. Her lips were parted and her eyes so full of desire they were almost closed.

He took the straps of her dress and slid them slowly off her shoulders and down her arms. The only movement was the rise and fall of her delectable breasts as she breathed deeply. He let the straps go as his hands lowered past her elbows and the dress slithered to the floor, leaving her in a black bra and panties.

Her eyes had widened and she looked at him, the innocent woman who'd slipped in and out of the limelight back once more. Then she smiled and the innocence was gone, the bold temptress returning as she reached behind and unfastened her bra, letting it fall away to expose full breasts, testing his control further. Then slowly, without breaking eye contact, she pulled her panties lower, wriggling with ease out of the black lace. Finally she stood and looked at him, a challenge in her mischievous smile. Was she daring him to resist her or daring him to make her his for tonight?

'You are even more beautiful now... I want to taste every part of you.' Just saying those words made his pulse leap with heated desire, but when she stepped towards him, her naked body highlighted by the pale light from outside, it was almost too much.

'I want you to.' She reached up and stroked the backs of her fingers over his stubble. It was such an erotic sensation he was glad he was still fully clothed, otherwise he would have pushed her back on the bed and plunged into her; all thought of making the pleasure last would have gone.

He caught her wrist, putting a stop to her caress before it pushed him over the edge. She looked up at him and for a second he thought he saw shock, but she recovered before he could analyse it, pressing her naked body against him wickedly. He let her wrist go and trailed his fingers down her arm and then to her breast, circling the tight bud of her nipple. She wasn't the only one who could be so wickedly teasing.

'And so I shall,' he said and lowered his head to tease her nipple with his tongue. She pushed her hands into his hair as he moved to her other breast to begin the torment again. Then he dropped to his knees and kissed down her stomach, holding her hips tightly as a spike of lust threatened his control. Gently he moved lower, teasing at the dark curls as she gasped her pleasure and gripped her hands tightly in his hair.

'I never knew,' she gasped, writhing beneath his exploration, 'that it could be so nice, so...'

'You make is sound like you've never made love.' He looked up at her, each breath she took making him want her all the more.

'Would that be so bad?' She looked at him and bit at her lower lip. He frowned in confusion, wondering if this was why one minute she was a temptress, the next an innocent. Was she telling him she was inexperienced—or even a virgin? After the moments they'd just shared, and her boldness, could that really be true?

'Why do you ask?'

'It's just that I've never...I'm a...' She blushed, unable to finish the sentence, the temptress gone.

'You are a virgin?' Shock rocked through him, followed by something else. She'd never made love and was choosing him to be her first lover.

'Yes,' she whispered and looked down at him, her eyes full of longing. 'And I want you to be the man who shows me what desire and passion is like.'

He stood up and took her hands in his, looking at her as she stood naked before him, uncertainty all over her beautiful face. He shouldn't want her, shouldn't want to be the man who showed her the pleasures of sex for the first time, but an overwhelming need to be that man flowed through him, making him want her more, testing his control beyond endurance.

'It wouldn't change anything, Emma.' He wanted her to be sure, wanted her to know that after this there wasn't anything else. 'If we have sex it will still be just tonight. I don't want a relationship. I don't intend to settle down any time soon.'

She pressed her palm against his face, her fingers running over the stubble, unleashing the same wild desire as before. 'I want nothing more than this moment in time.'

He pulled her to him, enjoying her soft skin beneath his hands and the feel of her nakedness against his clothed body. He kissed her gently, determined to make this as special as possible—for both of them.

In one swift movement he swept her up in his arms and carried her to the large bed he'd spent the last two nights alone in. As he placed her on the soft covers, he allowed his fingers to trail over her, his gaze fixed firmly on hers.

He stood before her and pulled off his clothes, enjoying the way she watched, her eyes widening when he stood before her naked and aroused. He picked up his wallet from the bedside table and pulled out the all-important foil packet. 'I assume this is the only con-traception we have between us?'

The impish smile which had been on her face as she'd watched him divest himself of his clothes slipped away as he rolled the condom on. 'It is, yes.'

He moved on to the bed, bracing his arms on either side of her head, his body tantalisingly close to her as he teased her with a kiss. 'Now that we've sorted that out, we can get back to the important issue of pleasure.'

She wrapped her arms around his neck, pulling him to her, and he had to fight hard to stop himself covering that delicious body with his and thrusting into her. As she stroked her fingers down his back, returning his kiss with ever more passion, he knew he couldn't hold out much longer and he moved on top of her. She wrapped her legs around him; if he hadn't known she was a virgin, he'd never have considered it possible, as she rocked her hips teasing him mercilessly.

His control snapped and all he could think about was making her his. She gasped out and dug her fin-gernails into his back as he took possession of her, sliding in as gently as his burning need for her al-lowed. She opened her eyes and looked up at him as he moved within her.

'Nikolai...' She whispered his name and moved her hips with him, encouraging him to deepen that posses-sion and pushing him over the edge.

He reached that edge, trying to hang on, trying to take her with him, and when she met him there he fi-nally let go, collapsing afterwards into her embrace, their breathing hard and fast.

CHAPTER FOUR

IT WAS STILL dark when Emma awoke, her body humming from the exquisite pleasure of making love with Nikolai. Movement caught her attention and she looked towards the window where the soft light of dawn was starting to creep around the blinds. Nikolai stood looking out through the blinds, his body partially in shadow and every sculpted muscle of his torso highlighted like a black-and-white photo. He'd pulled on a pair of jeans and in her mind Emma filed the image away as if she'd pressed the button on her camera and taken it.

His forehead was close to the blinds as he stood looking out. He was completely lost in thought and didn't hear the soft rustle of the bedclothes as she sat up. His jaw was tense and his brow furrowed into a frown. What was he thinking? Was he angry that she wasn't the experienced seductress she'd tried so hard to be? Had their one night been disappointing for him?

'Is it still snowing?' she asked as she propped herself up on her elbow, needing to say something to break the heavy silence around them. She hoped it was snowing too much for them to do what he'd planned today and, if it was, would he come back to bed?

She'd never expected to find what she had discovered last night in his arms, that completeness, as if they belonged together. The romantic inside her that she always tried hard to supress wanted more, so much more, but the ever-present realist that life had made her pushed those silly notions aside. Once she left Vladimir, there could be no more. This was just a fling for him, a way to amuse himself on a cold snowy night. It could even be a way to distract her from what she'd come here to do. That thought slipped uncomfortably over her but she refused to give it any importance; after all hadn't there been an undeniable spark of attraction between them since the moment she'd arrived?

Nikolai continued to look out at the snow, as if he hadn't heard her, and just when she thought she might have to ask again he turned and looked at her, lines of worry creasing his brow. 'It is.'

The roughness of his voice made her swallow hard against the disappointment which rushed through her. What had she expected? A declaration of undying love because she'd given him her virginity? Even she knew better than that!

'Will it stop us meeting your grandmother?' She tried hard to keep her voice soft and calm, as if discussing the weather with the man she'd just had the most wonderful sex with was as normal as the snow falling over the Russian landscape in winter.

He turned to look at her, so slowly she wondered if she'd said something really wrong. With casual ease he hooked his thumb in the belt loop of his jeans and fixed her with a deep and penetrating gaze, and the unmistakable stamp of suspicion was on his handsome face.

'Would that be a problem?'

It should be but Emma realised with shock that it

wouldn't be, not if she could stay cocooned here with Nikolai and lose herself in a moment she hadn't expected at all. A moment which had unlocked a passionate woman within her she'd never known existed, a woman she wanted to be again before the coldness of daybreak brought reality back.

'No,' she whispered softly. 'Let's not think of anything else until daylight.'

Her words lifted the tension which had folded around them, but as he stepped towards her, every muscle highlighted for her pleasure by the growing light from outside, that tension was replaced with something far more powerful.

'Looking at you right now, that is exactly what I want to do.'

Emma pulled aside the tousled sheets, inviting him back into bed, and as he pulled off his jeans and slipped in beside her she was in no doubt what he wanted to do. Heat uncoiled deep within her, lighting the flame of desire once more. Never in her wildest dreams had she expected to find this when she'd boarded the plane for Moscow and she knew that it would change her life for ever.

'I want to be yours til morning breaks,' she said as she moved against the heat of his body, relishing the strength of his arms around her as he pressed her into the bed, covering her body with his, passion exploding like fireworks around them.

'Until daylight,' he said as he kissed her lips, then made a blazing trail down her throat. 'You will be mine, Emma.'

Nikolai felt his control slip away as he pushed the reality of the world aside and kissed Emma. How could she make him feel like this—so lost unless he was holding her, kissing her, as if she truly was his? Her hands moved over his body and her warm skin pressed close against his and all he could think was that she was his, totally his.

The fire of desire ripped through him as her lips claimed his, demanding so much and giving even more. It was so wild, so intense, all he could think about was making her his. Nothing else mattered but that. All he wanted was to be deep inside her.

'Nikolai!' She gasped his name and arched herself up to meet him as he claimed her once more, a powerful urge almost totally consuming him. 'Don't forget...'

A curse flew from him as he pulled back from her and the release which threatened to come far too quickly. How could one woman obliterate his control? Undo him so completely? Feeling like a fumbling teenager, he dealt with the contraception as she looked up at him, desire-darkened eyes holding his.

'This time there is nothing to stop us.' His words were smothered as her lips claimed his and her body welcomed him, taking him deep within her.

An explosion of heated emotions erupted, making him shudder as his release came hard and fast. He kissed Emma, binding them ever closer as the same wave he was riding crashed over her. The sea of desire left him swirling in exhaustion and, as her hold on him turned to a soft caress of his back, he allowed himself to slip under, to give in to the pleasure of sleeping in a woman's arms in a way he'd never done before.

When he woke several hours later, Emma's body warm against his, he didn't want to move, didn't want to give up the moment. Never before had he allowed emotion into the bedroom. For him it had always been about lust and acting upon an attraction. He'd thought it would be the same with Emma when he'd taken her to his room, but the moment he'd taken her virginity, had become her only lover, something had changed.

Gently he kissed her hair as she lay against his chest. Immediately she lifted her head and looked at him, a shy smile on her face. 'You could always just tell me about your family and then we can stay here all day instead of going to see your grandmother.'

His mood was lighter than it had ever been and he stroked his hands through the softness of her hair. 'If I tell you too much, I will have to keep you here for ever.'

'Promises, promises.' She laughed, a soft, sexy laugh which pushed him further from reality.

'You know the basics,' he said as she kissed his chest, forcing him to close his eyes. 'I grew up in Russia and when my father died my mother and I left for New York.'

'That must have been tough.' Her slender fingers traced across his chest, easing the pain of the memories, the pain of telling them.

'My mother had help from a business acquaintance of my father's and, several years later, she married him.' The surprised rise of her brows made him think more deeply and the hum of passion dimmed.

'Did you mind? That she married again, I mean, replaced your father?' If there was one question sure to kill the desire which had rampaged through him, it was that one.

'I didn't mourn my father.' The pain from his childhood made his voice a harsh growl and Emma pulled away from him to look up into his face. Could she sense the tension in him just thinking about how he'd been conceived, that he had been the product of a violent rape?

'What happened?' There wasn't any disgust in her voice for his open admission, no judgement in those two words at all. Had she too known childhood heartache? Did she recognise it within him?

'It was not a happy marriage and one my grandmother, Marya Petrushov, very much wanted to continue. She made things difficult for my mother, prolonged the unhappiness.' He skirted around the truth, trying to explain without giving her any more of the sorry secret than she needed to know. She could even be storing away the information right now to put it in her damned article. He pulled away from her, broke the contact. It was the only way to be able to think straight.

'Is that why you have been distracting me from meeting her?' The bold question didn't match the soft innocence of the image she created naked in his bed and he fought hard against the urge to abandon this conversation and use the language of desire and passion. Her next words killed that thought, so instantly his body froze. 'I need the story, Nikolai, all of it. I have a job to do.'

How could she look so deliciously sexy when her words were like hail thrashing his naked body? Had he fallen for the oldest trick in the book? Had she acted innocent to ensure he took her to his bed and he was now spoiling her plans? Worse than that, had she bargained her virginity just to get the story she needed? He shouldn't be telling her the intimate secrets of his family, not when she could portray a family ripped apart by greed and power as it had risen to new heights of wealth.

It was precisely what had happened. His mother must have been an easy target for a power-hungry man whose own family had come from nothing. Bile rose in his throat at the thought of his father's mother selling the story. Did she expect it to keep her comfortable in her final years? Was she planning even now to blackmail him? It damn well wouldn't happen if he had anything to do with it.

'You'll get your story,' he growled as he stood up and stepped away from her, away from the temptation of her silky, soft skin. She was as devious as his grandmother. She'd only slept with him to get what she wanted. She'd crossed the barriers he'd long ago erected and had exposed his emotions to the light of a new day and, with it, the pain of who he was. 'But not now. Not until I know if there are consequences from your underhanded way of interviewing me.'

'Nikolai!' she gasped and reached out, the sheet slipping, giving a tantalising view of her breasts. The fact that it turned him on, sending lust hurtling through him faster than anything he'd known, disgusted him.

He turned his back on her, not trusting himself to leave her alone, and savagely pulled on the remainder of his clothes. He'd been a fool. He'd thought he'd glimpsed what life could be like if his past wasn't a permanent shadow hanging over him.

'You need to leave.' He turned to look at her, allowing the anger to sluice over him and wash away the lingering desire. She was as deceitful and scheming as his grandmother and he wouldn't allow her to expose the truth and hurt his mother. She'd suffered enough shame.

* * *

Emma blinked and recoiled at the change in Nikolai. Where had the tender lover gone? Anger rushed from him like a fierce tide crashing onto the rocky shore.

'No, we need to talk.'

'I'm not saying anything else to you.' He spat the words back at her, the dim light of the room only making his anger even clearer. What had she done to make him suddenly hate her? The questions had only been part of her job and she'd never hidden that from him.

He stepped closer to her and she became aware of her nakedness again, clutching the covers against her once more. From the hard expression set on his face, she knew their moment of intimacy was over. The connection between them they'd shared last night had been severed as surely as if he'd cut it.

He reached into his jacket pocket and seconds later tossed a business card onto the bed. 'If you want to pry into my life any more, you can contact me on that number.'

Ice shuttered around her heart, freezing the new emotions she'd allowed herself to have for this man. How had she been stupid enough to believe he was different, that like her he was hurting because of the past? She'd thought that made what they'd shared last night more intense, more powerful.

She took the card, holding it as if it might explode at any second. The bold black print in which *Nikolai Cunningham* was written was as hard as the man who stood angrily before her.

'One last thing,' she said before she could think better of it. 'Why do you no longer use your family name, Petrushov?' It was the one thing which had puzzled her since she'd been given the assignment on the Petrushov family and had been told the only grandson would meet her in Vladimir.

'I have no wish to use my father's name.' The harshness in his tone made his hatred and anger palpable. It filled the room and invaded every corner. 'And, so that you have your information correct when you use my family's sordid past to further your career, I changed my name to that of my stepfather when I was sixteen.'

'I'm not going to use any of what you've just told me, Nikolai. What kind of woman do you think I am?' She couldn't keep the shock from her voice or the hurt from cutting deep into her. Did he really think that badly of her?

'You are obviously the kind of woman who will trade her virginity to climb a career ladder.' The hardened growl of his accusation sliced painfully into her, sullying the memories of giving herself to him so completely last night.

'No,' she gasped, wishing she was wearing something so that she could go to him. How could he think that of her? 'It wasn't like that at all.'

He gave her one last frosty glare and then strode to the door. 'Now you have all you need to ruin mine and my mother's reputations, you can get the hell out of my life.'

The door slammed behind him and she was left, blinking in shock. Only hours ago they had been locked in the arms of passion. Nothing else had existed. A tear slid down her face as she threw back the covers and picked up the black dress from the floor, trying not to remember the burn of desire she'd had for him as it had slipped off her body last night. Angrily she pulled it on, not caring about her underwear. All she wanted was to get along the hotel corridor to the sanctuary of her room and lock herself in until her heart stopped breaking.

Still reeling from the shock of Nikolai walking out on her, she shut the door of her own room and made for the shower, needing the warmth of the water to soothe her. After standing there for what felt like hours, Emma finally turned the water off and wrapped herself in a towel, trying not to dwell on the accusations Nikolai had hurled at her. Did he really think she'd all but sold herself just to get information out of him?

Her phone buzzed on the cabinet next to her bed. Instantly she was on alert. What if it was Nikolai? With a slight tremor in her hands she reached for it and, as she looked at the text from her sister, she knew the day was going from bad to worse. Even with the limited words of the text Emma could sense Jess's distress, but it was the final word which really propelled her into motion:

I need you, Em, come now. Please.

Finally the overnight train arrived in Perm and Emma made her way straight to the ballet school. The tearful conversation she'd had with Jess during that long journey was still fresh in her mind, which at least had given her little time to think of the night spent with Nikolai and how it had drastically changed things, how he'd rejected her.

'I've missed you so much, Em,' Jess said, dragging her mind back from thoughts of the tall, dark-haired Russian who had lured the woman she'd always wanted to be out of the shadows.

'Is that what this is all about?' Emma kept her tone light but, for the first time ever, felt constrained by looking after her sister. If she hadn't had to rush and get a train ticket sorted, she might have seen Nikolai again. She'd at least wanted to try and explain, especially after the intimacies they'd shared. All she knew was that he'd checked out.

'You've been so far away and it's been months since I've seen you. I guess I couldn't stand the thought of you being so close.'

'Not exactly close.' Emma forced herself to forget her problems and laughed, pulling her sister into a hug, unable to be irritated by the intrusion into her life at the worst possible moment. 'It was a very long train journey from Vladimir. It took me all night.'

'I hope I didn't spoil anything for you,' said Jess, looking a little subdued suddenly, and Emma wondered if there was more to this.

'There wasn't anything to spoil.' Nikolai had already done that, accusing her of all but seducing the story out of him. Well, she'd show him. Nothing he'd said to her in his room would find its way into her article, although it did go some way to explaining his shock at seeing his family home again.

'That's all right, then,' began Jess, sounding brighter already. 'I only have the rest of today off class, then it's back to it.'

'Then we need to do something really good.'

Later that night, lying alone in a different hotel room, having spent the entire day with Jess, Emma's doubts crept back in. She remembered Nikolai standing at the window, the light shadowing his body, and wished she could turn back time. The only thing she wanted to change was the doubt on his face, the worry in his eyes.

Several times this evening she'd wanted to call him, wanted to reassure him that all he'd told her about his childhood would stay with her. She knew what it was to feel unloved and out of place. Was that why he'd gone to great lengths to put off the meeting with his grandmother? Was there another side to the story? Had she been fooled by his heart-wrenching admission of his past?

She had spent time on the train drafting out what she wanted to write and none of it would include the torture of the man who'd shown her what being loved could be like, even for a few brief hours. If she told him that, would he believe her? She relived the moment he'd accused her of seducing him for information and knew he would never believe her.

Tomorrow she would be taking the train back to Moscow and from there a flight home to London. There wouldn't be an opportunity to see him; maybe fate was trying to tell her that what she'd shared with Nikolai that night was nothing more than a moment out of time.

CHAPTER FIVE

NIKOLAI STOOD AT a window of his apartment, looking at, but not seeing, Central Park bathed in spring sunshine. All he could think about was Emma. It had been almost two months since that night but the only communication had been from *World in Photographs*, thanking him, although he was yet to see a copy of what Emma had submitted. That, however, was the least of his worries.

He'd replayed their night together many times in his mind and, once the anger that she'd slept with him to get her story had cooled, a new worry grew from an inkling of doubt. The more he thought of it, the more his gut was telling him they might have had an accident after she'd coaxed him back to bed...the hurried and last-minute use of the condom playing heavily on his mind.

As he stood looking out of the window early that morning, he kept telling himself that no news from Emma was good, that their night of passion hadn't had the consequences he'd dreaded despite the ever-increasing doubt in his mind.

It had been many weeks since he'd marched from the hotel room and braced the snow to cool his mind and body with a walk. When he'd returned to the room, Emma had gone, and that had told him all he needed to know: he'd been used. The only good thing to come out of the night was that he hadn't had to face his grandmother.

Angry that he'd put himself in such a position, he'd checked out and headed straight back to New York, but he hadn't stopped thinking about Emma. She had haunted his every waking hour and made sleep almost impossible. Something had happened to him that night, maybe even from the first moment he'd met her. She had changed him, made him think of things he couldn't have.

He'd done what he always did where emotions were concerned and avoided them. He still couldn't believe he'd almost told her all about his childhood. Those hours spent in bed with her must have muddled his mind. It should have just been a night of passion to divert her from the horrible truth of who he really was, but he'd almost told her exactly what he'd wanted to remain a secret.

He'd gone to Vladimir and confronted the ghosts of his past in order to save his mother the heartache of seeing her story all over the newspapers, exactly where it would end up once it was published by *World in Photographs*. What he'd found in Vladimir with Emma was something different.

Yes, he had been guilty of wanting to distract her from the truth, but somewhere along the way things had changed. She'd reached into the cold darkness of his heart and unlocked emotions he'd thought impossible to feel. Even the woman he'd once proposed to had failed to do that, but Emma had been different.

'What the hell were you thinking?' He snarled angrily at himself. One of the only times he'd let a woman close and she'd cheated him, used him for her own gain. He'd even begun to question if Emma was as innocent as she'd claimed. Had that too been part of the plan—to make him think he was the first man she'd ever slept with—in order to get the real story?

The fact that she'd run out on him only added fuel to the fire. Not only that, there hadn't been a word from her since that night when he'd stood there and looked at her, clutching the sheet against her. He'd had had to fight hard not to pull the damn thing from her and get back into bed. His body had been on fire with need for her and, despite having spent all night having sex, he'd allowed the anger he felt at himself for being used to have precedence. It had been a far more reliable emotion to feel, one which had propelled him from the hotel room without a backward glance.

Driven by that anger, he'd left quickly, tossing her a card as an afterthought. Or was it because even then, deep down, he knew things might have gone wrong? If their night together did have consequences, then he knew he would face up to them and be the father he'd always longed for in place of the cruel man who had filled his childhood with fear.

The fact that he knew what he would do didn't make Emma's silence any easier. It irritated him. Did it mean she wasn't pregnant? That the condom failure about which he'd since convinced himself hadn't had any drastic consequences?

He looked at his watch. Ten in the morning here meant late afternoon in London. He could ring her. It would be easy enough to get her number through *World in Photographs*, but what would he say?

He'd replayed again the scene in the hotel room early that morning. He'd woken to find her sleeping soundly next to him and had watched her for a while. Then, as the ghosts of the past had crowded in, he'd had to get up. For what had felt like hours, he'd stood watching the dark and empty street outside the window as if it held the answer or truth about his past.

Emma had stirred, her glorious naked body doing things to his, and he'd had to hold on to his self-control, wanting only to lose himself in her once more instead of facing the truth. That truth was not only the fact that she'd lured him to tell her things he'd wanted to keep well hidden.

His phone bleeped, alerting him to a text, and he ignored it, wanting to focus on what to do next. Call her? Go to London and demand to see her? He'd have to find out where she lived.

Insistently the alert sounded again and he swore in Russian, something he hadn't done for a long time before he'd returned to Vladimir. When he picked up the phone and read the text, he almost dropped it as if it were red-hot.

We need to meet. I'm in New York. E

He inhaled deeply. This could only mean one thing—the very worst thing. There was no way she'd come here, all the way to New York, to tell him the article had been accepted, or show him a copy. An email would be sufficient for that. She needed to talk. His suspicions about their night together must be right—she was pregnant with his child—and that changed everything.

He pressed his thumb and finger against his eyelids in an effort to think, but there was only one answer. The same answer that had come up each and every time he'd thought of Emma and that night together. The very thing he'd never wanted to happen. He just knew it: he'd fathered a child. Now he had to face his fears from childhood and prove to himself he wasn't his father's son…that he could bring up his child with love and kindness. The very idea terrified him.

Emma was late. She'd arrived at Central Park early and wandered around taking photographs until midday, the time specified by Nikolai in his reply to her text. She'd tried to put her reason for being in New York to the back of her mind and had almost succeeded when she had become engrossed in taking shots of the park. Now the impending meeting with him loomed large but she couldn't recall which way she'd come. She looked around at the tall buildings surrounding the park and wondered if she'd be able to find her way back out. She was tired from travelling and early pregnancy was not being so kind to her. Panic rose up. She'd have to ask someone for directions.

'Excuse me, is it this way to The Boathouse?' she asked a mother pushing a pram, trying hard not to look down at the child. It would be too much like looking into her future and she wondered how she was ever going to cope on her own. Nikolai had made it more than clear that what they'd shared was just one night. He'd been so adamant about it she began to question her reasons for telling him personally. It would have been much easier just to call him, tell him he was going to be a father. It was her conscience and knowing what it felt like to be rejected by her father that had made her come.

All through the flight one question kept going round in her head: would her own father have wanted to be part of her life if he'd been given the choice like this? The day she'd first met him, after she'd begged her mother to tell her who he was, rushed back at her, as did his icy words. *It's too late. I don't need or want you in my life.*

'Keep walking and you'll see it.' The mother's voice dragged her back to the present. She smiled at Emma before heading on in the other direction. With unease in her heart Emma watched her walk out of sight. That would be her by the end of the year, but she was certain she wouldn't be here in New York, looking happy with life.

She shook the thought away and looked at her watch again. She was fifteen minutes late. Would Nikolai still be there? With the pain of her father's rejection stinging her heart, the need to see Nikolai, to tell him and give him the chance to be part of his child's life, deepened. She quickened her step but within a few strides they faltered. He was standing where the path turned through the trees and, despite the distance, she knew it was him, as if her body had registered his, known he was close.

She could also tell from his stance that he was not happy about being kept waiting. She breathed in deeply, then let the breath out in a bid to calm her nerves and quell the nausea which threatened to rear its head yet again. Within days of returning to London she had woken each morning feeling ill and had at first put it down to all that had happened between her and Nikolai. After all, losing your virginity to a man, only to have him walk out in anger, was not the best experience in the world. Not once had she considered there was a lasting legacy of that night.

As days had turned into a week, she'd known she couldn't ignore the encroaching doubt any longer and had purchased a pregnancy test. The fact that it had taken several more days before she'd been brave enough to use it only served to increase the weight of dread which filled her from the moment she woke each day. When she'd finally had enough courage to use the test, her worry had increased as the ominous blue lines appeared, confirming that the hours spent with Nikolai had most definitely had consequences—for her, at least.

She walked towards him now and with purpose pushed those long, lonely weeks aside in her mind, focusing instead on what had to be done. She kept her chin lifted and her eyes on him all the time. Anything else would be to show uncertainty or, at worst, fear. She wasn't scared of her future any more and, although it was going to be a struggle, she was looking forward to giving her child all she'd never had. What she did fear was telling Nikolai and, from the rigid set of his shoulders, she'd been right to fear this moment.

He made no move towards her, not even one step, and she hated him for doing that. He could have made the moment easier for her. Was he punishing her for contacting him? For making their one night something more? Each step she took must have shown her anxiety a little bit more. She should have called him as soon as she'd taken the pregnancy test, but shock had set in. She hadn't even been ready to accept it herself, let alone blithely call him up and tell him their one night had created a child which would join them for ever.

How did you tell a man who'd made it blatantly clear he didn't want any kind of commitment that he was a father? Her mother obviously hadn't done it right, but could she? She was about to find out.

As she drew level with him, the inky black of his eyes held accusation, just as they had done in the hotel room the morning after they'd spent the night together, the night she'd lost her virginity to him. The firm line of his lips looked harder than they had that morning but she refused to be intimidated, just as she refused to acknowledge the hum of attraction rushing through her just from seeing him, being near him again.

She couldn't still want him; she just couldn't.

'You are late.' He snapped the words out and stood his ground. Six foot plus of brooding male towered over her, sending her heartbeat racing in a way that had nothing to do with nerves at what she had to say. She hated the way she still wanted him, her body in complete denial of the numbness in her mind. How could she still want a man who'd rejected her so coldly after she'd given him her most precious gift?

'I couldn't find my way through the park…' she began, trying to instil firmness into her voice, but he cruelly cut her off.

'Why are you here, Emma?' The hard glint in his eye sparked with anger but she wouldn't allow him to make her feel like a guilty child. What right did he have to stand there and dictate to her what she should have done and when? He was the one who'd strode from the hotel room in Vladimir without a word to her after tossing her his card. He was the one who hadn't handled this right.

'Did you think throwing a business card onto the bed was a nice way to end our night together?' Her words spiked the spring air around them, but he didn't flinch. His handsome face didn't show a single trace of any other emotion beyond controlled annoyance. This just prodded at her anger, firing her up. 'We need to talk, Nikolai. That's why I'm here.'

'About the consequences of our night together?' He'd guessed. Guilt and shock mixed together and she looked up at him, not yet able to say anything.

He moved towards her, dominating the spring air around them, and while she heard people walking past she couldn't do anything other than focus on him. If she looked away, even for just a second, all her strength would slip away.

'By consequences, you mean pregnancy.' Finally she found her voice. Her sharp words didn't make a dent in his assured superiority, but saying them aloud filled her with panic.

'Yes, exactly that. I assume you haven't flown halfway around the world to tell me about the article. You're here to tell me you are expecting my child.' He looked straight into her eyes, the fierce question in them mixing with accusation. Was he blaming her?

Emma looked away from the impenetrable hardness in his eyes and wished it could be different, but no amount of wishing was going to change those two bold lines on the pregnancy test she'd finally had the courage to use. She was pregnant with Nikolai's child and, judging by his response to her arrival in New

York, he did not like that particular revelation. It didn't matter what he said now, she had to face the truth: she was very much alone.

She let out a soft breath, trying to come to terms with what she'd known all along, finally accepting why she'd wanted to tell him in person. She'd had the faint hope that he would come around to the idea, be different from her father. But no. If the fierce glint in his cold black eyes was anything to go by, he didn't want to be a father at any price. She would do this herself. She didn't need him—or anyone. 'Your powers of deduction are enviable, Nikolai. Yes, I'm pregnant.'

Nikolai braced himself against the worst possible news he could ever be told. He couldn't be a father, not when the example he'd seen of fatherly love still haunted his dreams, turning them into nightmares if he allowed it.

He looked at Emma, the one woman who'd captured a part of his heart. Ever since she'd left he'd tried to tell himself it was because he'd shared a bit of himself with her, shared secrets he hadn't wanted anyone to know. He still couldn't comprehend why he'd done that when she'd had the power to make it completely public, shatter his mother's peaceful life and destroy his hard-won business reputation. He was thankful he'd stopped at the unhappy marriage bit, glad he hadn't told her the full horror of how that marriage had come about. How he'd come about. If she knew the truth she wouldn't want him to have anything to do with his child, of that he was sure. But, although he had shared some secrets, he would now do anything he could to ensure those she didn't know about stayed hidden away.

'And did you leave Vladimir in such a hurry because

you thought you'd discovered extra facts for the story? Perhaps you rushed off to get it in?'

The anger he'd felt when he'd realised she'd left not only his room and the hotel but Vladimir itself still coursed through him. He'd had to leave her in the hotel room because of the desire coursing through him. He'd needed the cool air to dull the heavy lust she evoked in him with every look. He hadn't intended it to be the last time he saw her. He'd intended to go back and talk calmly with her, hear what she would want if the worst had indeed happened.

'No.' She looked down, as he quickly realised she always did when confronted with something difficult, as if she too was hiding from past hurt—or was it guilt for throwing herself at him just to get a few snippets of inside information? When she looked back up at him, her eyes were shining with threatening tears. 'I had a call from my sister and left soon after you did.'

'A call from your sister? So, after we'd worked together on the article, you thought spending time with her was more important?' Her face paled at his icy tone and a rush of guilt sliced briefly through him before he pushed it aside. She'd run out on him to play happy families with her sister.

'She was upset.' Emma looked up at him as if imploring him to understand. 'We only have each other. I left her to go back to Moscow but there wasn't any time to contact you again. It's not as if I knew there were such consequences then.'

'When did you first discover these consequences?' The fact that she must have known for at least a few weeks infuriated him more than the fact that she'd used him, seduced him into taking her to bed and spilling secrets.

'I've only fairly recently had it confirmed…' He moved even closer to her, dominating the very air she breathed and halting her words in mid-flow.

'And now we have to deal with it.' His attention was caught by passers-by, happy in the spring sunshine when he now had the weight of guilt pressing down on him, all but rooting him to the spot like one of the large trees of the park.

This was his fault. He should have been more careful, more in control, but if he was honest with himself he should never have given in to the attraction in the first place. Not with the woman who had the power to destroy his and his mother's happiness. What the hell had he been thinking? What had happened to his usual self-control? Emma had happened. She'd completely disarmed him, which he strongly suspected had been her intention all along.

'Deal with it?' He heard the panic in her voice and turned his attention back to her, to see she'd paled even more dramatically. She needed to sit down. He did too, but the restaurant would be busy, far too busy to discuss an unplanned pregnancy and the ramifications of such news.

'This way,' he said as he took her arm, ensuring she came with him. He strode towards the edge of the park where he knew the horse-drawn carriages would be waiting for customers. They could talk as they toured the park and, more importantly, she wouldn't be able to run out on him this time. She would have to face their situation, just as he'd had to as he'd gone over this very moment in his mind during recent weeks. In the carriage she would have no choice but to listen to him and accept that his solution was their only option.

'Where are we going?' She pulled back against him as if she was on the verge of bolting again, backing up his reasoning for taking a carriage ride like a tourist.

'Somewhere we can talk. Somewhere you'll have no choice but to sit and hear what I have to say, how we are going to deal with this.' Still she resisted and he turned to face her, sliding his hand down her arm to take her hand in his. As he did so, that fizz of energy filled him once more and he could see her face again, full of desire the night she'd taken his hand in Vladimir. The night they'd conceived a new life. His child. His heir. 'You are not going to slip away so easily this time, Emma, not now you carry my child.'

The determination and bravado slipped from Emma and her body became numb. She was too tired to fight any more, too tired to worry and fret over the future, and Nikolai's suggestion of sitting down seemed the best option. She walked hand in hand with him through the park. To onlookers they would have appeared like any other couple, walking together in the sunshine, but inside dread had begun to fill her, taking over the sizzle of attraction from just being with him again. Exactly how did he intend to deal with it?

'We'll take a ride round the park,' Nikolai said as he stopped beside a horse-drawn carriage and she blinked in shock. Was this just another of his romantic pastimes to distract her? Then the truth of that thought hit her. That was exactly what he'd done in Vladimir. He'd gone out of his way to distract her and had even successfully managed to keep her from meeting his grandmother.

He'd been keeping her from knowing more about his family and, thinking back to the moment they'd met, she could see he'd been evasive about the story of rags to riches she was supposed to cover. Why, then, had he said the things he had that morning after they'd made love, giving her a deeper insight into the childhood which had shaped the man he now was?

She still couldn't shake off the sensation that he'd wanted to say more but had guarded against it. Had he really believed she would put all those details in the article? She'd just wanted to create a fairy-tale story to go with the amazing photographs she'd taken, but he'd accused her of manipulating everything to get what she wanted.

'Trying to make me all soft again, are you?' The words were out before she had time to think of the implications. If she'd been clever she would have never let him know she'd guessed his motives.

'There is nothing to go soft about. I need to know exactly what you submitted to *World in Photographs* about my family and then we can discuss what happens next.' He opened the door of the carriage and, with a flourish of manners she knew he was displaying for the purpose of getting what he wanted, waited for her to climb in.

Emma looked from his eyes to the park around her and beyond that to the tall buildings of New York, a place she'd never been to before. What choice did she have? She was alone in a city she didn't know and pregnant with this man's baby.

'I have my laptop at the hotel, I can show you exactly what will be in it.' The painful knowledge that he'd rather discuss an article she'd written than talk about their baby cut into her. She sat in the seat, wishing she hadn't got in the carriage. The idea of playing the tourist with him again brought back heated memories of that first kiss in the sleigh.

'Did you use anything to do with what we talked about after our night together?' His voice was deep and firm, quashing those memories instantly as he snapped out the question.

'No,' she said and looked directly at him, into the depths of eyes that were shuttered, keeping her out and his thoughts locked away. 'I never wanted to pry into your family history, more to show an insight into your country. It was what Richard had suggested in the first place.'

'Who is Richard?'

'A photographer I met while on my course. He works for *World in Photographs* and helped me get the contract to write the article about your family.' She had nothing to hide, so why shouldn't she tell him about how she'd got the contract in the first place? If he chose to see it in the wrong light, that was his problem.

'What do you owe this Richard for getting you the contract?' The sharpness of his voice made her look at him quickly, but the coldness of his eyes was almost as bitter as the wind in Vladimir had been.

'Nothing. All I wanted was to take the best photographs I could and showcase your country, weaving in some of your family stories, which I have achieved without adding in anything you told me in your hotel room.'

'Then for now I trust you,' he said as the carriage

pulled away, the sudden movement making her grab the seat to steady herself. Instantly his hands reached out to hold her and from the seat opposite she felt that heated attraction connect them once more. Their eyes met; she looked into the inky blackness and swallowed as she saw the glint of steely hardness had given way to something more dangerous—desire. She couldn't allow herself to fall for his seductive charms again; she just needed to deal with the consequences of their night together and leave before she fell even further and deeper for him. Irritated by the direction of her thoughts, she pulled away and sat back in the carriage seat, desperate to avoid his scrutiny.

If he didn't trust her with his secrets then why had he told them to her? Had that also been a way of manipulating her to do what he wanted, make her think what he wanted her to think? It had not occurred to her until now that what he'd said might not have been the complete truth.

'I wouldn't lie to you, Nikolai,' she said defensively, and looked away from the dark eyes, feigning an interest in the tall buildings clearly visible above the newly green trees of the park. Maybe if she took a few shots from the carriage he'd see she was as unaffected by him as he appeared to be by her.

The lens of the camera clicked but she had no idea what she'd taken. Concentration was impossible with his dominating presence opposite her and the looming discussion of their baby. She turned the camera off and looked at him to see he'd been watching every move she'd made.

'We need to talk about our predicament.' Still his

dark eyes watched her, assessing her reaction to his words.

'Predicament?' she snapped, giving him her full attention. 'Is that what this baby is to you? A predicament? Something else you have to deal with? Just what do you suggest, Nikolai?'

'It is a predicament,' he said calmly, far too calmly, and it unnerved her. What was coming next? 'One I never wanted but one which now means we must get married.'

'Married?' she said loudly, then looked around to see if anyone had heard her. From the satisfied expression on Nikolai's face, that was exactly the reaction he had been hoping for. 'We can't get married.'

'Give me one good reason why not.' He sat back and regarded her sternly.

'We live on different continents to start with.' She grasped at the first thing she could think of and, from the amused look which crossed his face, he knew it. Why did he have to look so handsome, so incredibly sexy? And why was she still so attracted to him?

'That can easily be sorted. I have a home in London if New York isn't to your liking.' His instant response unsettled her. Had he worked it all out already?

'It's not easy for me,' she said quickly, angry that everything seemed so cut and dried with him. 'I have my sister to consider and my job. I've only just been offered a job with *World in Photographs*.'

'Your sister is in Perm for the next few years and your job could be done from anywhere, could it not?' The tone of his voice confirmed her suspicion of moments ago. He did have it all worked out—completely to suit him.

None of what he was suggesting suited her. She needed to be in London, especially now she had a job with *World in Photographs*, a job she needed for financial security, now more than ever. Not only did she have Jess to help through the ballet school, she had a baby on the way, but deep down it was more than that. His so-called deal tapped into her deepest insecurities after growing up knowing that out there in the world was her father, a man who didn't want to know her.

Overwhelmed by the panic of her situation, she glared at Nikolai. 'I need to be in London if I'm to keep the job as a photographer with *World in Photographs* and I need that job to support Jess.'

'That is easily sorted.'

She frowned, not sure what he was getting at. 'For you, maybe.'

'Jess will have all the financial help she needs to ensure she can—what was it you said in Vladimir?— chase her dream.' The look on his handsome face was as severe as she'd ever seen it, not a hint of pleasure from the generous gift he'd just offered. Or was it a gift? Was it not dangling temptation in front of her?

No, it was more than that. It was a bribe and all she had to do was marry him. The thought filled her with dread. She'd dreamed of the day a man would propose to her, dreamed of it being a loving and romantic moment. Nikolai was being neither as he sat watching her; even the ride in the carriage couldn't lend a romantic mood to the moment.

'I can't accept that,' she said, still unable to believe what was happening. He was making a deal with her for their child: marry him and she, the baby and Jess would be financially secure. It hurt that she had very little chance of ever matching that, especially now her pregnancy would affect her ability to work. If she turned him down, said no, as instinct was urging her to do, she would be turning down so much more than just a marriage proposal. She would be saying no to something which would help Jess but, more importantly, give her baby what she'd never had: a father.

Turmoil raged inside her as he watched her, the motion of the carriage making her feel slightly ill, and the steady rhythm of the horses' hooves sounding like drums in her head. How could this be happening? How could all this come from one desire-laden moment in time? How could those few blissful hours have such an impact on her life?

'No,' she said again, more firmly. 'I can't accept that.'

For a moment he looked at her and the tension between them intensified, but she refused to look away. She wanted to challenge him, wanted to push him in the same way he was pushing her.

Finally he spoke. 'Just as I will not tolerate being pushed out of my child's life, and the only way to ensure that is marriage.'

He leant forward in the carriage and she looked away, not daring to look into his dark eyes a moment longer. He had touched a raw and open wound. She was here because she'd hoped he'd want something to do with his child, that he wouldn't turn his back on either her or his baby. She'd never expected this from a man who'd declared one night was all he could give. If she turned him down, didn't that make her worse than her mother?

She couldn't help herself and looked deep into his

eyes, seeing what she'd seen that night in Vladimir, and tried to plead with him again. 'But marriage—'

'Is the only option.' He cut across her once more. 'We will be married, Emma. I will not take no for an answer, not now you are carrying my child.'

CHAPTER SIX

THE REST OF the carriage ride had blurred into a shocked haze and now, as she stood in one of New York's most renowned jeweller's, that haze was beginning to lift. She couldn't marry Nikolai. What was she thinking, allowing him to bring her here to buy an engagement ring? It wouldn't change the fact that this wasn't what he wanted. Turmoil erupted inside her. She didn't want to make the same mistakes as her mother, not when she knew what it felt like to be the child whose existence a father denied.

Could she really do this—sacrifice everything to do the right thing by her son or daughter? If she walked away now would her child blame her later, as she blamed her mother for depriving her of a father?

She looked anxiously at the door but had to steel herself against the reaction Nikolai provoked in her as he stood right behind her, so very close she could feel the heat of his body. It reminded her of the night they'd shared in Vladimir. The passion had been so intense, so powerful. Didn't the undeniable attraction count for something?

'Not thinking of running out on me, are you?' The whispered question sent a tremor of awareness down her spine, which deepened as he held the tops of her arms, pulling her back against the latent power of his body.

She shook her head in denial, unable to put a sentence together as his touch scorched through her, reminding her of the passion they'd shared the night their child had been conceived. That thought chilled the fire he'd unwittingly stirred to life just by being near her. She had to remember the cruel way he'd bargained not only with Jess's future, but her past, exploiting the one thing which had been a constant shadow in her life. Because of that, whatever she did, she had to control the desire he evoked within her from just a touch.

'No, you have made it perfectly clear what has to be done.' She turned to face him, wishing she didn't feel the rush of desire which flooded her as she looked into his eyes. They were dark and heavy with passion, just as they had been that night in Vladimir. Would she ever stop seeing images in her mind of him like that? He'd become imprinted there and he invaded every thought. Had it been because he was the only man to have touched her intimately, the only man she'd made love with or simply the worry of facing him to tell him about the baby?

A heaviness settled over her as an ominous clarity finally allowed her to see that night for what it really was. It had just been a seduction, a way to keep her from whatever it was he was hiding, and for him it most definitely hadn't been about making love. For him it would have been purely lust.

'Then I suggest we select the ring that will seal the deal.' His voice sounded firm and in control. Yet again he was manipulating her, forcing her to accept his terms.

Panic filled Emma. This wasn't how she'd envisaged the moment she would get engaged. It had been very much more romantic than this demand that she choose a ring. But what choice did she have now? Not only would he provide the funds for Jess, he would be in his child's life. It was exactly how she'd always envisaged being a mother—supported by the child's father. The only difference was that in her dreams that man had been there for her too—out of love, not duty to his child.

'You're right,' she said calmly, reluctantly acknowledging this was the only way forward.

Further doubts crowded in on her, solidifying the need to accept Nikolai's deal, no matter what she felt. What if she couldn't cope, just as her mother hadn't been able to do? Would her baby be taken from her, as she and Jess had been? That wouldn't happen if she was married to the child's father.

'So, are we agreed?' he asked in a calm voice.

'Yes,' she replied, seeing no other option but this deal he'd given her. 'This is the best way.'

Before she could back out of the marriage she'd agreed to, with a man she'd never expected to see again after he'd left her at the hotel, she gave her full attention to the rings displayed before her. The sparkling stones blurred for a moment and she blinked to try and refocus them, horrified to realise it was tears filling her eyes that were distorting the almost endless display of expensive rings.

Once she'd selected one of the rings and was wearing it the deal would be sealed. She would have accepted his terms. She blinked quickly once more, trying to stop the threatening tears from falling. She couldn't cry. Not yet. She had to be as strong and detached as he was being.

'I think an emerald.' He moved to her side and put his arm around her, his hand holding her waist as he pulled her tighter against his body. 'To match your eyes.'

He'd noticed she had green eyes? That snippet of information shocked her, because it meant he had taken an interest in her beyond the seduction he'd obviously been planning since the ride in the troika. The memory of that day was now tarnished by the reality of the fact that he'd engineered it all—and she'd fallen for it. Had that wonderfully gentle yet powerfully seductive kiss been part of the plan too?

Of course it had and you fell for it.

'How about this one?' she asked, tiredness washing over her, brought on no doubt by the stress of everything, combined with the time difference and pregnancy. All she wanted to do right now was get back to her hotel room and rest, but she held the ring up by the delicate diamond-encrusted band, the emerald sparkling in the bright lights of the store.

'Are you sure you wouldn't prefer one of the larger ones?' He moved away from her and sat in a distinctly antique-looking chair to the side of the table. She tried hard not to look at his long legs as he stretched them out before him. He looked far too relaxed when she was as tense as she'd ever been.

'No,' she said and looked boldly into his eyes, not missing the way his gaze slid down her body before meeting hers. The tingle of awareness was disconcerting and she pushed it aside, determined to be in control of this moment at the very least. 'No, this is much more my style.'

He stood up and came back to her. He took the ring from her, looking at it, then, to her astonishment, took her left hand in his, raising it up. With deliberate slowness he slipped the ring onto her finger and she was amazed to see it was a perfect fit, as if it had been made for her. 'In that case, will you do me the honour of becoming my wife?'

It was the last thing she'd expected him to do after having all but put a deal to her and she stumbled over her words, aware of the store staff watching the exchange. Was this all for their benefit or his? She looked at him, wondering if she'd be able to speak, but finally the words came out in a soft whisper. 'Yes, Nikolai, I will.'

He kept hold of her hand for far too long and she watched as he looked down at the square emerald now sat neatly on her finger. Would he keep his side of this strange bargain? Would he provide the funds for Jess to continue on her chosen course in life and, more importantly, be there for his child?

If he doesn't you only have to walk away; you have nothing to lose by agreeing.

As that rebellious thought rocked through her he stepped closer and lowered his head; she knew, with every nerve in her body, that he was going to kiss her. Right there in the store.

When his lips met hers fire shot through her and her knees weakened and, as her eyes fluttered closed, she forced them open again. He moved slightly and she could see his lips lifting into a smile that was full of self-satisfaction. Then he spoke so softly only she could hear. 'A very sensible answer.'

Nikolai opened the door of the car he'd ordered while he'd completed his purchase for the engagement ring—an item he'd never envisaged buying again. But what choice did he have? He couldn't turn his back on his child. This was his chance to prove to himself he was a better man than his father. His child had not been conceived in the underhand way he himself had been, so didn't that already make him a better man? But it wasn't enough. He needed to prove to himself he was not like his father.

He watched as Emma slid into the back of the car, looking weary, and a pang of guilt briefly touched him. He had nothing to feel guilty about, he reassured himself. Emma was here to secure her and her child's future and, now that he'd also added her sister's into the bargain, she had everything she'd come for—and more.

She would become his fiancée and, as soon as possible, his wife. He wanted this particular deal sealed long before news of their baby broke. He wanted his mother to think he'd found love and happiness. It was all she'd ever wanted for him and now, due to one night when he'd been less than in control, he was able to give her that.

'Where are you staying?' he demanded as he joined her in the back of the car.

'A hotel on West Forty-Seventh Street,' she said without looking at him, provoking that twinge of guilt once more as he gave the driver instructions.

'This is the right thing to do,' he said as he took her hand from where it lay in her lap. She turned to look at him, her sable hair moving invitingly, reminding him of how soft it had been between his fingers.

'What if you meet someone you really want to marry?' The doubt laced in her voice did little to soften the emotions running through him. As far as he was concerned, that would never be an issue. The example of married life his father had set him was one which had stayed with him long after his mother had found happiness. He might have seen her marry for love when he was almost twelve years old but inside he knew he had his father's genes. The way to avoid testing that theory had been to avoid any kind of emotional commitment. By the time he'd become a successful businessman in his own right, he'd also become cold and cynical and knew he would never think of marrying— at least, not for love.

'That won't be an issue. I could, of course, ask the same of you.'

'Oh, I always dreamed of the fairy-tale wedding. You know—big white dress, flower girls and brides-maids, fancy location and a honeymoon in a tropical paradise.' At first he was taken aback by her soft, wistful voice, but the hard glint in those green eyes warned him it was just a cover-up. He knew all about hiding emotions, only he was better at it than she was; but he'd play the game her way. For now, at least.

'And now?'

'Now?' She pulled her hand free of his and glared up at him, defiance adding to the sparks in her eyes. 'Now I know better.'

'So you won't be looking for love and happy-ever-afters?'

'Never.' That one word was said with so much conviction he didn't doubt it for one minute.

'Then we agree on that too. You see, already we have a good base for our marriage. A child who needs us both and an obvious dislike of anything remotely romantic.'

She looked at him, questions racing across her beautiful face, and all he wanted to do was taste her lips once more. The memory of that kiss in the snow had lingered in his mind for the best part of two months, just as the hours spent making her truly his had filled his dreams night after night. It had been those memories which had made kissing her in the store impossible to resist, that and the smouldering anger, defused by an undeniable attraction in her alluring eyes.

'We're here,' she said quickly, the relief in her voice more than evident.

'I'll come with you whilst you check out,' he said as he got out of the car into the bustle of New York's streets.

'I'm not checking out,' she said sternly as she joined him, defiantly glaring up at him.

'We are now engaged—you will not stay here alone; besides, we have a party to plan.' Did she really expect him to leave her here after the news she'd given him today? He wasn't going to give her any opportunity to run out on him again, which he suspected was exactly what she wanted to do.

'What party?' The shock in her voice angered him more than he was comfortable with. It seemed everything today was out of his comfort zone.

'Our engagement party. I'll call the planner as soon as we get back to my apartment. I think the weekend would be best.' Before she could say anything, he took her arm and propelled her into the sleek interior of the hotel. 'But first you need to collect your luggage and check out.'

Emma couldn't believe how things were going. She'd had no idea what to expect when she'd made the journey to New York, but it wasn't this. She walked across the spacious apartment which gave stunning views over Central Park and that feeling of disbelief that he'd insisted she check out of the hotel intensified. 'There was no need for me to leave the hotel.'

'There is every need, Emma. Apart from the engagement party, which is scheduled for the weekend, I want you to rest.' The authority in his voice was unmistakable. She wanted to rebel against it but, just as she had done when she and Jess had moved from one foster family to another, she held it back. It was a skill she'd become adept at over the years.

Nikolai strode across the polished wooden floor to stand looking out of the large floor-to-ceiling windows and seeing his solitary figure reminded her of the photo she'd taken at his family home. He'd looked desolate and alone then. Now the firm set of his shoulders warned her he was far from desolate and very much in control of the situation and his emotions.

She wished she had her camera in her hands right now but instead walked softly across the floor to join him, her footsteps light. Just remembering him like that had calmed her emotions, made her want to find again the companionship they had experienced in Vladimir before they'd spent the night together. Maybe, if they could find that, then this marriage she was about to make had a chance of success.

She was fully aware the attraction was still there, the chemistry that sparked to life from just a single touch. His kiss as they were buying the ring had proved that, but if they were to make this work they needed to be friends; they needed to be able to hold a simple conversation without being on guard.

'That's quite a view,' she said as she stood next to him, hoping to make light conversation about something neutral. He didn't look at her and she glanced at his strong profile. 'I'd like to take some photographs, perhaps as the sun sets.'

'So that you can sell them?' Harshness had crept back into his voice and he turned to face her. 'Is that what this is all about? Extracting yet more from me and my family? Exposing even more details to bargain for money?'

As his words sank in she realised with shock what he was asking. 'It's not about that at all, Nikolai, I just wanted to take the photographs for my own enjoyment. I've never been to New York, let alone in a swanky apartment with views over Central Park.'

'I haven't yet seen what you submitted to *World in Photographs*.' He turned to look at her, his dark eyes black with veiled anger.

'That is easily sorted,' she said as she headed to the room he'd had her small amount of luggage delivered to. She'd been relieved to discover that he had no intention of spending the night in the same bed as her, but to her dismay that relief had been tinged with disappointment.

When she returned to the large open-plan living

space of the apartment, he was still looking out of the window, his shoulders more tense than ever. What was he so worried about? What could a few photographs and a small piece about his family really do?

She put her laptop down on the table and fired it up, the question as to what he was so worried about going round in her mind. All families had troubles they kept hidden from the world. She knew that more than most. She opened the piece she'd written for *World in Photographs* to go with the stunning images she'd taken and stepped away from the table.

'It's there for you. Richard liked it,' she said softly and sat down on the large cream sofa which dominated one corner of the apartment.

'Richard has seen it?' From across the room, Nikolai glared at her.

'He's been very helpful, and I wouldn't have got that contract without his help.' She fixed her gaze on the view of the park, not daring to look at him as he walked towards her laptop and began reading.

After five minutes of heavy silence he turned to look at her, his handsome face set in a forbidding frown. 'This is what you submitted?'

'Yes; what did you expect, Nikolai?'

'Not this light-hearted, romantic stuff about life in Russia. You have turned what I told you into something quite different.'

He walked towards her, his footsteps hard on the polished wooden floor, and she wished she hadn't chosen to sit down. He was too imposing, too dominating. 'You told me very little, Nikolai, and as I didn't get to meet with your grandmother I had to come up with something.'

'None of it true.'

'What is the truth, Nikolai? Why were you so worried I would meet your grandmother?'

He sighed and sat down next to her on the sofa, the air around them suddenly charged with something she couldn't yet fathom out. 'My family's story is complicated.'

'I know all about complicated, Nikolai. Jess and I have experienced it first-hand.' Why had she said that? She wanted to find out about him, not spill out her own sorry story. Would he still want her as his wife if he knew what kind of upbringing she'd had?

'Then we have that in common at least.' Sadness tinged his voice and her heart constricted, just as it had done when she'd taken the photo of him outside the ruins of what had once been his family home. She wanted to reach out to him, but kept her hands firmly together in her lap.

'Do you want to talk about it?' she asked, knowing full well he didn't, that he wanted to keep it all hidden safely away. It was what she'd done all through her childhood, mostly to protect Jess, who didn't know half of it.

'No but, as you are soon to marry into my family, then you should know.'

Her mouth went dry with fear. Would that mean he too would want to know about her childhood, her family? 'You don't have to tell me anything you don't want to.'

'You should know something of how I came to be living in New York and why I no longer use Petrushov, the surname I was born with.'

She looked at him, unable to stop herself from

reaching out to touch him. She placed her hand on his arm, trying to ignore the jolt of something wild which sparked between them from that innocent touch. 'We don't have to do this now.'

He ignored her and continued, his face a firm mask of composure. 'My mother's marriage to my father was not happy, neither was my childhood, and when he died it was a release for both my mother and I.'

'I'm sorry,' she said softly but her words didn't seem to reach him. Instead they only brought forward her own painful childhood memories—and she wasn't ready to share them yet.

'My mother was helped by a business acquaintance of my father and I guess it was one of those rare moments when love conquered all.' He looked down at her hand, still on his arm, and frowned, as if he'd only just realised she was touching him. Obviously her touch didn't do to him what his did to her.

'You say that as if you don't believe in such a concept.' She pulled her hand back and kept it firmly in her lap.

'I thought we'd already established that love is something neither of us believe in.' His dark eyes bored into hers, accusation and suspicion filling them, and she recalled their conversation in Vladimir. She remembered being blasé about looking for a fairy-tale wedding and happy-ever-after. She knew no such thing would ever happen to her, but from the way he was looking at her now he thought she wanted such things.

'We did; you just threw me when you said it was one of "those rare moments". As if you really believe they happen.' She smiled at him, injecting lightness into her voice. It was far better he thought she didn't believe in love in any shape or form. The last thing he needed to know right now was that she did believe in love and happy-ever-afters; she just didn't believe it would ever happen to her. It never would now she'd agreed to marry him as part of a deal.

'Well, whatever you believe, it happened for my mother. She changed from the constantly scared woman who lingered in the shadows of her marriage and blossomed into someone very different—and it's all thanks to Roger Cunningham. Even in my early teens I could see that, and at sixteen I changed my surname legally to his, although I'd already spent all my years here in New York as Nikolai Cunningham.'

'I did wonder,' she said, remembering his insistence that his name wasn't Petrushov when she'd first met him, and the card he'd tossed on the bed just before walking out on her. She pushed the pain of that moment aside and focused on the present. 'And now your child will take that name too.'

'As will you when we are married.' He looked at her hand, at the emerald ring on her finger, and she wondered if he was regretting what had seemed an impulsive move, telling her they would be married.

'We don't have to get married, Nikolai. I would never keep you from your child, not after having grown up without a father myself.' She swallowed down the nerves as she waited for his response. He looked into her eyes, as if he was trying to read her thoughts, and as much as she wanted to look away she held his gaze.

'Is the idea of being my wife that abhorrent to you?' His voice had deepened and a hint of an accent she'd never noticed before came through. The idea of being married was terrifying, but the idea of being this man's wife was less so. Was that because he was the only man she had truly known?

She shook her head, not able to speak.

He lifted his hand and pushed her hair back from her face. 'I will never do anything to hurt you, Emma; you do know that, don't you?'

The words were so tender she had to swallow down the urge to cry. His fingers brushed her cheek, bringing their night together vividly back to her mind. 'Yes, I know that.'

He leant towards her, his hand sliding round beneath her hair, holding her head gently, and before she could say or do anything his lips were on hers, the same gentle, teasing kiss as in the store. Her resistance melted like ice-cream on a hot day and she kissed him back. He deepened the kiss, sending a fury of fireworks around her body, reviving all the desire she'd felt for him and, if the truth were told, still felt even though she'd supressed it well.

She still wanted him, still yearned for him.

'We still have the passion we found in Vladimir,' he said as he broke the kiss and moved away from her, leaving her almost shuddering from the heat coursing through her. 'And that at least will make our marriage more bearable.'

She blinked in shock at his words. He'd been toying with her, proving his point. He obviously would never have chosen her to be his wife if it wasn't for the baby, but he'd told her he'd never wanted to be married when he'd first met her. She'd already accepted it was what she had to do for Jess as much as the baby. 'It will, yes.'

He smiled at her, but the warmth didn't reach those black eyes. 'Then we shall marry in three weeks. But first, there is the small matter of an engagement party.'

CHAPTER SEVEN

THE WEEK HAD flown by in a whirl of party arrangements and now it was time to face not only Nikolai's friends as his fiancée but his mother and stepfather. Emma's nerves jangled as she waited and she thought back to those two kisses on the day they'd become engaged. She had thought they were a positive sign, that he did at least feel something for her, but for the last week he'd withdrawn into his work and she had spent much of the time out with her camera.

Just this morning she'd been shopping in a store Nikolai had instructed her to visit for a dress suitable for the glamorous event the engagement party had turned into; now she stood looking out over a city which never slept, wearing the kind of dress she'd never imagined possible and feeling more like Cinderella every minute. The only thing she needed was Prince Charming to declare his undying love and sweep her away for a happy-ever-after but she doubted Nikolai would be willing to play that role.

She'd been in the beauty salon for the early part of the afternoon, nerves building with each passing hour. The cream dress, encrusted with beads, fitted to perfection and when she'd looked in the mirror before leaving her room she hadn't recognised herself. The woman Nikolai had met in Vladimir had gone, replaced by someone who looked much more polished and refined. What would Nikolai think of that? Or had it been his intention all along to mould her into the woman he wanted her to be?

She heard Nikolai's footsteps and nerves filled her so quickly she didn't want to turn round, but knew she would have to. When she did her breath caught in her throat. She'd seen him in a suit, but never a tuxedo, and the image he created stirred more than just her creative mind.

The fine black cloth hugged his broad shoulders, caressed his biceps and followed his lean frame downwards. The crisp white shirt set off the black tie to perfection, but it was his face which drew her attention far more. Stubble which had been tamed to look effortlessly sexy covered his jawline, emphasising the firm set of his lips. Dark hair was styled into conformity but a few locks were already breaking free and forming curls at his temples.

'You look…' he said softly as he stood and fastened his cufflinks, the movement showing off his wrists and designer watch. His dark eyes were full of controlled anger as he sought the words he was looking for.

'Very different.' She didn't want to hear what he thought and finished the sentence for him. All she wanted was to get his charade over with. She hated the pretence of it all.

He stepped a little closer, dropping his arms by his side, making the cloth of the tuxedo cling even more provocatively to him. 'I was going to say very beautiful.'

'I'm not so sure about that.' She blushed beneath his scrutiny and clutched her bag ever tighter.

She was about to walk past him when he caught her arm, the look in his eyes heavy with desire; as much as she wanted to look away, to avoid the way her body sizzled with pleasure, she boldly met his gaze. She stood there, locked in time, waiting for him to say something. He didn't and finally he let go of her, the connection gone, snuffed out like a candle, leaving a lingering scent in the air.

'We should go. My mother will be expecting us.' He turned away from her, as if he'd made a mistake even touching her, and she wasn't sure what worried her the most: the thought of meeting his mother and stepfather or that he couldn't bear to look at her.

'I'm looking forward to meeting her,' she said as she fiddled with her bag, anything other than witness his obvious discomfort at being around her.

'There is one thing I need to ask from you.' He stopped at the door of the apartment and looked down at her. 'My mother knows nothing of the baby and I'd like to keep it that way. For now, at least.'

He was ashamed of her, ashamed of the child she carried. That hurt her more than anything, but it also showcased the fact that this marriage was nothing more than a deal and she must never fall into the trap of thinking it was anything else.

She frowned and tried to smile, but she couldn't help but ask, 'Why?'

'She believes I am in love. We are in love. I want to keep it that way. I want her to believe we are marrying simply because we fell in love.' Each time he said the word 'love', his voice became harsher, as if he couldn't bear even naming such an emotion.

So he was ashamed he was to be a father. Was that why he wanted to get married as soon as possible—so that he could make it look like something they'd planned or at least wanted?

She shrugged, trying to hide her hurt at what he'd just said. 'If that's what you want.'

Nikolai watched as his mother hugged Emma, then held her hands and stood back to look at her, as if shocked that he'd finally brought a woman home to meet her. His gaze lingered a little too long on Emma's glorious body, encased in a gown which caressed her figure in a way that evoked memories of kissing her all over before making her his—truly his.

'I am so pleased to meet you.' His mother's words dragged his mind back from the erotic path they had taken, forcing him to concentrate on the present. 'I never really believed I'd see this day; and such a gorgeous ring.'

'A gorgeous ring for a very beautiful woman.' Nikolai spoke his thoughts aloud before he had time to evaluate them, but when Emma blushed and his mother smiled he knew they had been exactly what was needed.

'You must of course stay here tonight,' his mother offered Emma, just as she had done with him earlier in the week, but he'd refused, claiming a need to work the next day.

'Emma and I will be travelling back tonight,' he said sternly and felt Emma's gaze on him. Was she pleading with him to extricate them both from the invitation?

'I won't hear of it. How can you enjoy your engagement party if you have to travel back tonight? Besides, I've already had a room prepared, so there is no excuse.'

'I need to be at the office first thing in the morning.' Nikolai knew his voice sounded abrupt and, if the curious glance Emma cast his way was anything to go by, his mother would know he was making excuses.

'Nonsense. You work far too hard, and besides, it's the weekend and you should be spending it with your fiancée. Isn't that right, Emma?' His mother smiled at him, using her charm and tactics as she always did to get what she wanted, but he didn't want Emma pushed into a situation that she clearly didn't want. Also, staying here at his mother's house in The Hamptons would almost certainly mean sharing not only a room with Emma, but a bed. The fact that his mother had made a room ready suggested she'd already planned it all out.

'I don't have anything with me, Mrs Cunningham.' Emma's soft voice caught him unawares, as did the way it sent a tingle of awareness down his spine. He looked at her, at the worried expression on her face, and something twisted inside him, as if his heart was being squeezed.

He couldn't be falling for her. He didn't want that kind of complication, especially when she was here to celebrate their engagement only because he'd made a deal which would secure not only her baby's future but her sister's. A deal she'd been more than happy to agree on once he'd made her see that refusal would leave her child without a father. Something he knew she was all too familiar with.

'Well, if that's the only reason, I can soon sort that

out. My stepdaughter is here with her husband and between us both we can loan you anything you need.'

Nikolai's control on the situation was slipping through his fingers and he was torn between saving Emma from being forced to spend a night in the same room as him and allowing his mother to continue with the illusion that he'd finally succumbed to love.

'I couldn't do that…' Emma began, but before she could finish he spoke over her.

'Then we shall stay.' He pulled Emma against him, the fine fabric of her dress no barrier to the heat from her body as it seared through his suit, setting him alight with a desire he had no intention of acting on. Diversion was what he needed. 'We should mingle.'

At the extravagantly laid tables all around them were friends and members of his family, or rather his stepfamily. Everyone was enjoying themselves and their laughter mixed with the music from the live performers. He and Emma were the centre of attention, and that was something he hadn't thought of when he'd put the party planners in touch with his mother and let them loose together. A big mistake.

'I'm sorry,' he said as he took Emma's hand and led her to a table where they could sit and try and keep out of the limelight, for a while at least.

'For what?' She sat elegantly beside him and again that strange sensation washed over him.

'There isn't anyone here you know.'

'That's okay,' she answered as she looked around the marquee, hardly recognisable beneath its lavish decorations. 'It's not as if it's a real engagement.'

'It's very real, Emma.' Anger surfaced, smothering the simmering desire which brewed deep inside him.

She turned in her seat to give him her full attention and all he could do was look at her lips, red with lipstick, and imagine kissing them until she sighed with pleasure. He couldn't let her do this to him. He had to get back his control and fast. 'We are engaged and will be married by the end of the month.'

'But it's not for real, Nikolai, despite what you want your mother to believe. None of it is real—and I can't do this again.' A look of fear flitted across her face and he frowned in confusion.

'Do what?' He took her hands from her lap, where she'd clutched them tightly together. She looked at him, directly into his eyes, and he saw the anguish in hers.

'Be paraded around like this. When we get married, I want it to be with as little fuss as possible. I don't want to be the subject of everyone's scrutiny.' Her green eyes pleaded with him and the slight waver in her voice unsettled him. Was she having second thoughts about their deal?

'That suits me perfectly.' He snapped the words out and let her hands go, angered by the thought that she was at this very moment looking for a way out of their planned marriage—and the deal.

Emma didn't want the party to end. It was so lavish she could hardly have dreamed it up if she'd tried, and if she and Nikolai had truly been in love it would have been the perfect start to their life together. But they weren't in love. Nikolai's stern words as they'd sat talking at the beginning of the evening had been more than enough proof for her.

'Emma, Nikolai.' His mother came up to them, excitement all over her face. 'It's time for the finale, and

I want you to be in the prime spot when it happens. Come with me.'

'What have you done now?' Nikolai's deep voice demanded of his mother, but she wasn't listening, and she headed off through the crowds, leaving them no choice but to follow her out and across the lawns. Emma could hear the water in the darkness which surrounded the extensive garden, now lit up with hundreds of lights, and it was a relief to be away from the many people who had attended the party, none of whom she knew.

'I have no idea what this is about,' Nikolai said sternly, his irritation at such a public display of them as a newly engaged couple all too obvious.

'We should at least see,' she said to Nikolai, unable to supress a smile. How nice it must be to have a mother who would arrange surprises for you; it was exactly the kind of mother she wanted to be herself.

Nikolai didn't say anything, but took her hand and made his way to where his mother was talking to a group of people. His annoyance at the arrangement was very clear.

'Stand here, with the party as a backdrop. I want an engagement photo of you both.' The excitement in his mother's voice was contagious and Emma couldn't help but laugh softly. Nikolai didn't share her appreciation and wasn't in the least amused by it.

'That's not necessary.' Nikolai's brusque tone didn't make a dent on his mother's enthusiasm.

At that point Emma realised this wasn't just a snapshot for a family album, as a party photographer joined them and set about making them stand just where he wanted them to. Instantly she was uncomfortable. She hated being on what she considered the wrong side of the lens.

'Now, embrace each other,' the photographer said as he stepped back and started clicking, his assistants altering lights to get the best result. 'Kiss each other.'

Kiss.

Emma looked at Nikolai and wondered just what he was going to say about being forced to kiss her. The same kind of boldness which had come over her in Vladimir rushed through her again.

'We'd better do as we're told,' she whispered with a smile on her lips, amused at his hard expression. He wasn't doing a very good job of acting the part of a man in love, which was what he'd wanted his mother to think he was. 'We're in love, remember?'

His eyes darkened until they were so black and full of desire that she caught her breath as anticipation rushed through her. Her heart thumped harder and she was sure he'd see the pulse at her throat, but his gaze didn't waver. He pulled her closer against him and she could feel his thighs touch hers, his chest press against her breasts.

He moved slowly but with intent purpose until his lips met hers and, acting on instinct, her eyes closed and her body melted into his. His arms held her tighter still and she wrapped hers around his neck as he deepened the kiss. She didn't want to respond, didn't want to acknowledge the power of the passion racing through her, but she couldn't help herself. She opened her lips and tasted his with her tongue as fireworks seemed to explode around them.

'Perfect,' the photographer directed. 'Keep kissing her.'

Nikolai's hand slid down to the small of her back, pressing her against him, and the fire of desire raged through her. If she didn't stop him now she'd be in danger of giving herself away, of allowing him to see just what he did to her.

She let her arms fall from his neck and pushed against his chest, wanting to continue, yet not wanting him to know that just a kiss could make her his again. 'That's pretty powerful acting,' she said, alarmed at how husky her voice sounded.

A large bang sounded behind them and, startled, she looked towards the party. Fireworks filled the night sky behind the marquee and relief washed over her. She thought she had heard fireworks as he'd kissed her, ones created by this man's kiss. The relief at discovering that they had been real made her laugh and, still in Nikolai's embrace, she looked up at him.

'The same can be said of you.' Desire filled his voice as he responded.

Nikolai let her go as his mother walked towards them, a big smile on her face. 'That was perfect. I will see you both in the morning.'

Emma watched her leave, an ultra-glamorous woman who believed her son had found the love of his life. What would she say if she knew the truth, and why was it so important to Nikolai that she thought that? Questions burned in her mind.

'Shall we return to the party or retire to bed?' The question shocked her and she didn't know which was more preferable. She didn't want to continue to be the centre of speculation but neither did she want to go to their room.

'Perhaps we should just go back to your apartment.'

The suggestion came from her before she had time to think.

'I can see that my presence in your room is not going to be welcome, but I can assure you, nothing will happen. The pretence of being in love can be dropped once we close the bedroom door.'

'In that case, we should retire,' she said, trying to keep the despondency from her voice. He didn't want her, didn't find her attractive. The kiss of moments ago had been just an act. Pretence at attraction and love, purely to keep his mother happy.

Nikolai saw the expression of horror cross Emma's face, and wished he'd been firmer with his mother, but she'd looked so happy he just couldn't destroy that for her. This whole sham of an engagement was to make his mother happy and now he was guilty of making Emma unhappy. Strangely, that was worse, but it was too late to back out now. They would spend the night in this room and leave as soon as they could in the morning.

Emma crossed the room to the only bed and looked at the items his mother had instructed to be left for them. She held up a cream silk nightdress which would do little to conceal her figure and he closed his eyes against the image of her in it—and, worse, next to him in that very bed.

'It appears your mother has thought of everything,' she said as she looked up at him. 'It's almost as if she was planning on us having to stay.'

Emma had just echoed his own thoughts, but he brushed them away in an attempt to put her at ease. 'Whatever it was my mother had planned, she believes we are in love and, as I said earlier, I want to keep it that way. I also promised that nothing would happen between us, so I will sleep in the chair.'

He gestured to an easy chair which would be perfect for relaxing in during the day, but not so great to sleep in for a night. She looked from him to the chair and sighed, as if in resignation.

'I hardly think that will be conducive to a good night's sleep.' He was about to argue the point when a smile tugged at the corners of her mouth. 'We'll just have to manage together in the bed. We are, after all, both adults and have agreed that nothing is going to happen.'

He might have agreed, but he seriously doubted if he could carry through that promise. She stood before him now in the dress which shimmered in the lights of the room, and he wanted her more than he'd ever wanted any woman.

Maybe one more night in her arms would be enough to suppress the desire-laden thoughts he constantly had about her? That question sent a rush of lust sparking around him, but as he looked at her worried expression he knew it couldn't happen. Not after he'd been the one to set the time limit—just one night in Vladimir.

'In that case, I suggest we get some sleep.' He pulled off his tie and tossed it onto the chair he'd planned to sleep in, determined to prove to himself he was able to exercise firm control where this woman was concerned. Emma didn't move. 'Is there a problem?'

'Can you unzip me?'

She blushed and looked more beautiful and innocent than she'd ever done, but there was a hint of humour in her voice. Did she know just how much she was torturing him?

'I had help this afternoon, but I don't have a stylist to hand at present. Thanks for arranging all that; it was very thoughtful.'

He walked towards her, wondering if he trusted himself to be so close to her, undoing the dress he'd wanted to remove from her sexy body all night. She was testing him, pushing him to the limits of his endurance, whether she knew it or not.

'I wanted you to look the part,' he said, then added more gently as her perfume weaved around him, drawing him ever closer like a ship lured to the rocks by a raging storm, 'And you looked beautiful—so very beautiful.'

'I felt beautiful,' she whispered, as if letting him hear her thoughts. 'It was a fairy-tale night.'

'My mother believes in that fairy tale, at least,' he said firmly, desperate to remind himself why he was even here like this with her. 'You played your part well.'

She looked up at him as he stood in front of her, boldly locking her gaze with his in a fleeting gesture of defiance before lowering her lashes and looking away. She turned her back to him and lifted up her hair, which hung in a glossy veil down her back, exposing the silky, smooth skin he remembered from their night together.

His hand lingered on the zip. He couldn't let go, couldn't step away from the temptation she was creating. He could see her spine and curled his fingers tight against the need to trail them up it and then all the way down. He wanted to kiss her back, to take every last piece of clothing from her sexy body and kiss her everywhere, before claiming her as his once more.

He bit down on a powerful rush of desire which surged through him. Not only had she made it clear she didn't want him, he didn't want the complications of sex becoming something more. He had to ignore the lust which was rapidly engulfing him, if only to prove to himself he didn't want her, didn't feel anything for her.

He reached out and gently pulled the zip downwards, inwardly groaning as her back became visible. The heat of passion was rushing straight to his groin. If this was any other woman, or any other moment in time, he would be kissing that wonderfully bare back and sliding the dress from her, exposing her near nakedness to his hungry gaze. But this wasn't any other woman. This was the woman who was to become his wife and everything was so very complicated.

'Thank you.' She stepped away from him and he clenched his fingers tightly to prevent himself from doing anything else.

Passion pounded in his body, begging for release as she turned to face him. Her hardened nipples were clearly visible through the fine material and he wondered how he'd never noticed until now she was braless. The thought shifted the demanding desire inside him up several notches, ever closer to breaking point.

The air hummed with heavy desire as she picked up the nightdress his mother had magically found from somewhere and walked into the adjoining bathroom and closed the door. For a moment, relief washed over him until he realised that when she returned she'd be wearing even less. The cream nightdress would offer even less protection from him.

With an angry growl he took off his jacket and slung it over the back of the chair. What the hell was wrong with him? He'd never been a slave to desire. He was always in control. *Except with this woman.*

As the bathroom door opened he crossed the room, not daring to look at her, not wanting to see her wearing the silky nightdress which would reveal far more of her body than he could tolerate. He kept his back to her as he heard the bedcovers being moved and then headed for the bathroom. Once inside, he shut the door firmly and turned on the shower, selecting the coldest setting.

When he returned to the bedroom, invigorated from the icy cold jets of water, Emma was lying in the bed, as far to one edge of it as was possible, and either asleep or pretending to be. Wearing only his underwear, he slid beneath the cool covers, turned off the light and lay on his back, looking up at the ceiling through the darkness. Anger boiled up in him, thankfully dimming the throb of desire, allowing his usual stern control to return.

Emma sighed softly next to him and turned over, moving closer to him. He lay rigid in the bed as her breathing settled into the soft rhythm of sleep again. He could feel the warmth of her body, and in his mind all he could see was her naked in his bed in Vladimir. Nothing had changed. He couldn't relax. Damn it, he'd never sleep.

He closed his eyes, willing his body to relax, and, just when he thought he might achieve that elusive state, Emma stirred and moved again. Closer to him. Far too close. She put her arm across his chest and pulled herself closer, pressing her body against the side of his, and instantly his body was ready for her. He clenched his jaw tightly, fighting the throb of desire and the urge to turn to her, to wrap her in his arms and kiss her awake before making her his once more.

A feral curse slipped from his lips as she sighed once more, pressing herself tighter against him so that he could feel the swell of her breast against his arm. He couldn't move. He didn't trust himself to. He had to prove he was stronger than the desire he had for her, something he'd never had a problem with before.

How could he want her so much? What had she done to him? Questions raced through his mind and he focused on them instead of the heady warmth of Emma's sleeping body next to his.

Never in his life had he spent a night with a woman without having sex. How had it come to this? He tried again to sleep, to ignore the heat of her body, and it was more than torture as he lay rigid next to the one woman who threatened everything, from his sanity to his family. How the hell could he want her so badly?

CHAPTER EIGHT

EMMA BLUSHED AGAIN as memories from the few hours they'd spent in bed together came rushing back to her. She still couldn't believe that she'd been wrapped around Nikolai when she'd woken. She'd opened her eyes as spring sunshine had streamed into the unfamiliar room, wondering at first where she was. Then she'd realised they were entwined, as if they were lovers. Slowly she'd moved away from Nikolai as he slept, taking the chance to steal a glance at his handsome features before slipping away to put on a dress left for her last night.

Had anything happened? Had she embarrassed herself by saying or doing something stupid in a sleepy state? She hoped she hadn't let her growing feelings for him show—especially as he'd been adamant that nothing would happen between them. So many questions had raced around her mind as they'd left the beautiful house and started the drive back to his apartment in New York. A tense silence had enveloped them in the car and she hadn't been about to break it, especially not by asking about last night.

Now they were back in his apartment and she was lying in her bed alone, replaying the events of the party.

The kiss for their engagement photo had been so powerful, so very evocative, she'd thought it was real, but then he'd pulled away from her, the hardness of his eyes warning her against such thoughts. But it was when he'd helped her out of her dress that things really had changed. She'd seen raw desire in his eyes as he'd looked at her, and when he'd touched her she'd clamped her mouth tightly closed, worried she might say something and give herself away—because she'd wanted him to touch her.

She should be grateful he hadn't said a word about the previous night other than to make small talk about the party itself, but she wasn't. It didn't feel right, ignoring whatever it was that sizzled between them. With a huff of irritation, she flung back the covers. There was no way she could sleep now. Her mind was alive with questions and her body still yearned for a man who didn't want her.

Silently she left her room and padded across the polished wooden floor to the kitchen as the sounds of a city which never seemed to sleep played out in the background. Was this what her life would be like from now on? Would she be hiding an ever-deepening affection for the father of her child for ever? Could she live like that?

She poured some water and went to sit by the windows, needing the peaceful view of the park to soothe her tortured emotions. She just couldn't be falling for Nikolai, not when all she'd wanted was that happy-ever-after with a man who loved her. But she'd never get that happiness now, even by marrying Nikolai. He didn't love her and had made it clear their marriage was to be nothing more than a deal.

'Are you unwell?' Nikolai's voice startled her, but when she looked up she was even more startled. Just as he'd done that night in Vladimir, he'd pulled on a pair of jeans, and looked so incredibly sexy she had to stop herself from taking in a deep and shuddering breath.

'I couldn't sleep.' She tried hard to avert her gaze from his bare chest, but couldn't. All she could think about was lying with her arms across it last night. She could still feel the muscles beneath her palm and distinctly remembered the scent of his aftershave invading her sleep. What else was she going to remember?

'But you are feeling quite well?' The concern in his voice was touching and she smiled at him.

'I'm fine, just not sleepy.' She didn't have much chance of feeling sleepy now after seeing him like that. All her senses were on high alert, her body all but tuned into his.

His gaze travelled down her bare legs and she realised how she must look, sat on the sofa wearing only a vest top and skimpy shorts, but there wasn't anything she could do about it now, not without alerting him to the fact that she was far from comfortable having a discussion with him when they were both half-undressed. It was much too intimate.

'Is it because you are alone tonight? Nobody to curl up with?' The seductive huskiness of his voice held a hint of laughter. Was he making fun of her?

She looked up at him and knew that wasn't true. He moved closer and stood over her, his dark eyes seeming to penetrate deep inside her, searching for something. 'About—about last night...' she managed to say, but hated the way she stumbled over the words. 'What I mean is, did we...? Did anything happen between us?'

The air heated around them, laden with explosive sexual tension, but she couldn't look away, couldn't break the connection which was becoming more intense by the second.

'Trust me, Emma, you'd remember if it had.' A smile lifted his lips and a hint of mischief sparked in his eyes.

He was making fun of her.

'Oh,' she said softly, heat infusing her cheeks.

'You sound as if you're disappointed to discover that we slept in the same bed without having sex.' Like a brooding presence, he towered over her, suffocating the very air she breathed, making her pulse leap wildly. 'It can of course be rectified.'

This time she wasn't able to stop the ragged intake of breath or the shudder of desire. He wanted her. Just as she wanted him. It was like the night in Vladimir all over again. Then she had believed she was giving in to the allure of a powerful sexual attraction for just one night; even though they were to be married, she knew this was exactly that again. He didn't love her. This was nothing more than sex.

Her heart thumped hard, and warnings echoed in her mind, but she didn't want to heed them. She wanted Nikolai, wanted him to desire her, and the allure of that was more powerful than the prophecy of a broken heart.

The seconds ticked by and the power of the sexual chemistry between them increased as surely as if he'd touched her. Her body yearned for his touch, her lips craved his kiss, but most of all she wanted his possession. She wanted to be his.

Nikolai stood over Emma as she sat and looked up at him. Did she have any idea just how damn sexy she looked in that white vest top, her nipples strain-ing against the fabric? As for the white shorts, well, he couldn't go there or he'd drag her off to his room like a Neanderthal.

'We could rectify it now—tonight.' The lust cours-ing through him had got the better of him, and he spoke the words before he had time to think, but, judging by the sexy, impish smile, it wasn't something she was horrified by.

'Could we?' Her voice was husky, teasing him and testing him. Damn it. What was the point in denying the attraction which fizzed around them? He wanted her and, unless he was very much mistaken, she wanted him too.

'I want you, Emma,' he said and held out his hand to her, more emotionally exposed than he'd ever been in his life. He had no idea how, but this woman was dismantling every barrier he'd erected to shut himself away, to prevent himself from ever having to feel any-thing for anyone.

The silky softness of her throat moved as she swal-lowed, her gaze fixed on his. Then she parted her lips, the small movement so sexy he almost groaned out loud. Finally she took his hand, placing hers in his, and he pulled her gently to her feet and towards him.

Shock rocked through him as her body collided with his and he wrapped his arms around her, pulling her against him. Her body seemed to beg his for more, but he wanted to hear it from her lips, needed to know this was what she wanted. 'Is this what you want?'

She slipped from his embrace and he drew in a sharp breath as she crossed her arms in front of her and, tak-ing hold of her vest top and pulling it over her head, threw it carelessly to the floor. His gaze devoured her slender figure, her full breasts, and he clenched his hands into tight fists as he fought to hold on to control. But when she slithered the white shorts down her legs, kicking them aside, he knew that control was fading fast.

It was like Vladimir all over again. Except this time he didn't have to worry about consequences. This time he could make her his totally.

'Yes.' That one word was a husky whisper that sent fire all over him at the knowledge this woman was his, and the fact that she'd given him her virginity only increased the power of that idea.

He closed his eyes briefly against the need to take her quickly, to thrust into her and possess her more completely than he had ever taken a woman before. She'd only ever known his touch and because of that he had to take it slowly, make this a night of pure pleasure for both of them.

Slowly he undid his jeans, maintaining eye contact with her as he removed them to stand before her as naked as she was. A dart of satisfied pleasure zipped through him as she lowered her gaze to look at him, arousing him still further.

She moved back to him, looking into his eyes and taking on the role of seductress, just as she had in Vladimir; she wrapped her fingers around him, pushing him to a new level of control. He actually trembled with the pleasure of her touch and groaned as her lips pressed against his, her hand still working the magic.

When she let go of him and kissed down his neck, over his chest, he groaned in pleasure, but when she lowered herself down to continue the torture her touch had started it was nearly his undoing. He pushed his fingers deep into her hair but, as his control began to slip, he pulled her back and she looked up at him, her green eyes dark and full of question.

'My turn.' The gravelly growl of his voice was almost unrecognisable as he pulled her to her feet then pushed her back onto the sofa. With predatory instinct he knelt up before her and, leaning on her, pressed his lips to hers, taking in her gasp of pleasure.

'Nikolai,' she breathed as he kissed down her neck rapidly. She arched herself towards him as he took one nipple between his teeth, nipping, teasing, before caressing it with his tongue.

Again enforced restraint made him shake and he braced his arms tighter to hold himself over her. She writhed in pleasure beneath him as he turned his attention to the other nipple, her hands roaming hungrily over his body.

As he moved lower still, kissing over her stomach, she clutched at his shoulders, her nails digging in, the spike of pain so erotic he could hardly hang on to his control any longer. But he wasn't finished with her yet.

He moved his head between her legs, tasting her as she lifted her hips upwards, all but begging him for more. He teased her with his tongue, pushing her to the edge, but stopping as he felt her begin to tremble, not ready to let her go over just yet.

'Let's go to the bedroom,' he said between kisses as he moved back up over her stomach, over the hardened peak of her nipple and up her throat.

'No,' she gasped as she clung to him, wrapping her legs around him, the heat of her touching him; he knew that he was lost, that all control was gone.

In one swift move he filled her, thrusting deep into her and making her his once more. She gasped as she gripped harder onto his back, her hips lifting to take him deeper inside her. It was wild. Passionate.

Her body was hot and damp against his, but still it wasn't enough. He wanted more, much more. With a growl he thrust harder, striking up a fierce rhythm she matched. Her cries of pleasure pushed him further until he forgot everything except her. With one final thrust, he took her over the edge with him.

Darkness still filled the room as Emma lay contentedly against Nikolai after the hours of making love. They had moved from the sofa to the shower and then finally to his bed. She should be exhausted, but she'd never been so alive, so vibrant. It was almost too good to be true.

The doubts she'd had about accepting his so-called proposal had been blown away by the hot sex they'd shared. If things were that good between them, wasn't there hope he might one day feel something deeper for her? She certainly wanted that to be true because her feelings were definitely growing for him. They had become deep and meaningful. Did that mean she was falling in love with him?

As the question reared up before her, Nikolai stirred and she braced herself, remembering how she'd woken to find him staring out of the window in Vladimir. Had he regretted that night? A night which had changed both of their lives beyond recognition. More questions stirred in her mind as Nikolai propped himself up on his elbow and looked at her, his eyes filling with desire once more.

'I'm going to see some sights today,' she said, trying to fight the rise of a fresh wave of desire. She didn't want their time together to be all about sex. She wanted to get to know him better, but while he kept the barrier raised around himself that was going to be difficult. Did he ever let anyone get close?

'We'll go together.' He pulled her against him and kissed her and she almost gave in.

'That would be nice,' she said with a teasing smile and moved away from him. 'It will be a nice way to get to know each other better.'

'How much better do we need to know each other?' He was smiling but there was a hint of caution in his voice.

'There's so much we don't know about each other.'

'Such as?' The hard tone of his voice had become guarded and it was like being back in Vladimir that first night with him. The impenetrable wall was right round him, shutting her out.

'What we really want from this marriage.' She let the words fall softly between them.

'I know what you want. You want financial security. Why else would you come all this way? You also want for your child what you never had—a father figure.'

Did he have any idea he'd got it so right? Was he really that cruel he'd manipulate her insecurities so coldly?

'My offer of marriage is exactly what you wanted.' He spoke again and all she could do was take it, knowing it was all true. 'Even though you held out for a bit more, marriage is what you came here for, wasn't it, Emma?'

'What?' She couldn't believe what he was saying,

but neither could she move. All she could do was stay there and look at him.

'Is tonight part of a bigger plan?'

How could a night so perfect turn into a one so terrible? Emma shivered in the shadow of the gulf which had opened up between them at the mention of the deal they'd struck. 'Is that what you really think?'

'You have given me no reason to think otherwise.' He threw back the sheets and strode across the room to pull on his jeans, totally uncaring about his nakedness. He was running again.

'Nikolai.' She said his name more sharply than she intended. 'Don't go. Not again.'

He stood at the end of the bed in the semi-darkness of the room and glared at her. 'What exactly is it you want to know, Emma? And, more to the point, who is asking—the woman I am to marry, the one who is carrying my child or the woman who wants to get to the truth just for an article in a magazine?'

Emma recoiled at his fierce tone, but it proved he was hiding the truth, that whatever it was he'd gone to great lengths to conceal from her in Vladimir was still there, creating a barrier around him as physical as a wall of bricks and mortar.

'I'm asking, Nikolai—as your fiancée—because I care, because if we don't deal with this, whatever it is that's keeping you emotionally shut away, making you so cold, it will fester between us, always dominating, always threatening. Do you want your child to grow up under that cloud?' Her passionate plea didn't dent his armour.

'What do you want? My life story? I gave you that in Vladimir.'

'You gave me the version you wanted me to know, but things have changed. We are having a baby and, if we're to marry, then I want that marriage to be a success. I don't want our child to grow up knowing any kind of insecurities.'

'What do you know of insecurities, Emma?' His voice had softened, taken on a more resigned tone.

'Much more than you might think.' Her own childhood, the unhappiness of continuously moving to new foster homes, crept back to the fore, as did her father's rejection. She pushed it away. Nikolai must never know what sort of mother she'd been raised by. If he did, he might think she wasn't fit to be a mother herself, and she couldn't risk her baby being taken away, like she and Jess had been.

'Do you really think that's possible?' He glared at her and she knew he was angry that she was not only challenging him but being evasive herself.

'Tell me, Nikolai. I know some of your story but, as your fiancée, I want to hear it from you.' She spoke softly and held her breath as he paced the room and ran his fingers quickly through his hair.

Nikolai didn't know where to start. He was angry, at himself and Emma. She knew the basic facts so why did she want more? He looked down into her eyes and realised it didn't matter any more what he tried to keep from her; she knew half the story and he was sure that it would only be a matter of time before she'd know every sordid detail. Better it came from him—now.

'Why exactly do you feel it is necessary to know?' Why the hell was he doing this? It was far too deep, too emotionally exposing, and he just didn't do emotion. He'd learnt long ago how to keep fear, anger and even love out of whatever he was doing. Each time he'd come to his mother's rescue as his father had used his fists, he'd acted calmly and without emotion. It hadn't mattered whether he was wiping her bleeding nose or merely standing between them, he'd been devoid of any emotion. It had been the only way—and still was.

'You said before, in Vladimir, that your parents were forced to marry.' She nudged his memory with the start of the story he'd told her that night they'd first slept together. Then, just as now, being with her had threatened to unleash his emotions.

'Yes, they were, but only because she was pregnant with his child.' He watched her face pale and had the urge to kiss her, to forget the past and lose himself in her wonderful body once more. It surged through him like a madness. Thankfully, sense prevailed. Despite the fact that she looked so sexy sitting there naked in his bed, her hair no longer sleek but ruffled from sex, he was suffieiently in control to acknowledge things were already complicated enough without giving her hope of having a normal, loving marriage.

'That's hardly the crime of the century,' she said, sympathy in her voice and a smile lingering tentatively on her lips as he sat on the bed and looked at her.

He knew what she meant. She was pregnant with his child and they were going to be married; that fact only compounded his misgivings, making him ever more determined to keep emotions out of this deal they'd struck, because that was how he had to think of it: as a deal for his child. Just as his father had forced his mother into marriage, he was forcing her.

Now the one thing he didn't want to happen was

happening. Emotions were clamouring from his child-hood, demanding to be felt, and he hated it. Memories rushed back at him and he fought for control. What would she think of him if she knew the truth?

He should just say it. However he tried to dress it up, those words would be painful; knowing how he'd come into the world, how it had forced his mother into something she hadn't wanted, made him feel worthless. It was that sense of worthlessness which had driven him hard, making everything he did a success.

He looked at Emma and knew she had to know just who he was.

'He'd raped her.'

There, he'd said it. Finally said the words aloud. He was the unwanted product of a rape which had devastated his mother's life, forcing her into a violent marriage.

'Rape?' Her voice was hardly more than a whisper, and it helped to be near the warmth of her body as the cold admission finally came out, but strangely just saying those words wasn't enough. He wanted to tell it all now he'd finally started, as if he'd opened a door he could never close.

'My father was a family friend and had asked to marry my mother. He'd wanted the connections our family name and wealth would bring him.'

Emma didn't say anything but moved a little closer to him, heat from her body infusing him. He wanted to hold her, to feel the goodness within her cleanse the badness from him, but he couldn't, not yet, not until she knew it all. 'Did she refuse him?'

He gritted his teeth as he recalled the time he'd first found out what had happened, how his gentle and loving mother had become the wife of a vicious brute of a man just because of him. He had no idea why, but now he wanted to talk, to tell Emma everything, even knowing she could use it all and destroy him. He wanted to prevent it all coming out as a headline story in the press. That was why he'd flown from New York to a country he barely remembered to ensure a grandmother he'd come to hate didn't tell her the damned story. Now here he was, spilling it all out to the very woman who wanted to know his family story for that very reason.

'She did. And because of that he attacked and raped her.' He bit down on the anger which raged in him now, just as it had done the day he'd realised he'd been the reason his mother had married a violent man. Surely their life would have been better without a man like that in it? He'd never questioned his mother, never asked her about it. She didn't even know he'd overheard her and his stepfather talking. That would break her heart as much as the story being leaked to the world would.

'I don't understand. Why did she marry him after that?' Incredulity filled her voice as she once again looked up at him.

'That is something I have never understood.' Despite the warmth of her body his mind drifted back in time, to the many occasions when he'd cowered in a corner, hiding from his father's wrath. 'When my mother and I left Russia I was ten and I never wanted to go there again. I did all I could to fit in with our new life, to please my new father. It was like being given a new chance.'

'Why did your mother marry your father if he'd done that?' It was a question he'd asked himself so many times.

'Maybe she saw marriage to that brute as her only chance. She was from a well-known family and wouldn't have wanted to bring such a scandal out into the open.'

Emma moved and wrapped her arms around him, pressing her lips to his forehead. It was strangely comforting to be held by her, to feel her compassion wrapping around him. 'I'm sorry,' she whispered. 'For making you go there again.'

'Maybe I should have faced my father's mother when I had the chance, asked her why she helped to hide such horrible things from the world. From the outside we must have appeared a normal family. I want to know if she realises that by doing that she trapped my mother and I with an angry bully. Only his sudden death freed us.'

'It doesn't mean we shall be the same,' she said, homing in on the worry he'd had since the moment she'd arrived in New York with the news of her pregnancy. He wasn't fit to be a father with a past like that, but that just made him more determined to be a part of his child's life, to be a better father.

'How can you say that when you only agreed to marriage for the child's sake?' He began to build his barriers back again, using all the ammunition he had to push her away. As he spoke he looked into her eyes and saw the flash of pain within them, but buried it deep inside him.

'Our child was not conceived through violence,' she said firmly as she touched his face with the palm of her hand, a gesture he wanted to enjoy, but he couldn't allow himself that luxury.

'But it most definitely wasn't conceived out of love.' He threw the harsh truth at her and her hand stilled.

'No, it wasn't.' The softness of her voice, mixed with sadness, slashed at him harshly. What the hell had he been thinking of, talking about this with her?

She moved away from him, looking like a hurt and wounded animal, and that strange sensation squeezed his chest again. This was getting far too deep for him and he had to put a stop to it right now.

'I never want to talk of this again.' Anger boiled over inside him, threatening to spill out everywhere, turn him into a copy of the man who'd terrified him as a child, and she'd done that to him.

Emma looked up at him and he watched her bare shoulders go back as she sat a little taller, her chin lifting in that sexily defiant way of hers. 'I understand, and we won't.'

She understood? How could she understand? He wanted to ask her about her childhood, just what it was in her past that qualified her even to say that, but he couldn't deal with any more emotion. He needed space, time on his own. He strode from the bedroom as the light of dawn filled the apartment, thankful that she hadn't attempted to follow or ask anything else.

CHAPTER NINE

THE GENUINE CONCERN Nikolai had been showing her all week, taking time out from the office and going sightseeing with her, had definitely brought them closer in many ways. After the disastrous way last weekend had ended she felt a glimmer of hope and the uneasy sensation that she was doing the wrong thing marrying him melted into the background.

Today he'd chosen a trip on the Hudson River to see the Statue of Liberty. He'd hired a private boat and it was so romantic it reinstated the flailing hope. It was a perfect spring day but, even so, the motion of the boat was making her queasy. Just as she had done every day this week, she tried to hide it from him but, as if he'd become tuned into her feelings, he guessed she was unwell.

'This wasn't such a good idea,' he said as he stood behind her and pulled her close against him. She closed her eyes, enjoying the sensation of being cared for, being protected. Deep down it was all she'd ever wanted. Love and protection had been so lacking in her childhood it had become the elusive dream. A dream which right at this moment felt tantalisingly close.

'It's fine,' she said as she snuggled closer. The spring

wind not yet carrying any warmth didn't help, but, against the man she was most definitely falling in love with, she really didn't care about anything. Being here in his arms like this was so right, so natural, she didn't want anything to spoil it. 'I just don't think I can take photos today.'

'Then don't.' He kissed the top of her head and she smiled. Was he falling in love with her too? Could she be on the brink of her happy-ever-after? 'You should stop working and just enjoy the moment. Photographs can wait.'

'Can I ask you something?' She started speaking while watching the buildings of New York become ever taller and more modern as they made their way down the river towards downtown Manhattan. Before he had a chance to reply, she spoke again. 'Have you ever been in love?'

She needed to ask, needed to know if he'd ever let a woman into his heart before, but the tension in his arms as he held her warned her she'd gone too far.

'No.' The sharply spoken word told her more than she needed to know. 'You know what happened when I was a child. You even told me yourself that you didn't believe in such nonsense as love.'

'I didn't,' she said softly and swallowed down the disappointment. If his mother had found happiness after such a terrible marriage, then love must exist. Her heart was opening to the idea, but could his?

'I hope that doesn't mean you've changed your mind.' The sharpness of his words cut the air around them and she shivered, as if winter had returned.

Her heart went into freefall and she focused hard on the New York skyline, determined not to allow his throwaway comments to hurt her, but the truth was she had changed her mind. She'd changed it because of her deepening feelings for him, feelings that she knew for sure could only be love.

'Of course I haven't,' she said quickly, sensing that to tell him now wouldn't be sensible. She had to remember why she was here as his fiancée at all. She was carrying his child and he'd made a deal with her, a deal which gave her baby all she'd missed out on as a child, and she wasn't about to jeopardise that. 'We are doing this for our child.'

'And your sister.' His stern reminder left her in no doubt he considered his offer the deal clincher. It was nothing more than a deal for him, but his next words cut her heart in two, making her feel shallow. 'Funds for her "dream", as you called it, were the sealing factor in the deal, were they not?'

He let her go and moved to stand next to her, feigning an interest in the city's skyline, and she knew she'd got too close to the barriers erected around him, barriers to prevent him from being affected by any kind of sentimental feelings. Deep inside her that newly discovered well of hope dried up. She had thought he might be able to find it in his heart to feel something for her, as she was beginning to for him.

They'd created a child together in a night of passion, a child that would bind them together for evermore, but she wanted more than that. She wanted to be loved and love in return. Every night this week, since they'd returned from their engagement party, the hours of darkness had been filled with passion and her love had grown, but for him it had been nothing more than sex.

She'd let herself down, done the one thing he'd

warned her not to do. She wanted more; it hurt to admit it, but she loved him. She tried to distract herself with thoughts of her sister but they made her lonelier than she'd ever been. The last few times she'd called her, Jess hadn't been able to take the call, and she'd just received brief texts in reply.

'I'd like to see if Jess can make it to New York for our wedding.' She tried tentatively to steer the discussion away from the subject of love. Maybe it was a safer thing to talk about. 'Do we have a date yet?'

He laughed softly and looked at her, almost frazzling her resolve not to feel anything for him. 'Are you that keen to become my wife or are you just changing the subject?'

'There's nothing to be gained by waiting now we have agreed our terms.' It might be the truth, but her voice had a tart edge to it as she tried to stem the hurt and rejection growing within her.

He looked at her, studying her face for a few seconds, and all she could hear was the sound of the boat engine and the wash of water. The spring sunshine was warm on her face, but not as searing as his gaze. 'Then you'll be pleased to know it has all been arranged for this Saturday.'

'Saturday?' She whirled round to face him, not caring that she was missing the spectacular views he'd brought her here to see. Saturday was too soon. She'd never be able to organise Jess flying in from Moscow by then. Was he deliberately trying to cut her off from everything she held dear? 'Jess will never be able to get here by Saturday—and she's all I have, Nikolai.'

Before he could answer, her phone rang and she snatched at the chance of avoiding his scrutiny. She'd left so many messages for Jess, it had to be her, and she needed to speak to her now more than ever. She looked at the screen, but it wasn't her sister. It was Richard. Nikolai looked down at the screen while she thought of not answering. She didn't need to talk to Richard of all people right at this moment, no matter how much he'd helped her get her contract with *World in Photographs*.

'You had better answer that.' His voice was harsh, each word clipped with anger. She looked up at him in confusion but he turned from her and walked away a few paces.

'Richard,' she said as she answered the call. 'How lovely to hear from you.'

Nikolai didn't like the way Emma smiled as she spoke to Richard or the way she'd turned her back on him to take the call. He recalled he was the photographer who'd helped her get her career off the ground, but now he was beginning to question exactly what she thought of him.

'The article is out?' Emma's voice carried across the deck as she continued her call. 'That's brilliant. Thanks for calling to tell me—and, Richard, thanks for your help.'

Nikolai clenched his jaw against the irrational anger which bubbled up just from hearing her talk to this other man. Was it really possible that he was jealous? The thought was ludicrous. To be jealous of another man he'd have to have feelings for Emma—deep feelings he just didn't want.

He turned to watch her as she spoke on the phone. Her long silky hair was in a ponytail down her back, but the wind kept playing with it, reminding him how it felt against his skin while she slept. For the last week, since the night they had returned from their engagement party, she had spent every night in his bed. Each of those nights of passion had claimed them in its frenzied dance; afterwards she'd always slept wrapped around him and he'd enjoyed the closeness.

Her laughter as she responded to something Richard said only served to send his irritation levels higher and he turned from her, determined he wasn't going to be affected by it. Their marriage was to be one of convenience for the sake of his child and all he had to do was remind himself how easily she'd been talked into the marriage once he'd used the lure of funds for her sister.

Before Richard had called, he'd been about to tell her that he'd made arrangements for Jess to come to New York for the wedding. He'd put things in motion after the engagement party, which had been all about his family and friends, because he'd wanted her to have someone there for her. He'd also insisted that the wedding itself was limited strictly to close family, which had been a battle with his mother, but now the urge to tell her these details had gone.

'That was Richard,' she said as she joined him and he certainly couldn't miss the smile on her face. Irritation surged deeper through him at the happiness in her voice. 'The article is out and he said it's really good.'

'If it's what I have already read, then I am pleased for you.' He kept his voice neutral, not wanting a trace of any kind of emotion to be heard, especially the new and strange one he suddenly had to deal with.

'Why would it be any different?' She frowned up at him. 'You don't trust me, do you, Nikolai?'

Of course he didn't trust her and now, thanks to a

moment of weakness, she knew everything. She still had the ability to shatter his mother's happiness. That was something he wasn't going to allow to happen at any price and precisely why he'd flown to Russia in the first place.

'Is Richard a close friend of yours?' he asked, unable to keep his curiosity under control any longer, or the anger at the way the idea of Richard and Emma being close filled him with such strong emotions.

'Why do you ask?' Her cautious question was just what he'd expected—and feared. She was hiding something; of that he was certain.

Despite his suspicions, there was no way he was going to let her know how he felt, so he assumed an air of indifference he definitely didn't feel. 'I have limited the wedding guests to immediate family and close friends. I just wanted to know if he was a close friend.'

She looked down, not able to meet his gaze, and when she looked up again disappointment and sadness were in her eyes, but he refused to be made to feel guilty. 'He's helped me a lot and, yes, once I hoped we could be more than friends. I'm sure there are women like that in your past.'

He hadn't anticipated such honesty and it threw him off balance for a moment as he realised the truth of what she'd said. 'There was someone once, yes.'

Why had he said that? Why had he brought his ex-fiancée into this?

'Someone you loved?' she asked cautiously.

'No, someone I couldn't love, someone who needed that from me and I couldn't give it to her—or maybe it was because I didn't want to give it. Either way, the engagement ended.'

'You were engaged?' Her brows lifted in surprise and he regretted saying anything, but then maybe it would back up all he'd already told her, convince her that love was not something he could do.

'I was, yes.' He didn't want to have this conversation with her. It was something he never spoke of.

She clutched at her hair and looked away from him, as if she sensed his reluctance to talk. 'I've always wanted to see the Statue of Liberty. Thanks for this.'

Shocked by her change of subject, he looked up, and sure enough they were close to the statue as it reached up into the spring sky. He'd been so absorbed in her and the way he was thinking about her, feeling about her, that he hadn't even registered they'd got this far.

Emma turned and looked at him, her expression serious. What was it about this woman that muddled his senses so much? Every time he was with her he lost all clarity on what it was he wanted from her and from life.

'I don't expect love from you, Nikolai.' Her voice was as clear as a mountain stream but it didn't settle the unease he felt.

'What do you expect?'

'Nothing, Nikolai. You've made that perfectly clear from the very beginning. Our marriage is purely for the baby's sake.' She laid her hand lightly on his arm and, just as he had done before, he pulled back from her touch, not wanting such intimacy.

'We each have things to gain from the marriage, Emma.'

Emma looked at Nikolai and her heart began to break. She knew the whole thing was a deal, that their marriage was nothing more than a convenience, but always there had been a spark of hope fuelled by the heady passion they'd shared. Now that spark had gone, extinguished by his cold words.

'All I want is to be able to bring up my child, Nikolai. Do you promise me my ability to do that will never be questioned, even if we are apart?' She didn't want to tell him the truth behind her demands, but if it made him realise just how much she wanted this then it would have to be done.

She wanted her child to know who she was, not to think of her as a distant shadow in the background, as her own mother had become. It still hurt that a woman could turn her back so easily on the two children she'd given birth to, but she'd always told herself and Jess that their mother had been sick and didn't know what she was doing. Now, with her own baby on the way, she seriously doubted this. Her mother just hadn't wanted either her or Jess.

Nikolai's dark eyes searched hers but she couldn't look into them for fear he'd see the pain she felt about her mother and she looked beyond him to the passing city as the boat headed back along the river to the pier they'd left earlier.

'Why would I ever question that?' He moved a little closer, as if sensing there was much more to her demand.

She looked back at him, feeling the cooling wind in her face. 'I have already told you my sister and I were in care as children.'

He frowned and looked down at her, his mouth set in a firm line of annoyance. She was well aware now that he hated personal conversations, anything that meant he might have to connect emotionally. Did he think she was trying to make him feel sorry for her?

Before he could say anything which might stop the flow of words from her, she continued. Whatever he thought, this was something that had to be told. She couldn't spend the rest of her life, whether living with Nikolai or not, worried that she might be classed as an unfit mother and her child taken from her. She knew what it felt like to be that child.

'We were taken into care because my mother couldn't look after us. She'd rather have cuddled a bottle of something strong and alcoholic than hold my sister, and certainly hadn't worried about me.'

She looked directly at the passing buildings, into the mass of stone and windows that created a maze that ordinarily she'd long to explore. Now it was just something to look at. She couldn't look at Nikolai, didn't want to see the disapproval on his face. All she wanted was the promise that, no matter what happened between them, she could be a mother to her child.

'Do you really think I would keep a mother and child apart?' The stinging anger in his voice forced her to turn and look at him, and his dark eyes sparked with annoyance, heightening her own sense of anxiety.

'You made it virtually impossible for me to refuse the marriage deal.' Had he forgotten how he'd dominated that discussion?

'You were the one who quickly accepted the suggestion of funds for your sister.'

'It wasn't exactly a suggestion, Nikolai. It was more of a demand. It probably even comes much closer to blackmail.' She should tell him about her father, about the fear and rejection she'd grown up with.

Darkness clouded his eyes, as if the spring sun had slipped behind a cloud. 'It was not a demand and most certainly not blackmail. What kind of man do you think I am that I need to use such underhanded tactics?'

Defiantly she looked up into the icy blackness of his eyes. Her heart was pounding in her chest but she knew this had to be dealt with before they married. She didn't want to enter into a marriage, even a loveless one, with unresolved issues such as these. She couldn't live with that uncertainty hanging over her.

'I don't know, Nikolai. You have made it clear marriage isn't something you want to enter into freely, and yet you insist your mother lives under the illusion that we are in love. What kind of man does that make you?'

'I want only the best for my child. That's what kind of man I am.'

The boat bumped against the pier and Nikolai looked at Emma, wondering just what kind of monster she thought he was. Did she really believe he would separate her and their child, after all he'd told her about his childhood? Anger rushed through him and he couldn't look at her any more, couldn't take the accusation in her eyes.

Had he made a mistake, insisting on marriage? He couldn't walk away from his child, but none of this felt right.

No, it had to be this way. It was the only way he could prove he was not like his father, that despite the genes inside him he had his mother's goodness, he could be a good father. He wanted his son or daughter's childhood to be very different from what he'd known—and from what Emma had known, if what she'd told him was anything to go by.

'Do you really believe a loveless marriage is the way to achieve that?' she demanded hotly.

Her question caught him off guard and neither of them moved, despite the need to leave the boat. That word again. Why did love have to come into everything?

'Our marriage will achieve that precisely because it won't be swallowed up by nonsense such as love.' The hardness of his tone shocked her; he could see it in her eyes, feel it radiating off her.

'And what if one of us falls in love?' Her bold question challenged him from every side. Nikolai's suspicion about the ever-helpful Richard increased.

'If what you told me before is true, that will not happen. Neither of us believe in love—unless of course you are already in love with another man?' Again that irrational jealousy seeped into him as he thought of how happy she'd been talking to Richard on the phone. How she'd smiled and laughed.

'How can I love another man when I have known only you?' The hurt in her voice was clear, but his rational sense had jumped ship, replacing it with intense jealousy for a man he hadn't even met. A man who could make *his* fiancée smile so brightly that happiness danced in her eyes.

'Do you love Richard?' He couldn't think clearly, and didn't even register her words properly, but fired the question at her. She gasped in shock and stepped back from him.

'You think I am in love with Richard?'

'Why is that so implausible?' Impatience filled him at her act of innocence. She'd used that act once before.

'Because he's a friend. But I'll be honest with you—

it hurts like hell to feel anything for someone who feels nothing for you. But you wouldn't know what that's like, would you, Nikolai?'

Before he had a chance to ask more, she left him standing on the deck and he watched as she disembarked and strode away from him. What the hell had all that meant?

CHAPTER TEN

EMMA HAD TRIED to keep alive the flicker of hope that things had changed between them after returning from their engagement party. Nikolai had avoided the painful discussion they'd had that night, but had played to perfection the role of adoring fiancé. Yesterday on the boat had doused that hope and now the ever-increasing nausea was making everything so much more difficult to deal with.

'I've cleared the diary for today,' he said as he strode across the room to stand looking, brooding, out over the park and the vastness of New York beyond. His withdrawal from her made her feel insignificant and rejected, feeding into her childhood insecurities which were growing by the day.

'You did that yesterday; please don't feel you have to do it again.' A wave of nausea washed over her. She pressed her hand against her forehead, her elbow on her lap, and curled over as a sharp pain shot through her. She didn't feel well enough to do anything this morning, least of all play happy bride-to-be with Nikolai.

Was it the strain of everything: the way he'd manipulated the whole marriage deal, using the one thing she wouldn't wish upon any child, least of all her own?

Another cramp caused her to take in a sharp breath and she bit down against the pain. There was something wrong. Very wrong. Panic rushed through her like a river breaking over a waterfall. She wanted this baby so much, with or without Nikolai's support, but what was happening to her? What had she done wrong?

'Nikolai,' she said, her voice shaky. 'The baby. Something's wrong.'

She closed her eyes against another wave of nausea and tried to fight back the tears—not just tears of pain, but tears of fear for her baby. She couldn't take it if something happened. What if she lost her baby? In the back of her mind, as the fog of pain increased, the thought that it was exactly what Nikolai would want rampaged round like a wild animal, making her angry and more panicked.

'Emma.' Nikolai's stern voice snapped her back from that fog and she looked up at him as he stood over her, phone in hand. His brows were snapped together in worry and his face set hard in stern lines. 'I'm taking you to the hospital.'

A tear slid down her cheek as relief washed over her. He was in control. But could he stop what was happening, what she feared was the worst thing possible? As another pain stabbed at her stomach she closed her eyes and the need to give in to the blackness rushing around her was too much. Would that be the best thing to do for the baby? Further questions were silenced as she let go and did exactly that.

When she opened her eyes again she knew she was in hospital and panic charged over her like a herd of wild, stampeding horses. She tried to sit up, but Nikolai's hand pressed into her shoulder, preventing her from doing so. 'It's okay. Lie still.'

His voice was soothing and commanding without any of the panic she felt, but still she tried to get up. She wanted answers, wanted to know what was happening to her and her baby.

'My baby?'

He leant over her, forcing her to look into his face, his eyes. She smelt his aftershave, felt the warmth of his hand on her shoulder, and relished the calm control he had. 'The baby is fine. You are fine. So please, just relax. Stress won't help you or the baby at all.'

'Thank goodness.' She breathed and closed her eyes as relief washed over her.

What would she have done if she had lost the baby? A terrible thought entered her mind, slipping in like an unwanted viper. If this had happened just a week later, and it had had the most unthinkable consequences, she and Nikolai would have been married. What would he have done then, married to a woman who no longer carried the child he'd made a deal for?

'You have been doing too much,' he said sternly. 'Rest is what you need.'

'Maybe we should call off the wedding.' She couldn't look at him, couldn't bear to see the truth in his eyes. She'd been rejected by her father before he'd even seen her and then again as a teenager. For him marriage and fatherhood wasn't what he'd wanted in life and she knew it was the same for Nikolai; he'd made that more than clear. She couldn't trap him into something he didn't want but neither could she deny her baby the chance of knowing its father. A heart-wrenching decision, born out of the panic of the moment, grew in her mind. Who should she be true to—her child or herself?

'If the doctor agrees you are well and can come home, that will not happen.' There wasn't a drop of gentleness in his voice. The man who'd become more gentle and loving each night had gone and the cold, hard man who'd walked out on her in Vladimir was back.

'But this isn't what you want.' She hated the pain that sounded in her voice, hated the way she still clung to the hope he could one day love her.

'What we want is irrelevant.' He looked down at her, his dark eyes narrowed with irritation. 'It's what is best for the child, Emma. We will be married.'

Nikolai fought hard against the invading emotions as he helped Emma to sit up. This was more than the physical pull of sexual attraction that had surrounded them since the day they'd first met in Vladimir. This was something he'd never known before. Something he'd been running from since the night he'd made her his.

He cared, really cared, not just about the child who was his heir but about the woman he'd created that child with. When had that happened? When had lust and sexual desire crossed the divide and become something deeper, something much more powerful than passion?

He had no idea when, but all he knew was that it had happened. He looked down at Emma, her face full of uncertainty, and knew without doubt that he cared for her. And it scared the hell out of him. Caring caused pain.

'We will take Emma for a scan now.' The nurse's

voice snapped him back from that daunting revelation. A scan? Would he be able to see his child? Now?

'Is there something wrong?' The quiver in Emma's voice reached into his heart and pulled at it, making him want to hold her hand, give her reassurance. Making him want to love her. But how could he do that when he didn't know how to deal with the emotions that were taking over? Or even exactly what they were?

'Is there?' he demanded of the nurse.

'Everything is fine,' she said with the kind of smile meant to dispel any doubts. 'We just want to reassure both of you.'

'Thank you.' Emma's reply called his attention back to her and he looked down at her, noticing, as he had done several times in recent days, how pale she was. Should he have done something sooner? Guilt ploughed into him. He'd pushed her too hard, not taken enough interest to see how tired she'd become. He'd risked his baby.

His baby.

Those two words crashed into him and for a moment he couldn't draw a breath. Then he felt Emma's hand on his arm, the sympathetic touch almost too much. He didn't deserve that from her.

A short time later, and with no recollection of how he'd got there, he was in a small room with Emma. She lay on the bed, the soft skin of her stomach exposed as the nurse pressed the scanner probe against her. He noticed her hand was clenched as it held her top out of the way, as if she feared the worst. He watched as the nurse moved the probe, trying to get a clear image on the screen. He wouldn't have been able to tell Emma was pregnant with his child, her stomach was flat, but the first image filled the screen and he knew the machine didn't lie.

In his mind he tried to add up how many weeks' pregnant she was. How many weeks was it since they'd had the most amazing night which had had such far-reaching consequences. Before he could work it out, the nurse's voice broke through his thoughts.

'There we are. Baby at ten weeks.'

He looked at the screen, not able to take his eyes from it. The fuzzy image had a dark centre and in that darkness was his baby. Small, but unmistakable. He couldn't move, couldn't do anything but stare at it.

A tense silence filled the room as the nurse continued to move the scanner around, losing the image briefly. He couldn't look at Emma, couldn't take his attention away from the screen that showed him the secret of his baby.

'And everything appears normal,' the nurse added as she paused once more, showing an even clearer image. 'See it moving and its heart beating?'

Fierce protectiveness rose up in him like a rearing horse and he knew in that tension-filled moment he would do absolutely anything for his baby. He would go to the ends of the earth for him or her. It would want for nothing and he would love it unconditionally.

Love.

Could he love it? Could he give it the one thing his father had never given him? The one thing which terrified him?

Finally he looked at Emma as she watched the screen, a small tear slipping down her cheek. Did he love her? What was the powerful sensation of crushing around his chest and the lightness in his stomach each time he saw her or thought of her? Was it love? Had he fallen in love with a woman who could never love him? A woman whose heart was already elsewhere?

Emma looked at the screen and tears began to slide down her cheeks. They were in part tears of happiness: her baby was well. She'd seen it move, seen its little heart beating. But those tears of happiness mingled with tears of pain. Nikolai had been silent throughout. He hadn't uttered a word, had barely moved, and she could no longer look at him. Was he now seeing the reality of the deal he'd made?

She glanced up at him now as the nurse completed the scan and then left them alone. No doubt she thought she was giving them private time to be happy together, but then she didn't know the truth.

The truth was that Nikolai didn't want this baby. He'd stood stiffly by her side, his hard gaze fixed rigidly on the screen as the first images of their child had appeared. Now he couldn't move, couldn't look her in the eye.

The elation that filled her from seeing the baby, from knowing it was well, cooled as the tension in the room grew to ominous levels and she wished the nurse hadn't left. At least then she might have been able to avoid the truth.

'You must rest,' Nikolai said, his voice deeper and more commanding than she'd ever known it. Was he blaming her? Was he even now thinking she was as uncaring as her mother had been?

'I—I think we should at least postpone the wedding.' She stumbled over her words as his fiercely intense gaze locked with hers. If she could get him to agree to postpone it then it would give them both time to decide if it really was the right thing to do. She loved him but couldn't marry him, tie him to her, if there was never going to be a chance that he would one day feel the same for her.

'No, but you won't need to worry about anything. I will arrange for your final dress fittings to be at the apartment.'

He moved away as she sat up and slipped off the bed, but she felt more exposed than she had that morning she'd first woken in his bed. It was as if he knew everything about her. She knew he didn't, knew that she still guarded her fear of rejection—his rejection. Her father had rejected her. Richard had too, just by refusing to see her as anything other than a friend, and the last thing she wanted was to be rejected by the father of her baby, the man she'd fallen in love with.

'I'm not sure marriage is the right thing for us at the moment.' It was like standing on the shore, allowing the waves to wash over her toes, each wave taking her deeper into the conversation until it was swim or allow the depths to swallow her up.

His eyes narrowed. 'Why?'

'It doesn't feel right, Nikolai.'

'We made a deal, Emma.' The uncompromising hardness of his voice shocked her.

'It's almost as if you've bought me, bought the baby.'

'You agreed to the deal, Emma, and if my memory serves me right held out for just that little bit more. Not content with securing yours and the baby's future, you also wanted to secure your sister's.'

'But this isn't right. We don't love each other.' The plea in her voice must have reached him somehow because he moved closer to her and she waited with bated breath to see what he was going to do or say.

'Love isn't always needed, Emma.' He touched her cheek, brushing his fingers across her skin so softly she could almost imagine he cared. 'Sometimes passion and desire is a better base on which to build a marriage and we've proved many times that exists between us.'

'But that's not love, Nikolai.' She drew in a shuddering breath as he moved even closer. Why couldn't he just admit he didn't love her, that he would never feel that for her?

'I don't care what it is, we made our deal with it.'

'But will it be enough?' She stepped away from him, wanting to get out of this dimly lit room and away from the sudden intensity in his eyes.

Nikolai looked at Emma as she tried to evade him. Was she that desperate to get away from him? Was he doing the right thing, insisting the marriage deal went ahead?

'For me, yes.' There was no way he was going to reveal the depths of the emotions seeing his baby had unlocked. He wanted to protect his child, always be there for it. He also wanted to do the same for Emma, but after the call from Richard he doubted Emma felt the same way.

She'd come to New York to secure her and her child's futures. She must have done her homework on him because she'd then held out for more than that when all he'd wanted was to keep his child in his life.

Fatherhood might not be something he'd looked for, or even wanted, but now that it had happened he wasn't about to let any man or woman stand in the way and prevent him from being a father. He had to prove to himself he had not inherited his father's mean streak.

'And what if one day that changes?' She challenged him further, deepening his resolve to make it work, to be the father he'd never had.

'It will not change, Emma. We have created a child together and that will bind us for all eternity; nothing can change that now.' The truth of his words sounded round in his head and he knew he couldn't let her walk away from their marriage, their deal.

'So there's no going back?' An obstinate strength sounded in her voice, as if sparring with him was making her stronger.

'Never.'

CHAPTER ELEVEN

THERE WERE JUST two more days until she married Nikolai and Emma was restless. She'd been taking it easy since returning from the hospital but today felt different. She'd had lots of time to think and, although Emma knew brides had nerves, she didn't think they had the serious doubts she was being plagued with.

She still cringed with embarrassment at how close she'd come to revealing she loved him whilst they were on the boat, but those tense few minutes in the hospital had highlighted how bad the idea of marrying him was.

His reaction at the scan emphasised clearly that marriage was the wrong thing to do. She could feel him pulling away from her emotionally, locking down those barriers again, and she braced herself for his rejection.

It didn't matter how many times she let the question wage a battle in her mind, she still came back to the same answer: how could she marry a man who didn't love her? Each and every day she had fallen deeper in love. If only they hadn't spent that night together after they'd returned from the party. If only he hadn't stirred her emotions up and awakened her love for him, then maybe she could have merely acted the part of adoring and caring fiancée. Such thoughts were useless when each night spent with him filled her heart with more love.

Her phone bleeped on the table and she abandoned the view of the park she often contemplated and opened the usual daily text from Jess, missing her more than she thought possible. If Jess were here, sharing this moment with her, she might be able to deal with it better.

With a sigh she picked up the phone and read the text from Jess. As she read the words, her heart leapt with excitement.

Surprise! Be with you in five minutes.

Jess was here? In New York? How had that happened? She recalled the lighter conversations with Nikolai when they'd taken the boat along the river. He must have arranged for Jess to come over for their wedding. Why had he done that? He confused her. Such actions made him look nice, as if he did have some feelings for her, making everything even harder. She couldn't back out of the marriage now if Jess was here, knowing that by doing so she'd be letting Jess's chance of a worry-free future slip away as well as depriving her child of its father.

Ignoring the inner churning of her heart, she sent a text back to Jess. Excitement almost took over the nauseating worry that filled her. She wondered again about Nikolai's motives for organising it. With a huff of frustration, she sent a text to Nikolai to say thank you. Two could play at the relationship game.

Before Emma had a chance to do anything else, the apartment door opened and Jess stood there, a big smile on her face. Disbelief kept Emma rooted to the spot for a moment and emotions overwhelmed her. Jess let go of her case and walked towards her and, as she'd always done, Emma enveloped her in a hug, not able to believe she was actually here.

'How did you get here?' she asked when they'd finally let each other go.

'Your wonderful fiancé.' Jess's excitement was palpable and Emma couldn't even think straight. Of course she would think he was so wonderful; it was exactly what she'd wanted her to think. She couldn't let Jess know the real reason she'd accepted the marriage.

'Nikolai?' she asked and Jess laughed.

'How many do you have? Of course Nikolai.' Jess walked around the apartment, taking in the luxury of it all, something neither of them were used to. 'He arranged everything, right down to the key to get in. He's amazing, Em, you're so lucky. He must love you so much.'

Jess's enthusiasm for her soon-to-be brother-in-law was so zealous it almost brought Emma's world crashing down. Despite the miles that had separated them, he'd charmed Jess, made her see what he wanted the rest of the world to see. She'd never felt more trapped in her life.

'He didn't tell me, though,' she said, quickly pushing away the doubts, not wanting them to creep in and spoil this time with Jess.

'Because he wanted to surprise you. He made me promise not to say a word. Have you any idea how hard that's been the last few weeks, keeping it a secret from you?'

Last few weeks? He'd organised this long before they had the discussion about Jess attending the wedding? Had he done it even before their engagement party? Was that why he'd been so concerned that she had nobody there for her that night?

'Well, he's certainly done that,' she said as she took Jess off to her room, determined not to let Nikolai's motives spoil this unexpected moment with her sister.

Nikolai arrived back at his apartment to the sound of women's voices drifting through the open plan living area from the bedroom Emma had used on her arrival, which her sister would now use. For a moment he was taken aback and stood listening to them, grateful that Jess had managed to keep her arrival a secret. The lack of anyone for Emma at their engagement party had made such a surprise important, but the visit to the hospital had reinforced it.

'You're having his baby?' Jess's unfamiliar voice was filled with shock and he remained silent and still, waiting to hear Emma's reply, but none came. Was she smiling and nodding her confirmation to her sister or giving away the truth of it all? Would she let Jess know this was nothing more than a marriage of convenience?

Silence echoed around the apartment for what seemed like hours, but he knew it was merely seconds. He stood still, not daring to move, not wanting them to hear his footsteps on the polished wooden floor. Finally the silence was broken by Jess's voice.

'But you love him, right?' Jess asked, concern in her voice, and Nikolai held his breath, hoping Emma would act the same part she'd acted for his mother, that of a woman in love.

'He's a good man.' Emma's subdued answer was not at all what he'd expected her to say. It seemed her

acting skills were not on form today and disappointment flooded through him. The last thing he wanted
was Emma's younger sister letting slip to his mother
that the marriage was not a love match. That would
make his mother feel guilty for what had happened in
his childhood. The only thing she'd ever wanted was
for him to find the real love she had.

'I thought you wanted true love.' Jess's voice lowered so he was hardly able to hear it and right now he
certainly didn't want to hear Emma's answer. He recalled her light-hearted view on love when they'd first
met and knew it must have been true and not the throwaway comment she'd allowed him to think it was. She
did believe in love, and was looking for it, but love was
something he couldn't give her.

He strode across the room, his footsteps loud on the
polished floor, and perfect for blocking out the answer
he didn't want to hear. He poured himself a much-
needed glass of brandy. The voices had gone silent
and now he wished he had waited to find out what she
thought. Would it be so bad to be loved by the woman
who was carrying his child, his heir? Somewhere deep
inside him the idea stirred those emotions from the day
at the hospital and for a brief moment of madness he
wanted exactly that.

'I didn't hear you come in.' Emma's voice sounded
cautiously behind him and he turned his back on the
view to face her. She looked pale and he wondered if
she was well enough to have Jess here.

'I've only just arrived,' he said grimly, wishing she
didn't have such an effect on him. With just one questioning look she cracked the defensive shield around

him, made him feel emotions, which as far as he was concerned was dangerous.

She walked closer to him and, for the first time since they'd arrived back from their engagement party, she looked shy and unable to meet his gaze. She'd had the same look in her eyes as she'd met him in the hotel lounge the night after the sleigh ride. That shyness hadn't lasted long. It had soon been replaced by the temptation of a seductress. Had it been that which had pushed his limits of control beyond endurance?

'Thank you,' she said softly.

'For what?' She looked at him with big green eyes and to see the emotion within them was too much. He didn't want the complication of emotion in his life. Never. It was why he hadn't looked at her as they'd seen their baby on the scan.

She smiled shyly. 'For getting Jess here. You have no idea how much that means to me—and Jess.'

As she said the words a young, dark-haired girl came into the room and smiled, the similarities between the sisters striking. 'And you must be Jess?'

Emma turned round as he spoke and held out her hand to her sister. 'We are both grateful for everything, but this is such a surprise. Getting married will be easier with Jess at my side.'

Irritation surged through him. She thought getting married to him was going to be difficult? From what she'd just said, it was obvious Jess was in full possession of the facts; no pretence at love for her sister's benefit was needed now. Didn't that show she was as cold and calculating as he was? It certainly proved she was only marrying him because of the baby.

'You helped me with my mother. It was only fair you got something out of our deal too.' He then turned his attention to Jess, needing to put some barriers back up between him and Emma, uncomfortable at the effect she was having on him. 'Did you have a good flight?'

'I did, thanks. I've never flown first class before,' Jess replied, grinning enthusiastically. He felt Emma's curious gaze on him, but ignored it, and the way his body warmed just from her nearness. He had to get out of here now.

'I'll leave you two girls to it, then. You have dress fittings later.' Before Emma could say or do anything, he left them alone. It was more than obvious to him now that he had to leave and check into a hotel until his wedding day. His wedding day. After ending his first engagement, he'd never thought he'd ever get married, let alone be a father.

He turned at the door. 'I've booked into a hotel until after the wedding, so you will not be disturbed by my presence.'

'You don't have to do that,' Emma said, alarm in her voice.

'Of course he does,' Jess chipped in. 'It's bad luck to see each other before the wedding.'

'In that case, I will go now.'

Emma watched Nikolai leave, angry that after all she'd done for the benefit of his mother he'd made no attempt to act the part of loving fiancé in front of Jess. He'd looked angry and irritated by her presence and their thanks, and she worried how that would look to Jess.

Especially when she'd made every effort to make it appear they were in love when she'd met his family at their engagement party.

Why had he chosen that precise moment to drop the caring façade he'd hidden behind all week? She'd only just told Jess she loved him and that she was happy to be his wife as well as a mother. Then he'd arrived back at the apartment like an angry lion whose authority had been challenged and made it obvious that the marriage was a deal that was going to unite them and definitely not love.

'I'm not stupid, Em, I know what's going on.' Jess's voice broke through her thoughts.

Emma whirled round to look at her sister and saw a frown of worry creasing her brow. What did she know? That the pregnancy was a mistake and that she'd abandoned her dreams of love and happiness to do what was right for the baby?

'Nothing's going on. Every bride and groom is nervous before the big day.' She bluffed her way out of the corner Jess was backing her into. But it was too late. Emma's fragile faith in her love for Nikolai was fading fast. Was she really doing the right thing by her child, marrying a man who didn't want her around, much less love her?

'Tell me, Em, please.' Her sister's pleas showed wisdom beyond her years, wisdom born out of the hardships they'd faced growing up.

Emma sighed heavily. 'I can't marry him, Jess. I can't marry a man who doesn't want love in his life. But, more than that, I can't live each day waiting for him to reject me and his baby.'

Any further attempt at spilling out her sorry story

was halted as the dress fitters arrived. Emma let them in, amazed at the quantity of dresses that hung wrapped up on the rail they were quickly setting up. The fact that they were here also made what she was doing seem even more real. She was actually going to marry a man who didn't want love in his life, who could never give her what she'd always dreamed of finding.

But he can give Jess a chance to be something.

Emma tried to shrug off those thoughts and walked over to stand by the tall windows. She looked but didn't see the view which usually captivated her so easily as she battled to halt the doubts which were growing by the second. She heard Jess come to stand beside her.

'What makes you say that?' Jess asked, shock obvious in her voice.

'He's never told me how he feels,' Emma said quietly, not quite able to add that he'd already told her he didn't want love, that the deal they'd struck was one which would benefit Jess.

'I don't think it's something men say,' replied Jess confidently, and Emma turned to look at her, finding it odd that she could even smile at such a remark. 'What?'

'Do you actually know what you are saying?' Emma laughed, trying to lighten things up. She shouldn't be talking to Jess like this. Not if she wanted to prevent her ever finding out the exact terms of the deal.

'Of course I do—I watch films, listen to people talk.' Now Jess laughed, but it was edged with relief. Guilt rushed over Emma. She must have worried Jess for a moment.

Emma pushed all her doubts to the back of her mind.

She was doing this for Jess as well as her baby, which meant she couldn't let on how much she doubted her sanity for accepting the terms of the deal.

'What colour do you think?' She strolled over to the rail of bridesmaid dresses and touched a pink one.

'Blue.' Jess joined her. 'You always said blue was your lucky colour.'

'But I thought you liked pink?' Emma was touched by her sister's acknowledgement that it was her day.

'I do, but I want you to have all the luck in the world, so I want blue.'

As Jess spoke, the dress fitters pulled out several dresses, but a pale-blue strapless gown caught hers and Jess's attention at the same time. Moments later, Jess was twirling round the apartment. 'It's a perfect fit. This has to be the one.'

'You look gorgeous, Jess. All grown up.'

'And I am, so you can go off into the sunset with your very own Prince Charming and not worry about me.' The reproach in Jess's voice brought a mixture of tears to Emma's eyes and a soft giggle of happiness.

'I guess I'd better decide on my dress,' said Emma. 'This is so last minute, I can't possibly find one to fit.'

Cream silks blended with white on the rail and Emma didn't know which one to look at first. Should she even have a full-length gown? What about cream? Or should it be white?

'This is the one,' said Jess as she pulled the skirt of a beautiful white gown towards her and grinned. 'Try it on.'

Helped by the fitter, Emma tried on the white lace gown with a strapless bodice that matched Jess's perfectly; it was almost too good to be true. As she was zipped into it, she looked at herself in the mirror and saw, not plain Emma, but a beautiful bride. The dress was simple yet elegant with a small train; she'd never imagined herself in such a dress.

'It's all meant to be,' Jess gushed. 'First my dress, now this one. You and Nikolai are going to make the perfect couple.'

CHAPTER TWELVE

EMMA WOKE EARLY with a start, the big bed cold and empty, just as it had been since the day Jess had arrived and Nikolai had moved into a hotel. He was stepping back from her as if he too had doubts. Why hadn't she tried harder to sort things when they'd been at the hospital?

She looked around her. The early-morning sun shined with wicked brightness into her bedroom, seeming to highlight the wedding dress hanging in readiness for that afternoon, when she would step into it and seal the hardest deal of her life.

Could she do it? Could she put on the white gown of lace and become Nikolai's wife, knowing he would never love her?

She pulled on her jeans and jumper and put on a pair of flat pumps. She couldn't stay and look at the wedding dress any longer. She had to get away, get out of the apartment and think. The sensation that she was doing the wrong thing had taken over, blocking out everything else.

'Where are you going?' Jess asked, quickly taking in her casual clothes as she went into the bedroom.

'I need to go for a walk. I need to think, Jess. I need

to think really hard before I make a terrible mistake.'
Emma looked at the long pale-blue dress she and Jess
had selected the day she'd arrived. It hung in readiness,
mocking, from the wardrobe door. During those few
hours when she'd tried her own dress on for the final
time, Jess had enjoyed herself so much selecting styles
and colours that her enthusiasm had become infectious
and for a while Emma had believed everything was
going to be all right.

But it could never be all right. Nikolai could never
love her as she loved him. If she married him it would
be the worst mistake of her life.

'What's the matter, Em?' Jess crossed the room
quickly and Emma wondered how she was ever going
to tell her. How did you look your sister in the eye and
tell her you were throwing away her chance of fulfill-
ing her dream, of being what she wanted to be, and
worse, subjecting a child to a life without a father?

'I'm not sure I can do this.' Emma felt ill at the concern on her sister's face and wished she hadn't said
anything, but she had to. In about six hours she would
have to put the wedding dress on. What if she couldn't?
What if she couldn't unite herself with Nikolai in marriage? She had to tell Jess something, had to give her
some warning that things weren't as they should be.

'I thought you were happy, that you loved him,' Jess
said, a hint of panic in her voice, and that was the
last thing Emma wanted her sister to do. They'd had
enough panic and upset in their lives. How had this
turned into such a mess?

'I was,' she said with a sigh as she looked past her
sister and to the view of the green trees of the park beyond. 'And I do love him.'

I love him too much and I can't face his rejection.

'So what's wrong, then?' Jess touched her gently on the arm, pulling her back from her thoughts, back to what she had to do.

She closed her eyes against the pain of knowing she'd fallen in love with Nikolai even after he'd readily confessed he couldn't love anyone. She couldn't stop the words any longer, couldn't hold them back. 'He doesn't love me.'

She felt Jess's hand slip from her arm, but she couldn't look at her and tell her what it was all about, why they were really getting married, so pulled away. Even when Jess spoke again she couldn't look at her. She'd failed her. If she ran out on Nikolai now, she'd be throwing away the chance for her baby to know a different life. 'I think you are wrong about that.'

'Don't, Jess, you don't know the half of it.' Emma's hot retort left her lips before she had time to consider what she wanted to say.

'Last night he looked as if he'd wanted to eat you alive.' Jess's bold words, so out of character for her little sister, didn't ease the doubt; instead, it increased it. Lust had been responsible for that look on Nikolai's face. Nothing other than desire-fuelled lust.

'That's not love, Jess, and it's not something to build your future on. Don't ever fall for that.' But wasn't that what she herself had done—fallen for the power of raw lust?

'You're wrong, Em. What I saw in his eyes last night was love. Anyone can see that.'

'Don't be so silly. You're not even seventeen. How can you know what love looks like?' Emma was becoming irritated with this conversation. All she wanted to do was leave the confines of the apartment. She needed time to think what to do next—after she'd told Nikolai they wouldn't be getting married.

'I know it was love, Em, I just know it. He loves you.' Jess pleaded with her, but it was too late. She'd made up her mind. 'Don't let your past stand in the way of your future. You are not Mother and he's not your father.'

That was so painfully close to the truth, she didn't want to hear it. 'I have to get out of here.'

For nearly an hour Emma all but marched around the park but none of it gave her any joy, any release from the feeling of impending doom which loomed over her. All she could think about was that she had to tell Nikolai it was over. She stopped walking and found a bench and, sitting down, took out her phone. Her hands shook and, even though her heart was breaking, it was what she had to do. This sham of an engagement had gone on long enough. It was time to end it.

She pressed Nikolai's number and listened to the ringing tone, part of her wanting him to pick up, part of her wishing he wouldn't, that she could hang up and walk away. The message system took over, and for a moment she nearly ended the call without leaving a message, but if she didn't do this now, didn't say what she needed to, it would be too late. He'd be waiting for her to arrive at the church he'd booked for the small, intimate ceremony with only his family and Jess as guests. They might have struck a cold deal for their child's sake, but she couldn't marry him knowing he'd never love her.

'It's me, Emma,' she said, not liking the quiver in

her voice, and she tried to sound much sterner. The message she left had to be decisive and firm. 'I can't do this, Nikolai. It was wrong of me to accept your deal. I can't marry you. I'm going back to London with Jess—tonight.'

She ended the call and stared at the phone as if it might explode, but inside she knew she'd done the right thing. She couldn't marry a man who didn't love her, not when her love for him grew deeper and stronger each day. All along she'd thought she was doing the right thing, but now she couldn't see any happiness for her or the baby in a loveless marriage.

She looked at the time on her phone: almost ten. The wedding was due to take place at three. Nikolai had plenty of time to sort things out and make all the necessary cancellations, just as she had time to get a flight back to London booked for her and Jess. She hoped he wouldn't come and try and persuade her to go through with the wedding. Would he really do that when marriage and fatherhood were the very things he'd admitted not wanting? She wanted to be able to leave in peace. Of course, they'd have to settle things to do with the baby, but that could wait until she was more in control of her emotions, more able to be strong and hold back her love.

It was what she had to do, but she couldn't move, as if by doing so it would make it worse. But how much worse could it get? She was pregnant with the child of the man she'd lost her heart to and all he wanted was a loveless marriage, a convenient deal. The spark of sexual attraction wouldn't keep the marriage alive for ever, and once it dwindled to nothing she didn't think she could continue to live the lie—or hide her love.

She turned off her phone and as she sat in the peace of the park, letting the birdsong soothe her, she wished she could turn off her emotions as easily. All she needed was a few minutes to compose herself and then she'd go back to the apartment, book the flights and leave New York. She could explain to Jess on the long flight home, admit it had been a mistake to come here, and an even bigger mistake to accept Nikolai's deal, whatever extras he'd thrown her way.

Nikolai tried to get Emma on the phone again as he strode through the park. Jess had told him to try there after he'd called at the apartment. Anger boiled up inside him as he heard her message going round and round in his head. She didn't want to get married. *I can't do this, Nikolai:* that was what she'd said.

Each time he replayed the words in his mind anger sizzled deep inside him. Anger and rejection. He should have seen it coming. What she'd said at the hospital after the scan suddenly made sense. While he'd been bonding with his child and liking the idea of fatherhood, of settling down with Emma, she'd been thinking of ending the engagement and calling off the wedding.

Anger simmered, pushing him to walk hard and fast through the park. He had no idea where to begin looking and savagely pulled out his phone and tried to call her again. Nothing. She'd turned it off. If she thought a switched-off phone would be enough to deter him, she was very much mistaken. He wasn't used to people backing out of a deal and he certainly wasn't accustomed to being denied what he wanted—and he wanted Emma.

The thought trickled through him like a mountain

stream thawing after a long, hard winter. He wanted her, really wanted her. Not just with the hot lust that had driven him mad, but with something much deeper. It wasn't anything to do with the baby. He wanted Emma.

The park was full of morning joggers and dog walkers wrestling with groups of dogs as he stopped and looked around for Emma. She'd been so enamoured with the park since her arrival; she could be anywhere. A strong curse left his lips as he marched on towards the lake; then, as he rounded a corner, he could see her through the trees. She was sitting on a bench, looking away into the distance, totally absorbed in thought.

He reined in the instinct to rush over to her and demand to know just what the message had been all about, and instead walked slowly towards her, taking advantage of the fact that she was looking the other way. Her long hair gleamed in the morning sunshine as he got closer and he rubbed the pads of his thumb and finger together, remembering the silky softness of her hair. Would he ever feel it again?

Emma turned to look his way and he stopped walking, frozen to the spot with something that seemed horribly like fear, but fear of what? He saw the moment she realised it was him, saw the tension make her body stiffen, and the realisation that he did that to her hurt more than he knew. She was either afraid of him or hated him for what he'd done to her.

She didn't move, but she did look down, as she always did when something was difficult to do. Was her reluctance to leave an invitation for him to join her? He didn't care what the hell it was. He was going to sit with her regardless.

I can't let the woman I love walk out on me.

That thought crashed into him and he stopped again, his heart pounding as he realised exactly what that thought meant. He'd felt the same at the hospital. Why hadn't he seen it then?

He looked at her, sitting on the bench in the morning sunshine only a short distance away, yet it was like a chasm had opened up right there in the park. It yawned between them, becoming greater with each passing second.

He couldn't move, couldn't cross it.

He'd pushed her to the other side of it right from the very beginning and she'd been more than happy to be there. She'd agreed with everything he'd said about commitment and love, accepted the cold terms of his marriage deal. She scorned love or happy-ever-after just as much as he had, but now, as if he'd finally opened his eyes and seen what was real, he had to accept that he did want all that. He did want Emma in his life, as his wife and the mother of his baby, but not out of any obligation—out of love.

Did he risk everything and tell her how he felt, that he loved her after all he'd said to her? Or did he try and persuade her to keep the deal in the hope he'd got it wrong? Maybe panic had filled his head with such nonsense as love.

But he didn't just feel that desolate distance in his head. He felt it in his chest—in his heart. That sensation he'd experienced since the moment he'd first met Emma was back, squeezing tighter than ever, as if trying to get him to acknowledge the truth, acknowledge it as love.

She looked at him, apprehension clear on her face, and finally he managed to move towards her. Each step was harder than the previous one. How could he tell her what he really felt when he'd only just realised the truth of it himself?

'Did you think a quick phone message would be enough to extricate you from our deal?' That wasn't what he wanted to say at all, but the protective barrier around his heart wasn't just keeping her out, it was locking the truth inside him, preventing him from saying what he had to say, what he wanted to say.

She looked up at him as he came to stand in front of her, those gorgeous green eyes narrowing against the sun. Or was it the harshness in his voice? 'I didn't expect you not to answer.'

'I was in the shower,' he said quickly, banishing the memories of the time they had spent in the shower together not so many days ago.

She looked down and away from him again. Was she recalling the same thing, the same heated passion? He sat down next to her and once again her gaze met his. 'It doesn't matter, Nikolai, because I can't marry you.'

'Not even for the baby?' He flung the question at her as he clenched his teeth against the panic which flowed through him like a river in flood. He couldn't let her go, let her just walk out of his life, not now he knew what he really felt for her. How long had he loved her? The thought barely materialised before he knew the answer. He'd loved her from the first night they'd spent together in Vladimir, maybe even the first moment he'd seen her.

'No.' She shook her head and looked directly ahead of her, as if distracted by the surroundings, but he sensed she was holding back on him. But why? And what?

* * *

Emma looked at the pain in his eyes and knew he was blaming his past, his father's mistakes. Her heart wrenched and she desperately wanted to reach out to him, to reassure him it was nothing to do with that. But, if she did, she'd weaken and the last thing she wanted to blurt out was that she couldn't marry anyone who didn't love her as she loved them, that she couldn't put herself in the path of such rejection.

'No. I know it sounds very clichéd, but it's me.' She looked into his eyes, seeing their darkness harder than they'd ever been.

'So you are quite happy to back out of our deal.' His voice was deceptively calm and that unsettled her even more. Was he just going through the motions of asking her to reconsider when he'd rather book flights back to London for Jess and her himself?

'For our child's sake, yes.' She skirted around the truth, her heart pounding harder than ever, and despite the warm spring sun she shivered as skitters of apprehension slithered down her spine.

'Our child will benefit from the marriage, but will it benefit from being brought up by you alone, while I am on the other side of the world?' The scorn in that question was almost too much for her. Was he deliberately trying to make it harder for her or was he finding a way to make her worst nightmare come true and take her baby from her?

Whatever he was doing, this had to be sorted now. She couldn't go on for the rest of her pregnancy wondering what he would do next. 'Our baby will be better off with two parents who are apart and happy than two living under the same roof that are unhappy.'

'And will you be happy?' The question threw her off guard, as did the change of his tone. He sounded defeated. She'd never heard Nikolai sound like that.

'All I want is for my child to grow up happy, to never feel the sting of rejection from its father.' She wanted to say more, to make him aware just how anxious she was, but stopped the words and the pain from flowing out.

'And you think I will reject my son or daughter?' Hurt resounded in his voice, but his eyes narrowed with annoyance. 'After all I saw and witnessed as a child, do you really think I want to hurt my own child?'

She looked down, knowing her words had been taken the wrong way, and she hated herself for hurting him. He'd done all a young boy could to protect his mother and even now, as a grown man, was doing the same. That was why he'd insisted on the pretence of love at the engagement party and why he'd gone to Vladimir in the first instance.

Instinctively she reached out to him, placing her hand on his arm. 'No, Nikolai, that's not what I thought. I don't want my child to know what I've known. I can't stand by and let you reject them when they are no longer any use in your life.'

He took her hand in his, the warmth of it briefly chasing the apprehension away 'I would never do that, Emma, never.'

She looked at him as his eyes softened and she almost lost her resolve, but his next words brought it hurtling back to her.

'I'm not about to let you walk away. I want to see my child grow up and, just as I never want to be like my father, I promise I will never do what yours has done to you.'

'It doesn't mean we should marry, though.'

'We will marry as planned, Emma.' He looked at his watch. 'In less than four hours, you will be my wife.'

CHAPTER THIRTEEN

'I'M SORRY, NIKOLAI.' Emma jumped up away from him, breaking the tenuous connection he'd just forged. Her hard words hit him like a speeding truck. 'It's too late.'

He watched as she stood up and looked down at him and, when he couldn't respond, couldn't say what he wanted her to hear, she turned and began to walk away. It seemed as if he was watching each step she took happen in slow motion, but each one took her further from him.

He couldn't let that happen. She couldn't walk away from him until he'd told her what he'd only just realised himself. Nerves sparked through him, briefly making it impossible to say or do anything except watch her begin to walk away.

'Emma, wait.' The demand in his voice rang clearly through the morning air but she didn't slow, didn't turn. She was leaving him, walking out of his life. He had to make her see reason, had to make her understand, and there was only one way to do that.

He walked briskly after her, catching up with her as she began to cross Bow Bridge. 'I need you, Emma.'

Had he said that aloud? He stood still at the end of the bridge and watched as her steps faltered, then she stood, her back to him in the middle of the bridge. Seconds ticked by but it felt like hours as he waited for her to turn to look at him. When she did, he could see she was upset, see she was on the verge of tears, and he hated himself for it. He'd handled this all wrong, right from the moment he'd woken after that first night they'd spent together. The night that had changed not only their lives but him.

'Don't say what you don't mean, Nikolai.'

'I mean it, Emma, I need you.' Inside his head a voice was warning him that that wasn't enough, that he had to say more, he had to put himself on the line and tell her he loved her. He couldn't do that, not knowing she loved another man, but it was his baby she was carrying and he'd been the only man who'd made love to her. Surely that meant something?

'It's not enough,' she said firmly, her chin lifting in defiance. 'I want more than that, Nikolai. I want to be needed for who I am, not for the baby I carry. But more than that I need love.'

His stomach plummeted as she said those final words. Was she going back to London to be with Richard? Did she love him that much?

'I always thought love was nothing more than a word.' He took a step towards her. That chasm he'd felt earlier now had the thinnest of wires across it, but could he use it? Did he have the courage to reveal his emotions when they were still shockingly new to him?

'You made that more than clear from the very beginning.' Still she stood there in the middle of the bridge, looking at him with fierce determination. She didn't even notice a couple walking across the bridge towards him. Her gaze didn't leave his face for one second.

He had done exactly that; there was no denying he'd made it absolutely clear he didn't want love. Such a denial was what had kept him safe. It meant he'd never have to give a piece of himself to someone who could use it and destroy him emotionally—something Emma had had the power to do from the moment they'd first met. As a teenager he'd spoken just once about his father to his mother and she had confessed she'd loved him when they'd first met, before he'd shown his true self. From that moment on he'd vowed to keep such destructive emotions as love locked away.

He couldn't do that any longer. He had to acknowledge them and set them free, even if Emma did have the power to destroy him. If she didn't feel the same burning love for him, then he would be nothing, but he couldn't just tell her, not when he wanted her to be happy—with or without him. If she truly loved someone else, then he would have to let her go. It shook him to the core to realise he loved her enough to do that, enough to set her free into the arms of another man.

He thought back to their discussion on love, to the day she'd laughed at such a notion existing. It had been that denial of what she'd truly wanted that had forged the path forward for them.

'You made a joke out of love and happiness. You scorned it as much as I did, Emma.' He took several tentative steps closer, encouraged when she didn't move, didn't turn and walk away. Inside, his heart was breaking. He was a mess, but he kept his stern control, retaining that ever-present defensive shield.

'I can understand why you want to shut love out of your life, Nikolai, but the things I experienced as a child made me want that kind of happiness even more.'

She took a step towards him and hope soared inside him. 'We want different things. You want to be free of commitment and emotion, but I want love, Nikolai.'

Those last words goaded him harder than he could have imagined, pushing him to ask just what he needed to know, even though the answer would be like a knife in his newly revealed heart. 'And does Richard give you that love?'

'Richard?' Emma's mind whirled in shock. Why did Richard have anything to do with this? She struggled to think, struggled to work out how he'd come to that conclusion, and then it hit her as she remembered their afternoon on the river trip. She'd taken a call from Richard and had been so happy the article was out and that he liked it, approved of what she'd done, but Nikolai's mood had darkened the instant she'd told him who was on the phone. She'd thought he was angry with her, but was it something more? Had he felt threatened by Richard, even though he'd been on the phone?

That wretched flicker of hope flared to life within her once more and kept her where she was. She looked at Nikolai, standing now at the end of Bow Bridge, as if to continue to walk towards her was something he couldn't do.

'Do you love him, Emma? Is he the man you are leaving to go back to?' Nikolai's voice was hoarse with heavy emotion in a way she'd never heard before.

She blinked at him in total shock. He seriously thought she was in love with Richard? *You used to, before he rejected that young love and adoration.* The taunt echoed in her head and she saw it from Nikolai's perspective. She saw the easy friendship she and Richard had established over the last few years, saw how it might look to someone on the outside. But, like Nikolai, Richard had made it more than clear he didn't want anything serious, squashing that first crush until it withered and died, leaving nothing but friendship—a working friendship.

'Richard and I are just friends. Always have been.' She frowned at the scowl which crossed his face. Did such a reaction really mean he saw Richard as a threat? But to what—their marriage born out of a deal or something more?

'But that isn't what you want, is it, Emma? You told me as much on the boat.'

'I did?'

'"It hurts like hell to feel anything for someone who feels nothing for you". Those were your exact words, Emma.' He calmly repeated what she'd told him, his dark eyes watching every move she made, every breath she took.

Emma's knees almost buckled beneath her and she moved to the side of the bridge, clutching at the ornate balustrades for support. She'd been talking about him, not Richard, but he'd interpreted it as something quite different. No wonder he'd become distant to the point of coldness since that day. The closeness they'd begun to share, which she'd hoped would give rise to love, had vanished—because of what she'd said.

Waves of nausea rushed over her and her head swam. She couldn't think any more, could barely stand. She hadn't eaten anything yet, too anxious earlier to face anything, and now it was all too much. She couldn't do this now.

She felt as though she was falling then strong arms folded around her as Nikolai wrapped her in the safety of his embrace. To feel his arms around her, holding her against his body, was almost unbearable. It was like coming home—and it broke her heart a little bit more.

'You're not well.' The deep, seductive timbre of his voice radiated through her and she closed her eyes, allowing herself a brief moment in the haven of his embrace.

'Maybe we can talk later.' She clutched at the life-line the moment had given her, not wanting to have this discussion any more. It was bad enough that he didn't love her, that he was about to reject her, but to accuse her of loving Richard was too much.

'No, we talk now—or not at all.' She looked up into his dark eyes and saw myriad emotions swirling in them, emotions she'd never seen in them before. 'It's your choice, Emma.'

She didn't want to talk now, didn't feel well enough to think, let alone talk, but she couldn't walk away and say nothing. Not when he held her so gently and looked at her so longingly. Was it possible he did feel something for her? Could it ever be love?

She needed to make herself clear, to let him know how wrong he'd got it all. She looked up at his handsome face, fighting the urge to reach up and touch his cheek, feel the smoothness of his freshly shaven face. 'It wasn't Richard I was talking about that day.'

Nikolai had moved quickly, taking Emma in his arms, holding her against him before she'd slithered completely to the floor. He'd inhaled her sweet scent, felt the warmth of her body, and his senses had exploded despite the worry he had for her health. How had he not seen it before? How could he not have known he loved her?

Because you shut your heart away.

She leant against the balustrade and looked up at him, as if waiting for him to say something, expectation mingling with desperation in her eyes. She'd just spoken, as his mind had whirled and his body had gone into overdrive just from holding her. Whatever it was she'd said, she obviously expected a response, but his ability to think rationally had left him the moment he'd held her.

'What did you just say?' he asked gently, unable to resist the urge to brush her hair from her face and then stroke the silky length of it down her back.

She looked up at him, tears beginning to brim in her eyes. 'I said that it wasn't Richard. When I said that on the boat, it wasn't him I was talking about.'

His hand stilled at her back and he held his breath, willing her to say more, but she looked down, her head dipping against his chest. If it wasn't Richard, who was it that didn't love her in the way she loved him? Had she been referring to him? Was it possible she loved him?

'Emma,' he said and lifted her chin forcing her look up at him. 'Have you ever told that person you love them?'

Still he couldn't say that he loved her, couldn't admit his deepest emotion. She searched his face, her gaze flicking over every part of him, as if committing him to her memory in the same way a camera did at the touch of a button.

She shook her head. 'It's not what he wants to hear. He doesn't believe love exists—at least, not for him. I could never tell him. I just can't.'

There was nothing else to do. He had to prove he loved her by telling her right now just how much. He had to risk having got it wrong, risk making a fool of himself. If he didn't tell her he loved her now, he'd lose her for ever.

'Maybe he just has to tell you,' he said as he looked deep into her eyes, the tears now dissolved and hope glowing from them. 'Maybe he needs to be bold and admit something he'd never thought possible.'

'Maybe he does,' she said as she watched his lips, as if willing him to say it, and his heart began to thump hard with trepidation.

He took a deep breath and swallowed, trying to instil calm into his body. This was the one thing he thought he'd never say. 'I love you, Emma Sanders. Completely and utterly.'

She closed her eyes, her body relaxed in his embrace and he couldn't resist her any longer. The temptation to kiss her was too much and he lowered his head and pressed his lips against hers. The soft sigh which escaped her did untold things to his body, but passion and desire could wait. This was a kiss of love.

Emma sighed as Nikolai kissed her, so tenderly it almost made her cry. He loved her. It wasn't only that he'd told her, but it was the way he was kissing her which proved it more than anything else. This kiss was different. It wasn't hot and filled with lustful desire that stoked the fire of passion within her. This kiss was very different. It was gentle and, more importantly, it was loving.

She wrapped her arms around his neck and kissed him back, finally allowing all the love she felt to pour from her. He stopped kissing her and pressed his fore-head to hers, the gesture so unguarded emotionally she couldn't say what she wanted to say for a moment.

'I thought you didn't want love.' She smiled, her voice teasing and light.

'That was before I met you. Everything changed the moment you stepped off that train in Vladimir.' His eyes were so tender, so filled with love, it was heart-rending and his voice broke with intense huskiness that sent a wave of pleasure breaking over her.

She closed her eyes and revisited the memory of the day they'd met, but even more importantly the knowl-edge that he had felt something for her from the mo-ment they had met seeped into her. It had been no different for her. There had been something between them from that very first moment at the station in Vladimir, and he'd admitted that had turned to love even before she'd been carrying his child. That could mean only one thing.

'So our child was conceived out of love, Nikolai.' She breathed the words against his lips as he once more claimed them in a deep and meaningful kiss, his hands holding her face as if he couldn't bear not to kiss her.

Around her life went on: voices of people in the park, the ripple of the water beneath them and birds singing their joy of spring all blended into the most perfect backdrop for the moment the man she loved with all her heart confessed his love for her.

As he pulled back from her, she let her palms slide down to his chest, feeling the beat of his heart beneath her right palm, a heart which was filled with love for her. He'd had the courage to admit his love even though he'd been convinced she was going to walk away from him. How had she got it all so wrong?

'I love you, Nikolai Cunningham—with all my heart.' She smiled up at him as he smiled back at her, then kissed her tenderly, his lips gentle and loving. She wanted to melt into the moment, enjoy the kiss, but she needed him to know how much his words meant to her. She pushed against his body and pulled away from him, away from the temptation to deepen the kiss.

'You have no idea how relieved I am to hear that. The thought that you were in love with another man has been eating me up for days.' His deep, sexy voice held a hint of seriousness and she knew it had been hard for him to talk about his feelings, no matter what they were.

'Is that why you really moved out of the apartment?' she asked as shyness crept over her. 'I thought you wanted me out of your life.'

'Like your father? No, Emma, that will never happen. I figured I needed all the luck I could get after what Jess had said, so didn't want to tempt fate by flouting tradition. I knew even then I couldn't risk losing you, but I was too blinded by my past to realise why—that I'd fallen in love with you.'

'Really?' She looked up at him to see amusement sparkling in his eyes, mixing with the newly acknowledged love.

'Yes, but I also wanted you and Jess to have time to catch up and have girl chats about me.' The laughter in his voice was contagious; she laughed softly and when he stroked her hair back from her face she almost melted all over again.

Then what he'd said finally registered and embarrassment flooded her. 'You heard us talking?'

How much had he heard? She recalled telling Jess she loved him with all her heart, and she'd meant it, but they wouldn't be here like this, with the worry of the last few days behind them, if he had truly heard what she and Jess had spoken about.

'Only a little bit,' he said and his brows rose, his eyes filling with that sexy amusement that had captured her heart in the first place.

'Well, you obviously didn't hear the part where I told Jess I loved you so much that it almost hurt; that marrying you was what I wanted to do,' she said with an impish smile on her lips, taunting him mercilessly.

The humour left his face. 'No, I didn't hear that, but it could have saved me a lot of heartache if I had.'

She laughed softly, wanting to lighten the mood. 'I'd much rather just tell you myself.'

'In that case, don't let me stop you.' He pulled her against him once more and pressed his lips briefly to hers.

'I love you, Nikolai, so very much, I just want to marry you. Today.'

'Is that so?' he teased. 'In that case, you are in luck; I have everything planned for a perfect wedding for the woman I love.'

She looked at her watch and let out a shocked gasp. 'I have to go now. The man I love with all my heart is going to make me his wife and the happiest woman alive. I just hope he'll be there waiting for me.'

'I have every faith that he will be, because he's madly in love with you.'

EPILOGUE

EMMA PULLED ON an elegant black gown and looked at her reflection. The last time she'd studied herself so intensely had been the day she'd tried on her wedding dress. Now, over a year later, she was a mother to a beautiful little boy and so happy the doubts she'd had in the days before her wedding seemed like a bad dream.

'As ever, you look amazing, Mrs Cunningham.' Nikolai kissed the back of her neck and looked into the mirror at her. The usual flood of love for him filled her and she smiled back at him as he continued to compliment her. 'It will be an honour to escort you to the ballet tonight.'

A quiver of apprehension ran through her as she thought of Jess being given a chance to dance as the lead ballerina so early in her career. 'I hope Jess isn't too nervous. This is her first leading role.'

'And what better place than here in Russia, at its greatest school? She is the rising star of the company. She will have a wonderful life.' Nikolai's reassurance helped to quell the nerves she had for Jess and she knew he was right.

Emma still couldn't believe that Jess was now half-way through her training and already other ballet companies were interested in offering her a place. She had the world at her feet. It was more than she could ever have hoped for her baby sister.

'I do wish we could have brought Nathan.' Emma turned to Nikolai, wrapping herself into his embrace.

'He is just fine with his grandma.' Nikolai kissed her gently—stirring sensations she couldn't allow to take over moments before they were due to leave the hotel. She blamed it on how amazingly sexy Nikolai was in a tuxedo.

'But it's the first time we've left New York without him.' She smiled as his brows rose in a suggestive way, hinting at the plans he had to fill that time without a six-month-old baby making demands on their attention.

'Which is precisely why I intend to take full advantage of the fact. Once we've seen Jess in her starring role, I intend to bring you back to this room and that very large bed. I want to make love to you all night, just to make sure you know exactly how much and how completely I love you.'

'Is that wise?' Emma teased as she kissed his freshly shaven cheek, not daring to press her lips to his.

'What makes you ask that?' His eyes darkened with desire and an answering heat scorched inside her.

She shrugged nonchalantly. 'You know what happened last time we made love in Russia…'

'This time will be different,' he said as he kissed the back of her neck. She watched him in the mirror until she had to close her eyes against the pleasure.

'In what way?' she asked in a teasing voice.

'This time you will know how much I love you with each and every kiss.'

She turned in his arms and looked up into his handsome face, hardly able to believe how happy she was. 'Everything you do for me, Nikolai, shows me that— from bringing me here to see Jess dance, to supporting me with my photography. I couldn't be happier.'

'But I'd still like to show you,' he said softly.

'Then who am I to argue?' She laughed up at him.

Nikolai looked down at her, a seriousness brushing away the humour of moments ago. 'You are my wife, the mother of my son and the woman I love with all my heart.'

* * * * *

A DEBT PAID IN
THE MARRIAGE BED

JENNIFER HAYWARD

For my Dad –
A gifted surgeon, teacher, woodworker and
master of anything trivia, you were also the
greatest father I could have hoped to have.

There is a piece of you, Dad, in every hero
I write because you were larger than life. I can't
imagine a world without you, that I can't ever
pick up the phone again and pick your brain
on a storyline. I only know if I live a life half
as courageous and remarkable as yours,
I will be happy. xx

CHAPTER ONE

"Sir."

Lorenzo Ricci pocketed his phone and lengthened his stride, pretending he hadn't witnessed the appearance of his portly, balding, middle-aged lawyer in the hallway behind him. Fifty minutes back on US soil, the last thing he needed was to discuss the fine print of the complex acquisition deal he had been negotiating, a subject bound to make his head ache even more than it already was.

Tomorrow, after a shot of his favorite whiskey, a steam shower and a face-plant into the Egyptian cotton sheets his housekeeper had procured for his very comfortable king-size bed, would be soon enough to endure that brain-throbbing task.

"Sir!"

Dio. He pulled to a halt, turned and faced the man doing his best to catch up to him on short, stubby legs, his outward appearance the very antithesis of the pit bull he was in the boardroom.

"I've been traveling for sixteen hours, Cristopher, I'm tired, I'm in a vile mood and I need sleep. Trust me when I say tomorrow is better."

"It can't wait." The edge to his lawyer's voice commanded Lorenzo's full attention. Not once in five years of completing difficult and sometimes downright antagonistic deals together had his legal counsel ever looked this rattled. "I need five minutes of your time."

Expelling a long sigh, his stomach souring at the thought of attempting to interpret the finer points of legalese when what his brain officially needed was sleep, Lorenzo waved a hand toward his office. "*Bene.* Five minutes."

Cristopher followed him into the sleek, black-and-chrome offices of the Ricci International executive team. Gillian, Lorenzo's ultraefficient PA, gave him an apologetic I-tried look. He waved her off. "Go home. We can go through everything in the morning."

She murmured her thanks, got to her feet and started gathering her things. Cristopher followed him into his office, hovering in front of his desk while he dropped his briefcase beside it and shrugged off his jacket. The apprehension skittering up his spine deepened. His lawyer didn't hover. *Ever.*

He walked to the bank of floor-to-ceiling windows framing a magnificent view of a dusky, indigo-lit Manhattan—one of the perks of being CEO of his family's international Italian conglomerate, a shipping dynasty he had evolved into a diverse empire that included hotel chains, cruise lines and real estate arms. He loved the view, but tonight, it barely penetrated the fatigue clouding his brain.

Turning, he leaned back against the glass and crossed his arms over his chest. "All right," he said, "give it to me."

His lawyer blinked behind gold-rimmed spectacles, flicked his tongue over his lips and cleared his throat. "We have a…situation. A *mistake* that's been made we need to rectify."

He frowned. "On the deal?"

"No. It's a personal matter."

Lorenzo narrowed his gaze. "I didn't invite you in here to play twenty questions, Cris. Spit it out."

His lawyer swallowed. "The legal firm that handled

your divorce made an error with the filing of the papers. An *omission*, actually…"

"What kind of an omission?"

"They forgot to file them."

A buzzing sound filled his ears. "I divorced my wife *two years ago*."

"Yes, well, you see…" Another long swallow. "You didn't actually. Not in the technical tense because the papers were never filed with the state."

The buzzing sound in his head intensified. "What are you saying?" He asked the question slowly, deliberately, as if his brain was having trouble keeping up. "Just so we're clear?"

"You're still married to Angelina." Cristopher blurted the words out, a hand coming up to resettle his glasses higher on his nose. "The lawyer who handled your divorce had an insane caseload that month. He thought he'd asked his clerk to file the papers, was sure he had, until we went back to look at the specifics after the conversation you and I had recently."

When it had become clear Angie was never going to touch a penny of the alimony he gave her each month.

"My wife announced her engagement this week. To *another man*."

The lawyer pressed a hand to his temple. "Yes… I saw the piece in the paper. That's why I've been trying to track you down. It's a rather complicated situation."

"Complicated?" Lorenzo slung the word across the room with the force of a bullet. "How much do we pay that firm an hour? Hundreds? Thousands? To *not* make mistakes like this. *Ever*."

"It's not acceptable," Cristopher agreed quietly, "but it is the reality."

His lawyer squared his shoulders, looking ready to be verbally flogged to within an inch of his life, but Lorenzo had lost the power of speech. That his short-lived marriage to his wife, a disaster by its ignominious end, had, in fact, never been legally terminated was too much to take when heaped upon the other news his father had delivered today.

He counted to ten in his head, harnessing the red-hot fury that engulfed him. *This* he did not need as he attempted to close the biggest deal of his life.

"How do we fix this?" he asked icily.

Cristopher spread his hands wide. "There are no magical solutions. The best we can do is hope to expedite the process. But it could take months. It will still mean— I mean you'll still have to—"

"Tell my wife she can't marry her boyfriend so she doesn't commit *bigamy*?"

His lawyer rubbed a palm across his forehead. "Yes."

And wouldn't that be fun, given Angelina was set to celebrate that engagement in front of half of New York tomorrow night?

He turned to face the jaw-dropping view, blood pounding against his temple in a dull roar. He was shocked at how much the idea of Angie marrying another man repulsed him even though he had once convinced himself if he never saw his wife again it would be too soon. Perhaps because her vibrant, sensual, Lauren Bacall-style beauty haunted him every time he thought about taking another woman to bed... Because every time he tried to convince himself he was ambivalent about her, he failed miserably.

The conversation he'd had with his father before leaving Milan filtered through his head like some sort of cruel joke, had it not been of an entirely serious nature. The chairman of Ricci International had fixed his impenetrable, ice-blue stare on him and dropped a bombshell. "Your brother Franco is unable to produce an heir, which means it's up to you, Lorenzo, to produce one and produce it soon."

His dismay for his younger brother, his bewilderment Franco hadn't told him this the night before over dinner, had evaporated under the impact of his father's directive. *Him marry again?* Never happening. Except, he conceded with bitter irony, he was apparently *still* married. To the woman who had walked out on him and said he had no capacity to love. The woman who had stolen the last piece of humanity he'd possessed.

"Sir?"

He turned around. "Do you have any more bombshells to add to the pile or is that it?"

"That's it. The deal is fine for the moment. We're still negotiating the smaller points and you need to clear those last couple of tricky items with Bavaro, but other than that we're on track."

"Bene." He waved a hand toward the door. "Go. I'll take care of Angie."

His lawyer nodded. "Do you want me to file the papers? Get the process started?"

"No."

Cristopher gave him a stupefied look. "Sorry?"

"I said leave it."

His lawyer left. A wise decision. He walked to the bar and poured himself a whiskey. Padding back to the windows, he lifted the glass to his mouth and took a sip. Began to feel vaguely human as the spirit warmed his insides and smoothed out the raw edges—raw edges that had been festering ever since one of the clippings in his daily press briefing had buzzed about his former wife...*current* wife's betrothal plans to a prominent Manhattan lawyer.

He had pushed the news of Angie's engagement aside. Refused to acknowledge how it sank its claws into his skin, dug into his insides—inspired dark, inexplicable thoughts he couldn't have identified if he'd tried. Angie had ended a marriage that had descended to the very deepest depths of acrimony, a marriage many would have left for dead. So why did it still sting so much?

Why was he still so angry, still so damn angry it was like a disease inside of him, eating away at his soul? He *itched* he was so angry.

Why hadn't he asked Cris to file those papers? Ended something that should have been ended two years ago?

He stared out the window for a long time, sipping the whiskey, watching night fall over a light-strewn Manhattan. Considered his duty to the Ricci line. The fifteen-billion-dollar acquisition deal in front of him—a deal that required every bit of his concentration—that would make Ricci the top luxury hotel chain in the world if he landed it.

The solution to his predicament, when it came, was shockingly, simplistically clear.

Why wasn't there any air in this room?

Angie took the glass of champagne the bartender handed her, turned and leaned against the lit glass surface, surveying the cocktail-dress-attired crowd mingling in the elegant, whitewashed art-gallery space. Shimmering light from the antique chandeliers cascaded onto gleaming black marble floors, while directed lighting spotlighted the stunning artwork on the walls. A perfect, sophisticated backdrop for her and Byron's engagement party, everything they'd envisioned to celebrate their upcoming nuptials. Why then did the room seem to have drained of oxygen as the night wore on? Why this restless pull in her veins she couldn't explain?

She *should* be ecstatic. She had the career of her dreams as one of New York's most buzzed-about new jewelry designers, the freedom she'd always craved from life as a Carmichael and a wonderful man waiting in the wings. What more could she ask for?

And yet something still felt…missing.

It did not, she told herself firmly, have anything to do with the man who haunted the edges of her happiness. Who had shown her what having everything looked like, then taken it away in the next breath. Because she knew now that kind of an adrenaline rush was for fools. What went up must come down, and in her and Lorenzo's case, had come crashing down.

A searing pang throbbed in her chest. She took a deep breath of the nonexistent air. Perhaps that's what she needed—oxygen to clear her head.

Byron engaged with a business colleague across the room, she seized the moment. Winding her way through the buzzing crowd, around the live jazz band to the elegant staircase that led to the second level, unused tonight, she climbed the stairs and headed for the small terrace that opened off the upper level.

Hot, thick summer air hit her like a wall of heat as she stepped outside. She walked to the edge of the beautifully landscaped space, rested her elbows on the railing and drank it in. The frenetic activity in the street below as cabs and pedestrians battled for supremacy on a sticky Manhattan night was a familiar refrain that soothed her senses.

Another sensory impression seeped in. Spicy, masculine, it was imminently familiar. *Disturbingly, distantly familiar.*

Cold fingers clamped down on her spine. Her heart a drumbeat in her throat, she turned around. Her brain flatlined as she took in the tall, dark-haired, olive-skinned male dressed in an exquisitely tailored suit standing in front of her. She lifted her gaze to his hard, dark eyes, as treacherous as black ice. Moved them down over Lorenzo's prominent Roman nose, the day-old stubble lining his jaw, his beautiful, sensual mouth that knew how to wound and pleasure in equal measure.

For a disturbingly real second or two, she thought she'd conjured him up. That he wasn't actually here, but was a product of the strange, restless mood she was in. That, in this fantasy of hers, he'd heard about her engagement and come here to stop it. That he still cared about her, because once, during the stormy complexity of their marriage, she'd sworn he had.

A panicked pulse echoed through her. What if he had? What would her answer be? She was terrified she'd cave like a ton of bricks.

She pressed her champagne glass to her chest before her shaking hands spilled it. Before she allowed herself to start conjuring up the fairy tales she'd always had about this man. That maybe he'd wanted *her* when he'd married her. That what they'd had in the beginning *had* been magic, instead of the reality that had materialized like a harsh slap to the face.

That he had married her for political expediency, to secure his heir, and when she'd lost their baby he'd lost all interest in her. *Shattered her.*

She took a deep breath, shifted her weight to both feet in an attempt to gain some equilibrium. "What are you doing here, Lorenzo?"

His lethally handsome face twisted in a mocking look. "No 'Hello, Lorenzo'…? 'You look well, Lorenzo'…or even a 'How are you, Lorenzo?'"

Her mouth tightened. "You've crashed my engagement party. I hardly think pleasantries are in order. We abandoned those at about month six of our marriage."

"Did we last that long?" He crossed his arms over his chest and leaned back against the railing. She forced herself not to follow the ripple of muscle in that powerful body. To acknowledge how he seemed to have hardened into an even more dangerously attractive version of the man she'd known.

He lifted a shoulder. "My apologies for showing up out of the blue, but I have business we need to discuss."

"Business?" She frowned. "Couldn't we have discussed it over the phone?" She flicked a nervous glance toward the door. "Did Byron—"

"No one saw me. I blended in with the paint. I did get a chance to listen to the speeches, though. Touching as they were."

She stared at him, horrified. "How long have you been here?"

"Long enough to see you clearly have *Byron* roped and tied, as my rancher friend, Bartlett, would say. Fully enamored with your considerable charms...ready to let you run the show. Is it everything you ever dreamed of, Angie?"

Her blood heated, mixing with the panic fizzling her veins. "I never wanted to run the show. I wanted equal billing in our relationship—something you, in your arrogance and chauvinism, refused to give me."

"And our good friend Byron does?"

"Yes."

"What about in bed?" His eyes glittered with deliberate intent. "Does he satisfy that insatiable appetite of yours? Does he make you scream when you wrap those long legs of yours around him and beg? Because he doesn't look *man* enough to me, *cara*, to deliver it the way I know you like it. Not even close."

Lust slammed into her hot and hard. An image of Lorenzo's beautiful, muscular body imprinted itself on her brain, filling her, pushing her to the limits of her pleasure, his voice a hot whisper at her ear, demanding she tell him if it was good, not satisfied until she'd begged to let him know it was, until she'd screamed, because yes, he *had* made her scream.

Blood rushed to her cheeks, her stomach contracting in a heated pull. She'd been so desperate for his love, for his affection, she'd taken whatever crumb he'd been willing to throw at her. In the end it had been all they'd had.

She sank her teeth into her bottom lip. Lied. "I have no complaints in that area, either."

His eyes hardened, a dark glimmer stealing across their ebony depths. "Too bad it just isn't going to work out."

A frisson of apprehension swept through her. "What are you talking about?"

"Well, you see, there's been a…hiccup in the paperwork for our divorce."

"We *are* divorced."

"So I thought. The firm handling the paperwork failed to file the correct papers with the state. The error was brought to my attention yesterday after I asked them to review the document."

Her knees went weak. "What are you saying?"

"We're still married, Angie."

The floor gave way beneath her feet. She grasped the railing, wrapping her fingers around cool metal to steady herself. Blinked as she tried to work through the fog enveloping her brain. *Married?* She and Lorenzo were still married?

She swallowed past a paper-dry throat. "I'm marrying Byron in three weeks…in St. Bart's. We're eloping."

His stare was bold, aggressive, like the predator he was. "Unless you plan on committing *bigamy* that would be impossible."

She struggled to get her brain in working order. "You need to *do* something. *Fix* this. It's your firm's fault. *They* should fix it."

An indolent shrug. "There's only so much they can do.

These things move at a snail's pace. It could take months to push it through."

"But you *know* people. You have influence in all the right places...you could make it happen."

"Perhaps."

Her blood ran cold at the hard, unforgiving lines of his face. "But you don't plan to use it."

"No. It would be an unnecessary calling in of favors."

Unnecessary? A red mist descended over her vision. "I am getting *married* in three weeks. It's all planned. How is that *unnecessary*?" She shook her head, pinned her gaze on his. "Are you still angry with me? Is that it? You want to punish me for walking out on you? For God's sake, Lorenzo, you knew our marriage was doomed. You knew it was never going to work. Let me move on."

He stepped closer, six foot three inches of far too intense male vibrating just centimeters from her. His expression, when he looked down at her, was full of leashed aggression. "Our marriage was not *doomed*. Our marriage failed because you were too young and selfish to realize that marriages take work. *Effort*, Angelina. Instead you put all your energy into rebelling against what I asked of you. Into ignoring what *I* needed."

She lifted her chin. "You wanted a perfect society wife without a mind, a *purpose* of her own. You should have hired a beautiful robot to fill the role. It would have been the perfect match for you."

His eyes flashed. "Don't be sarcastic, *cara*, it doesn't suit you. I liked your mind, you're well aware of that. I offered you all sorts of chances to get involved in the charitable efforts Ricci supports, but you didn't have any interest in them, no matter how challenging." He pointed his glass at her. "As for being my society wife, you knew what you were getting into when you married me. What the reality of my life was."

Had she really? Twenty-two, pregnant and wildly infatuated with her husband, she'd had no idea she'd been exchanging one lonely existence for another. That instead of finding the love she'd craved, she'd be giving up the very independence she'd been searching for, the dreams she'd had of being a jewelry designer. That she'd be following in her mother's footsteps in falling for a man who had no capacity to love—the one mistake she'd sworn never to make.

She lifted her chin, chest tight. "I thought you, of all people, would understand my need to pursue my passion. My need to *be* something."

"I did understand it. You had a fledgling online business. I helped you nurture it. What wasn't going to work was to play start-up with a boutique that would take up the lion's share of your time. Our life was too busy."

"*Your* life was. It was never about *my* life. Yours was more important."

"That's not true."

"It damn well is." Champagne sloshed the sides of her glass as she jabbed it in his direction. "All you wanted was for me to stay in line, to look the part…to warm your bed. And even then, I was a possession to be enjoyed and discarded according to your whims."

His jaw hardened. "Our intimate relationship was the one thing about us that didn't need fixing, *cara mia*. Don't sully it with your sharp tongue."

"Didn't it?" Her mouth twisted. "You never truly let me in—not in bed or out of it. Emotional intimacy was simply not on the table with you."

A glimmer of something she couldn't read passed through those dark eyes. "You are right," he agreed in a clipped tone, "that I, too, bear responsibility for the breakdown of our marriage. We *both* bear responsibility for it. Which is why we're going to fix it together."

Her jaw dropped. "Wh-what?"

"Franco cannot produce an heir. That responsibility falls to me now. Since we are still married, it leaves me with only one option."

Oh, no. She backed away from him. "That's insane. *You* are insane. I'm sorry for Franco, but I am engaged to be married."

"I've just explained why that's impossible."

She absorbed the hard set of his jaw. *My God, he's serious.*

"Lorenzo." She adopted her most reasonable tone. "It can't work between us. We've been through too much. We want different things. I have a life I've built, a career. I'm not giving that up."

"I'm not asking you to give up your career. We'll find some middle ground on that. But I do intend to have my wife back, that part is nonnegotiable."

She bit down hard on the inside of her cheek, the salty tang of blood staining her mouth. Once, she would have given anything to hear him say that—that he wanted to fix what they'd broken. In those first few weeks after she'd left, terrified she'd made an irreversible mistake, it had been *all* she'd wanted to hear. But she knew from experience people didn't change. You couldn't heal them no matter how much you loved them. People broke your heart over and over again.

"I won't do it," she said quietly. "You can drag the divorce proceedings out as long as you like, but you're crazy if you think you can just snap your fingers and I'll come back to you and deliver you an heir. I'm engaged, Lorenzo. I'm in love with my fiancé."

Lorenzo absorbed his beautiful wife's lie with the confidence of a man who'd had enough practice reading her reactions to know it was exactly that. A woman didn't pronounce her love for another man and mean it while she ate you up with her eyes like she'd been doing with him. When he could tell he had every nerve in her curvaceous body on edge.

The thought of her offering *that* body to another man made his blood burn. *Watching* her make that toast to her fiancé when she was technically still his. When she would *always* be his.

He dropped his gaze to the thrust of her breasts beneath the delicate silk of her dress. Down over the swell of her hips…the length of her amazing legs atop stiletto heels. His body throbbed with a need that had eluded him for so long his skin went tight at the intensity of it. The injustice of it. *Always Angelina. Never anyone else.*

He returned his gaze to his wife's face, studied the heat that stained her cheeks with a savage satisfaction. "You think," he drawled, "that if I touched you, I couldn't make you forget about him in about sixty seconds? Because you know I could. There's this thing that happens between us, Angelina, that is undeniable. Pure biological chemistry."

Her mouth tightened, a layer of ice settling over her face. "I'm not playing any more of these games. Byron will be looking for me. I'd advise you to go ahead and have your lawyers fix their mistake or I will sue you and your law firm for incompetence."

A smile twisted his lips. "The thought crossed my mind, too. Then I realized it must be a sign we are meant to fulfill the responsibilities we assumed three years ago."

"You *are* crazy." She spun and walked toward the door. "Get out, Lorenzo, before anyone sees you."

The antagonism in him darkened. She had walked out on him at one of the lowest moments of his life, left him to face a firestorm of Manhattan gossip, to break the news to their family and friends while she'd gone vacationing in the Caribbean. Left their marriage in ashes…

She would not walk out on him again.

"Oh, but I'm not finished." His quiet words stopped her in her tracks. "You didn't think I came here empty-handed did you? Without some bargaining power?"

His wife turned to face him, blue eyes apprehensive. "The Carmichael Company is bleeding money," he told her. "Has been for quite some time. I've given your father two large loans to keep things afloat."

She blinked. "That's impossible."

That had been his reaction when Angie's father had come to him for help. That the Carmichael Company, an over two-hundred-year-old textile dynasty, an American icon with its name on the main campus of one of New York's most prestigious design schools, could be in the red, *deeply* in the red, had been inconceivable to him.

He watched the color drain from his wife's face. "If you bothered to go home, you would know. So many countries are in the mix now, producing high-tech fabrics. Things haven't been good in some time."

She shook her head. "If this is true," she said faintly, "why would you help my family?"

His lips curled. "Because I am loyal to the relationships I form, unlike you. I don't run when things get rocky. Who do you think is underwriting your studio?"

She frowned. "*I* pay the rent on my studio."

"You pay one quarter of the rent. It's my building, Angie."

Her mouth slackened. "I hired that real estate agent. Found the space…"

"You found what I wanted you to." He waved a hand at her. "It made me sleep better at night knowing you were in a safe part of town."

Her face crumpled as realization set in. "What are you insinuating? That you will pull the plug on the aid you're giving to my family, toss me out on the street if I don't agree to come back to you?"

"I prefer to think of it as *incentive*. We owe our marriage a fair shot before we relegate it to the history books. You come back to me, we try and make it work, I pull Carmichael out of its financial difficulties before it becomes a footnote in a list of great American dynasties. It's a win-win."

A win-win? She stared at him, disbelieving. "You would really hold that over my head?"

"You didn't play fair when you walked out on me, *tesoro*. You just cut and ran. So yes, I will use whatever means required to make you see the light. To do the right thing."

"I *asked* you to go to counseling. I *begged* you to. I tried to save our marriage and then I left."

He ignored the stab of guilt that piece of truth pushed through him. "You expected us to solve things overnight. It doesn't happen that way."

Her fingers curled tight around the delicate stem of her champagne flute. "Putting the two of us back in a marriage where we'll destroy one other is not doing the right thing."

"We are both older and wiser. I think we can make it work."

She shook her head. "That's where you're mistaken. That's where you've played the wrong card, Lorenzo, because I will never become your wife again."

She turned on her heel and left. He let her go, because he knew she'd be back. He'd never gambled on a deal he couldn't win.

CHAPTER TWO

ANGIE RETURNED TO the party, shaken to her core. Palms damp, heart thrumming in her chest, a frozen numbness paralyzing her brain, she made a beeline for Abigail. Mouthing an apology to the well-known philanthropist her sister was speaking to, she extracted Abigail from the conversation and pulled her toward a quiet corner of the room.

Her sister eyed her. "What's wrong? You look like you've seen a ghost."

"Lorenzo is here."

Abigail's eyes widened. "At your *engagement* party?"

"Someone screwed up our divorce papers, Abby. We're still married."

"Married?" Her sister's jaw dropped. "What do you mean 'screwed them up'? Who?"

"Lorenzo's legal firm. They forgot to file the papers with the state."

"Is he fixing it?"

She closed her eyes. "He won't."

"What do you mean 'won't'?"

"Franco can't have a baby. Lorenzo needs to produce an heir. He wants me to do my duty and put our marriage back together. Give him a baby."

A gasp escaped her sister. "That's outrageous. You're engaged."

"Am I?" Panic skittered up her spine. "If I'm legally

married to Lorenzo, what does that make Byron? My *illegitimate* fiancé?"

Her sister looked dumbfounded. "I don't know… Regardless, we'll sic our lawyers on him. This has to be negligence."

"He's angry," she said quietly. "So angry at me for leaving."

"You did what you had to do. Lorenzo wasn't an innocent victim in all this. You both had a role to play in what happened."

Angie pushed a hand through her hair. Fixed her gaze on her sister. "Is the Carmichael Company in trouble? Is there something you haven't been telling me?"

A guarded look wrote itself across her sister's face. "What does that have to do with this?"

"Lorenzo says he's given Father two loans. That he will bail Carmichael out of its financial problems if I try and make our marriage work. *Incentive*, he called it."

Abby's eyes turned into hard, bright sapphires. "That bastard."

"Is it true? Did he give father those loans?"

"Yes." Her sister's admission made her stomach plunge. "At first it was the need to switch over equipment to compete with other high-tech manufacturers. But Carmichael never really recovered from the new technologies taking over the market."

Angie's breath left her in a sharp exhale. She'd been hoping against hope it wasn't true.

Abigail's lips firmed. "You aren't doing this. Father's been burying his head in the sand for years. He didn't want to see the writing on the wall. It's his problem to fix, not yours."

"Why didn't you tell me?" She swallowed past the lump swelling her throat. "You promised you wouldn't carry the load alone."

"You needed time. You were shattered when you walked away from Lorenzo. The last thing you needed to know was that your ex-husband was bankrolling the Carmichael Company."

Blood pulsed against her temple. "And Mother? How is she handling this?"

Abby frowned. "Ange—"

"Tell me."

"She's become more unstable since the financial difficulties began. It—" She waved a hand. "It may be time to check her into a program. She doesn't want it. She swears she won't go, but I got a call from Sandra last week while they were on a girls' night out. I had to pour her into bed."

Emotions she'd long held at bay welled up inside of her, causing her throat to constrict and the knots in her stomach to twist tighter. "What was it this time?"

"Gin."

She closed her eyes. She'd distanced herself from her family for her own self-preservation—because picking up her mother again and again had left her in a million pieces. Because she just couldn't do it anymore while she'd been trying to pull herself back together after the demise of her marriage. But the guilt surrounding the difficult decisions she'd made was always there in the background, impossible to escape.

It wrapped itself around her now—tight, suffocating. For when Della Carmichael started sliding down her slippery, alcoholic slope, the bottom came fast and furious.

"Angie." Her sister's firm voice brought her head up. "I won't allow him to do this to you. This is not on you."

But Angie knew her sister was wrong. The only solution to this was *her*. Her convincing Lorenzo this was insane, that it would never work. Because she knew tonight hadn't been the end of it.

* * *

Her dilemma was still raging in her head as she put down the phone the following evening having assured Byron she was fine—that the headache she'd pleaded to extract herself from the party just before midnight was gone. The same headache that had made her slide out of her fiancé's kiss and leave him on her doorstep, a frown on his face.

Dammit. She gave up on the idea of work, pushed to her feet and walked across her bright studio space to stand looking out at the street. SoHo at night was still busy with foot traffic, the city thick with tourists at the height of the summer. A good thing for the boutique she ran below the studio that featured her work. The bell announcing visitors had been ringing all day.

The purple awning bearing her name whipped in the breeze below. *Carmichael Creations.* It rankled, more than she could say, to know this studio she loved, that she was so proud of, had been contaminated by Lorenzo's powerful reach. She'd wanted—*needed*—to prove so badly she could do this by herself. To follow her heart and forge a successful career as a designer after Lorenzo had dismissed it as a hobby, when in fact, self-expression was as necessary to her as breathing.

She watched a group of young girls walk by, laughing and jabbing each other in the ribs as they pointed at a slick-suited handsome male in front of them. Her heart gave a painful squeeze. She'd been like that when she'd met Lorenzo—desperately innocent, utterly swept away by his powerful aura.

The memories flooded back, tumbling one over another in painful succession until she was standing by the pool at her parents' legendary winter party in Nassau clad in the sexiest silver lamé gown she owned, butterflies in her stomach knowing the gorgeous, ruthless corporate raider Lorenzo Ricci would be in attendance. Her father had been doing friendly business with Lorenzo rather than serving as one of her husband's hostile take-over targets, but Alistair Carmichael's directive had been clear to his daughter—*leave Lorenzo alone, you're way out of your depth.*

And she had been. But smarting from an argument with her father, needing to escape her miserable, lonely existence for just one night, she couldn't resist. Every woman had wanted to catch Lorenzo, the most desirable widower in Manhattan, perhaps because none ever had. She'd taken her best friend Becka's dare to ask him to dance and shockingly he'd said yes. That dance had led to a kiss in the garden and a hot, heated assignation that had shaken her innocent foundations to the core. She'd gotten her one night with Lorenzo Ricci plus way more than she'd ever bargained for.

She closed her eyes, an ache pulsing low in her chest. She'd thought she could be *the one*, the one who could make her husband love again because what they'd had had seemed earthshaking to her twenty-two-year-old self. That by offering him her unrequited love, she could help him get over his late wife, Lucia, who popular consensus had said he was still hung up on. Until Angelina had learned love was an emotion her husband reserved exclusively for his late wife, an emotion that would never be on offer to her.

Blood throbbed at her temples. She couldn't change the past as much as she wished she could, but she *could—* would—fight Lorenzo on this.

She could postpone the wedding until her divorce came through. Move to a cheaper studio space. But that still didn't address the financial difficulties the Carmichael Company was in. The responsibility that lay on her shoulders.

A chill crawled through her at the thought of the cold,

hard stranger she'd faced on the terrace last night. Lorenzo had always been tough, carved by his experiences, shaped by the cutthroat scion of the Ricci family, Salvatore Ricci, but last night she'd seen a whole new lethal side of him.

Had her walking out on Lorenzo made him this heartless? Or was that just the man he'd become?

Guilt fought a battle with anger. Anger won. She'd been right last night—too much had passed between her and Lorenzo to ever resurrect their marriage. He needed to see reason.

She stalked to her desk, pulled her purse out of the bottom drawer and headed for the door. She was not letting Lorenzo bully her, steal her happiness. Force her back into a life that had nearly destroyed her because he needed an heir for the illustrious Ricci dynasty. She had grown too strong over the past couple of years to let him ride roughshod over her.

Her husband was about to find out just how much she'd changed.

Lorenzo was easy to find. Another hot, steamy Manhattan night bathed the city in a smoky heat as Angie stepped through the doors of her husband's Park Avenue building. The doorman's face lit up when he saw her. Federico's gray brows rose just a fraction before he lowered them back into place and ushered her into the private elevator.

Lorenzo didn't bat an eyelash when the doors opened on the top-floor penthouse. He waved her in as he talked on his headset. As if he'd been expecting her.

Dressed in black jeans and a T-shirt, he looked less corporate shark tonight and more deadly male, the jeans riding low, hugging his lean hips and muscular thighs, his black T-shirt skimming rock-hard abs he kept in premium condition at the gym where he pushed himself as hard as he did everywhere else.

Hell. She banished the frisson of sexual awareness that pulsed through her and walked past him into the luxurious dark brown and chrome space. Lorenzo in casual clothes, which made him look like a mere mortal rather than the deity Wall Street painted him as, had always been her weakness. Perpetuated her belief he had a heart when in fact he did not.

Eyeing the bottle of wine and two glasses that sat on the marble bar, she wondered if he'd been that confident she would show up or whether he'd been expecting someone else. Her stomach contracted into a tight ball. Bringing her back teeth together, she walked to the bar and looked for a bottle of sparkling water in the fridge. Lorenzo covered the microphone and told her to open the wine.

She did. If only to give herself something to do other than absorb the pure physicality of the man pacing the room. She poured two glasses of wine, picked up one and took a sip. Lorenzo rattled off a series of instructions for whoever was on the call and ended it.

"Scusami," he murmured, as he pulled off the headset, tossed it on a chair and walked toward her. "I'm in the middle of negotiations for a company we're looking to acquire."

When wasn't he? "You didn't know I was coming," she said, holding out a glass of the expensive French red he'd provided to put a physical barrier between them. He noted it with an amused twist of his lips.

"I apologize if you were expecting company."

"I was expecting you." Instead of taking the glass, he wrapped his elegant, long-fingered hand around hers and drew her to him.

Her heart slammed against her chest. "Lorenzo…"

He dipped his head toward hers, a dark glimmer of intent in his beautiful eyes. "We forgot our manners last night. Perhaps we should start again."

Her breath caught in her throat. He was going to kiss her. She opened her mouth to protest, to say *absolutely not*, but his firm, sensual lips landed on her cheek instead. Lingered just a little too long for civility's sake…

An electric current charged through her as he repeated the gesture on her other cheek, little pinpricks of heat exploding across her skin. Thoroughly flustered, she stepped back. "I'm not here to accept your proposition."

He lifted a brow. "So you are here to…"

"Talk reason with you."

"All right," he said calmly in the placating tone he'd always used to soothe her like some high-spirited racehorse he'd paid millions for. "Over the wine, then. I've had a hellish day."

Was she allowed to find that secretly enjoyable? She handed him the glass and followed him to the sitting area, where she sank down into one of the chocolate-brown leather chairs she'd always loved to read in.

"What company are you acquiring?"

"The Belmont Hotel Group." He lowered himself into the sofa across from her, splaying his long legs in front of him.

The Belmont? One of the world's most historic luxury hotel chains, it boasted boutique properties in some of the world's most glamorous, exotic locations.

"I'm shocked it's for sale."

"It's not."

"Ah." She took a sip of her wine. "A hostile takeover, then."

"More like a reluctant bride that needs to be brought to heel. She wants to be there but she can't bring herself to admit it."

She eyed him coolly. "Isn't it all the same? It's your specialty, after all. Find a vulnerable company, strip it of its assets, then relegate the rest to the scrap heap. Symbolism, tradition, be damned."

He cocked a brow. "Is this you setting the tone, *cara mia*? I thought you wanted to keep things civil."

She lifted a shoulder. "I don't care for what you do."

"You didn't always feel that way. You used to think it was hot, the power I wield. It was an *aphrodisiac* for you."

Heat stained her cheeks. "And then I grew up. I saw the hundreds of people you put out of jobs. How you relegated iconic companies to the history books if you could profit from it. It was always about the almighty dollar."

"Most of the companies I acquire would eventually fail. It's only a matter of time. In Belmont's case, they have lost sight of what the luxury traveler is looking for—their profits have nose-dived. Call it being cruel to be kind."

"A wolf in sheep's clothing is still a wolf…" She pointed her glass at him. "The question is, when is it all going to be enough, this obsession you have with owning the world?"

He rested his glass on his thigh. "What would you have me do? Rest on my laurels? Tell my shareholders I've proven myself—'so sorry, but that's all the profit you can expect this year…'"

She set her gaze on his. "You could try addressing the demons that drive you."

His dark, spiky lashes swept down. "We aren't here to talk about the past. We're here to discuss our current situation."

"Oh, that's right," she murmured, "that subject is off-limits. I forgot the rules of the game."

His jaw tightened. "Stop baiting me, Angelina, and tell me what's going on in that head of yours."

"Your proposition is outrageous. To expect me to dissolve my engagement and come back to you, simply to ensure the continuation of the Ricci line…"

He shook his head. "I told you, it's about more than that. It's about both of us putting the effort into this marriage we should have in the first place. About living up to the vows we made."

"You *divorced* me."

"It was a mistake."

Her heart skipped a beat. "What do you mean 'a mistake'?"

"I mean you like to run from your problems, *cara*. And maybe I was running, too. But given the current circumstances, given we are still married, technicality or not, we need to rectify that mistake. I did not intend on marrying twice. I certainly don't intend on marrying a third time."

She came back to reality with a crashing thud. "You don't want me," she said flatly, "you know that. You want a nice little Italian wife your mother will love who will host your dinner parties, charm your business acquaintances and greet you at the door every night in sexy lingerie. *That* would be your idea of perfection."

An amused glint entered his gaze. "I'm fairly sure I would be bored with an obedient wife after you. But you are right on the lingerie—that *would* be my idea of perfection."

She said a very bad word in her head. "You don't even know who I am anymore. I'm different. Changed. Not the woman you married, nor will I ever be again."

"Then I look forward to finding out who that woman is." He gave her an appraising look. "I'm prepared to make concessions to make this work. Your career is a case in point. You've clearly become very successful. You've worked hard to get where you are. As long as it doesn't interfere with our important commitments, we'll make it work."

We'll make it work? Heat rose up inside of her. He had no idea what her work meant to her. The sanity it had been throughout her rocky life.

"As for my mother," he continued, "she had certain... *preconceived* notions regarding our marriage you never dispelled with your behavior. You also never made an effort with her. If you do so, I expect you'll find her a different woman."

Her fingers curled into a fist. "She thought I deliberately trapped you into marriage."

"Not an unreasonable assumption when our one night together resulted in a pregnancy. I did, however, make it clear that the responsibility lay on both of us."

"How big of you." A red mist of fury wrapped itself around her brain. "What other *concessions* are you prepared to make, Lorenzo? Are you prepared to let me beneath that impenetrable layer of yours? Talk to me instead of shutting me out? Confront our issues instead of pushing me to the outer fringes of your life until I cease to exist?"

"Yes." The low rumble in his voice vibrated through her. "I understand I was distant at times...emotionally unavailable if you like. I recognize that as a fault of mine I need to work on. But let's just be clear, Angelina, you locked me out just as surely as I ever did you with those cast-iron defenses of yours."

After the big chill had begun. Because eventually it had become too painful to give and never get anything back.

Hurt contracted the muscles around her heart. The wine warming her blood, loosening her inhibitions, made her reckless. "If we're going for the brutal truth here," she growled, "if we're not going to pull our punches, then let's get all the skeletons out on the table shall we? The real reason our marriage failed was Lucia. Because you would have preferred to stay in your cave, pining for your dead wife. Instead you had to marry me."

The color leached from his olive skin. His face tightened, cheekbones standing out like blades. The cold fire that engulfed his dark eyes told her she'd gone too far this time. "It was *your* obsession with Lucia that you wouldn't let go of, not mine."

Her chin lifted, heart pounding in her chest. "Tell yourself that enough and you might even start to believe it."

The silence in the room was deafening. Chest tight, she pushed to her feet and crossed to the floor-to-ceiling windows that framed a magnificent view of Central Park lit up at night. Hugging her arms around herself, she took a deep breath and attempted to regain her equilibrium.

"You aren't this heartless," she said after a long moment, turning to face him. "I don't believe you will let the Carmichael Company fail. You like my father too much."

His eyes were a purposeful, dark velvet cool. "Then don't make me. I meant what I said, Angie. I want you back. I want us to give this marriage the shot it deserves. You come back to me with your heart and head fully in it and I will ensure your legacy survives."

The confusion swirling in her head deepened, thickened. She wrapped her arms tighter around herself, struggled to contain her emotions, but they spilled outside of the edges of her barely shored-up walls. "Wasn't it enough for you?" she asked, voice trembling. "Every second, every minute of those last excruciating months together? We couldn't even be in the same room without tearing each other's throats out. And when we did, it didn't feel any better…it felt worse."

He got to his feet and prowled toward her. "We lost a baby. It was painful, Angelina, it *hurt*."

A rock climbed into her throat. "And here we are hurting each other again."

He stopped centimeters from her. Her body reacted to the heat of him, the familiarity of him, vibrating with an internal memory she couldn't control. She pressed her fingers to her cheeks, trying to hold it in, trying to stop the insanity midflow, but he saw it, read her as he always had, eyes darkening with heat.

"The point is to get past the pain. To deal with what we should have dealt with years ago."

"No," she said, shaking her head, fear bubbling up inside of her like magma, threatening to push her on a course she knew she'd regret. "I'm engaged, Lorenzo. I love him."

Fire licked his gaze. "You know that's a lie."

"It's not a lie. It's the truth."

"You are my *wife*." Curving an arm around her waist, he drew her to him. She swallowed as her vibrating body swayed perilously close to the wall of heat that drew her like a moth to a flame. She flattened a palm against his chest, but her feet wouldn't seem to take her anywhere and her eyes locked on his. "Kiss me like you don't belong to me," he said huskily, "and I might reconsider."

"No." Her sharp response sounded as panicked as she felt. "Why are you doing this? Why are you being so cruel?"

"Because I should have stopped you the first time you walked out. Because the thought of you with another man drives me insane…because you *haunt* me, Angelina, every time I'm with another woman. All I can see is those beautiful blue eyes of yours and those vows we recited…" He cupped her jaw in his hand, fingers closing possessively over her skin. "Because we are not over, *mi amore*. We never will be."

Her heart stuttered, an ache enveloping her that seemed to go soul-deep. "You can't do this to me," she said hoarsely. "Throw threats at me one minute, then say these things the next and just expect me to—"

He lowered his head, breath mingling with hers. "Prove

you feel nothing for me. Prove what I'm saying isn't true and I'll walk away."

"No." But even as she said it, his mouth was covering hers in a whisper-soft caress that switched on every cell in her body. She closed her eyes. *Just do it, Angie. Prove it to him, then walk away.*

He slid a hand up her back, flattened his big palm against her spine. Warm, possessive, his touch seeped into her senses, stroked a wounded, jagged part of her that had never healed. Warning bells went off in her head, a blaring, unmistakable cautionary signal she should stop this now. But she had to convince him it was over.

Slow, infinitely gentle nudges of his mouth demanded a response. She held herself rigid, determined to end it. Tightening his fingers around her jaw, he tilted her head back and took a deeper possession of her mouth. The alarm bells in her head grew louder as the sweet intoxication of his kiss melted her bones.

"Lorenzo—"

He slicked his tongue across her lower lip. Erotic, intimate, it sent shock waves of pleasure rocketing through her. Her mind blanked, stomach clenched, fingers curling around a handful of his T-shirt. He did it again, stroking soft, vulnerable flesh with a deliberate possession that made her quiver.

When he flicked his tongue along the seam of her lips and demanded entry, she obeyed, lost in a sea of sensation. He rewarded her with a hot, toe-curling caress that made her moan low in her throat, grab hold of him more firmly.

He brought her closer with the palm of his hand at her back. Swept it down to cup the flesh of her buttock. The kiss turned needy, desperate, her hips arching against his burgeoning arousal. Thick, hard, he was so potently virile he turned her blood to fire.

Reality slammed into her like a bucket of ice dropped

over her head. She shoved a hand against his chest and pushed back. Breathless, her mouth bruised from his kisses, she stood staring at him.

How had that happened? How had she *let* that happen?

"I hate you," she breathed. "I really do."

His mouth twisted. "That makes two of us. Sometimes I really hate you, too, *tesoro*. It's the rest of the time that messes us up."

She shook her head. Backed away from him. Turning, she snatched her purse off the chair and walked out without looking back.

What had she done?

CHAPTER THREE

New York Daily Buzz
Society Shocker!

Word has it the engagement of up-and-coming designer Angelina Carmichael and district attorney candidate Byron Davidson is off after a flashy soiree to celebrate the couple's betrothal just two weeks ago.

The buzz about town is the prominent lawyer is clearly devastated at the split, perhaps suggesting it was Angelina who called it off?

One can't help but wonder if the reason for the break comes in the form of none other than Angelina's ex: sexy corporate raider Lorenzo Ricci. The two were seen dining at Tempesta Di Fuoco last week, conjuring up images of the couple's tempestuous marriage that offered this column a regular supply of juicy news over its fiery but short duration.

Given the much lusted-after Lorenzo has been curiously devoid of a woman on his arm since the split, suspicion is running rampant that Angelina could be the cause.

The question on everyone's lips is…are the Riccis back on?

OH, FOR GOODNESS' SAKE. Angie tossed the salacious tabloid on the coffee table in her studio, blood heating. Did those people not have better things to do with their time? Her heart sank as she imagined what Byron must be thinking. *Feeling.* How he was coping with the barrage of gossip that had spread through town faster than a forest fire eating up dry timber.

She hadn't talked to him since the night after her confrontation with Lorenzo, when she'd given him back his ring. Since that *kiss* with her husband had made it clear she couldn't marry her fiancé. Even if Lorenzo had miraculously changed his mind and offered to expedite their divorce, she still couldn't have married her fiancé. Not after everything she'd done to prove she was over her husband, that she didn't care about him anymore, had been exposed for the lie it was.

Her mouth turned down. *That* was why she'd felt so off the night of the engagement party. Because she'd been trying to convince herself she was in love with her ultraintelligent, grounded fiancé, that she wanted the opposite of her roller-coaster ride of a marriage, when in fact she had never truly gotten over Lorenzo—the man who had made her feel as if her emotions were out of control.

The movers, currently emptying her apartment above the studio of her possessions, stomped back in to take the final load of boxes out to the truck parked on the street. The ball of tension in her stomach grew as she witnessed what was left of her carefully constructed existence disappear before her eyes.

A conversation with her father had provided no alternatives to her husband's proposition, only a suggestion by her father to repair the marriage she never should have left in the first place.

Potential investors were too spooked by Carmichael Company's recent performance to touch the once lauded company, nor would her father's pride allow him to hunt other offers of assistance. Which meant, as she'd feared, she was the only solution to this problem if her brother, James, who would someday soon run Carmichael Company and her sister, Abigail, were to have anything left of the company to inherit.

She picked up her coffee, taking a sip of the steaming brew and cradling the cup in her hands. Allowing Abigail to bear all the responsibility for her mother was also something she needed to fix. She had her life together now. She was strong. It was time to start assuming some of the responsibilities she'd been shirking so her sister could have a life, too.

Which didn't negate the fear gripping her insides. The anger keeping her awake at night, tossing in her bed, leaving her hollow-eyed in the morning. That Lorenzo was forcing her into this reconciliation, using her family as leverage, made his intentions very clear. This was a power play for him like every other he executed on a daily basis. He wanted her back, needed his heir, so he'd made it happen.

It was not about his feelings for her. Or lack of them… About a sentimental, real desire to give what they'd had a second chance. It was about him repossessing what he felt was his. Staking his claim.

She set down her cup in its saucer. If she was going to do this, she needed to do it with her eyes wide-open, naïveté firmly banished. On *her* terms. She wasn't going to allow him to take control, to overwhelm and intimidate her as he had the first time around. She wasn't sacrificing the independence and freedom she'd carved out for herself and she wasn't letting her husband break her heart again. Those were her *rules*.

Defiance drove her back to her worktable when the movers left, where her anger fueled a furious burst of productivity. By the time she finished up a couple of pieces for Alexander Faggini's Fashion Week show, her watch read 7:00 p.m. *Oops*. She was supposed to be home having dinner with Lorenzo right now—their first night together again in the penthouse. Unfortunately, she was going to be at least a half hour late.

"How's the deal going? Still mired in legalese?"

"Sì." Lorenzo cradled his mobile between ear and shoulder while he poured himself a drink in deference to the end of the week. "There's a few small points Bavaro and I have to work through. He's been a bit of a wild card."

"Bene." Amusement danced in Franco's voice. "I love watching Father on this one. To make Ricci the largest luxury hotel chain in the world is an accomplishment even he can't match. It kills him to think of you surpassing his achievements."

Lorenzo smiled. His father, retired now and serving on the boards of other companies, had an endless thirst for competition. That included the one he had with his sons. It had made the bonds between him and Franco even tighter as they had united to combat their father's powerful personality, with Franco running the shipping operations out of Milan, while Lorenzo oversaw the rest of the company from New York.

"He needn't worry he'll be forgotten. He has more than his fair share of achievements." Lorenzo lifted the whiskey to his mouth and took a sip. "So," he said, as the fiery spirit burned a soothing path through his insides, "when were you going to tell me about the IVF? I have to hear it from the old man?"

A low oath. "I should have known he'd jump the gun.

We didn't get the results on the latest procedure until today. I was waiting until we knew for sure before laying that on you."

"I figured it was something like that." He paused a beat, searching for the right words. "So what was the verdict?"

"It didn't work. Likely never will."

A knot formed in his throat. "*Mi dispiace.* I know how much you and Elena wanted this."

"It is what it is."

The raspy edge to his brother's voice gutted him. It always hurt to be so far away but right now it felt like the sharp blade of a knife. "How is Elena taking the news?"

"Not well. She's claiming it's her fault even though I've told her it could just as easily be me."

He closed his eyes. He didn't know the pain of being denied what he'd always assumed to be his, but he did know what it was like to lose a baby. How deeply it had cut when just a week after being given a clean bill of health, Angelina had inexplicably lost their child. How you didn't know how much you wanted something until it was taken away from you.

"Be there for her," he said quietly. Do what he hadn't done.

Franco exhaled. "We might adopt. I don't know…it's a big step."

"It is. Take your time with it."

A pause. Franco's tone was wary when he spoke. "Your reconciliation with Angelina… The timing is…"

"It's not because of this. Yes, there is that, but it's become clear to me Angelina and I have unfinished business between us."

"She walked out on you, *fratello*. How much more finished do you want it to be?"

Lorenzo winced, pressed a hand to his temple. "I bear

responsibility for the demise of my marriage, too. You know I have my ghosts."

"*Sì*. But she changed you, Lorenzo. You shut down after she left. You don't trust like you used to—you aren't the same man."

No, he wasn't. His wife had taken a piece of him with her when she'd walked out that door on the heels of the loss of his child, his fledgling trust in life and love, his half-built bond with Angelina vaporizing on a tide of bitterness so thick he'd wondered if he would ever move past it. But with time, as his grief over Lucia had subsided, his own faults had been revealed. It would be delusional of him to lay the blame solely at his wife's feet.

"Angie was young. She needed time to grow. I intend for our marriage to work this time."

"Or you will take the house down around you as you try." A wry note stained his brother's voice.

Lorenzo asked about his mother's upcoming birthday celebrations. They chatted about that for a few minutes before his brother signed off. Lorenzo leaned against the bar and nursed his drink while he waited for his wife to deign to appear.

The thought that he would have to produce the Ricci heir no longer evoked the violent reaction it had when his father had lobbed that grenade at him. Instead of feeling *roped and tied*, he felt strangely satisfied. As if his father's directive had been the incentive he had needed to rewrite a piece of history that hadn't gone down as it should have.

Two years after the death of Lucia, he had still been without a taste for women the night he'd met Angelina in Nassau. Plagued by demons, if the truth be known, over the wife he hadn't protected. Until Angie had walked out on the terrace while he'd been talking to one of her father's associates and he'd felt as if he'd been struck by lightning.

All it had taken was one dance, his hands taking purchase of her lush curves, before he'd found himself in an isolated part of the gardens taking over the seduction, driven by a need he couldn't name. His libido had woken up like a five-alarm blaze by the time they'd made it to his luxurious room on the Carmichael estate. Somehow, in the haze of his still ever-present grief, Angie had brought him back to life.

His mouth twisted as he brought the whiskey to his lips. Little had he known that the passion they shared would devolve into the plot from *The War of the Roses*. That the only place he and his young wife would be in sync was in the bedroom, where they'd solved every argument with hot, burn-your-clothes-off sex.

The clock chimed seven thirty. His good mood began to evaporate. The elevator doors swished open a couple of minutes later, his wife breezing in dressed in black capris and a sparkly, peasant-style blouse. Her hair pulled back in a ponytail, face devoid of makeup, she was still the most exquisite woman he'd ever known.

"Long day?" he drawled, leashing his anger.

Pink color stained her cheeks. "It was. I had to finish up some pieces for a show. I'm sorry I'm late."

No, she wasn't. But for the sake of their fresh start and given everything he'd thrown at her, he cut her some slack. "Go change." He cocked his head toward the bedroom. "Constanza unpacked your things. She left dinner in the oven. It'll keep while we have a drink."

Her eyes darkened at the order. Firming her mouth, she dropped her purse on a chair and swept by him.

"Angie?"

She swung around.

"Put your wedding rings on."

She lifted her chin. "Is this how it's going to be, Lorenzo? Just like old times? You firing orders at me? Expecting me to run and do your bidding?"

"Married people wear wedding rings." He held up his left hand, the elegant, simple gold band she had given him glittering in the light.

Her face tightened. Turning on her heel, she disappeared down the hallway. When she returned, she was dressed in the comfortable black leggings she favored and a cream-colored tunic that fell just below her curvaceous derriere. *Unfortunate*, he decided. He'd have to fill in that part from memory.

"Drink?" he asked, walking to the bar.

"Mineral water, please."

"It's Friday night."

"I'd still like mineral water."

And the battle lines were drawn... He poured it for her, added a slice of lime and carried it out onto the terrace, where Angie had drifted. Strategically placed lanterns lit up a thirty-five-million-dollar view of the park.

He handed her the drink. Noted she wore her sapphire engagement ring and wedding band. "Which show?"

She blinked. "Sorry?"

"Which show are you designing for?"

"Oh." She wrapped her fingers around the glass. "Alexander Faggini's Fashion Week show."

"That's impressive."

She lifted a shoulder. "A friend of mine introduced us. He thought my designs worked well with his. It's an honor for me."

"I'd like to see the collection."

"Would you?" She turned those beautiful blue eyes on him. "Or are you just making an effort to appear interested?"

"Angelina," he growled.

"It's a fair question." Her chin set at a belligerent angle. "I am, after all, *playing at a start-up* business that has somehow, magically, found success."

He rested his gaze on hers. "Three-quarters of new businesses fail in this city. They don't even last until their second year. You have done something extraordinary with yours. I'm proud of you. But at the time, it seemed like a long shot."

"You didn't think I had the talent? Not even with you *nurturing* me?"

There was a distinctly wounded edge to her eyes now. He blew out a breath. "I could see you were talented. But you knew I wanted my wife at home. We were having a baby."

"You were like that after we lost the baby. When I desperately needed something to occupy my brain."

His mouth flattened. "I could have supported you better, there's no question about it. I *should* have. But someone had to run our life. I needed the sanity of you at home."

"And I needed the sanity my work provided me." She turned her gaze to the lush canvas of green spread out before them, Central Park in full, glorious bloom.

He studied the delicate line of her jaw, the stubborn set of her mouth, silhouetted in the lamplight. *Defensive. Protective.* It made him wonder about all the pieces of his wife he hadn't known. Didn't know. Had never attempted to know.

"Sanity from what?"

She shrugged. "My life. All of it."

He frowned. He understood what being the offspring of a dynasty meant, because his family was as much Italian aristocracy as the Carmichaels were American royalty. Understood how the pressure of the relentless press coverage, the high expectations, the *rules* in their world could weigh a person down. What he had never understood was what about it his wife reacted so violently to.

"Why do you hate it so much," he asked, sweeping

a hand through the air. "This world? Why has being a Carmichael been so difficult for you? I could never figure it out. I know you have a combative relationship with your father and that having his affairs plastered across the media couldn't be easy for you...but it always seemed like it was more."

A cynical light shone in her gaze as she turned toward him. "Did it need to be more? Those affairs devastated my mother, cut her so deeply she never recovered."

"No," he agreed, "it doesn't. My father worships the ground my mother walks on and rightly so. I can't imagine how painful it must have been to watch your father disrespect your mother like that when she has stood by his side the entire time."

Her dark lashes swept over her cheeks. "You see what everyone else sees. The glittering, perfect world of the Carmichaels. You don't see the dysfunction on the inside."

"So tell me about it," he countered. "Help me understand."

"They are private family issues. I would be betraying confidences if I did."

"You are my *wife*. You can confide in me."

Her mouth formed a stubborn, straight line. An oath left his lips. "This is one of those areas we need to fix, Angelina. How can we make this marriage work if there are big pieces of you I don't know?"

"Like those big pieces of you I don't know?" Her eyes flashed, a storm rising in their gray-blue depths. "You can't press a button and summon emotional intimacy. *Trust.* It doesn't work like that. It takes time and effort. If you want that from me, you have to lead by example."

Heat seared his belly. He knew she was right. Knew he'd been operating on automatic pilot in the years after Lucia's death, cauterizing his emotions, refusing to feel. But it wasn't the easiest thing to admit.

"Bene," he conceded harshly, opening his arms wide. "Consider me an open book, then. No subject is off-limits. Anything is fair game. But we *are* going to learn how to communicate—in ways that do not involve the bedroom."

The stare she leveled at him rattled every nerve ending. Made him ache to resort to tried-and-true methods. But he wasn't going there. He was making good on the promise he'd just given her.

"I think," he said evenly, deciding a change of subject was in order, "we should host a party in the Hamptons over the long weekend. Marc Bavaro, the CEO of the Belmont chain, has a place there. I'd like to try and soften him up a bit. Get a few outstanding issues resolved. It would also provide an ideal opportunity to formally announce our reconciliation given the gossip that's running rampant."

She muttered something under her breath. His brow lifted. *"Scusa?"*

"I *said* to put your stamp on me. That's why you want to have this party."

"I already did that," he murmured, eyes on hers. "Why would I need to make a public display of ownership when we both know the truth?"

A flush stained her cheeks. "Go to hell, Lorenzo."

"I've already been there, *cara.* At least this time there will be a great deal of pleasure along with the pain."

Her eyes locked with his. A long, loaded moment passed as they took a step into uncharted territory. Lashes lowered, his wife studied him, as if deciding whether to continue the charge.

Her chin dropped. "Everyone's calendars will be full on the Labor Day weekend."

"They'll be doing the rounds. What's one more stop? Speculation about us alone will pack them in."

She gave him a pointed look as if to say that was exactly the issue. "I have to finish the pieces for Alexander so he can match them up with the show. If something doesn't work, I'll need to come up with an alternative."

"It's one weekend. There's nothing pressing between now and then. Work around it." He pointed his whiskey glass at her. "This is where we learn to compromise, Angie. You give, I give—that's how it works."

Her mouth flattened. "Fine."

"Good. Gillian will plan it, you will contribute your guest list and the staff in the Hamptons will execute. All you need to do is show up."

Her expression remained frozen. He sought the patience he was not known for. "I expect you to invite your family. Whatever's going on between you and your parents, you need to fix it. This will be a good opportunity to do so."

"No." The word flew out of her mouth—swift and vehement. He lifted a brow. "I went to see them last week," she explained. "They aren't in the Hamptons much anymore in the summer. There's no point in inviting them."

"I'm sure they'll make the effort to come. It will look strange if they're not there given I do business with your father." He took a sip of his whiskey. "Speaking of parents, mine will be visiting the week after the party. They'll stay at their apartment, but we'll host them here for dinner. Decide on a date with Gillian that works for you."

Her face fell further, if that was possible. "What did you tell them? About us?"

"That we've decided to make this marriage work. That we made a decision in haste at a time when we were both in pain and now we are rectifying it."

"So you chose to leave out the part where you're *bullying* me into becoming your wife again?"

"I prefer to think of it as a mutually beneficial arrangement. *Motivation* for us to make this marriage work." He leveled his gaze on her combative face. "We made a deal, a commitment to each other, Angelina. I meant it when I said your heart and soul have to be in it, but I'm not so unfeeling that I don't understand you need time to adjust. After that settling-in period, however, I expect an *attitude* adjustment, because this is not how it's going to be."

An attitude adjustment? Angie was still fuming after she and Lorenzo had shared a tense, mostly silent dinner on the terrace, where she ate little and talked less. It had been so *generous* of him to concede she needed time and space after what he'd done to her. *Clearly* she should be falling into line, looking forward to spending more time with his PA than she did her husband.

Her mouth twisted. *I meant it when I said your heart and soul have to be in it.* He didn't even *have* a heart… or a soul for that matter. What would he know about it?

Lorenzo was ensconced in his home office to finish some work, so she elected to have a hot bath and go to bed. Constanza had unpacked all her things in the light, airy master bedroom, with its gorgeous vistas of the park, the housekeeper's usual ruthless efficiency putting everything back as if she'd never left.

It was eerie to pull a nightgown from a puddle of silk in a drawer and untangle her hair with the pearl-backed brush that sat on the dresser in the exact same place it used to be. On edge, her nerves in disarray, she headed for a rose-scented bath in the Italian-tiled en suite, immersing herself up to her ears in hot, cathartic bubbles.

All sarcasm aside, she was relieved with her husband's acknowledgment they needed time—that he didn't expect her to jump into bed with him as seamlessly as her brush had landed back on the dresser. But clearly, she thought, stomach knotting, given that her things were where they were, he expected her to share that bed with him. The thought made her search desperately for something else to focus on, like why he had rose-scented bath bubbles in here.

Either Constanza had been thoughtful, as she was wont to be, or they had belonged to one of his lovers. Because surely, the tabloids couldn't be right? Surely her highly sexual husband, who'd thought he was divorced, had had other women?

You haunt me, Angelina, every time I'm with another woman... Her heart sank, a numb feeling settling over her. He'd pretty much admitted he had. Lorenzo wouldn't have spent two years pining after her as she had him. Going dateless until Byron wouldn't take no for an answer.

The thought of her husband with other women lanced her insides. She sank farther into the bubbles and closed her eyes. They had been so happy in the beginning. That's what hurt the most. What *might* have been.

After Lorenzo had accepted the consequences of what a broken condom had produced, he'd submitted willingly to her mother's ostentatious society wedding—what he'd considered a politically advantageous match, she suspected. She'd been too crazy about him to care.

They'd spent the first months of their marriage in a pheromone-induced haze, tuning out the world. In Lorenzo's arms, her worries about why he'd married her had faded to black. He'd hungered after her with an intensity that had made her feel as if she'd been the most important thing on the planet to him, their addictive obsession with each other inescapable, unassailable. The wounded pieces of her, the parts that had been convinced she was unlovable after a childhood devoid of emotion, had begun to heal. For the first time in her life, she'd felt whole, as if she was *worthy* of love.

And how could she not? Having her husband focus on her, choose to engage, had been like having the most powerful force in the universe directed at her. Suddenly all the pieces of her life had been falling into place and happiness had seemed attainable after years of wondering if it even existed.

Until reality had interceded—one of Lorenzo's big, flashy deals had come along, he'd immersed himself in it and their cozy cocoon had become her husband's insanely busy life.

She'd learned being Mrs. Lorenzo Ricci had meant wining and dining his business contacts multiple times a week, their social schedule so exhausting for a pregnant Angie she'd barely been able to keep up. She'd begun to feel as if she was drowning, but Lorenzo hadn't seemed to care, was too busy to notice.

It had all come to a head when they'd lost their baby. Her increasingly distant husband withdrew completely, rendering him a virtual stranger. He'd descended into the blackness, whatever hell had been consuming him, and they'd never recovered. But, apparently, she thought bitterly, it was *her* obsession with Lucia that had crippled their marriage—not his.

The water cooling, a chill descending over her, she got out of the bath and got ready for bed. Slipping the silk nightie over her head, her eyes were half-closed by the time she stood in front of the beautiful, chrome, four-poster bed.

Too many memories crowding her head, a burn in her chest so painful it was hard to breathe, she fought back the hot, fat tears that burned her eyes. *I can't do it.* She could no more get into that bed as if the last two years hadn't happened than she could convince herself that coming back to Lorenzo hadn't been a big, huge mistake.

She padded down the hall to the guest room. Done in soothing pale blues and yellow, it evoked none of the master bedroom's painful echoes. Pulling back the silk coverlet, she slid between the sheets. Peace descended over her. She was out like a light in minutes.

She woke to a feeling of weightlessness. Disoriented, half-asleep, she blinked against the velvet black of night. Registered the strong arms that cradled her against a wall of muscle. *Heat.* The subtle, spicy, familiar scent seduced her into burrowing closer. *Lorenzo.*

Lost in the half-awake state that preceded full consciousness, bereft of time and place, the dark, delicious aroma of her husband seeping into her senses, she flattened her palm against the hard planes of his chest. Reveled in his strength. Registered the rigid set of his body against hers.

Her eyes flew open, consciousness slamming into her swift and hard. The taut line of Lorenzo's jaw jolted her the rest of the way to full alertness. Cold, dark eyes that glittered like diamonds in the dim light.

"Wh-what are you doing?" she stuttered as he carried her down the hallway and into the master bedroom.

He dumped her on the bed. "You can have all the time you need but you will sleep in here. We are moving *forward*, not backward."

She pressed a hand into the mattress and pushed herself upright. "I—" She slicked her tongue over her lips. "I couldn't get into this bed. There were too many memories, too many things I—"

"What?" he responded harshly. "Too many things you want to forget? Too much backstory you'd like to erase instead of facing it?"

She blinked, her eyes becoming accustomed to the light. Anger pulsed in his face—a living, breathing entity that made her heart tick faster. "Why are you so angry?"

"You weren't in bed," he said tersely. "I didn't know where you were."

He'd thought she'd left. Again. The realization wrote

itself across her brain in a dazed discovery that had her studying those hot, furious eyes. She'd known instinctively that walking out on Lorenzo hadn't been the right thing to do, but she hadn't been equipped with the emotional maturity at twenty-three to handle the destruction they had wrought. Instead she had left Lorenzo alone to face the fallout of their marriage while she'd spent a month in the Caribbean with her grandmother. She'd never quite forgiven herself for it.

"I'm sorry," she said quietly, reminding herself he had things to be angry about, too. "For leaving like that. I didn't handle it the right way. I did what I thought was necessary at the time. I needed to find myself—to discover who I was. But it wasn't right. I know that."

He reached for the top button of his shirt, eyes on hers. "And did you succeed? Did you find what you were looking for?"

"Yes." She laced her fingers together, eyes dropping to the sapphire that blazed on her finger. "I found me."

"And who is she?"

"The true me," she said quietly. "The one who spends her evenings with a sketch pad beside the bed, who gets to get up every morning and make those ideas into reality, tells a story someone might find beautiful. That's what I love, Lorenzo. That's when I am at peace."

He stared at her for a long moment, then finished unbuttoning his shirt. She told herself to look away as he stripped it off, but her sleepy, hazy brain, her senses, still filled with the scent of him, the parts of her that still craved him like a drug demanded she watch. Absorb every lean, cut line he exposed, angling down to the V that disappeared into his belt line.

Heat lifting to her face, she lay back against the pillows. It didn't matter how many times she'd seen Lorenzo naked, it still had the ability to fluster her beyond reason.

Seeking to distract herself, she voiced the one question her still unguarded brain needed to know as she lay staring at the ceiling. "Those women you talked about... did you sleep with them?"

Lorenzo balled up his T-shirt and tossed it in the hamper, struggling to get his anger under control. A part of him, the bitter, wounded part that hadn't been able to enjoy the one woman he had taken to bed during their time apart, while she had apparently found her fiancé more than satisfactory, wanted to see her flinch, *hurt*. But something stopped him. He thought it might be the knowledge that if he followed through on that desire, it would haunt them forever.

Setting his knee down on the bed, he joined his wife. "I don't think we should go there," he said softly. "I said, forward, Angie, not back."

Her face crumpled. "I want to know."

A knot formed in his chest. He drew in a breath. *Dannazione*—he was not the injured party here.

"One," he said evenly, "and no, I won't tell you who she is."

"Why?"

"Because you don't need to know."

She closed her eyes.

Heat seared his belly. Blood fizzling in his veins, he threw a thigh over his wife's silk-clad body and caged her in, forearms braced on either side of her head. "Angelina," he murmured, watching as her eyes fluttered open, "you asked. And while we're at it, let's not forget about our friend Byron."

Her lashes shaded her cheeks. "I didn't sleep with Byron. We were waiting."

He rocked back on his heels. "Waiting for *what*?"

"Until we got married."

Incredulity that any man would marry a woman without knowing whether they were sexually compatible warred with the infuriating knowledge that she had lied to him.

"And yet you deliberately let me think you'd bedded him," he murmured. "'I have no complaints,' was how I think you put it."

Her eyes filled with an icy blue heat. "You blackmailed me back into this marriage, Lorenzo. If you think I'm going to apologize, think again."

What he *thought* was that he had no idea what to think. Knowing his wife remained his and only his satisfied him on a level he couldn't even begin to articulate. That she might be as haunted by him as he was by her...

He traced his gaze over her lush, vulnerable mouth. Across the enticing stretch of bare skin the askew neckline of her nightie revealed, down over the smooth flesh of her thighs where the silk had ridden up...the dusky shadow between her legs. *Unbearable temptation.* Hard as rock, he ached for her.

"Get off me." His wife drew his attention back up to her flushed face.

His lip curled. "What's the matter, *mia cara*? You afraid I'm going to penetrate those defenses you cling so desperately to? That make you feel so *safe*?"

A defiant look back. "Just like yours do?"

"Ah, but *I* am promising to open up." A lazy smile twisted his lips. "I'm a caterpillar poised for transformation. You get to come out of your cocoon, too, and try your wings."

"Very funny." She pushed at his chest. *"Off."*

He dropped his mouth to her ear. "An open book, Angelina. That's what you and I are going to be. The brutal truth and nothing but. We might just survive this little experiment if we can offer each other that."

He levered himself off his sexy, furious wife and headed for the bathroom. It occurred to him, then, as he stepped under a hot shower, his emotions a tangled mess, that he might have underestimated the power his wife still held over him. That both of them might end up getting burned before this was over.

CHAPTER FOUR

ANGIE SPENT THE WEEK leading up to the Hamptons party attempting to avoid any further confrontations between her and Lorenzo. That combustible scene in their bedroom had convinced her engaging with her husband was not a good strategy. Avoidance was. And with Lorenzo immersed in his big deal, it hadn't proven difficult. It was almost like old times.

Except it wasn't. She had been working long hours, too, at the studio getting Alexander's collection ready, with Lorenzo's support. Her husband, however, had insisted they share dinners together, even if they had to work afterward. He was intent, it seemed, on making this marriage work. They talked, shared things about their day, managed, for the most part, to be civil. But soon afterward, Lorenzo retreated to his office to work, not coming to bed until the early hours, ensuring her strategy had worked perfectly.

Tonight, however, she conceded as she watched a perfect East Hampton sunset stain the sky, there would be no escaping—not from her combustive relationship with her husband, nor the past she'd worked so hard to leave behind. Tonight they would host the toast of high society for cocktails at their sprawling waterfront estate, an event that had the gossip hounds frothing at the mouth and her insides curling in an intense, visceral reaction that begged her to retreat.

But it was too late. It had been too late ever since Gillian had sent out the cream-and-silver embossed invitations via courier and the RSVPs had started flooding in by the dozens, proving Lorenzo's point that a helping of titillating gossip would always command the day.

She watched a graceful, forty-foot sailboat navigate past on the gray-blue Shinnecock Bay, the high waves and white foam a perfect mirror for her churning insides. She adored the peace and tranquility of this exclusive enclave, the ability to escape a tourist-infested, muggy Manhattan and enjoy the cool breezes that tempered the island. What she didn't enjoy was the microcosm of Manhattan society the Hamptons were at this time of year. Taking part in the requisite social circuit, forging the right contacts through her and Lorenzo's recreational activities, *being seen with the right crowd*.

"You might as well be at work," her entrepreneurial friend, Cassidy, had once said, referring to the intense networking that went on here 24/7. "At least in Manhattan, you can disappear into your town house, plead a prior engagement and no one will ever know. In the Hamptons, *everyone* knows."

Her mouth twisted. And the cliquishness? The competitiveness? The feckless alliances that changed with the wind? She had seen the devastation they could wreak, had watched her mother shredded by their vicious bite and yet Bella Carmichael had, unfathomably, always gone back for more because headlining an American dynasty wasn't something you just walked away from.

Her mother had learned to grit her teeth and smile as all Carmichaels did, even when her world was falling apart, pretending the gossip chasing through the room about Alistair Carmichael's infidelities, which of his "assistants" he was sleeping with now, didn't faze her in the least. That her husband's predilection for twenty-five-year-old blondes and the power that came along with his ability to command them was par for the course in the world they lived in.

She smoothed clammy palms over her cranberry-red silk dress, praying her father's indiscretions would not come up tonight. She'd already briefed the waitstaff her mother was not to be served alcohol under any circumstance. Watching her go off the rails in front of the upper echelons of Manhattan society was the last thing she needed.

"I like this dress." Lorenzo materialized behind her, his hands settling on her hips. "Although," he drawled, turning her around, his inspection dipping to the plunging neckline of the dress, "I'm not sure I'm going to appreciate every other man in attendance tonight enjoying the same view."

Her pulse fluttered in her throat. Heat radiated from the light spread of his fingers to forbidden places, *dangerous* places, warming her insides. She took a step back, putting some distance between them.

The dress *was* provocative—the flesh revealed by the low neckline leaving a hint of the rounded curves of her breasts bare. It was more than she would normally put on display.

"It's one of Alexander's designs. He insisted I wear it tonight."

"I'm not surprised. It was made for you."

The sensual glitter in his eyes sent a skittering up her spine. Or maybe it was how good he looked in a silver-gray shirt and dark trousers that set off his spectacular dark coloring and beautiful eyes.

Her gaze dropped away from his. He curved his fingers around her jaw and brought it back up to his. The appraising look he subjected her to made her feel like glass—utterly transparent and far too vulnerable. "You've been off all day. What's wrong?"

She pulled free. "Nothing. I'm fine."

"No, you aren't." Irritation clouded his expression. "There's this thing that happens when we socialize, Angie. You turn into a plastic version of yourself. Aloof. Unreadable. Why?"

"That's hardly true."

"Every time, *cara*." He shoved his hands in his pockets and leaned back against the sill. "You can tell me or we can keep your parents waiting. It's all good with me."

Heat sizzled her blood. "Perhaps because it's always about a goal, a *business* transaction, rather than us enjoying ourselves. I was graded on my ability to accomplish those goals. Romance a partner of yours, flatter his wife, impress a potential target with my impeccable lineage…" She waved a hand at him. "Tonight it's Marc Bavaro—what's the goal with him? What would you like me to *be*, Lorenzo? Amusing? Intellectual? Cultured? Flirtatious?"

His gaze narrowed. "Not in that dress, no. And here we are getting somewhere, *bella mia. Communicating.* Because I had no idea you felt that pressure. *I* enjoy the thrill of the chase, accomplishing something by the end of the evening. To me it's us being a team. But I would *prefer* for you to be yourself…for you to be the woman I have always appreciated that never seems to show up on these occasions."

She leaned back against the sill, fingers curling around the edge. "And which woman is that? I'm intrigued despite myself, since I never seemed to get it right."

"The vibrant, spirited woman I met that night in Nassau who didn't seem to care what anyone else thought of her. Where has she gone, Angie? Where has that light gone?"

She blinked. Who did he think had snuffed out that spirit by asking her to be something she wasn't? By shutting her out when she displeased him? By constantly making her aware she wasn't measuring up?

She lifted her chin. "Why this sudden obsession with what makes me tick? It never seemed to concern you before."

"Perhaps because I'm realizing the woman I thought I knew has all these vulnerabilities lurking beneath the surface, vulnerabilities I think might be the key to why she is the way she is, and yet she won't let me near them."

"I think you're overthinking it."

"I think I'm not." He scowled and pulled his hands from his pockets. "I had some things to work through before, things I *have* worked on. It has proven illuminating to me. I would like to learn from it."

Things like Lucia? Her heart beat a jagged rhythm in her chest. To allow herself to believe that, to believe he truly cared, that he wanted to know her, *understand* her, that he truly wanted this time to be different between them, threatened to poke holes in the composure she desperately needed as she faced her old social set tonight. Not to mention her parents, who were waiting for them downstairs.

"We should go," she said quietly. "My parents will be waiting."

He pushed away from the sill. "We'll continue this later," he warned, setting a hand to the small of her back to guide her from the room. His warmth, his undeniable strength, bled into her skin. She swallowed hard. Somehow in the midst of all the chaos in her head, among all the conflicted feelings warring inside of her, his touch anchored her as it always had. Perhaps that was why it had hurt so much when he'd taken it away.

The poolside terrace was lit with flaming torches as they joined her parents outside, the lights from the sprawling, Italian-inspired villa reflected in the infinity pool that served as the star attraction of the space. Sleek waitstaff dressed in black hovered at the ready, the marble-and-brick bar stocked with rows of the perquisite champagne on ice.

Della and Alistair Carmichael were already holding drinks, listening to the local band they'd hired to play. Angie gave her mother, who was looking her usual elegant self in a powder-blue cocktail dress, her silver-blond hair a perfect bob to her ears, a perfunctory kiss on the cheek. Her gaze slid down to the drink her mother held as she drew back, the tightness in her chest easing when she saw that it was sparkling water.

"You look beautiful, Mother."

"Thank you." Her mother gave her a critical once-over. "Faggini?"

"Yes." A wry smile twisted her lips at their practiced small talk. It was how they'd learned to coexist after their fiery relationship during Angie's teenage years, when her mother's alcoholism had emerged and everything between them had been a war of wills. Their practiced détente still didn't quell the pain of losing the mother she'd once had, before Bella Carmichael's disease had devastated her, but at least it was a norm she knew how to maneuver within.

"Lorenzo." Her mother turned her attention to Angie's husband, the feminine smile she reserved for handsome, powerful men softening her face. "It's so lovely to see you." She kissed him on both cheeks. "Although," she said in a pointed tone as she drew back, "I think we've seen you more than our daughter over the past couple of years. Perhaps your reconciliation will remedy that."

"We're counting on it," her father said, stepping forward. Tall and distinguished with a hint of gray at his temples, his eyes were the same slate blue as his daughter's. That was where their similarities began and ended.

Eschewing the embrace he knew Angie would reject, he shook Lorenzo's hand. "Angelina knows how thrilled I am to see her back where she belongs."

Back where she belongs? A surge of antagonism pulsed through her. She wouldn't be in this situation if her father hadn't allowed his arrogance to blind him to the business realities staring him in the face. He was using her as a pawn and showed not the slightest conscience about it.

Lorenzo read the tension in her body, his palm tightening at her back. "My parents are in town next week," he said smoothly. "Perhaps you can join us for dinner? It would be nice for us all to reconnect."

Angie's back went ramrod-straight as her mother gushed on about how lovely that would be. It wasn't lovely, it was the worst idea ever. To put Saint Octavia, Lorenzo's supremely dignified mother, in a room with her own, given Della Carmichael's loose-wheel status of late, was a recipe for disaster.

Thankfully they were saved from discussing it further as the first guests began to arrive.

Hand at his wife's back, Lorenzo greeted the arrivals. Guest after guest arrived in cars piloted by drivers who would spirit them from party to party that evening. His wife grew stiffer and stiffer with each new arrival and the open curiosity about their newly resurrected relationship. By the time Marc Bavaro, the CEO of the Belmont Hotel Group, arrived with his beautiful redheaded girlfriend, Penny, Angie had perfected her plastic self.

Lorenzo's inability to understand what was happening to her, as his need to connect on a personal level with Bavaro pressed on his brain, made his impatience boil over.

"That's Marc Bavaro and his girlfriend walking in now," he murmured in his wife's ear. "Can we try for happy just for the next few minutes? Less like you're facing the executioner being by my side?"

Angelina pasted a smile on her face. "Of course," she said sweetly. "Your wish is my command."

Even without her real smile, his wife captivated Marc Bavaro. The CEO's leisurely once-over of Angelina's red dress, despite the stunning date at his side, made his wife's cheeks redden. So Marc Bavaro did have a roving eye, as advertised. Lorenzo couldn't necessarily blame him, given Angie's ability to mesmerize any red-blooded male with whom she came into contact.

He tightened his fingers around her waist. "Great that you could make it," he said to Marc. "Good to get out of the boardroom."

"Agreed." But Bavaro still wore the cagey expression that had been making Lorenzo mental as they debated the last few points of the deal.

"Your necklace is beautiful," Penny said to Angie. "Is it one of yours?"

"Yes. Thank you. It's one of my favorite recent pieces."

"I love your stuff." Penny threw Marc a wry glance. "I've given him lots of hints on what he can buy me for my birthday."

"Perhaps you'd like to come in to the studio and I'll design something for you?"

The redhead's eyes widened. "Would you?"

"Of course." Angelina slid Lorenzo a glance that said she was playing the game for now. "Why don't I introduce Penny around while you two talk business?"

Penny agreed and the two women set off through the crowd. Bavaro's eyes trailed after Angelina. "That's quite a dress."

"It is," Lorenzo agreed, amused. He didn't doubt the connection he and Angie had. It ruled out any other male as a threat. He was content to play the waiting game when it came to bedding his wife. Figuring out what was going on in her head was another matter entirely.

He nodded at Marc. "Let's find a quiet place to talk."

* * *

By the time Angie had introduced Penny around to anyone the real estate broker might have found interesting or
useful, she'd had enough of this party for a lifetime. She
hated small talk with a passion, had always dreaded the
legendary Carmichael parties she'd been forced to attend,
not to mention the fact that all roads seemed to lead back
to her and Lorenzo's unexpected reconciliation in the sly
side conversations she was drawn into.

"I thought maybe there was a baby in the works," joked
their next-door neighbor. "But clearly that can't be true.
That dress is *amazing* on you."

After the last, thinly veiled attempt to pry the story out
of her, she returned Penny to Marc. The Belmont CEO
asked her to dance in turn, and Penny didn't seem to mind,
so Angie accepted, eager to get away from prying eyes.
Marc was a good dancer and conversationalist. He was
charming, despite Lorenzo's depiction of him as a shark.

They danced two dances before Lorenzo cut in. "I'm
not sure if I should lock you up or use you as a weapon,"
he murmured as he took her in his arms. "Bavaro is like
a puppy salivating after a bone."

"Ah, but I don't have a purpose tonight." Sarcasm
stained her voice. "I'm just supposed to *be me* in all my
glory. The woman you *appreciate*."

His lips curved. Bending his head, he brought his
mouth to her ear. "I do appreciate you in that dress. It
screams 'take me,' *mia cara*. Too bad we are still learning
to communicate *verbally*. The timing is all off.*"*

Fire licked up her spine. He pulled her closer, a possessive hand resting on her hip, his splayed fingers burning into her skin. A slow curl of heat unraveled inside of
her. She'd enjoyed her dance with Marc—he was handsome by any woman's standards and equally charismatic.

But being in Lorenzo's arms was a whole different story. Dancing with her husband was…*electrifying*.

Her nerve endings sizzled as her hips brushed against his muscular thighs, erotic tension in every muscle. The masculine warmth of him bled into her, heating her blood, weakening her knees. She took a deep breath to center herself, but it was his dark, delicious scent that filled her head, heightening her confusion.

She stepped back, putting some distance between them, heart thudding in her chest. His ebony eyes glittered with a banked heat, moving over her face in a silent study. "Thank you for offering to design the piece for Penny. You didn't have to do that."

"It's fine." The husky edge to her voice made her wince. *You hate him, remember?* He had just turned her life upside down.

"Perhaps we will make that superior team," he suggested on a speculative note, eyes holding hers. "If you manage to move past that anger you're holding so tightly to."

Her gaze dropped away from his. She focused on the other guests, sticking determinedly to her vow to keep her shields bulletproof when it came to her husband.

A high-pitched laugh stole her attention. The blood in her veins turned to ice. Whipping her head around, she found her mother in the crowd, talking to a well-known society columnist, a glass of champagne in her hand. Oh, no! She'd found someone to enable her.

Panicked, she scanned the crowd for her sister. Abigail was all the way across the terrace in a group of people. She looked back at her mother, champagne sloshing from her glass as she laughed at something the columnist had said. It was not her first drink.

"Your mother is in fine form," Lorenzo said mildly.

Her brain frozen, she just stared at him. When the

music ended, she slipped out of his arms. "Keep socializing," she said, nodding at Marc. "Abigail's just waved for me to go meet someone."

He frowned at her. "Are you okay?"

"Perfect. Back in a minute." With as blasé a smile as she could manage, she set off through the crowd. Approaching the group her sister was in the middle of, she caught her eye. Abigail disentangled herself and came over. "You okay?"

"It's Mother. She has a glass of champagne in her hand. It's not her first."

Abigail frowned. "I've been watching her all night. She's been drinking sparkling water."

"She found someone to enable her." Angie's stomach lurched. "She's talking to Courtney Price, Abby."

Her sister's face grayed. Leading the way, Abigail wound her way through the crowd, Angie on her heels. Her mother had drained the champagne and procured another glass by the time they reached her. Her loud voice penetrated the din of the crowd, drawing glances from those around her. Angie's heart plummeted.

"You grab her," Abigail muttered. "Get her out of here. I'll do damage control."

Angie nodded. Heart in her mouth, she headed toward her glassy-eyed mother. Her mother glared at her. "Oh, look!" she declared in that far too loud tone. "My daughters are here to cut me off before I say something I shouldn't. I haven't, have I, Courtney? We're just having a nice conversation."

Courtney Price had a half fascinated, half horrified look on her face. *Brilliant column fodder.* Angie reached for her mother's arm. "Actually I have someone I'd like you to meet."

Her mother yanked back her arm. The force of the movement sent the champagne flying from her glass, splattering the dress of the woman beside her. Paralyzed, Angie stared at the silk dress, then lifted her gaze to the woman's bemused face. She was the wife of one of Lorenzo's business acquaintances.

Oh, hell.

Gasps rang out around her. The shocked sounds spurred her into action. Grabbing her mother by the arm, she propelled her through the crowd, people gawking at them as they went. Angry and humiliated, her mother kept up a verbal barrage the whole way.

"It was *your* fault that happened, hauling me out of there like that."

Angie kept her mouth shut. Nodding her thanks at the butler who opened the patio door for them, she marched her mother inside and up the stairs toward her parents' suite, keeping her mother's weaving steps on course. Where the hell was her father? Somehow this just never seemed to be his job.

Guiding her mother inside her suite, she flicked on the light. Her mother stared at her belligerently, hands on her hips. "All I wanted was to have some fun," she said, her speech slurred. "All I wanted was to be *happy* tonight, Angelina. But you won't even give me that."

A lump formed in her throat. "You're an alcoholic, Mother. You can't drink. *Ever.*"

"I am fine." Her mother put her arms out as she lost her balance and weaved to the side. "I would have been fine. I only had a couple of drinks."

A lie. Angie had heard so many of them, about the drinking, about the pills, about every secret her mother had wanted to hide—it had become her normal state of being.

Her mother headed toward the bar in the lounge. Threw open the door of the fridge. "There's nothing in there," Angie said quietly, stomach churning. "You need to go back for treatment, Mother. You know that."

Her mother swung around. Fear pierced her hazel eyes. "I told Abigail I won't go back there. *Ever. Never* again."

"You need help. Professional help."

"I won't go."

"Yes, you will." Rage vibrated through her. "You will not destroy all of us in your quest to annihilate yourself. Abigail needs a life. *I* need a life. You need help."

"You," her mother said, fixing her with a vicious look. *"You* who don't care. You who turned your back on me and walked away."

"Because I couldn't stand it anymore. Because you were taking me apart piece by piece, Mother."

Her mother's gaze darkened. She pressed her fingers to her mouth. "I don't feel well."

Angie moved fast, sliding an arm around her and helping her to the bathroom. When her mother had upended the contents of her stomach multiple times, Angie cleaned her up and put her to bed.

"I'm sorry." Her mother started to cry, her transformation from angry to sad happening with its usual rapid-fire swiftness. "I'm so sorry."

Heat burned the back of Angelina's eyes, the pieces of her heart she'd finally healed shattering all over again. "I know." She clasped her mother's hand in hers, hot tears escaping her stinging eyes and sliding down her face. "I am, too."

For everything. For all of it.

Turning off the light, she let herself out of the room. Tears blinding her vision, knees shaking, she slid down the other side of the door until she sat on the floor, hands pressed to her face.

She couldn't do this again.

CHAPTER FIVE

"ANGELINA?" LORENZO PULLED to a halt when he saw his wife sitting in the hallway, legs drawn up, head in her hands. Her quiet sobs tore loose a piece of his heart.

He squatted down beside her. "What's wrong?"

No response. He tipped her face up to his. "Angelina," he said more urgently, "what happened?"

Her beautiful blue eyes were red-stained, unfocused. Heart jamming in his throat, he cupped her jaw. "*Dio*, Angie. Talk to me. What's wrong?"

She shook her head as if to clear it. Lifted a hand to push her hair out of her face. "I—" Another tear streaked down her cheek.

He cursed. Slid his arms beneath her knees and back and scooped her off the floor. Carrying her down the hallway to their suite, he shouldered the door open and set her on the sofa in the sitting room. Her beautiful red dress was wet, stained with something. Champagne, he assumed, from the story he'd heard.

He sat down beside her. "What the hell happened out there?"

She frowned. Rubbed a palm over her brow. "I'm so sorry about Magdalena's dress. Did Abigail smooth it over?"

"Magdalena's dress will survive. What the hell happened with your mother, Angie?"

Her gaze slid away from his. "She had a bit too much to drink."

His brow rose. "She was drunk. *Blotto.* She could hardly stand up. I'd say it was more than a bit too much."

She bit her lip. "So she was drunk. It happens. I apologize for the scene she caused."

"I don't care about the scene." A flash of heat consumed him. "I just found my wife crumpled in a ball in the hallway crying her eyes out... *Dio mio*, Angelina, what is going on?"

Her chin dipped. "It's nothing. I'm just...emotional. It's been a tough night."

He pulled in a breath. Counted to five. "You can either tell me why you've been such a disaster tonight, what is going on with your family, or I will go outside and ask Abigail. In the spirit of making our relationship work, I'd prefer, however, if the truth came from *my wife.*"

She stared at him for a long time. He held her gaze, ready to follow through on his threat.

"My mother is a functioning alcoholic," she said finally. "She's been that way since I was fifteen. We've managed to keep it from being public knowledge, have taken her to rehab twice, each time thinking it would be the last. This recent dry spell lasted two years. She started to slide backward when the money troubles began."

A red tide swept through him. "You were carrying this around with you our entire marriage and you didn't tell me?"

"My mother swore us to secrecy. It was the only way she'd agree to go for treatment. It was decided it would remain locked within the walls of the Carmichael family vault. If we didn't speak of it, didn't acknowledge it, it ceased to exist."

He frowned. "Who *decided* this?"

"My father."

"I'm assuming your sister's husband doesn't know, then, either?"

A flush swept her cheeks.

"*Dannazione*, Angelina." His hands clenched into fists by his sides. "Why didn't you feel you could trust me with this?"

She waved a hand at him. "You have the perfect family, Lorenzo. I was worried you would look down on us. You have such a disdain for a lack of discipline."

Heat seared his skin. "I would have *helped* you, not looked down on you. That's what a husband and wife do for each other."

"And we had that aspect of our relationship perfected, didn't we?" Her eyes flashed. "I never felt good enough for you, Lorenzo. Appreciated by you. *Ever.* Not after those first few months when you started tuning me out. Treating me like an afterthought. At least when you wanted me, I felt I had some value. When you lost interest in even that, it *decimated* me. Why would I tell you about my mother? Air my family's dirty laundry? All that would have done was make you regret your decision to marry me even more."

"I did *not* regret my decision to marry you. *Ever.*" He stared at her, stunned. "Is that what you think?"

No response.

Confusion warred with fury, the red tide in him winning. "You are so off base, Angelina. *So* off base. I might have been distant, we agree that I was, but do you really think I would have thought any less of you because of this? That I wouldn't have supported you?"

Her mouth pursed. "I don't know."

His breath hissed from his lungs. His marriage was suddenly illuminated in a way it had never been before. What the cost of his emotional withdrawal had been on his wife. What he should have *seen*. He didn't like what he saw.

He took hold of her hand and pulled her to her feet. Turning her around, he reached for the zipper of her dress. She jerked away from him, eyes wide. "What are you doing?"

"Putting you to bed."

"I can't go to *bed*. The party's still going."

He moved his gaze over her face. "You're a mess. You can't go back down there. Things are winding down, anyway. I'll go finish up."

He turned her around and slid down the zipper. She pulled away, arms crossed over her chest. "I can do the rest."

He headed for the door. "Did Abby talk to Courtney Price?" she called after him. "She can't print this in her column tomorrow."

He turned around. "She pulled her aside. I saw them talking."

Her face relaxed. "Abby will fix it. She always does."

Abby will fix it. She always does. The words rang in his head as Lorenzo went back to the party. Is that what Angelina and her sister had spent the past decade doing? Fixing their mother's lapses before they made it to the tabloids? Preserving a family secret that was tearing his wife apart, a secret he hadn't known about because he'd been too caught up in himself, in his own stuff, to see the warning signals?

The tension that had always lain between his wife and her parents, the distance she'd put between herself and them this past couple of years, his wife's refusal to ever have more than one or two drinks no matter what was put in front of her—it all made sense now.

Anger at his own blindness fueling him, he found Alistair Carmichael and ensured he went and checked on his wife. What kind of a man was he to leave it to his daughters to pick up the pieces? To ignore what was clearly a cry for help from his wife?

Perhaps, he thought, the same kind of man *he* had been during his marriage. A man who had simply not been there.

Angie willed herself to sleep after Lorenzo left, curling up into a ball under the cool satin sheets and squeezing her eyes shut. But the scene with her mother kept replaying itself over and over again in her head.

You who don't care. You who turned your back and walked away.

A knot tied itself in her stomach. She *had* walked away. Because going through what had happened tonight again and again, never reaching that place inside of her mother that was in so much pain she couldn't heal, had taken a piece of her soul.

She burrowed into the pillow, an ache consuming her insides. Lorenzo's anger, his *fury*, twisted the knot tighter. Perhaps she should have told him. Perhaps she was as guilty of holding things inside as he was. Except it was difficult to communicate with a brick wall and that's what he'd been near the end.

She hugged the pillow tighter. Tried to force herself to sleep, because it hurt too much to be in the here and now. But she couldn't settle. She was still awake when Lorenzo came in just after one, stripped off his clothes, showered and came to bed.

He smelled so good, so achingly real and familiar, she had to fight the urge to beg him to hold her. Closing her eyes, she curled her fingers into the sheets. Lorenzo sighed, reached for her and turned her toward him. Feeling utterly exposed with her tearstained face and puffy eyes, she closed her eyes.

He ran a finger down her cheek, making her lashes flutter open. "Angie," he murmured, "*mia cara*. Things between us have to change. You have to learn to trust me. I have to get better at reading you…at knowing when you need me, because clearly I am terrible at that."

She searched the angular shadows of his face in the moonlight. "You're serious about this."

"You think I would have done what I've done if I wasn't? I want you back because you are meant to be with me, Angie, not because I have some cruel desire to make you suffer. I *married* you because you are beautiful and intelligent, because you were what *I* wanted in a wife, not simply because you were pregnant. Because for the first time since Lucia died, I felt alive. *You* made me feel alive."

Her heart stuttered in her chest. If she had sensed that this was the case, felt that intense connection that had bonded them together, he had never once verbalized it. When he had begun to shut her out, she'd convinced herself she'd imagined it, that she was delusional and hopelessly naive where he was concerned. But this, *this*, she didn't know how to process.

His fingers traced the edge of her jaw, commanding her attention. "If we had disagreements about how our relationship worked, it didn't mean I found you *lacking*— it meant we had issues to resolve. To say we didn't do a very good job of that is an understatement."

She bit her lip, the salt tang of blood filling her mouth. She'd been convinced he'd wanted her because she'd been a politically viable Carmichael, as a wife who could open doors for him in alternate social circles. For what he'd *thought* he'd been signing on for. If it really had been more than that, if he had wanted her for *her*, what did that mean?

Had she walked out on a marriage that had been reparable if she'd just stuck? It was an overwhelming, earth-shattering prospect to consider. She sucked in a deep breath and lifted her gaze to his. "Every time you withdrew I felt it as a rejection. It hurt, Lorenzo, badly."

"I know. I realize that now."

A long moment passed. His fingers slid to her cheek, thumb tracing over the tracks of her tears. The ache inside her grew until it was almost all-encompassing. The need for everything they'd had. Everything they'd never had. For this to be different this time as he was promising it would be. But she didn't know if she could trust him, wasn't sure she could go through another of his Jekyll-and-Hyde routines. Didn't know if she could trust her *own* instincts anymore.

Fear invaded her, coiled its way around her insides. She pushed a hand into the mattress to move before she did something she would regret. Something she wasn't ready for. Before she *did* beg him to hold her. Lorenzo hooked an arm around her waist and tucked her into the warmth of his body before she could, her back nestled against his chest. "Go to sleep," he murmured, brushing his lips over her shoulder in a fleeting caress. "Tomorrow we'll deal with what happens next."

Except she couldn't relax. Couldn't slow down her brain. Not with him so close, clad only in the sexy hipster briefs he'd added to his routine in deference to their *adjustment period*. Not when tomorrow would mean deciding what to do with her mother. Convincing her to go back to the treatment facility in California she swore she wouldn't return to.

Silent tears slid down her face. She reached up to brush them away, shocked there were any left. Lorenzo muttered an oath. *"Don't,"* he murmured, shifting so she lay back against the pillows. "We're going to solve this—I promise."

She should have protested when he set his mouth to

her jaw. As he kissed and licked away her tears, working his way up one cheek, then down the other. But the erotic, soul-searing comfort he offered eased the ache inside of her. Lit her up in a way only Lorenzo could.

A low sound escaped her throat. Her eyes locked with his in a hot, heated moment that held time suspended. Murmuring her name, he closed his mouth over hers, taking her lips in a slow, sweet kiss that drove everything from her head but him. How much she missed this. How much she missed everything about it.

He captured her jaw in his fingers, held her as he dipped deeper into her mouth, his tongue sliding against hers. The taste of him exploded through her, dark and dangerous as she tangled her legs with his, a tight fist of need forming in her stomach. She twisted closer, seeking, *needing* the oblivion he could give her because this, *this* had always been right.

She rocked against him. His obvious arousal, covered only by the thin cotton briefs, sank into her softness, the delicate material of her panties no obstacle. She gasped as he moved against her with possessive intent, the friction turning her insides molten.

"Lorenzo..."

He threaded a hand through her hair, held her still as he lifted his mouth from hers. "Angie," he murmured softly. "No."

No? Her eyes flew open.

"You will hate me tomorrow, *cara*. I guarantee it. You're emotional. I won't take advantage of that."

Her brain right-sided itself with a swiftness that made her dizzy. She pushed a hand against his chest, humiliation and confusion flaming through her. Lorenzo levered himself off of her. She scrambled to the other side of the bed, pressing her hands against her cheeks. "You started it."

"I wanted to comfort you," he said softly. "It got out of hand."

She turned her back on him and curled up in a ball.

"Angie." He laid a hand on her shoulder.

"Leave me alone." She took a deep breath as her fractured breathing slowed. She had no idea what she was doing. Thinking. Nothing made sense anymore. Everything she'd thought was true was now a massive gray area she had no idea what to do with.

Pain throbbed at the back of her eyes, her heart a rock in her throat. Lorenzo was just as much of an addiction for her as the alcohol her mother consumed. Just as dangerous. She would do well to remember that before she started making life-changing, potentially disastrous decisions to sleep with him again. Her husband was right in that.

She closed her eyes. This time sleep came swift and hard with the need to escape.

CHAPTER SIX

ANGIE WOKE THE next morning heavy-headed and bleary-eyed. Apprehensive about what lay ahead, confused about what had happened between her and Lorenzo last night, she dressed in jeans and a tunic, threw her hair into a ponytail and headed downstairs to the breakfast room, hoping it would be empty so she could spend a few minutes composing herself over coffee.

Her wish was not to be granted. Her husband sat by himself in the sun-filled room that overlooked the bay, the morning's newspapers spread out in front of him. He looked gorgeous in jeans and a navy T-shirt, his thick, dark hair still wet and slicked back from his shower. It was utterly disconcerting the way her heart quickened at the sight of him, as if it had a mind of its own.

He looked up, gaze sliding over her face. "You slept in. That's good. You needed it."

She took a seat beside him at the head of the table, even though her brain was screaming for distance. It would have looked churlish to do otherwise.

"Constanza made your favorite," he said, waving an elegant, long-fingered hand at the freshly baked banana bread on a plate. "And the coffee's hot."

"Thank you." She poured herself a cup of coffee. "Where are my parents?"

"Your father went for a run. Your mother's still in bed."

And would be for a while, she figured, taking a sip of

the hot, delicious coffee. His brow furrowed. "Your father, he is always this...*distant* when it comes to dealing with your mother?"

"Always. He thinks she is weak. That she should be able to conquer this addiction. When she slips it infuriates him."

"That's no way to get to the heart of the problem. Your mother needs support above all things."

She eyed him. "You were the king of distancing yourself when I displeased you."

"Yes," he agreed, dark gaze flickering. "And we've talked about how I'm going to work on that."

Right. And she was just supposed to take that at surface value? Forget the big stretches of complete alienation that had passed between them when he'd retreated into that utterly unknowable version of himself? How every time they'd made up in bed she'd thought it would be *better* just like she'd thought it would be better every time her mother promised to stop drinking, only to discover nothing had really changed.

She twisted her cup in its saucer. "It's always been that way in my family. We are the exact opposite of the Riccis—instead of expressing our emotions we bury them. Instead of talking about things we pretend they don't exist."

He frowned. "Ignoring an addiction, continuing to perpetuate an illusion that everything is fine when it isn't, is inherently damaging to all involved."

"I told you my family is dysfunctional."

The furrow in his brow deepened. "You said your mother started drinking when you were fifteen. What do you think precipitated it?"

She lifted a shoulder. "She always had the tendency to drink to cope with all the socializing. But I think it was my father's affairs that did it. Ask her to represent the family three or four times a week—fine. Ask her to do that when everyone is talking about who my father is screwing that week...to suffer that humiliation? It was too much."

"Why didn't she leave him?"

"She's a Carmichael. Image is everything. A Carmichael never concedes defeat. *Ever*. If we don't get her help, she will drink herself into the ground proving she can make this marriage work."

"That's nuts."

She arched a brow. "Didn't you say there's never been a Ricci divorce? It's what our families do."

He sat back in his chair, a contemplative look on his face. "That's why you don't like this world. Why you hate parties like the one we had last night. You hate what they represent."

"Yes."

"So you decided to leave me so you would never end up like your mother. You crave independence because you need to have an escape route in case our marriage falls apart like your parents' did."

Her mouth twisted. "That's far too simplistic an analysis."

"Perhaps, but I think your experiences drove your thinking with us. My withdrawal from you evoked shades of your father. Leaving you alone to cope while I went off to manage an empire. Except my vice wasn't other women, it was my work."

Her lashes lowered. "There may be some truth in that. But *saying* you're going to be more present and doing it are two different things."

"True," he conceded. "We can start with your mother, then."

"That's my issue to handle."

"No," he disagreed. "It's *our* issue. Like I said last night, we are going to handle this together. As a team. The way we should have the first time. You are not alone in this."

She shook her head. "It gets messy with my mother. It will be awkward for you."

"Exactly why I should be there." His jaw was a stubborn, unyielding line. "I saw you last night, Angie, crumpled on the floor. You were a wreck. This isn't going to be easy for you."

She pushed a hand through her hair. "You want to solve this like you want to solve everything, Lorenzo. Snap your fingers and *poof*, it's fixed. But it's far more complex than that."

"I know that. That's why the power of two will be better than one."

She exhaled a breath and stared out at the water, sparkling in the sun like the most electric of blue jewels. "We need to convince her to go back to the treatment facility in California. She's refusing to go."

"I may have an option. I called a friend of mine this morning. He had a brother in a facility in upstate New York that's supposed to be a leading edge program. If your mother was closer, perhaps it wouldn't be so difficult for her. You could visit her more often."

Her throat locked. The visits to see her mother in rehab had been the worst. Angry, bitter Della Carmichael had not gone easy despite recognizing the help she was getting. To put herself through even more of that with regular visits? The coward in her shrank from the idea, but she was starting to realize running from her problems hadn't gotten her anywhere—not with her mother and not with her marriage.

"We could go see it," her husband offered. "Then you can decide."

She eyed him. Her husband wanted to solve her problem because it was just one more obstacle between him and what he wanted—a wife able to devote her full attention to him. And yet, when he had comforted her last night she could have sworn he truly cared. That she meant something to him.

Perhaps she needed to exhibit a show of faith in them if this was going to work—a tiny, baby step forward, with her head firmly on her shoulders, of course. Last night had proven the need for that.

"All right," she said. "Let's go see it."

Angie and Lorenzo flew to upstate New York the next morning and met with the staff of the treatment center. Nestled in the foothills of the Adirondacks, the setting was lovely. By the time they'd finished touring the facility and meeting with the staff and doctors, Angie had an immediate comfort level with it.

They flew her mother up there to see it later in the week. If Della approved of the choice, the center could take her immediately. Surprisingly, her mother liked it. Angie's emotions were torn to shreds by the time her mother cycled through the anger and sadness that was her pattern before agreeing to stay. But, somehow, with Lorenzo at her side, it wasn't as much of a nightmare as she'd expected. Her husband was endlessly patient with her mother, commanding when he needed to be, caring when Della required a softer touch. Where had this man been, she wondered, during their marriage?

By the time they'd boarded the jet, headed for home, she felt numb.

"You okay?" Lorenzo looked at her from the seat beside her, his laptop conspicuously absent on the console.

She nodded. "I hate leaving her there. Please let this be the last time we have to do this."

He closed his fingers over hers. "Hopefully it is. If it's

not, we'll keep doing it until she's better. You're strong, Angie. You can do this."

She looked down at his hand curved around hers. Warm and protective, as he'd been all day. Her confusion heightened until it was that thick gray cloud, blanketing her brain. "Thank you," she murmured huskily, "for being there for me this week. I swore I'd never do this again because it hurts too much. But I'm learning running doesn't solve anything."

"No, it doesn't," he agreed, eyes darkening. "But sometimes we need to do things in our own time. Allow ourselves the space to heal."

Lucia. He was talking about Lucia again. A tight knot formed in her stomach. She couldn't ignore it any longer—this ghost that had always lain between them. She knew it was at the heart of figuring them out.

She pulled her hand out from under his. "What you said the night before the party—that you had worked through some things. Was one of them Lucia?"

A guarded expression moved across his face. "Yes. When I met you, I thought I had moved on, gotten through the worst of the grieving process. But after you left, I realized I hadn't left that process behind as fully as I'd imagined. That perhaps I had carried some of that baggage into our marriage—baggage which did make me emotionally unavailable at times."

She frowned. "You told me it was *my* issue with Lucia that was the problem."

His mouth twisted. "Because you made me furious. Pointing fingers at the ghost of Lucia was your favorite card to play when you were angry with me, *cara.*"

Her eyelids lowered. She couldn't deny that. She'd lashed out in whatever way she could to get a response out of him. Something, *anything* to show he'd cared. She'd known it was wrong to use Lucia as a weapon against him, but their fights hadn't exactly been rational ones.

"Tell me about her," she said quietly. "Tell me about what happened. I need to understand, Lorenzo. Maybe if I had, things would have been different."

He sat back. Rubbed a palm against his temple. "Where to start? Lucia and I were childhood sweethearts. We spent the summers together in Lake Como. Eventually our childhood crush developed into an adult romance. Our families were all for it, it seemed...*predestined*, in a way."

Her stomach clenched. She had felt that way about him when they'd met, their connection had been so strong, so immediate. But Lorenzo's heart had belonged to someone else.

"We didn't marry right away," he continued. "I needed to sow my wild oats. I wasn't sure I could marry the first girl I fell in love with. But after a few years, I knew it was her. We married when I was twenty-six. I was in New York by then, she joined me here." His dark lashes arced over his cheeks. "She was like a fish out of water, missing her family, missing Italy. I did the best I could to make her happy. She kept saying once she had a baby, once we started a family, everything would change. We were trying for that when she..."

Died. Her chest seized tight. She curled her fingers over his. "It's okay. You don't have to talk about it."

"No—you're right. You need to know what happened. It's...a part of me." He palmed his jaw, dragging his fingers over dark stubble. "The incident at the town house happened when I was in Shanghai on business. We had an excellent security system there. Impenetrable—like the one we have now. But the men who broke in were professionals—*violent* professionals. They knew how to talk their way into someone's home, knew the stories to tell. Lucia was so innocent—she never stood a chance."

Her stomach curled in on itself. "She let them in."

He nodded. "They put her in my den. Told her to stay there while they went and cleaned out the place. They left her alone for a few moments and she called for help on her cell. One of them came back, saw what she was doing and hit her with the blunt end of the gun." His fingers flexed on his thigh, his knuckles gleaming white. "The blow to the head caused a severe bleed on her brain. She never regained consciousness."

Angie pressed her fingers to her mouth in horror. "How do you know all of this?" she whispered.

"Surveillance video."

Her stomach dropped, a sick feeling twisting her gut. "Please tell me you didn't watch it."

"I had to. I had to know what happened."

The raspy note in his voice, the raw emotion in his dark eyes, tore a piece of her heart loose. What would it do to a person to go through that? To lose someone you love like that? It would change you forever.

"I'm sorry," she said quietly, a sinking feeling settling through her for all the wrongs they'd done each other. "For being so insensitive. I knew what happened to Lucia was horrible. I knew I should make allowances for it. But every time you retreated, every time you turned off, I hurt so badly, I just wanted you to hurt like I was hurting. It became instinctual, *reflexive*. But it didn't make it right."

He shook his head. "We were *both* experts at slinging arrows. It became easier than dealing with what was in front of us."

She caught her lip between her teeth. Stared out the window at a sea of blue, her ragged emotions begging her to stop. But to do that would stall them where they stood, suspended in a state of perpetual animation. It would not *fix* them.

"I know Lucia will always be in your heart," she said

quietly when she turned back to him. "I wouldn't expect any less. The issue between us was the emotional distance it caused, the emotional distance you put between us. I need to know you are over her, Lorenzo."

His cheeks hollowed. "I have let her go. I have moved on. That's what this is all about, Angelina—moving forward. I'm asking you to do that with me."

Her chest went tight. She knew they needed to let go of the past if they were going to make this work. But could she do it? Could she trust her instincts where Lorenzo was concerned? Could she trust that he had changed? Or was she setting herself up for an even greater fall than she'd taken the first time?

"Maybe what we need," he said quietly, a contemplative look on his face, "is a fresh start. A blank slate. No ghosts, no animosity, just us."

Her heart contracted on a low, painful pull. It was so tempting to believe they could recapture the good they'd had. That she could claim that piece of his heart she'd always craved. Because when it had been good between them, it had been good in a way nothing else could touch. And when it had been bad, he had eviscerated her.

Blood pumped through her veins, her breath caught in her throat. Suddenly her baby steps seemed like a heart-pumpingly, scary big leap.

"All of you," Lorenzo said evenly, eyes on hers. "That's what I'm asking for. A real shot at this. Can you give me that?"

She swallowed past a paper-dry throat. Took the leap. "I can try."

Lorenzo put his emotionally exhausted wife to bed after a light dinner, then headed to his study to work. The logistics with Angelina's mother had taken a big bite out of his week. He was behind and his inability to connect with

Marc Bavaro, who had disappeared on a multiweek trip to South America, meant the acquisition was still in limbo.

Resisting the temptation to drown his frustration in a potent shot of something strong because it would also dull his brain with hours of work ahead of him, he fixed himself a cappuccino in Constanza's steel marvel of a kitchen, returned to his study and picked up a report he had to review before his morning meeting, but the numbers blurred before his eyes.

His thoughts were consumed, instead, by his wife's haunted face as he'd put her to bed. With the fact that he had clearly never known her. Far from being the spoiled young woman he'd thought he'd married who was incapable of compromise, she was instead a vulnerable, emotional woman he'd never looked deep enough to see. A woman who had gone through hell under the purview of parents who had, in reality, been nothing of the sort.

That his wife had been strong enough at fifteen to police her mother at parties, to keep up a facade for as long as she and Abigail had, to take her mother to rehab not once but *twice*, by the time she was twenty, little more than a girl herself, boggled his mind. It was courage on a scale he couldn't imagine. Made him feel as if he'd just taken a hard shot to the solar plexus.

He sat back in his chair and closed his eyes, guilt twisting his insides. Twice now he'd failed to react when the most important women in his life had cried out for help. Failed to recognize what they'd been trying to tell him. *Failed to protect them.*

It shamed him on the most visceral of levels, raked across the dark presence that seemed to lurk just beneath the surface of his skin, searching for a way to the top.

Angie had always believed Lucia had his heart, that he wasn't over her and that was what had caused him to hold back with her. Instead the truth was something far worse. If he'd listened to Lucia, if he'd been *present* for her as Angelina liked to cite as his greatest fault, then she would still be alive.

Agitation drove him to his feet and to the window, where he stood looking out at a floodlit view of Central Park. The darkness pressed against his edges—relentless, *hungry*. He would never forgive himself for what had happened to Lucia because he didn't deserve it. But he could do things differently with Angelina this time.

He pressed a palm against his temple. If there was guilt for not being able to give his wife the love she so clearly craved, *deserved*, the love she'd never been shown, he would have to appease himself with the promise he would give her everything else. He would *be there* for her this time.

Because to allow his marriage to descend into the emotionally addictive union it had once been? To allow himself to feel the things for Angelina he once had? To experience more loss? Not happening.

Emotion had destroyed them the first time around, rationality and practicality would save them. That and the combustible chemistry he had slammed the breaks on in the Hamptons.

The lush, heady, spellbindingly feminine taste of his wife as she'd begged him to take her filled his head. He wanted to dull the edge, kill the need that drove him whenever he was within five feet of her. With a clean slate ahead of them, an agreement from Angelina to leave their ghosts behind them, he intended to accomplish that goal in short order.

He *would* have his delectable wife back in his bed, in every sense of the word. Would make this marriage into what it always should have been.

CHAPTER SEVEN

"Damn." Angie scooped the bracelet off the bedroom floor and attempted to refasten it around her wrist. She had been late coming home from the studio, where she'd been putting the final touches on Faggini's collection, which would debut at Fashion Week next week, not an ideal night to be running behind with Lorenzo's parents coming for dinner.

The clasp slipped from her fingers *again*. She grimaced. Was she that unnerved by the thought of a visit from Octavia the Great or did it have more to do with the fact she'd agreed to give her marriage a real shot? She suspected it was a combination of both.

"Need help?" Lorenzo emerged from the dressing area, rolling up the sleeves of the crisp white shirt he'd put on.

"Yes." She handed him the bracelet. "Please."

He slid it around her wrist, making quick work of the clasp. His gaze met hers. "Are you stressing about tonight? You have to stop doing that. Everyone wants us to work, including my parents."

"I'm not stressed, I'm late."

"You're not late. They're not even here yet."

He slid an arm around her waist and tugged her close. Smoking hot in dark pants and the white shirt, he made her heart thud in her chest. "I appreciate the fact that they are late, however," he drawled, "since I have not had time to greet you properly."

Her stomach clenched, heat radiating through her insides. He had a distinctly predatory look in his eyes tonight, one that suggested their adjustment period was officially over.

"Your parents will be arriving any minute,"

"Plenty of time." He slid his fingers into her hair, cupped her scalp and kissed her. A long, slow shimmer of a connection, it was leisurely and easy, a magic dancing in the air between them that stole her breath. Her palms settled on his chest, grabbed handfuls of shirt as her knees melted beneath her.

"Lorenzo," she murmured when they came up for air, "you are ruining my hair, not to mention my lipstick."

"Mmm." He slid his mouth across her jaw, down to the hollow of her throat. Pressed his lips to her pulse. It was racing like a jackhammer, revealing every bit of the tumult raging inside of her. He flicked his tongue across the frantic beat, his palms clamping on her hips to draw her closer.

He was all hard, solid muscle beneath her hands. The most exciting man on earth to her—always had been. She swayed closer, molding herself to his hard contours. He returned his attention to her mouth, each nip countered by a soothing lave of his tongue over tender flesh.

Drowning. She was drowning.

The doorbell rang. Jolted out of her pheromone-induced haze, Angie stiffened and dragged herself out of his arms. Lorenzo watched her with a satisfied look as he straightened his shirt. "Now you look like a proper wife."

She ignored him, walked to the mirror to straighten her hair and reapply her lipstick. It took several deep pulls of air to get her breath back. Her equilibrium.

Hand at her back, he guided her out to the foyer, where Constanza was greeting his parents. Lorenzo shook his father's hand, kissed his mother's cheeks, then drew Angie forward. She opted for the less threatening target first, Lorenzo's father, Salvatore.

Graying at the temples, shorter than his son by a couple of inches and stockier in middle age, Salvatore Ricci had always been much more approachable than his wife despite his fearsome business reputation.

"Buonasera, Angelina," he murmured, bending to brush a kiss against both of her cheeks. *"È bello rivederti."*

It's good to see you again. She forced a smile to her lips. *"Altrettanto."*

She turned to Lorenzo's mother, perfectly turned out as usual in an eggplant silk wrap dress that came to the knee and sleek Italian heels on her dainty feet. With her short, silver hair and her son's dark, dark eyes, she was still a stunningly beautiful woman. *"Buonasera, Octavia."*

"Buonasera." Octavia brushed a kiss to both her cheeks. "Thank you for having us."

"It's so lovely you are in town." Angie summoned the perfect manners she'd been taught since birth as she ushered Lorenzo's parents into the salon and offered them a drink. She had bemoaned all those social niceties as a teenager, finding them false and disingenuous, but right now, in this moment, she was exceedingly glad to have them to fall back upon.

It seemed everyone was on their best behavior as they enjoyed a cocktail before dinner. Lorenzo kept a palm to her back, a protective gesture Angie welcomed. Octavia didn't miss it, her shrewd dark eyes moving between the two of them every so often as if to assess what the real truth of them was.

Angie told herself she wasn't that twenty-two-year-old girl who'd been hopelessly intimidated by her mother-in-law. She was a successful business owner, every bit a match for Octavia Ricci. The thought settled her nerves as she sat beside Lorenzo at the table on the terrace Constanza had set with an elegant candelabra blazing in the final, hazy light of day. Lorenzo's parents sat opposite them, the humidity-free night a perfect choice for dinner outside.

The wine flowed freely, as did the conversation. By the time their salad plates were cleared, Angie had begun to relax, if not enjoy herself.

Octavia set her gaze on her daughter-in-law. "Lorenzo tells me you're partnering with Alexander Faggini on his show. That's impressive."

"Providing the jewelry," Angie amended carefully. "Alexander is the star. But yes, thank you, it's very exciting. Would you like to come?"

Octavia frowned. "We have dinner plans." She turned to her husband. "We could move them, couldn't we?"

"I'm sure that won't be a problem. It would be fun for you."

"Bene." Octavia flashed one of her queen-like smiles. "I would love to, then. Is your mother coming?"

Her heart skipped a beat. "I'm afraid not. She's out of town."

"Oh, that's too bad." Her mother-in-law looked anything but sad. "Where is she?"

"The south of France with family." She gave the cover she and Abigail had agreed on.

Octavia wrinkled her nose. "Isn't it *hot* there this time of year? I can't wait to escape the heat in the summer."

"We have a house there. She loves the flowers in the summer."

"I see."

"You must come with Lorenzo the next time he's in Italy," Salvatore inserted. "It would be nice for you to reconnect with the family."

"That would be lovely." She had no intention, however, of putting herself in the midst of Lorenzo's big, gregarious family until she and her husband had proven they could make this work. "It may be next year, I'm afraid. As soon as Fashion Week is over I'll be ramping up for the Christmas season. Things will be crazy right through January."

"I expect," Octavia interjected smoothly, "you will have to scale back once you and Lorenzo are expecting. My son tells me the pace you've been working at. That can't be good for a pregnancy."

Angie stiffened. Shot a sideways look at her husband. "Lorenzo and I are taking our time with that. But I see no reason not to keep working. I think it's healthier for a woman to stick to her usual lifestyle."

"Yes," said Octavia, "but it's common knowledge women who work too much have more difficulty conceiving. They are more stressed and the process doesn't happen so easily."

The *process* hadn't even happened between her and Lorenzo yet... How dare Octavia interfere like this? Lips pursed, she picked up her wine and took a sip. Lorenzo set a palm on her thigh.

"Give us time, Mamma. Angie and I have just reconciled. There will be plenty of opportunities to make babies."

"Angie is approaching twenty-six," Octavia countered. "You may need time."

Blood rushed to her cheeks. They were discussing her like she was a broodmare. Completely disregarding the fact that she wasn't *ready* to get pregnant, as her career was at a critical juncture. Or that she had miscarried the last time she had carried Lorenzo's baby, a soul-clawing experience she never wanted to repeat again. Not to mention the fact that her husband had shut down emotionally afterward, the impetus to the end of their marriage.

Lorenzo set a hard stare on his mother. "We had no problems conceiving before. We're not in any rush."

His mother lifted an elegant shoulder. "Angie was

young then—at the prime of her fertility. I'm simply giving you my advice. Women think they can wait forever these days and it just doesn't happen that way."

Angie drew in a breath. Lorenzo's fingers tightened around her thigh. He gave his mother a look that said that was enough and changed the subject.

She tried to shake it off as the meal wore on, but couldn't. Of all the things she and Lorenzo were battling through right now, a baby was not a priority.

Unable to do justice to the delicious chicken dish Constanza had cooked because her stomach had coiled up into a tight little ball, she set down her fork. By the time the elder Riccis got up to make their departure just after ten, she was fuming. She managed a few more minutes of civility, discussing the current theater runs with Octavia while Salvatore pulled his son aside in the study.

"*Maledizione*, Lorenzo, who the hell leaked this deal?"

Lorenzo leaned against his desk and crossed his arms over his chest. He'd been hoping to avoid this discussion, had almost managed it, until his father had pulled him aside.

"I have no idea," he said flatly. "There's only been high-level people involved. But you know what it's like—when there's a juicy story waiting in the wings, someone is always willing to spill."

"And if we don't close it?" his father countered. "This is Ricci's reputation you are gambling with. It's one thing to pursue a company that wants to dance, another thing entirely to drag it kicking and screaming onto the floor."

"I will close it," Lorenzo growled. "We will dance the final waltz, Papà. But I am not a magician. I cannot summon Mark Bavaro back from South America with a snap of my fingers. You need to give me time."

"I have given you time. A year this has been dragging

on, *figliolo*. This needs to be done before the next board meeting. Before they start wondering if we know what we're doing in the corner office or not."

Lorenzo scowled. "They are a bunch of overreactors with too much time on their hands."

"Who can make our lives hell if they choose to." His father crossed his arms over his chest, mirroring his pose. "I am beginning to think your ambition has got the best of you on this one."

His back stiffened. Bavaro's disappearance was raising his blood pressure. He didn't need the added pressure of his father trying to control everything around him even though he was no longer in charge of Ricci. But going head-to-head with Salvatore, he reminded himself, was like two stags locked in a fight to the finish. It never ended well.

"I am CEO of this company," he said, eyeing his father. "I will get the deal done. Back off and let me do my job."

His father gave a haughty tilt of his head. "October, Lorenzo. This needs to be signed and sealed."

Too riled up to sleep, Angie put on a swimsuit and headed for the hot tub on the terrace while her husband returned a phone call. Maybe it would unwind the Octavia-induced knots in her shoulders.

Built into the deck, with a sensational view of the Manhattan skyline, it was her favorite way to relax after a long day. She dropped her towel on the deck, set her half-finished glass of wine beside the tub and stepped into the hot, bubbling water, immersing herself up to her shoulders.

A sigh left her. Closing her eyes, she let the jets unwind the knots, ease the band of tension encircling her skull.

"In a better mood?"

Her eyes fluttered open. Her husband stood on the deck in navy trunks, a perfect male specimen in the prime of his life. Her heart rate skyrocketed as he tossed a towel over the railing. He was leaner than he'd been before, muscle and sinew arranged in a spectacular grid pattern across his pecs and abdomen. The perfect symmetry of it made her stomach curl.

She swallowed past a suddenly dry mouth. "I thought you had to make a call."

"It was a quick one." He lowered himself into the water, taking the seat opposite her. Her heartbeat calmed. His slow inventory of her, however, sent it ratcheting back up again. The bikini she had on, a halter top and briefs, wasn't overly revealing by any means, but her husband's thorough perusal made her feel as if there wasn't enough material to it. Not nearly enough.

"What happened with your father?" she blurted out, needing to distract herself from that…*heat*.

His dark gaze slid up to hers. "He is anxious about the Belmont deal. He is used to swallowing up tiny fish to build his empire. He doesn't have the patience to stalk a bigger prey, one that might not be quite so willing."

"You still haven't been able to tie down Marc Bavaro?"

"No." He exhaled a long breath and laid his head back against the tub. "He is MIA."

She studied the intensity that came off him like smoke. "What?" he asked, brow raised.

"I'm just wondering where this all-consuming drive comes from? This never-ending need for more."

He lifted a shoulder. "I was born with it. It's in my blood. Franco's, too."

"Franco has a sense of balance. A safety valve. You don't."

His gaze narrowed. "I am not my brother."

"No," she agreed. "But you weren't always like this. Franco told me that before Lucia you knew your limits. You knew how to live."

The glint in his eyes took on a dangerous edge. "My brother likes to play amateur psychologist. My ambition is strictly my own sin, *cara*, recognized and owned."

"It's not a badge of honor," she countered. "You push yourself to unsustainable levels, Lorenzo. You are going to drive yourself into the ground someday if you don't watch it. Maybe you should take a page out of your brother's book and allow yourself to be human once in a while."

"And maybe you should tell me what happened tonight." He raised a brow. "You knew my mother was going to bring up babies. It was a foregone conclusion. Why the overreaction?"

Heat seared her belly, her concern for him dissipating on a wave of antagonism. "It was not a foregone conclusion your mother would hammer me to the wall about a subject you know I am sensitive about. Knowing that, *you* should have diverted her. *We* haven't even discussed it yet."

He inclined his head. "Perhaps I should have. But you know you and I having a baby is a reality with Franco unable to conceive."

She lifted her chin. "It's not going to happen if you keep putting this pressure on me. We've promised to try this again, Lorenzo, and I will put my heart and soul in it, as you are asking. But I need time to adjust to *us* before we think about a baby. Not to mention the fact that I need to take advantage of the career opportunities in front of me. *Now* is not a good time for a baby. You said so yourself, we have time."

"We do," he agreed. "I'm not sure I'd say we have *lots* of it because my mother is right, it could take us time to conceive. Also—" He stopped in midsentence, a wary look in his eyes.

Her stomach bottomed out. "Also *what*?"

"We miscarried last time. It could happen again. Which is why we need to give ourselves *time*."

Fear and anger balled up inside of her. "I am not ready to have this discussion."

"Because you're scared?" he countered softly. "I understand if you are, Angie. I am, too. But we have to talk about it. We can't push it away as if it doesn't exist."

She pinned her gaze on his. "I'm *saying I'm not ready.* That we need to work on *us* before we start talking babies."

"Bene." His eyes glittered in the moonlight. "I am in full agreement on that point. So why don't you come over here? You're much too far away."

Her heart slammed against her ribs. "I don't think so."

"Oh, I think so," he murmured. "The only question is if you are coming over here or I'm coming over there. You make the choice."

Her blood pulsed through her veins in a restless purr. That kiss earlier, his hands on her all evening, had stirred her senses. But she was angry, too—furious about that baby conversation and being treated like a...*vessel* for the Ricci family.

"Time's up." He pushed away from the side of the tub, snared an arm around her waist and pulled her onto his lap, wrapping her legs around his hips.

Her breath caught in her throat, heart slamming against her ribs. "What are you doing?"

"Getting to know each other again. Just like you suggested..." He shot her a look filled with sensual heat, his throaty tone arcing straight between her thighs. "Relax, *mia cara.* I intend only to kiss you. *A lot.*" He lifted a brow. "What do you Americans call it? *Making out? Necking?"*

"Lorenzo," she said faintly, overwhelmed by all that heat and muscle singeing her skin, "stop playing with me."

"I don't think so," he murmured, laughter dancing in his eyes. "Isn't kissing the universal language? Maybe it will work for us, too."

She opened her mouth to tell him she was still angry with him. He lowered his head and caught her lips with his before she could get the words out. She set her palms on his shoulders to reject him, to tell him *absolutely not*. But his soft, seductive kisses seduced, persuaded. He nipped her bottom lip, sucking gently on her top one, sliding under her defenses like warm, sweet honey.

Melting from the inside out, she dug her nails into his muscular, sinewy shoulders. *Hard.*

"What?"

"I'm still mad at you. *You* can't avoid the baby issue by kissing me. I need time, Lorenzo. You have to give me that."

"Okay." He brushed his thumb over the pulse pounding at the base of her neck. "I'll give you time."

She blinked. "You will?"

"Sì."

Not expecting such an easy capitulation, she was momentarily silenced. He tucked a wisp of her hair behind her ear, dark eyes on hers. "What else is going on in that beautiful head of yours? It's like smoke coming out of your ears."

She shook her head.

"Angelina." His low, sensual tone promised retribution if she didn't spill.

"I'm scared," she said finally. "Terrified."

"Of what?"

Of letting herself want him again, *need* him again. Of letting herself feel the things she hadn't let herself feel since she'd left him because she could get hurt, because he would *see* beneath her skin as he always had. Of letting him make her whole again, then shatter her apart, because this time she wasn't sure she'd be able to pick up the pieces.

She closed her eyes. Pulled in a breath. "We were so good together. Then it all fell apart. I'm afraid of letting myself go there again only to have you shut down."

He shook his head. "I am not perfect. I have my moods, you know that. But I promise you it will not be the same. We will talk through our stumbles, work through them together. This is not about what *was*, Angelina, it is about what we are *building* together."

She swallowed past the fear bubbling up inside of her. The trust they'd built over these last emotional weeks together made her think they might be able to do it.

He tilted her chin up with his fingers. "*We* decide where this goes. But you have to commit. You have to trust. You have to believe we can do this."

"I do," she said quietly. "But we need to take it slow."

That wicked gleam in his eyes reappeared. "What do you think I'm doing?"

She didn't protest when he slid his palm to the nape of her neck and brought her back to him, his beautiful mouth claiming hers. Delivered on the leisurely, sensual make-out session he'd promised until her toes curled with pleasure. Full of heat and oh, so much promise, sweetness and play devolved into a deeper, fiery need.

She opened to his demand, his tongue stroking and licking while his hands kept her in place for his delectation. She curled her fingers in his hair, sighed his name and pulled him closer still. It had been too long, far too long since he'd touched her like this. It was like returning to heaven—a most dangerous paradise, she knew, but she couldn't deny she wanted it…wanted to revel in it.

Her husband shifted beneath her, his highly aroused body brushing against her thighs. Shock waves coursed through her nerve endings, lighting her on fire.

He lifted his mouth from hers, a wry smile curving his mouth. "This would be where the make-out session ends and something else entirely begins. Unless," he drawled, "you've changed your mind?"

Heat claimed her cheeks. All it would take was one more kiss, one sign from her she was ready and she could have him. But unleashing that kind of intimacy with her husband would bring all her walls tumbling down—it always had. And she wasn't ready for that. Not yet.

"I can wait," he murmured, tracing a knuckle down her cheek. "But be prepared, Angelina. When this does happen, one tame roll in that bed in there will not be enough."

CHAPTER EIGHT

ANGIE SPENT THE following week immersed in a flurry of activity leading up to Alexander's show. Likely a good thing given the confusing mixture of anticipation and apprehension engulfing her at the evolution of her and Lorenzo's relationship.

Their sizzling encounter in the hot tub had proven she was still as susceptible as ever to his expertly executed seductions, but had done nothing to illustrate they could make their marriage work. *That* they were going to have to prove in the days ahead.

Her husband, true to his word, was giving her the time she'd asked for. Not that he hadn't kept up a slow and steady campaign to put his hands on her whenever he could find an excuse to do so. She'd been so distracted at yesterday's rehearsal thinking about it, Alexander had had to ask her a question three times.

Determined to keep her focus, she'd buried herself in a couple of last-minute fixes to tailor her pieces for a model being substituted into the original lineup, keeping her mind firmly off her husband. Before she knew it, it was 7:00 p.m. on the night of the show, the lights had dimmed in the high-ceilinged Skylight Modern space, one of the premium, architecturally perfect Fashion Week venues, and Alexander's first model had begun her walk down the spotlit runway.

Anticipation built as one model after the next, with

a few supermodels thrown in for good measure, strutted their stuff, showcasing the collection the critics said would catapult Alexander to the top of the design world this season. The buzz and applause was electric as her friend's brilliance shone, his pieces the perfect backdrop for her jewelry.

It seemed like only a few minutes had passed instead of an hour before the show was drawing to an end.

Her blood fizzled in her veins as Astrid Johansson, the world's current *it* girl, stood spotlighted at the end of the runway to wrap the show, Angie's ruby necklace glittering against her alabaster skin. A shiver chased up her spine. It was perfect, a marriage made in heaven the way the necklace framed the square neckline of the sleek, avant-garde dress.

Lorenzo leaned down from his position beside her in the front row, bringing his mouth to her ear. "The highest paid model in the world wearing your jewelry. How does it feel?"

"Amazing." And her husband looked equally stunning in a charcoal-gray Faggini suit, his swarthy coloring set off perfectly by the light blue shirt he wore beneath it. She'd seen more than one of the models eye him as they'd walked by, eating him up with their confident gazes.

Astrid made her final pass down the runway, returning hand in hand with Alexander as the music died away and the lights came up, her fellow models falling into place behind them. Cheers and applause greeted the designer, who took it all in with a big smile on his expressive face.

She was shocked when he beckoned to her, motioning for her to join him. Oh, no, she couldn't.

Lorenzo gave her a gentle shove. "*Go.* Have your moment."

She found herself moving forward on legs that felt like jelly. Taking Alexander's hand, she followed him into the spotlight. The designer turned to her, gave a little bow and clapped his hands. Her chest swelled with happiness, a hot warmth stinging the backs of her eyes as the audience applauded. Her jewelry had been her light in the darkness when everything else had been falling apart. She would never be able to express what it meant to her. She only knew in that moment, it felt as if a piece of her was sliding into place.

She gave Alexander a kiss on the cheek, stood back and returned the applause. The lights went down. Alexander pulled her backstage for interviews with the media while Lorenzo and his mother went to enjoy a cocktail. She had expected only a smattering of media would be interested in speaking to her in the shadow of Alexander's presence. She was shocked when a handful of them chose to interview her, too.

She did a couple of broadcast interviews for television, then something with a leading newspaper's style section. Surprisingly, the media's focus remained mostly on her jewelry rather than on her lineage, the critics giving her collection an enthusiastic thumbs-up.

She was pretty much floating on air by the time Alexander hooked an arm through hers, propelled her into the crowd at the after-party and introduced her to the designers, fashion editors, models and actors starring in his next spring ad campaign, forging so many valuable connections it made her head spin.

An impenetrable glow filled her. Her career was skyrocketing, her marriage on the mend. It felt as if anything was possible.

Lorenzo watched his wife shine, her bubbly, animated demeanor taking him back to that night in Nassau when she'd transfixed him like the brightest star in the sky. The haunting, mysterious Northern Lights had had nothing on his wife that night as she'd flashed those baby blues at him, silky long lashes brushing her cheeks in a coquettish look she hadn't quite mastered, and asked him if he was going to brood all night or dance with her instead.

But even then, he realized, underneath all that sultry confidence and gutsy bravado, there had been a vulnerability to the woman in his arms, a sadness he hadn't quite been able to put a finger on—a knowledge beyond her years.

He had connected to that, even if he hadn't known it at the time. They had both been looking to escape their pain that night, he from his memories, Angelina from the inexplicably complex relationships that had formed her world. What they had found had been so powerful that for a while they had.

She caught him staring. Smiled. It was a blindingly bright smile that did something crazy to his heart. He had denied her this, the chance to be this shining light. To prove she was more than the sum of her parts. It was a mistake he refused to let haunt him.

He saw her say something to Alexander, nod at the woman they were speaking to and slip away, her long strides eating up the distance between them.

"Did your mother leave?"

"Yes." He swiped two glasses of champagne off a tray and handed her one. "She said to say thank you. To tell you your collection was impressive. And, yes," he added, a wry smile twisting his mouth, "she meant it."

Angie blinked. "Well, that's...*nice*. Did she have a good time?"

"She was in her element. Who knows," he murmured, lifting a brow, "there might be hope for the two of you yet."

"Don't get too hopeful."

He brushed a thumb across the delicate line of her jaw. "Positivity, *cara*. That's what we need here."

Her lashes lowered. "We should circulate if you don't mind."

He nodded. Kept a possessive hand at the small of her back as they made a couple of passes of the room. By the time the lights came down and the apparently wildly popular band Lorenzo had never heard of took the stage, he could feel his wife's energy level fading, her reservoir of small talk emptied out.

Tugging her into one of the intimate lounge areas, he plucked the wineglass out of her hand and pulled her onto his lap.

"Lorenzo," she murmured, "we are in public."

"At a party in full gear where no one is paying any attention to us." Setting a palm on her thigh, he pulled her closer, absorbing the tantalizing feel of her lush curves plastered against him. She looked insanely beautiful in Alexander's black dress with no back to it. Had turned every male head in the room. The need to have his hands on her was like a fire in his blood.

Bending his head, he traced the shell of her ear with his lips in a feather-light caress. His wife shivered. He moved lower, capturing her lobe between his teeth, scoring it lightly. "You are lit up tonight, *mia cara*. This is the woman I *appreciate*. The woman I was looking for."

She pulled back, eyes on his. "I needed this. For you to understand how important my work is to me."

"I do now." His voice was sandpaper-rough. "I am listening now, Angelina. Better late than never."

Needing to protect, to possess her in a way he couldn't even begin to articulate, he cupped the back of her head and kissed her. Passionate, infinite, it was a connection between them on an entirely different level than before, as if they were finally beginning to understand each other.

She slid her palm to his nape and kissed him back, the kiss turning hot and fiery. *Needy.* He moved his hand higher on her thigh, fingers tightening around the sleek, satiny skin he discovered. A primal heat consumed him, his body pulsing to life beneath her bottom. She shifted against him, a low moan leaving her throat.

"I want inside you," he whispered. "Inside this sweet, hot body of yours. Until you feel nothing but me, *cara*."

Blood roared in Angie's head. Light exploded in her eyes. She blinked against the sudden onslaught. It took her several seconds to realize it was a photographer's flash.

Lorenzo brushed a knuckle against her cheek, a wry twist to his mouth. "That must be our cue to leave."

Her legs felt like spaghetti as he set her on her feet. He kept a firm hand on her waist as he guided her through the thick crowd, stopping to say good-night to Alexander before they exited into the cool night air.

Wrapped in a sensual haze, she curled her arms around herself as Lorenzo retrieved the car. The sports car was deposited purring at the sidewalk moments later. Lorenzo tucked her into the passenger seat, then took the wheel to drive them home.

Her pulse hummed, her blood fizzled amidst the cacophony of sirens and honking horns that was New York, all of it blanking in her head as her senses focused on the man beside her. His quiet intensity as he controlled the powerful car and the hand he kept on her bare thigh were all she could register.

When this does happen, one tame roll in that bed will not be enough.

Her pulse jolted faster, her cheeks heated with anticipation. Her head might be wary about them, but her body was not. It wanted to experience the hunger he had promised. To feel alive again in the way only Lorenzo could make her feel.

Finally they were home. Parking the car in the garage,

he helped her out, ushered her into the lift that arrived in a whir of expensive machinery. Up they went to the penthouse, where she threw her purse on a chair, legs shaking. Walking to the bank of windows that looked out on the roughly drawn skyline of Manhattan, she took a deep breath, attempted to center herself.

The soft thud of her husband's jacket hitting the chair reverberated through the room. The tread of his footsteps across the hardwood floor sent a quiver up her spine.

"You are so damn beautiful," he murmured, setting his hands on her hips. "You make my heart stop in my chest."

Her breath caught in her lungs. Frozen, paralyzed, she couldn't move, her fears, her anticipation, blanketing her in a cloud of emotion. But this wasn't about the past, she reminded herself, it was about the future. And right now, it felt like they had one. A bright, shining light she was terrified to touch.

She did it anyway. Twisting around in his arms, she took in the dark, sometimes brooding man who'd stolen her heart once and threatened to do it again. His eyes tracked her, hot and focused. Her stomach contracted. Lifting her hand, she traced the sexy stubble shadowing his jaw. It was too tempting not to touch. She pressed a kiss to the abrasive canvas, sliding over the hard line of his jaw, *knowing* him again.

He let her play, drink her fill. Then impatience won out as he slid his fingers into her hair, tilted her head back and closed his mouth over hers. Greedy, laced with sensual purpose, his carnal kiss telegraphed his intent to know all of *her* tonight. To erase the pain.

She curled her fingers into the thick muscles of his shoulders, opened to his stark demand. The slow, erotic strokes of his tongue against hers coiled the muscles in her abdomen tight, his dark, sensual taste filling her senses, seducing her with its rich male flavor.

Fingers digging into his shoulders, she hung on tight. Lorenzo slipped a hand lower to her bottom, shaping her against him. The hard thrust of his desire, a thick, pulsing heat beneath his trousers, pulled a low sound from the back of her throat. She pressed closer, drunk on the feel of him. He rocked against her, slid his steely heat against her most sensitive flesh, scoring her through the thin material of her dress. "Feel how much I want you," he murmured against her mouth. "You make me crazy, Angelina."

A shudder went through her, her knees nearly buckling beneath her. He backed her up against the windowsill, kneed her legs apart so he could stand between them. Supported by the wall, she welcomed the hot press of his flesh. Allowed him to tease her, play with her until she thought she might go up in flames.

Her hands moved to his belt, greedy, desperate for him. Yanking the leather free of the buckle, she undid it, unbuttoned his trousers and slid down the zipper. Pushing her hands inside his pants, she cupped the thick length of him in her palms.

Lorenzo cursed low and hard. Removed her hands from him. "*Mi bellissima.* You need warming up or I will hurt you."

"No," she said, trying to free her hands. "I need you inside me."

"*Sì.*" Hard, uncompromising. He captured her hands, placed them palms-down on the sill. "Keep them there."

Eyes on hers, he sank his fingers into the knot of his tie, pulled it loose and stripped it off. Tossing it on the floor, he reached for the top buttons of his shirt and pulled them free. Her heart thrummed the frantic beat of a bird trapped in a cage as he dropped to his knees in front of her.

Reaching for her foot, he worked the delicate clasp of her shoe open, slid her foot out and tossed the stiletto aside. He did the same with the other. Setting his hands on her ankles, he trailed them up her calves to her knees. Pushed them apart with a deliberate, firm motion that had her sucking in a breath. "Lorenzo," she breathed, feeling far too exposed.

He looked up at her, an implacable expression in his dark eyes. "Stay still."

Oh, dear Lord. A shudder went through her. He pressed a kiss to the inside of both her knees, worked his way up the sensitive flesh of her inner thighs, caressing her with his mouth, the scrape of his teeth. She bit her lip, willing him on.

She was aching, pulsing for him by the time he got to where she wanted him. Ready to beg. Mouth dry, she watched as he pushed up her dress and tucked it beneath her hip, baring her lacy, black panties. A wisp of nothing— meant to seduce.

Hand on her thigh, he considered her. *Bold. Focused.* "You wore these for me?"

"Yes."

A smile tugged at his mouth. "I thought you said you weren't going to wear lingerie for me."

"I said I wouldn't greet you at the door wearing it."

A play of laughter in those dark eyes. "Appreciate the distinction."

Shifting his attention back to the job at hand, he lowered his head and caressed her through the silk with one long stroke of his tongue. Her knees buckled. Sinking back on her palms, she braced herself against the wood. Closed her eyes as he stroked her again and again, desensitizing her, she knew, for the pleasure he would give her.

When she stopped bucking under his tongue, he pressed a kiss to her trembling abdomen, slid his fingers under the edges of the silk and stripped the panties from her. Moving back between her thighs, he spread her wide.

Ran his thumb through her cleft. Blood surged from her fingertips to her toes as he examined her flesh.

"Already wet for me, *cara*." He looked up, eyes blazing. "Maybe I should stop."

She reached for him. Received a reproachful look as he put her palms back on the wood. "Move them again and I will."

She closed her eyes. Felt the heat of his breath before his tongue found the hard nub at the center of her, nudging it with sensual precision. Back and forth, up and down. When her legs started to shake, her voice a low plea, he licked her slowly, deliberately, talking to her as he did it, telling her the taste of her made him hard. Hot.

Insane for him, at the very edge, she curled her fingers into the wood. He circled her with his finger. Delved inside of her. Her muscles clenched around him, drawing him in. Slowly, relentlessly, he moved his finger in and out of her, another kind of pleasure stirring to life that was deeper. More intense.

"Look at me." His husky command brought her eyes fluttering open. Seeing him between her spread legs, pleasuring her, sent her right to the edge. "You want it like this? Or with me inside your beautiful body?"

She swallowed past the need constricting her throat, the raging hunger he inspired in her. "With you," she rasped, keeping her hands on the wood. "I want it to be with you."

Lorenzo removed his hands from his wife, swung her up in his arms and carried her into the bedroom, working to blank his mind from the emotion pouring through it. But his wife had always cast a spell over him and tonight was no exception, despite his attempts to tell himself going there was unwise.

He set her down near the bed and moved behind her to lower the zipper of her dress. Pushing it off her shoulders, Alexander's creation hit the wood floor in a swish of feather-light material.

Hands on her shoulders, he turned her around. Drank in his wife's mouthwatering curves. Lushly feminine in all the right places, her breasts were more than a handful, perfectly shaped and high, her delectable hips flaring above long, fantastic legs he wanted wrapped around him so badly, it was all he could do to keep this the leisurely seduction he'd planned.

Stripping off his shirt and pants, his gaze never left her. Kicking his clothes aside, he snaked an arm around her waist, pulled her to him and plastered her curves against the length of his body. Fingers curving around her jaw, he dropped a lingering kiss on her mouth. Shared with her the essence of their mutual passion until the raw, unvarnished truth of their connection swelled him so hard he thought he might break in two.

This time when she reached for him, her touch like silk around his throbbing length, he arched into it, desperate for more.

"That's it." His breath was hot against her ear. "I've missed your hands on me, *mia cara*. I *crave* them."

His skin began to burn, *tremble*, her exploration of his body firing his blood. He closed his eyes, primal sounds leaving the back of his throat as she stroked him to the edge.

When he could take it no longer, he pushed her hands away, sank his palms into her hips and lifted her onto the bed. The moonlight spilling in the French doors edged across her face, illuminating the beautiful vulnerability he was starting to believe was the truth of her.

He slid his hands around her back, released the catch of her bra and threw it to the floor. Her full, swollen breasts were a temptation he couldn't resist. A shudder raked through her as he swept his thumbs across the tips.

"Like ripe, delectable fruit," he murmured, lowering his head to her. He took a nipple in his mouth and sucked hard. She gasped, threw back her head and pushed her flesh farther into his mouth. He devoured her, satisfied his hunger. Played her other nipple between his thumb and forefinger while he brought the hard bud to a swollen erectness with his lips and teeth.

She moaned as he lavished the same attention on her other breast, digging her fingers in his hair. *"Please."*

Her broken plea contracted his insides. He joined her on the bed, shackled his fingers around her ankles and bent them back so she was open to him. Moving between her thighs, he palmed his length, brought himself to her slick entrance and rocked against her so just the tip pushed inside.

"You want me, *cara*?"

She nodded, her big blue eyes glued to his.

"Tell me how much."

"All of you," she gasped. "I want all of you."

Bracing a palm on the bed, he tipped his hips forward and filled her with another inch. "Lorenzo," she breathed, arching up to meet him, "I need you."

A primal satisfaction claimed him. All of those nights since she'd left when no one else would do, when her memory had made a mockery of his libido, were vindicated as she lay begging beneath him, beautiful and oh, so vulnerable. Exactly as he'd wanted her. And yet, as he rocked forward again, her body clenching around him like a hot, silken glove, he would have been delusional to deny he was as affected as she was.

He leaned forward, slicking his tongue across her bottom lip in an erotic caress that made her clench tighter around him. "There is no going back," he rasped, "only forward. Tell me you understand that."

"Yes." She arched her hips, eyes glazed. *"More."*

He buried himself inside her with a smooth, powerful stroke. Her gaze met his in an electric, soul-destroying connection. "You feel like heaven, *cara*. Perfection."

Her slick, aroused body absorbed him, stretched to accommodate his length and girth. He gritted his teeth, forced himself to hang on. Fine tremors snaked through her body, her inner muscles rippling around him. He moved inside her then with hard, powerful drives designed to drive her to orgasm. He lacked his usual finesse, but was beyond caring. Her fingers clutched his hips as his big body rode hers, claimed her, found that spot deep inside her that made her moan with pleasure.

She arched into it, wanting everything he had to give. He braced himself on one arm, slipped the other hand between her legs and found the bundle of nerves at her center. "I can feel you clenching around me," he murmured, stroking his thumb teasingly over her clitoris. "Like that," he whispered when she jerked beneath his touch. "And that," he said as another shiver raked through her. "Come for me, *cara*."

His next firm caress set her off. Her husky groan, the way she gloved him in a tight squeeze, pushed him into a violent, body-shaking release. Relinquishing control, he tightened his fingers around her hips, drove into her and made her come apart a second time.

Lorenzo was awake long after his wife fell asleep in his arms. Soft and warm, her body curved against his, their fit together was so perfect it was as if she'd been made to fill in his missing spaces. To complete the parts of him that had been empty so long he'd had no idea they still existed.

A knot fisting his stomach, he disentangled himself from his wife and lay staring at the sky through the window overhead. He'd crossed a line tonight—allowing this thing between him and Angelina to become emotional when he'd promised himself he wouldn't. It had been that kind of a night, to be sure, but he knew if he wasn't careful, he'd start walking down a path he could never go and it would be Angelina who got hurt, not him.

He'd been falling in love with his wife when she'd left, his instincts warning him if he let himself, he would have fallen harder for Angelina than he had ever fallen for Lucia. His love for Lucia had been a pure, untainted first love that lacked the passion and emotion he and Angelina had shared. The depth of his feelings for Angelina, the betrayal those feelings had seemed to Lucia, the youth and unhappiness Angelina had displayed that had made her an unsure bet, had made him cauterize his feelings, refuse to acknowledge them.

And his instincts had been dead-on, he thought, staring up at the cloudy night sky. Angelina had walked out as soon as the going had gotten tough, had made a mockery of the vows they'd made. And that was why certain lines could never be crossed.

If he was smart, he would follow his original plan. Burn out the attraction between him and his wife until it no longer held any power over him.

Now that he had her back in his bed, he intended to do exactly that.

CHAPTER NINE

"HOW ABOUT YOU come to Mallorca in a couple of weeks? I have to be at our flagship property for a few days. You can meet with the management team and we can go through the last few points face-to-face."

Lorenzo blew out a breath. He'd spent two weeks anticipating Marc Bavaro's return from South America and now he wanted him to gallivant off to *Spain*, Belmont's global headquarters, to make this deal happen? He ran a global corporation, for God's sake, three times the size of Bavaro's. How the hell did he have time for that?

"As much as I'd love to," he said in an even tone, "my schedule is insane. We can't do it before then?"

"I'm headed to London as we speak. I'm not back to New York until mid-October."

Too late, with the board meeting looming. "I'll see what I can do," Lorenzo conceded. "How long are you thinking?"

"Come for a couple of days. We can have dinner with my brother, Diego, the night you arrive, then we'll do the management meeting the next morning. Oh—" the CEO's voice dropped to an intimate purr "—and bring your beautiful wife...she can keep Penny company."

He wasn't sure Bavaro lusting after Angelina was going to go over so well in his current mood. "Angie is in her busy period. I'll have to check her schedule."

"Let me know." The roar of a jet engine fired in the background. "I should go."

He cut off the call. Turned the air blue. Gillian popped her head in his office and asked if he needed help. He told her to clear his schedule for the time in Mallorca, then turned his thoughts to his wife. How to get her to agree to go to Spain was the challenge. She was so busy with commissions after Faggini's show she'd even hired a couple of part-time designers to help with the rush. She would balk at a trip, no doubt about it.

He sat back in his chair and contemplated a solution. Things had been better than good between them. They were learning to compromise, to manage their expectations of each other. They were communicating both in bed and out of it. His marriage was *working*. The last thing he needed was to rock the boat.

But this, he thought, tapping his fingers on the desk, was necessary.

A plan came to him. It was a good one. Satisfied, he picked up the phone.

"I have a proposal for you."

Angelina cradled her mobile against her ear as she put down her pliers, the intimate, seductive edge to her husband's voice unleashing a wave of heat beneath her skin. The huskiness, she knew, came from the inhuman working hours he was keeping.

"If it involves sleep for you, I'm all for it," she said lightly. "What time were you up this morning?"

"Five. And, yes, it involves sleep for both of us," he replied in a throaty tone that sent goose bumps to her heated skin. "Well," he amended, "it involves a bed and *us*. Sleep not so much."

Her heart beat a jagged rhythm. They hadn't been able to get enough of each other since Alexander's party, thus contributing to *her* sleeping deficit. Not that she was complaining. She was so happy she was afraid to blink, because history had taught her something *would* implode in her face if she did.

But she wasn't *thinking* that way, she reminded herself. "What are you proposing?"

"The only way I can pin Marc Bavaro down is to hook up with him at his property in Mallorca in a couple of weeks' time. Penny's going. He wants you to come, too."

She pressed a palm to her temple. "Lorenzo... I have so much work to do before Christmas."

"That's part of my proposal. You come with me to Spain and I will absolve you of any social obligations until the hotel opening in October."

"What are you going to do? Go to them alone?"

"Sì."

She didn't like the idea of her gorgeous husband attending all those events alone the way women fell all over him. Leaving the country for a week was also an unwise idea given the work in front of her.

But how could she say no after everything Lorenzo had done for her? He had been her rock as she'd navigated her emotional visits with her mother, pushed her to hire a couple of assistants to keep her sanity with all the work pouring in. And when she was exhausted from managing them, he deposited her bodily into bed when she no longer recognized her limits. She wasn't sure what she would have done without him.

"I will take you to Portofino for a couple of days afterward." Her husband's voice lowered to a sexy rasp. "We can do walks through the village. I'll take you to that seafood restaurant you love..."

Her heart turned over. By far her most magical memories with Lorenzo were from that heavenly week they'd spent together in the tiny fishing village on the Italian Riviera on their honeymoon, the view from the Riccis' villa perched in the hills spectacularly romantic. It had been impossibly perfect with their strolls through the cobble-stone streets, leisurely, seaside dinners and long, uninhibited nights of lovemaking in which her husband had taught her wicked things, *delicious* things her innocent mind could only have dreamed of.

Going back would be like walking into a piece of the past she wasn't sure she was ready for, but perhaps that was exactly what she needed to do.

"Well?" her husband prompted. "Say yes. It will be good for us, *cara*."

She blew out a breath. "Okay. But I can't be gone longer than a week. And I'm holding you to your promise."

"Bene." Satisfaction laced his tone. "I'll get Gillian to work with you on the details. *Grazie mille, bella.* I should go."

She hung up. Stared at all the pieces on her desk that needed to be finished. Thought of the massive influx of orders to be filled. She was a tiny operation—she wasn't built for this.

Panic clawed at her insides. She couldn't afford to mess up this chance she'd been given. The interest in her work following Alexander's show was a once-in-a-lifetime opportunity to make her name. But neither was she prepared to mess up her marriage.

She could do this. She just needed to lean on the designers she'd hired and make a plan.

Angie worked like a demon over the next two weeks, making a good dent in the list of commissions. Reserving the trickier pieces for when she got back, she handed the rest of the work over to her assistants and stepped on the jet for the trip to Mallorca with Lorenzo.

Shocked at how exhausted she was, she put the reclining seat back as soon as dinner had been served and slept while her machine of a husband worked.

When she woke, it was to the darkest of ebony eyes and a very seductive kiss from her husband. "Wake up, sleeping beauty. We're about to land."

She blinked. "We *aren't*."

"We are. A half hour tops. Go freshen up so you can have some breakfast before we land."

She slid out of her seat and headed for the bedroom, where she changed her top, so she wouldn't look so wrinkled when they met the driver, and freshened her hair and makeup. Breakfast, however, wasn't to be. Her stomach still felt like it was 2:00 a.m. Coffee and orange juice would have to suffice.

The driver took them up into the lush green mountains of Mallorca's peaceful northwest coast to the Belmont Mallorca, considered to be one of the world's finest hotels. Nestled into a valley surrounded by soaring peaks, its two stone manor houses offered a spectacular view of a medieval village.

Still inordinately tired, she took a nap in the afternoon in their beautiful airy suite to arm her for a late dinner while Lorenzo spent the afternoon with Marc. But even after she woke and pulled herself out of the white-silk-draped canopy bed and showered, her limbs still felt as if they were weighted with lead.

She hadn't felt this inexplicably tired since the first trimester of her pregnancy, she mused as she stood at the wardrobe selecting a dress to wear for dinner. Ice slid through her veins… *No. There was no way.* She couldn't be. She was on the pill. She had been so careful.

Rationality, however, did not stop her from flying into the bedroom to find her purse, where she retrieved her birth control pills and found they were all accounted for. Slackening with relief, she saw the antibiotics she'd been taking following a dental procedure. Remembering she hadn't taken one today, she popped one into her mouth, swallowed it with a gulp of water, then padded back to the wardrobe to choose her dress.

A cream-colored jersey sheath called to her. She pulled it off the hanger, then froze, her stomach bottoming out. *Antibiotics and birth control pills...* Hadn't she heard somewhere...

Lorenzo watched Angelina in the mirror as he did up his shirt. Stunning in a knee-length ivory dress with a floral scarf draped around her neck, she was amazing to look at as always, but it was the preoccupied air about her that held his attention. He hadn't seen it in weeks.

"You okay?"

She nodded. "Just tired. Sorry, I'm quiet I know."

He did up the last button of his shirt and tucked it into his pants. "You don't ever have to be sorry about being quiet. I just want to make sure you're okay."

"I'm fine." She turned back to the mirror and spritzed some perfume behind her ears.

"Is it work?"

She shook her head. "It's fine. I'll catch up when I get back."

"Then what is it?"

She spun around, a frown creasing her brow. "You don't have to treat me with kid gloves, Lorenzo. I'm *fine*."

He lifted a brow. She expelled a breath. "I am a little stressed about work. And the time change kills me."

He crossed over to her. "Try and put it out of your head and enjoy the week," he murmured, tracing a thumb over her cheek. "It's only a few days. You deserve a break."

She nodded.

"There is no goal tonight, *amore mio*. Unless you count paying attention to me," he added huskily, thumb sweeping over the lush fullness of her lips. "That is most definitely on the agenda."

Color stained her cheeks. He lowered his head and pressed his lips to her temple, breathing in the sexy, Oriental fragrance of her, her perfume the perfect match for his strong, sensual wife. They were intoxicating, both the scent and her.

For a moment, he just held her, drank her in. Knew, in that moment, he felt more for her than he would ever admit. More than he should.

Her head dropped against his chest. "We should go," she said quietly, but she didn't move.

His mouth curved. Sliding his fingers through hers, he moved his lips to her ear. "Hold that thought."

Dinner with the Bavaro brothers took place in the Belmont's famed terrace restaurant, with its spectacular view of the mountains, the live piano music lending a distinctly sophisticated atmosphere to the setting. Marc's brother, Diego, the Belmont's other controlling shareholder, joined them for dinner along with his wife, Ariana. With Penny to round out the table of six, it was an entertaining and lively dinner.

Diego, who had been a bit of a dark horse during the negotiations, content to let Marc take the lead, could have been a double for his brother with his swarthy, dark Mediterranean looks and lean build. But that was where the similarities ended. Whereas Marc was cagey, careful in what he revealed, Diego was an extrovert who liked to hear the sound of his own voice.

If Lorenzo got the younger Bavaro brother talking, he might make some progress. He waited until the fine Spanish wine had had a chance to mellow all of them, and an amiable, content atmosphere settled over the table. Sitting back in his chair, wineglass balanced on his thigh, he eyed Diego.

"I'm sensing some hesitation on your part. If the regulatory issues aren't going to be a problem in most jurisdictions, perhaps you can tell me where the pause is coming from?"

Diego took a sip of his wine and set down the glass. "My father is concerned the Belmont legacy will cease to exist with the sale. That you will absorb what you desire of our marquee locations to fill the empty dots on the map, then dispose of the rest."

A warning pulse rocketed through him. That was exactly what he intended to do—certainly the Bavaros had been smart enough to figure that out?

"We'll have to see what our assessment says," he said coolly. "But since I am offering to pay you a fortune for this chain, more than half again what it's worth, I would think it would keep you from lying awake at night worrying about it."

"It's not always about money," Diego responded. "It's about family pride. National pride. Spaniards look up to Belmont as a symbol of international success. It is bad enough to have it eaten up by a foreign entity, but to have its name extinguished along with it? It negates a hundred-year-old legend."

"It's always about the money," Lorenzo rejected. "Nothing lasts forever. You wait a few more years and you'll get half what I'm offering."

"Perhaps." Diego lifted a shoulder. "You want to make my father happy? Put a clause in the deal that you will keep the name."

Heat surged through him. He kept the fury off his face. *Just.* "What sense would that make?" he countered. "This deal will make Ricci the number one luxury hotel chain in the world. To split the brands would be counterproductive."

Silence fell over the table. Lorenzo eyed the younger

Bavaro brother. "May I ask why this is coming up at the eleventh hour?"

"My father's feelings have grown stronger on the issue." Diego pursed his lips. "I'm not saying it's a deal breaker. I'm saying it's a major twist in the road."

Lorenzo's brain buzzed. His own father would do the same, he knew—would refuse to see his legacy destroyed. He couldn't necessarily blame the Bavaros. What infuriated him was that this hadn't come up earlier. It changed the entire landscape of the deal.

"This acquisition needs to happen," Lorenzo said evenly. "If this is the issue, you need to get your father onside. There will be no postsale conditions attached to it. It is what it is."

Diego's eyes flashed. "It was never our intention to sell, as you know."

That was when Lorenzo knew he had a big, big problem on his hands.

Angie paced the suite while she waited for her husband, who was having an after-dinner cognac with the Bavaro brothers. After the tension-filled end to the meal, she was glad to have escaped, but now she had a much bigger issue on her hands than her combustible spouse.

Penny had driven her to the local pharmacy on the pretext of finding some allergy pills. She'd shoved two pregnancy tests on the counter instead, two *positive* pregnancy tests that now lay in the bathroom garbage can, irrefutable evidence that fate had once again taken a hold of her life in the most indelible way.

How could this possibly have happened? What were the odds? What was she going to do?

Unable to breathe, she crossed to the windows and stood looking out at the dark mass of the mountains. She knew this baby was a gift. Even as sure as she'd been at twenty-two she hadn't been ready to have a child, as terrified as she'd been she wouldn't be a good mother given her own history, she'd developed a bond with her unborn child, a wonder at the life she and Lorenzo had created together.

She felt the same way now. But she was also scared. *Terrified.* The timing was all wrong. There was no way she could run her business, be a mother and juggle her and Lorenzo's busy social schedule all at the same time. And then there was the thought of losing another baby that sent panic skittering through her bones.

It was too soon. *Too much.*

Anxiety clawed at her throat, wanting, needing to escape. The click of the suite door brought her spinning around. The look on her husband's face kept all the anxiety buried inside.

"What happened?"

He walked to the bar, threw ice in a glass and poured himself a drink. "Preserving the Belmont name is going to be an issue."

"You don't think they'll give on it?"

He took a long gulp of the Scotch. Leaned back against the bar. "I don't know."

"Maybe you need to talk to the father? He seems to be the roadblock."

"I'd have to go over Marc and Diego's heads. It would be a last resort."

She frowned. "They didn't mention *any* of this before? Surely they knew it might be an issue?"

"I'm fairly sure I would remember if they had."

The biting sarcasm in his voice straightened her spine. She absorbed the incendiary glow in his eyes, the flammable edge to him she remembered so well from the past. *This* was the old Lorenzo—the one who could transform into a remote stranger in the blink of an eye, focused only on the end goal and to hell with anyone in his path.

Tension knotted her insides, the need to know this wasn't devolving into the old them burning a hole in her insides. Not now, not with the news she was holding inside.

She wrapped her arms around herself, fingernails digging into the soft flesh of her upper arms. "It was a rhetorical question," she said quietly. "I know this deal is important to you, Lorenzo, but it either works or it doesn't. You need to be able to find a way to walk away from these things and not let them get to you like this. *Consume* you."

He gave her a scathing look. "It's a fifteen-billion-dollar deal, Angelina. Ricci's reputation rides on it."

"And yours," she said quietly. "Isn't that the real issue here? You losing face? You becoming anything less than the unbeatable Lorenzo Ricci, king of the blockbuster deal?"

"This is not about me," he growled, voice sharp as a blade. "It's about my family's reputation. Rumors about the deal are running rampant…investors are getting antsy. It is my responsibility to close this acquisition."

"And if you don't?" She shook her head. "One of these days you *will* lose. You are only human. Then what? Would it be the end of the world? You have fifty of these deals you *have* landed, Lorenzo. Isn't that enough to command the confidence of your investors?"

His jaw turned to stone. "You have no idea what you're talking about."

"Maybe not," she agreed. "But I do know how I feel. You like this—I've seen it before. *This* always marks the beginning of one of your binges—it scares me where it will end."

"I'm good," he said harshly. "*We* are good. Stop trying to make problems where there aren't any."

Was she? The jet lag was killing her, her head too achy and full, her emotions all over the place. But now was not the time to tell Lorenzo about their baby. To make him understand why getting this right was so important to her.

"You wanted us to be an open book," she said, lifting her gaze to his. "Here I am, telling you how I feel."

He prowled over to her and pressed a hard kiss to her lips. "And I'm telling you, you don't need to worry. We are fine. I just need a few minutes to take the edge off."

She sank her teeth into her lower lip. Nodded. He ran a finger down her cheek, his eyes softening. "You're exhausted. You need rest. Go to bed. I'll join you in a few minutes."

"You should come, too. You didn't sleep at all last night."

He nodded, but it was an absentminded nod that told her he wouldn't be coming for a while. She went to bed, but it was hard to sleep, empty in the beautiful bed without him, the intimacy that had wrapped itself around them the past few weeks missing, leaving her chilled and scared to the bone about what lay ahead.

Lorenzo went to bed at two. Extinguishing the lights, he slid into bed with his sleeping wife, no closer to a solution to his problem than he had been two hours before. The urge to wake his wife, to bury his agitation in her beautiful, irresistible body, was a powerful force. But she was so peaceful, so deeply asleep, he couldn't do it.

He thought about how quiet she'd been earlier, his instincts telling him something was still off. He was so scared of missing something again, of not *seeing* what he should see.

Inhaling her scent, he slipped an arm around her waist and pulled her against him, her back nestled to his chest. She murmured something in her sleep and cuddled closer.

A smile on his lips, he pressed his mouth to the sweet curve of her neck. To the silky soft skin of her cheek. The salt that flavored his lips caught him off guard. Levering himself up on his elbow, he studied her beautiful face in the moonlight. She had been crying.

His fingers curled, the urge to shake her awake and make her tell him what was wrong a furious current that sizzled his blood. They had promised to be open books with each other and still she was keeping things from him.

He forced himself to resist waking her, drawing her back against his side. Tomorrow in Portofino would be soon enough to discover what was eating his wife.

CHAPTER TEN

PORTOFINO WAS AS lovely and picturesque as Angie remembered, with its narrow, cobblestone streets, pastel-hued houses dotting the Italian Riviera and bustling shops, restaurants and luxury hotels lining its half-moon-shaped harbor.

Lorenzo had taken her to their favorite seaside restaurant following his meetings in Mallorca and their short plane ride over from Spain. He had come down from his volatile mood of the night before, his attention focused solely on her. Too much so, she thought nervously, fidgeting with her water glass as he slid her another of those long looks he'd been giving her. The secret she carried was burning a hole inside of her.

She had been waiting for the right time to tell him her news, but it just hadn't seemed to come. Lorenzo had been working the entire plane ride and something about "Could you pass me the tartar sauce, and, oh, by the way, I'm pregnant" wasn't working for her.

Her stomach did a slow curl. So here she was, making every attempt to look like she was enjoying herself and hoping her husband bought the performance.

Lorenzo snapped the spirit menu closed and handed it to the hovering waiter. "I think we'll take the check," he said in Italian.

Angie's heart skipped a beat. "I thought you said you wanted a brandy."

"I'll make an espresso at home."

The deliberate look on his face made her heart beat faster. She had the feeling he hadn't bought her act for a minute. Blood throbbed at her temples as he settled the bill, wrapped his fingers firmly around hers and they walked up the hill toward the villa.

Embraced by fuchsia-and-coral-colored bougainvillea that climbed its whitewashed walls, Octavia's retreat from her busy city life was paradise personified. Although, Angelina allowed, as Lorenzo slid the key in the door and ushered her in, her mother-in-law's description of it as her "simple abode" hardly seemed apt. The dark-wood, sleek little villa with its cheery, colorful accents that matched its vibrant surroundings, was hardly *simple*.

She walked out onto the terrace while her husband made an espresso. Hands resting on the railing, she drank in the spectacular view as a breeze lifted her hair in a gentle caress. *Paradise.* If only she could just get the damn words out.

Lorenzo returned, settled himself into one of the comfortable chairs arranged for an optimum view of the sea and deposited the coffee cup in his hand on the table. Her heart lurched in her chest at the stare he leveled at her. "You going to tell me what's wrong?"

His neutral tone did nothing to lessen the intensity of his expression. Heat stained her cheeks.

"Lorenzo—"

"*Dannazione*, Angelina." His fury broke through his icy control. "How many times do we have to have this discussion? I can't help you, *we* can't do this, unless you talk to me. I have spent the entire dinner waiting for you to tell me whatever it is that's eating you. Do you think I can't read you well enough to know that something is?"

Her tongue cleaved to the roof of her mouth. "You

weren't in the right state of mind last night and it wasn't a discussion for a restaurant."

"How about before dinner in the very *private* suite at the Belmont?" Fire flared in his eyes. "I asked you if something was wrong. You said no. Then I come to bed only to discover you've been crying."

She blinked. "How do you know?"

"I checked on you when I came to bed. You had tearstains on your face."

Oh. She wrapped her arms around herself. Took a deep breath. "I couldn't understand why I was so tired yesterday. Jet lag always gets me, yes, but I hadn't felt like that since my pregnancy. I went to check I'd taken my pills after my nap and found the antibiotics I've been on in my purse. It made me put two and two together."

His face went utterly still. "To equal what?"

"Antibiotics can interfere with birth control," she said quietly. "I'm pregnant, Lorenzo."

A behavioral psychologist could have scoured his face and found nothing it was so blank. It was in his eyes that she saw his reaction—deep, dark, raw emotion that made the knots inside her tie themselves tighter.

"How do you know?"

"Penny drove me to the pharmacy."

He was silent for so long she couldn't stand it. "What are you thinking?"

"I'm trying to absorb it," he said huskily. "In my mind, we were waiting."

Not so much.

"You're scared?"

She nodded. Her chin wobbled, the emotion welling up inside of her threatening to bubble over. "I know I should recognize this as a wonderful thing and I do, but all I can feel is the fear right now. I *hate* that I feel that way, but I do."

His gaze softened. "Come here."

She moved to him on unsteady legs. He pulled her onto his lap, wrapping his arms around her. "You're allowed to be scared," he murmured against her hair. "We lost our baby. It was scary, it was unexpected. It wasn't supposed to happen."

She closed her eyes and burrowed into his warmth. Waking up to those severe abdominal cramps, the spotting, *knowing* something was wrong had been so scary. The loss of something so special like losing a piece of herself. But it was the fear she had somehow precipitated it that haunted her the most. Her mixed emotions, her worry she wasn't ready to be a mother, that she wouldn't be a *good* mother. It was a fear she'd never shared with Lorenzo because she had been too ashamed to even think it, let alone *admit* it to him.

She curled her fingers around a handful of his T-shirt, tugged at the soft material. "I worry about what this is going to do to *us*. We're in a good place right now. What's going to happen when the stress of this kicks in?"

"We're going to manage it," he said quietly. "Just like we've managed everything else. Life isn't going to stop throwing curveballs at us, Angelina. That's the way it works."

"I know." She bit her lip. "But what about my career? I have worked so hard for what I've achieved. I can barely keep up with the demand as it is. How am I going to handle it with a child?"

"Keep your assistants on a full-time basis. Do what you need to do. We're lucky money is no object for us."

"And if I want to get a nanny?"

His face stilled. "We can talk about it."

She read his reluctant expression. "You want me home raising our child just like your mother was."

"I know I need to make concessions," he conceded

stiffly. "I'm just not sure I want a nanny bringing up our child." He lifted his hand in a typically Italian gesture. "A child needs its mother. You, of all people, should know that."

She wasn't sure what sparked the violent reaction that rose up inside of her—fire licking her spine, heat flaming her cheeks. Whether it was because this was Lorenzo and his perfect family he was using as a benchmark, or whether he saw her as a deficient product of her mother's lack of maternal ability and wanted to make sure his child had better.

She pushed a hand against his chest, rolled to her feet in a jerky movement and stood facing him, hands planted on her hips.

"Angelina—"

"No, you're right." Fury crackled beneath every syllable. "I do know what it's like. I also know what it's like to feel as if my life is utterly out of control—to navigate those curveballs you talked about on a daily basis, to not know what's going to blow up in my face next. I am an *expert* at navigating the perils of childhood, Lorenzo. So trust me when I say, I will never neglect our child."

His jaw hardened. "I didn't say that."

"Yes, you did." She lifted her chin. "A part-time nanny would not be detrimental to our child's development."

"You didn't say part-time, you said 'a nanny.'"

"Well, I'm saying it now. I *will* be in control of this, too, Lorenzo. You will not decide how this works and negate all my decisions or I will take the Ricci heir and walk so fast you won't know what hit you."

His gaze narrowed, an icy black flame burning to life. "You need to settle down and not say things you'll regret, *cara*. You are overreacting."

"Overreacting? You are the one who *blackmailed* me back into this marriage."

"Sì." A flash of white teeth in his arrogant face. "A marriage you promised to make work. And just to point out—*you* have sprung this on me just this minute. *I* have not had the time to process the fact that I am going to be a father. You might give me some time to do that."

Guilt lanced through her. She thought she *might* be overreacting as she stood there, chest heaving with God knew what emotions, but it was all just too…*much*.

Lorenzo snagged an arm around her waist and pulled her back down on his lap.

"We," he said, visibly pulling himself back under control, "are going to figure this out. *You* are not going to create one of your dramas to throw us off track. There will be no decrees from me, Angelina, but we *will* talk this out in whatever way we need to to reach common ground."

She stared at him for a long moment. Took a deep breath and nodded.

"That said," he continued, "what was it about what I just said that set you off?"

She was silent for a moment. "Part of it is Octavia. How you build her up to be this mythical creature who can do no wrong—the earth mother who created the perfect family. The other part of it is about me, I think. I worry about being a good mother. I worry I don't have the skills to do it—that it isn't in my DNA."

His gaze softened. "You have a deep, loving relationship with your sister. You have mothered your own mother since you were fifteen. How is that not a sign you will be a caring mother?"

The adrenaline surging through her veins eased, her breath escaping in a slow exhale. She'd never thought of it that way. She'd thought she'd had no choice but to take care of her mother because that's what family did. But in reality, she could have done the opposite as James had—

as her father had—and pretended the problem didn't exist, that the disease ravaging her mother wasn't tearing her apart. But *that* hadn't been in her DNA.

Her tendency to sabotage the good before it disappeared was suddenly cast in a bright, blinking light. "I'm sorry," she said quietly. "It's my instinct to reach for anger, to lash out when I don't know how I feel…when my emotions confuse me."

"I know you now." His stare was level, unwavering. "I'm not going to let you drive wedges between us because of your fears. This baby is our second chance to do this right, Angelina. But you have to fight for us like I'm fighting for us. Fight for what we are building here."

She nodded. Rested her forehead against his. "I know. I'm sorry. Old habits die hard."

He lifted a hand to cup her jaw. Brought his mouth to hers. She met his kiss hungrily, wanting, *needing* him to wipe away her fears. Because she knew in her heart they could do this—that what they were building was more powerful, more *real* than what they'd been before. She just needed to get past the fear.

He slid a hand into her hair, held her more securely while he consumed her, *feasted* on her. She kissed him back, giving of herself without reservation. Hotter, brighter, the flame between them burned until it was an all-consuming force that engulfed them both.

Undoing the buttons that ran up the front of her dress, he exposed her body to his gaze. She shivered as he took the weight of her in his palms and teased her nipples into hard, aching points with his tongue, his teeth, nipping then laving her with soothing caresses. Moaned when he drew her deeper into the heat of his mouth, his hot, urgent caress turning her core liquid.

His eyes were hungry when he broke the contact, devouring her face with an intensity she felt to her toes. "My child will suckle at your breast," he rasped. "Do you know what that does to me? How much that makes me want you? How can this not be right, Angelina?"

Her heart slammed hard against her breastbone, stealing her breath. Her gaze locked with his for a long, suspended moment before he lowered his head and covered her mouth with his. Sliding his hand up the inside of her thigh, he found the strip of silk that covered her most intimate flesh.

She spread her thighs wider, giving him better access. Sweeping aside the silk, he dipped inside her heat, stroking her with a touch that made her arch her back, mewl a low sound of pleasure at the back of her throat.

Nothing, no feeling on this earth compared to being in Lorenzo's arms. He had become her addiction again as surely as she'd known he would. And yet it was more, so much more this time.

He sank two fingers inside of her. She gasped, her body absorbing the intrusion. He worked them in and out, his urgent, insistent rhythm sweeping her along with it until she was clenching around him. Begging him to let her come.

He pressed a kiss to her temple. "We should go inside."

"Here," she insisted, desperate to have him.

She slid off him, moved her hands under her dress and shimmied her lacy underwear off. Straddling him, she left enough room between them to find the button of his trousers and release it. He gritted his teeth as she slid the zipper past his throbbing flesh, closed her hands around him.

"Angie," he groaned, eyes blazing. "The neighbors could see us."

She ignored him, stroking her hands over him, luxuriating in the velvet-over-steel texture of him. He was made to give pleasure to a woman and she wanted him to lose control as surely as she did each and every time he drove her to it.

Her husband closed his eyes. Let go. Told her how much he loved it, how good it felt, how much it turned him on to have her hands on him. Her blood burned hotter, so hot she thought she might incinerate.

He let her have her fill, then he took control, snagging an arm around her waist and pulling her forward. Lifting her with one hand anchored around her hips, he palmed himself, brought his flesh to her center and dipped into her slick, wet heat.

His penetration was controlled and so slow it almost killed her. She shuddered, clenching her fingers around his nape. The look of pleasure written across his beautiful face, the naked play of emotion he couldn't hide were all she needed to fall tumbling into him. And this time she did it with all of her.

She caught his mouth with hers. "More."

He gripped her hips tighter and impaled her in one impatient movement that made her gasp. Clutching his shoulders, she absorbed the power of him. How he filled her in ways she'd never been filled before. How what they were becoming accessed even deeper pieces of her than she'd even knew existed.

She knew in that moment she'd never stopped loving him. Wondered how she ever could have denied it. The admission sent a frisson of wild, unadulterated fear up her spine.

Eyes on his, she rode it out, anchored herself to him with the contact, trusted him with all of her. Circling her hips, she took him deep. He was hard as a rock and thick enough to stretch her muscles to the very edge of her pleasure. She sucked in a breath as the power of him caressed her with every hard stroke, pushing her toward a release she knew would be intense and earth-shattering.

The glazed look in his eyes told her he was just as far gone as she was. Banding his arm tighter around her hips, he drove deeper, harder.

"*Lorenzo*—" His name was a sharp cry on her lips.

He shifted his hand to the small of her back, urging her to lean forward, to grind against him, to take her pleasure. She moaned low in her throat as his body set her on fire. He drove up into her shaking body until he hit that place that gave her the sweetest pleasure. Nudged it again and again until she splintered apart in a white-hot burst of sensation that knocked her senseless.

Her husband joined her on a low, husky groan, his big body shaking with the force of his release. It was erotic and soul-searing in a way that sucked the breath from her lungs.

She wasn't sure how long they stayed like that, joined with each other, before Lorenzo picked her up and carried her to bed. The dusky shadows of the room enveloped her as sleep carried her off to unconsciousness, her limbs entangled with his.

He had to move faster.

Lorenzo pressed his finger against the biometric scanner, heart pounding in his chest. The lights of the sports car, still running in the street, illuminated the number 29 on the red door.

The system flashed green. Jamming his hand on the handle, he swung open the door and strode inside, scanning the dimly lit main floor. Nothing.

Lucia had called from his study.

Running for the stairs, he climbed to the second level. Deep voices echoed above. The intruders were still there...

Back against the wall, he scaled the length of the narrow hallway until he reached the pool of light sprawl-

ing from his study. Silence, black silence, pumped ice through his veins.

He pushed the half-ajar door open. Levering himself away from the wall, he slipped inside. Stopped in his tracks. Blood—red, sharp, metallic, everywhere. His heart came to a shuddering halt. He followed the trail that dripped slowly to the mahogany floor up to the woman at the center of it all, slumped over his desk.

The world began to spin. Snapping out of the trance he was in, he started toward her—to help her, save her. A flash of movement—fingers banded around his arm. He lifted his other arm to strike. The glimmer of the officer's gold badge froze his hand in midair.

He was too late. He was always too late...

Lorenzo sat bolt upright in bed, sweat whipping from his face. His heart, gripped by terror and grief, stalled in his chest. It took him a full two or three seconds to realize the woman beside him was not Lucia, it was Angelina.

He was in bed with Angelina in Portofino.

She stirred now, putting out a hand to touch him. He set a palm to her back and told her to go to sleep. Making a sound in the back of her throat, she curled an arm around her pillow and went back to sleep.

He sucked in deep breaths, attempted to regulate his breathing. Soaked with sweat, he slid out of bed and put himself under a cool shower in the guest bedroom so he wouldn't wake his wife.

Water coursing over him, he stood, head bent, palms pressed against the tile as the brisk temperature of the water cooled his skin. When the hard spray had banished the worst of the fog, he stepped out of the shower and dried off.

Wrapping a towel around his waist, he walked out onto

the terrace, the lingering fragments of his dream evaporating as the pink fingers of dawn crawled across the sky. They had used to come nightly, his nightmares. He couldn't remember the last time he'd had one.

He watched the sun rise over the hills, a fiery yellow ball that crept into the hazy gray sky. *I'm going to be a father.* It had been the goal, of course, but he hadn't expected it to happen so quickly, not when they hadn't even been trying. His brain, his emotions, needed time to catch up, because they were mixed just as his wife's were.

There was joy, undoubtedly, at something he'd at one point decided might never be his. Bittersweet regret his brother would never have that opportunity. And fear. Fear that what happened before might happen again. The fear of more *loss*.

Losing his unborn child on the heels of Lucia had pushed him into a red zone where any more emotional deficits were too much. Where any more losses could push him over the line. So he'd shut down—refused to feel, and avoided any chance of that happening. In doing so, he had pushed Angelina away when she'd needed him the most—when *she* had been at her most vulnerable. No wonder she was so terrified to do this again.

His jaw locked, a slow ache pulsing beneath his ribs. This time would be different. This time he'd made sure he and Angelina's relationship was built on a solid, realistic foundation of what they were both capable of. He would make sure he kept them on track—he would be the steady, protective force she needed as they went through this pregnancy together.

If he worried his emotions for his wife were wandering into dangerous territory—into that red zone he avoided—that his efforts to exorcise her power over him weren't having any effect at all, he would just have to make sure he was extravigilant he never crossed that all-important line.

* * *

Angelina awoke to the sensually delicious smell of coffee and spicy, hedonistic male. "Breakfast," her husband intoned in her ear, his sexy, raspy tone sending a shiver up her spine, "is served."

She wasn't sure which she wanted to inhale more—him or the coffee. She opened her eyes to find him dressed and clean-shaven. The kiss he pressed to her lips was long, leisurely, the kind that squeezed her heart. Curling her fingers around his nape, she hung on to the magic for as long as possible.

He finally released her, sprawling on the bed. "I bought pastries in the village," he said, gesturing to the tray he'd tucked beside her.

"Is that a chocolate croissant?"

"What do you think?"

Yum. Her husband knew all of her weaknesses. She picked up her espresso and took a sip. Eyed him. Not as bright-eyed and bushy-tailed as she'd first imagined with those dark shadows under his eyes. "Were you up last night? I thought I heard you."

"I woke early." He plucked a croissant off the plate. "An annoying habit I can't seem to get rid of."

She watched him over the rim of her coffee cup as he inhaled the croissant. "I had a thought on the walk back," he said.

She lifted a brow.

"We're going to have to renovate the Belmont locations before we fold them into the Ricci chain. Your clientele is a perfect match. Why not open Carmichael Creations boutiques in them?"

"You haven't even landed them yet. Aren't you getting a little ahead of yourself?"

"It will happen. It's a perfect marriage of brands, don't you think?"

He was serious about this. Her heart contracted. Once she would have given anything to hear him say that. To know he believed in her work that much. But their child needed to take precedence now.

"That's a big compliment," she said carefully, "but I have more business than I can handle at the moment and I want to remain hands-on. Plus, with the baby, I think we'll have our hands full."

"True." His brow creased. "I suggested the hotel boutiques because you've always said you wanted a partnership between us. But the point is for you to be happy, Angelina. That's what I want for you."

A glow inside her sparked, grew to almost scary proportions. She'd never imagined they could be this good. This *amazing* together.

She didn't want to be afraid of loving him anymore. She wanted to trust that this was going to work out, that they were meant to be together, just like he'd said that night in the Hamptons. Taking that last step, however, making herself completely vulnerable, was painfully hard.

His eyes darkened with a sensual heat that made her pulse leap. He nodded toward the half-eaten croissant in her hand. "You going to eat that?"

She shook her head. Put it down. He reached for her, covered her mouth with his in a kiss that was pure heat. Pure possession. She relaxed her grip on the sheets as he stripped them off her, working his way down her body, tasting, idolizing every inch of her.

It was the most leisurely, spine-tinglingly good buildup he'd ever lavished on her. The most perfect thing she'd ever experienced. By the time he joined their bodies, she was so far gone she was never coming back.

Mouth at her ear, his hand closing possessively over her breast, he started to move, seducing her with words as well as with his body. Heart stretching with the force of what she felt for him, she refused to consider the possibility her husband would never love her. She was through sabotaging her happiness.

CHAPTER ELEVEN

THE WEEKS FOLLOWING her trip to Italy were as busy as Angie had expected as she caught up on the backlog of commissions that had come in. She ploughed through the work with the help of her fellow designers, knowing it was a *good* problem to have—growing pains for a business that seemed to have come into its own.

Burying herself in her work allowed her to achieve her other goal of putting her pregnancy into a manageable box and not let the fears eating away at the fringes of her psyche take control. The doctor had confirmed her pregnancy upon their return home, giving her a clean bill of health. She wasn't going to fret about it. Or at least she was *telling* herself that.

Her husband, however, had clearly elected to take the opposite strategy. Although he was giving her the time to work he'd promised her, he had been monitoring her eating and sleeping habits like a hawk, enforcing periods of rest. When he happened to be around, that was. Ever since they'd come home, he had been working day and night to close the Belmont deal. Add to that another acquisition Franco was negotiating that required her husband's counsel and Lorenzo wasn't doing any eating or sleeping himself.

She knew it was an inordinately busy time, but the feeling that their life was sliding into its former self was growing stronger with every day. Their bond was too new, too nascent, not to allow the warning signals to affect her.

Another long day at the studio behind her, she walked into the penthouse just after eight, kicked off her shoes and made herself a cup of tea. Carrying it into the living room, she sat reading a book while she waited for her husband. But the book failed to keep her attention.

Weeks like this were the worst when Lorenzo was gone for nights on end. Old fears crept around her unsuspecting edges, insecurity set in. Given their dinners together at home had vaporized with her husband's insane schedule and he refused to wake her up when he came to bed so late, she didn't even have the comfort his passionate lovemaking offered, that seemed to make any obstacle seem surmountable.

The minutes ticked by, her agitation rising. Perhaps now that Lorenzo had had his fill of her, now that he'd gotten everything he wanted, he would lose interest again. Perhaps whatever client he was out wining and dining tonight was a convenient excuse to stay away. Perhaps the emotional distance she'd sensed in him since Portofino was a reality.

The clock struck ten. Discarding the book, she decided to take matters into her own hands. To be proactive rather than reactive. To take control of her relationship, something she hadn't done the last time.

In her bedroom, she dug out the lingerie she'd bought earlier that week and slipped it on. The sexy cream-and-black baby doll that just covered her pertinent assets was fairly indecent. She stared at herself in the mirror, rosy color stinging her cheeks. The cream lace bodice did nothing to hide the bold thrust of her nipples, the silk encasing her curves a seductive caress that was pure temptation.

She pulled the elastic from her hair and let it fall around

her shoulders the way her husband liked it. A slow smile curved her mouth. *If this didn't bring him running, nothing would.*

Lorenzo arrived back at the table at the trendy restaurant in the meatpacking district, where he and his CMO were entertaining his Japanese business partners to find his phone sitting on his chair.

An amused smile curved his CMO's mouth. "Figured you might not want the whole table seeing that," he said, nodding toward the phone. He leaned closer. "PS—I'd go home if I were you."

Lorenzo glanced at the screen. Almost choked on the sip of beer he'd taken. His wife dressed in a piece of lingerie he'd never seen before—an outrageously sexy piece, by any male's standards, occupied the entire screen. Hair loose around her shoulders, the lingerie doing little to hide the dark shadow of her nipples beneath the transparent lace, she was the twenty-first-century version of a pinup poster. *Times ten.*

He glanced at the message.

Are you coming home?

Heat claimed his cheeks. It took very little of his creative ability to imagine peeling that silk off of her. How she would taste under his mouth. He'd thought his crazy social schedule might prove an ideal cooling-off period for the two of them given the depth of the emotion they'd shared in Portofino. But this, *this* was too much to resist.

"You didn't see that," he muttered to his CMO.

"What?" Gerald said innocently. "I'll cover for you if you want to make an exit."

Lorenzo tucked his phone into his pocket. Put his exit strategy into motion. Except his Japanese colleagues were intent on taking in the entertainment the club provided. It would be rude for him to cut the night short.

He texted his wife back.

Hold that thought.

It was close to midnight, however, by the time he walked into the penthouse. Devoid of light, it was cast in shadows. He let out a low oath that turned the silent space blue and threw his jacket on a chair.

Body pulsing with frustration, every ounce of his blood so far south it was never coming back, he reached up and loosened his tie. A flash of movement near the windows caught his eye.

He took in his wife, silhouetted against the New York skyline, the sexy negligee plastered to every centimeter of her voluptuous body.

Her breasts were bigger with the advance of her pregnancy, their lush, creamy expanse drawing his eye. That tantalizing glimpse of nipple beneath sheer, gauzy fabric made his mouth go dry.

"You waited up." His voice was husky, laced with a need he couldn't hide.

"I was on my way to bed."

Chilly. Distinctly chilly. He gathered his wits as he moved toward her. "I tried to get away, but my business colleagues were in from Japan. It would have looked rude to leave."

"It's fine." She crossed her arms over her chest, amplifying the view of the bare flesh he ached to touch.

He reached for her. She stepped back. "I don't think so."

"There was nothing I could have done, Angelina."

"I'm tired. I'm going to bed."

He caught her hand and pulled her to him, content to

work his way back into her good graces. Her perfume drifted into his nostrils, a tantalizing tease that stroked the heat in him higher. "Clearly you're angry," he murmured. "Let me make it up to you. I'm so hot for you, *cara mia*. I will make it so good."

She lifted her vibrant blue gaze to his. "No."

He blinked. "What do you mean 'no'? You sent me a photo of you in lingerie."

"That offer expired an hour ago."

"You are my wife," he barked. "Offers don't expire."

A mutinous set of her lips. "This one just did. Maybe next time I'll be a compelling enough attraction that you will be home before midnight. Maybe next time you won't blow off those dinners *you* insisted on. Maybe when I remember what my husband *looks like*, the offer will be available for redemption."

He scowled. "You are being completely unfair."

She shook her head. "This *is* history repeating itself, Lorenzo. I don't like it, and I'm not imagining it this time."

He drew his brows together. "It's nothing like the past. We have been great together. We're talking, we're communicating. Just because you have hurt feelings that I didn't jump when you sent me that photo doesn't mean I'm ignoring you. It means I was *busy*."

Her eyes darkened to a stormy, gray blue. "Just because you've had a few drinks and you're hot for a booty call doesn't mean you get to act like a child when it doesn't go your way. Learn your lesson and maybe next time it will work out for you."

Dio, but she was beautiful when she was angry. He loved this strong, sexy version of his wife—it turned him hard as a rock. The problem was, he needed her to give so he could get his hands on her.

"Bene." He lifted his palms in a conciliatory gesture. "I've learned my lesson. Mission accomplished. You've

made your point." He trained his gaze on hers, hot, deliberate. "What would you like me to do? Get down on my knees and beg?"

Her confident swagger faltered, a blaze of uncertainty staining her beautiful eyes. He took a step closer. "Just say yes," he murmured, raking her from head to toe. "While I'm there, I'd be happy to indulge you. Mouth, hands, name your pleasure."

A blaze of sensual heat fired her eyes before the ice made a swift reappearance. "I am not a possession to be used and discarded according to your whims."

"You've said that before," he murmured, his good mood rapidly dissipating. "I find it as objectionable as I did the first time. That is *not* what this is, Angelina. These are extraordinary circumstances trying to land this Belmont deal."

"There will always be another deal...another pot of gold at the end of the rainbow. It never stops, Lorenzo. It never will."

"It will. Once we land Belmont, I will be able to breathe again."

She shook her head. "I've watched my mother go through this a thousand times, wondering when my father will deign to pay attention to her again, always putting her second, *third*, if he happened to be having an affair at the time. I've lived through it with you. I won't repeat these hot and cold patterns again—that roller-coaster ride we do so well."

"I am *not* your father." Irritation edged his voice. "And I've put you first every time since we've been back together in case you hadn't noticed."

"Yes," she agreed, "you have. Which is why I'm speaking up. Because we've built such a great thing together... because I refuse to see things go back to the way they were."

He shook his head. "You're being too sensitive."

"No, I'm not."

He crossed his arms over his chest, too tired, too frustrated to know how to respond. He was giving her all he had and still she wanted more.

Her lashes lowered. "I need sleep. I have a long day tomorrow."

He let her go, refusing to run after her, tongue wagging, like some desperate fool, despite the way he burned for her. Pouring himself a glass of water, he collapsed into a chair, too wired to sleep even though he couldn't remember the last time he had enjoyed that particular human luxury.

Things *would* get better after he landed Belmont. His wife was completely overreacting—a guilt trip he didn't need when making sure she was okay, that she and their baby were healthy, had been his primary obsession amidst the insanity of his life.

He sat back in the chair. Downed a long swallow of water. His wife's indignation, quite honestly, was the least of his problems. Losing the Belmont deal was a real possibility. It was becoming more and more clear the branding issue might be a deal breaker. The business pages were ripe with speculation on the potential megamerger, Ricci stock was on a roller-coaster ride, the board meeting was looming and he needed to get Erasmo Bavaro, the Bavaro scion, onside. But the Bavaro brothers weren't offering access to their father. He had to play the situation very, very carefully and it was driving him mad.

Oh, the world wouldn't end if the deal fell apart, he conceded, but Ricci's stock and reputation would take a serious hit. Confidence would be shaken. And it would be his fault.

I am beginning to think your ambition has got the best of you on this one.

A nerve throbbed at his temple, his fingers tightening around the glass. Had his father been right? Had he finally overstepped himself? Gotten too confident? Cocky?

He rested his head against the back of the chair and closed his eyes. His culpability was a moot point at this stage. All that mattered was getting the deal done. Pulling it out of the ashes.

As for his wife? He'd never promised her perfection—had warned her this was who he was. He'd vowed to be there for her and he would. But perhaps she was right. Perhaps he'd dropped the ball on his promise to be present of late, had let their dinners together slide.

He could rectify that—take her out for dinner tomorrow night. Calm the waters at home.

CHAPTER TWELVE

IT WAS GOING to be a late night.

Angie set the almost completed, black-and-white diamond bracelet on her workbench, sat back in her chair and rubbed her eyes. *Almost there* wasn't good enough when the bracelet was due to one of Manhattan's most noted philanthropists tomorrow, a woman who could make or break her reputation. And since she had already pushed the delivery date back because of her trip to Europe, then had to wait for some stones to be delivered, it needed to get done tonight.

She headed for the coffee machine, thinking maybe java might perk her up. But she suspected what was really bothering her was the fact that although her husband had made an effort to reinstate their dinners at home whenever his schedule permitted, although he was making an effort to be *physically* present, he had become even more emotionally distant over the last couple of weeks.

Keeping the faith, believing in them, was growing increasingly difficult when not knowing if he'd ever love her was burning a hole in her soul. She wanted him to say those three words so badly, it was almost painful. But she knew if he ever did, and it wasn't a given he would, it would take time.

"Do you want me to stay and work with you tonight?" Serina threw her a glance as she put on her coat.

Angie poured herself a cup of coffee. "You have a

date." She gave the diminutive blonde an amused look. "That exciting is he?"

Serina made a face. "Friends set us up."

"Then you should definitely go. That's how all the good matches are made."

She wasn't so sure how love at first sight was going to work out for her.

Picking up her coffee, she nursed the steaming cup between her hands. "I have to finish Juliette Baudelaire's bracelet. The clasp I'd envisioned isn't working."

She and Serina conferred on the issue, the other designer agreeing her current design wouldn't work. They tossed around a couple of alternatives, then Serina headed out for her date.

No sooner had Angie settled into her work than her cell phone rang—it was her husband's name on the caller ID.

"Yes," she purred, craving a taste of his raspy, delicious voice to ease her jagged emotions. "I thought you had to work late."

"Marc Bavaro's invited us to the opera tonight. I need you to come."

No hello. No preamble. No sexy rasp. Cool, rapid-fire words thrown at her with that hint of edge he'd been wearing all week.

She bit her lip. "I can't. I'm sorry. I have a bracelet due to an important client in the morning."

"It's a bracelet. Not life or death. Finish it tomorrow."

She stiffened. "It's *due* tomorrow. I've already put her off once because of Marc Bavaro."

"A few hours isn't going to make a difference. Stop being so contrary and get ready. I'll be there in fifteen minutes to pick you up."

The line went dead. She stared at the phone. Had he just called her *contrary*? *Dismissed* her like that?

She put down the phone. Took a couple of deep breaths.

Seriously considered calling him back and telling him what he could do with his opera invitation. Except Marc Bavaro was driving him crazy. She could see it on his face when he walked in the door at night…in the dark circles under his eyes he was wearing like a badge. He was under immense pressure to close this deal and the strain was showing.

She exhaled a long breath. Even though her own work would suffer, she would *not* be the one to sabotage their relationship this time.

Juliette's nearly done bracelet glittered on her desk. She supposed she could send her an email and let her know it would be done in the morning, afternoon at the latest. Surely that would be fine?

Decision made, she sent the email and gathered up her things, her animosity growing by the minute. By the time Lorenzo pulled up at the sidewalk in front of her studio, her blood was boiling.

"Ciao." He leaned toward her to give her a kiss when she got into the car. She gave him her cheek instead. His ebony gaze narrowed. "What?"

"If you don't know what, you don't deserve an answer."

He eyed her. "Is it because I called you contrary?"

She didn't deign to respond to that.

A muttered oath. "It's one night, Angelina."

She turned a furious gaze on him. "I have a commission due tomorrow. How would you feel if I insisted you attend a party with me when you had a security filing the next day? I can just see you now—'Pff, it's just a security filing…the lawyers have this. Be right with you, honey.'"

"Now you're being ridiculous."

She turned to look out the window.

He gave up after that, getting them home in record time. She changed into a cap-sleeved, navy classic sheath dress, adding elegant gold sandals and jewelry to spice it up. Lorenzo looked devastatingly handsome in a dark suit, white shirt and an ice-blue tie he had clearly put on to match her dress, but she was in no mood to acknowledge it.

They met up with Marc and Penny outside the stunningly beautiful Metropolitan Opera House, with its white travertine stone facade and five massive, graceful arches that, lit up at night, made it a sight to see. It had always been one of Angie's favorite places to go for its sheer magnificence. Her first trip there, to see a ballet as a little girl, had been full of wide-eyed wonder. But tonight she was too annoyed to register much other than the fact that she was itching to shrug off the hand her husband held at her back, but couldn't.

They shared a cocktail with the other couple in one of the bars. Sparkling water, sadly, for Angie, when a glass of wine might have mellowed her out. She focused all her attention on the Belmont CEO and his girlfriend, ignoring her husband completely, to the point where Penny jokingly asked her if Lorenzo was in the doghouse as they settled into their seats in the Belmont box to watch Puccini's *La Bohème*.

She denied it, of course. Made a joking comment that Penny would see what it was like when the honeymoon phase was over. Lorenzo must have heard it with that laser-sharp hearing of his because his face turned dark. A mistake, she recognized, as the whisper of a chill rose up her spine. She had insulted his male pride.

She focused on the performance. He had earned that one.

La Bohème was one of her favorites, but tonight it couldn't have been a worse choice. The story of Mimi and Rodolfo, the fiery, star-crossed lovers, sung to perfection by the visiting Italian soprano and her American tenor— had always moved her. But tonight, given her rocky emotions, her insecurities about her and Lorenzo, it affected her in a way she couldn't hide. By the time the two lovers decided to stay together in the face of Mimi's heartbreaking illness at the end of the third act, her imminent death on the horizon, tears were running down her face.

Lorenzo put a hand on her thigh. She ignored him, kept her eyes focused on the stage. When the act came to a close, she rooted around desperately in her bag for a tissue, a necessity at the opera, and *dammit*, how could she have forgotten them?

Lorenzo shoved the handkerchief from his front pocket into her hand. "Excuse us, will you?"

"What are you doing?" she whispered as he grabbed her arm and propelled her out of the box.

A tight, intense look back. "We are going somewhere to talk."

"I don't want to talk."

"Well, that's too bad, *amore mio*, you don't get to choose."

Into the multistoried lobby they went, past the two glorious murals Marc Chagall had painted. Somewhere along the way, Lorenzo dropped the general manager's name. The next thing she knew, he was directing her down a hallway and into an empty dressing room marked Visiting Performers.

Lorenzo twisted the lock on the door and turned to face his wife. What the hell was wrong with her? Watching her cry like that had made him want to crawl out of his skin, because he didn't think all of it had to do with the admittedly heartbreaking opera.

Angie swept her hand around the room, dominated by the sofa that sat along one wall and a dressing table and mirror on the other. "We can't be in here."

"I was just told we could." He crossed his arms over

his chest. "Explain to me why you are so angry, *cara*. I asked you to do me a favor. You know how important this deal is to me. What's the problem?"

She jammed her hands on her hips, eyes flashing. "You *ordered* me to come. You know how important my career is to me and yet you completely discounted my work. The bracelet I'm creating is for Juliette Baudelaire—a huge commission, particularly if she spreads the word to her friends. It's not just a bracelet, it's a *stepping stone* in my career. And yet here I am, not delivering on time—*twice*—because of you and your needs."

His irritation came to a sudden, sliding halt. "I had no idea it was for her."

"*How could you?* You hung up on me before I had a chance to tell you."

He muttered an oath. Pushed a palm over his brow. "*Mi dispiace.* I'm sorry. I wasn't thinking when I called you. I was behind, annoyed because I had prior commitments I, too, had to cancel."

She hugged her arms around herself. Glared at him. He scowled back. "You," he said, waving a hand at her, "are so emotional tonight. What's going on? Is it the pregnancy effect?"

The daggers in her eyes would have sliced him to shreds if they'd been real. "*You*, Lorenzo Ricci, are so oblivious, so *emotionally unaware* sometimes it blows my mind."

He didn't think that was fair. He thought he was *very* emotionally aware at times and had been with her *a lot* lately. They were talking. *Communicating.* Being honest with each other. The last couple of weeks had just been particularly brutal.

The thought vaporized from his head as his wife headed for the door. Moving with a swiftness born of his superior height and muscle, he made it there at the same time she did. Jamming his palm against the wood, he looked down at his very beautiful, very angry wife.

"We aren't done talking."

"Oh, yes, we are."

"No," he said deliberately, "we aren't."

She crossed her arms over her chest. "What else would you like to say?"

"I'd like to say I'm sorry again. I sincerely feel badly that I did not check to see what it was you were working on. If I'd known, I would have come by myself."

Her stormy blue gaze softened.

"I would also like to know how I am being *emotionally unaware*."

She pursed her lips. "You're kidding, right?"

"No." He frowned. "I thought we had the pregnancy thing out in the open. We're dealing with it."

"It's not that." She shook her head. "Women cannot *stand* when a man plays the hormone card, Lorenzo. It's like waving a red flag in front of a bull."

"Oh. *Certo*," he said, nodding. "I will remember that for the future. I had no idea. I thought pregnancy hormones were a documented thing."

"*Lorenzo.*" She glared at him. "I'd stop while you're ahead."

"*Bene.*" He snagged an arm around her waist and pulled her close. "Is there anything else you would like to tell me? Why you are so upset?"

Her gaze dropped away from his. "You haven't been emotionally present the last few weeks. I don't know where your head is. I don't know where *we* are. I miss you."

Guilt tied a knot in his chest. In trying to pull back, to not lead them down a path he couldn't go, he'd hurt her.

"I'm sorry." He bent his head and buried his mouth in the curve of her neck. Drank in her irresistible scent. "Things have been crazy. I will do better."

"It's… I—" She sighed. "We should go. Find Marc and Penny."

"Not until you say you're not angry with me anymore." He slid his hands down over her bottom and pulled her closer. "I hate it when you're angry with me."

Tracing the line of her neck with his lips, he sank his teeth into the cord of her throat where it throbbed against her skin. Her breath hitched. "Fine. I'm not angry at you anymore."

"I'm not convinced." He dragged his mouth up to hers. Pushed his fingers into her hair and kissed her. Dominant, persuasive, he sought to fix whatever was going on with her. To fix *them* in the only way he knew how.

She melted beneath his hands. "Okay," she whispered against his lips. "You're forgiven."

But he was too far gone now, his body pulsing with the need to restore the natural balance of things. Denying himself Angelina was carving a hole inside of him he didn't know how to fill.

He backed her into the wall, pushed his thigh between hers, imprinting her with the throbbing evidence of his need. She gasped. *"Lorenzo."*

"What?"

"We can't do this here."

"Why not?" He slicked his tongue over her lush bottom lip, tasting her. "You liked it in Portofino. The element of risk…"

"Yes, but—"

He delved inside the sweetness of her mouth. Made love to her with his tongue like he wanted to do to her body. Her bag clattered to the floor, a low moan leaving her throat. Lust coursing through him, he nudged her legs farther apart and swept her dress up her thighs. She was damp when he cupped her between her legs, as turned on as he was.

He ran his palm over the hot, wet silk that covered her. Moved it aside to find her slick and ready for him.

"I need to have you," he rasped.

Her stormy blue gaze locked with his. *"Yes."*

He stroked her. Readied her. She made more of those sexy sounds at the back of her throat, arching into his hand. Shallow strokes of his fingers inside her tight channel to tease, insistent circles against the tight bundle of nerves at the heart of her with his thumb. Throwing her head back, she said his name in a broken voice that ripped right through him.

Urging one of her legs around his waist, he released himself from his pants, pushed aside the wet silk and entered her with a hard, urgent thrust. She gasped, the sensation of her tight, velvet warmth gripping his swollen flesh indescribable. It had never been so good.

"Okay?" he murmured.

"Yes."

Bending his knees, he drove up inside of her with an urgent desire that annihilated anything but the need to have her. His erection pounded in time with his heartbeat, his control shredding. He captured her hand in his and brought her fingers to the hard nub that gave her pleasure.

"Touch yourself," he whispered. "Come with me, Angelina."

She closed her eyes. Rotated her fingers against her flesh. He kept his hand over hers, absorbing the tiny quakes that went through her. Held on to the very threads of his control while she pleasured herself. When she was close, when the deeper shudders came, moving from her through him, he gripped her hip tighter and stroked deeper, setting a hard, wild rhythm that blew his brain apart.

His body tightened, swelled, his breathing hoarse in the silence of the room. In perfect sync, they came together in a soul-shaking release like none he'd ever experienced before.

Mouth buried in her neck, he held her as her legs gave out. He wasn't sure how long they stayed like that, wrapped around each other, before he recovered enough to straighten and push back.

Bracing a palm against the wall, he leaned in to kiss her, to acknowledge what that had just been. His heart stopped in his chest at the tears streaming down her cheeks.

"Angelina?" He cupped her face with his hands. "What is it?"

She shook her head. Pushed away as she straightened her clothes. "It's nothing. I'm emotional from the performance."

The bell sounded to end the intermission. He ignored it, focusing on his wife's tear-streaked face as he zipped himself up. "It's a hell of a lot more than that."

She swiped the tears from her face with the backs of her hands.

"Angelina," he roared. "Out with it."

She bent and scooped her purse off the floor. Straightening, she rested her blue gaze on his. "I'm in love with you, Lorenzo. Silly me, I forgot the rules."

CHAPTER THIRTEEN

LORENZO'S JAW DROPPED. "Angie—"

The bell rang again. His wife turned, unlocked the door and walked out. Blood pounding at his temples, he straightened his shirt and followed her out.

How he sat through the last act, he wasn't sure. It was like someone was driving nails into his head in some kind of ancient torture. When it was finally, mercifully over, they bid Marc and Penny a good night and acquired the car from the valet. Neither of them spoke in the loaded silence of the car.

The penthouse was in shadows as they entered, Manhattan spread out before them in all its glory. He threw his jacket on a chair and headed straight for the bar and a stiff shot of whiskey.

Angelina kicked off her shoes. When she headed for the bedroom, he pointed to the sofa. *"Sit."*

She lifted her chin. "What's the point? I know you can't tell me what I want to hear. You would have said it to me in that dressing room if you could."

It was a truth he couldn't deny. He wanted to—he wanted to tell her everything she wanted to hear if it would wipe the hurt from her eyes, but he'd promised her honesty and they'd come too far to give each other anything but.

He set down the whiskey. Pushed a hand through his hair. "To lose someone you love like I loved Lucia changes a person. You *know* too much. Things you should never have to know…things that make you question everything you once took for granted—the *natural order* of things. It isn't a faith I'll ever have again. Loving someone like that isn't something I'm *capable* of doing. But it doesn't mean I don't care for you. You know I do."

Her eyes grew suspiciously bright. "Not capable," she asked quietly, "or simply unwilling to try?"

He lifted a shoulder. "It is who I am."

The brightness in her eyes dissolved on a blaze of fire. "You know what I think, Lorenzo? I think it's a cop-out, this 'I am who I am' line of yours. Saying you can't love again is easier than making yourself vulnerable…easier than exposing yourself to the potential for pain, so you choose not to go there. You choose to believe you are incapable of love."

He shook his head. "I won't tell you lies. We promised each other that. But what we have, Angelina—is something *more* than love. What we have is based on rationality, on that great partnership you've always wanted, on the affection we have for each other. It is *real*. It's what's going to make this marriage work. *Last*."

She wrapped her arms around herself. Turned to look out the window. He closed the distance between them, curled his fingers around her shoulder and turned her to him. "We have a good thing," he said softly, "an electric connection—a special connection. The kind that rarely, if ever, comes along. We will be great parents to our child because we know the gift it is. What more could you ask for?"

"The love of a lifetime," she said quietly. "You had yours. Maybe I want mine. Maybe *this* isn't enough."

His stomach contracted, her words sucking the breath from him. He inhaled, dragged in a breath. Searched for something, *anything* to say. But he knew what she was saying was true. She deserved to have that untainted love—everything he couldn't give her. But he'd thought he could make her happy by giving her everything else. He should have known it would never be enough.

Naked pain wrote itself across her beautiful face. "I have to go to bed. I need to deliver that bracelet to Juliette tomorrow and I still have to figure out the clasp."

He watched her leave the room, a heavy, hollow ache in his chest, because he wasn't sure he could fix this. It was the one thing he *couldn't* fix.

Bleary-eyed from a restless, sleepless night, Angie forced herself into the studio shortly after her husband left for the office, putting on coffee just as the birds were beginning to sing.

She sat down at her desk with a cup of the strong brew, numbly processing the events of the night before. She hadn't meant to confront Lorenzo. She'd meant to give him time. But somewhere along the way, her emotions so raw, it had just come tumbling out. Maybe it had been the way she'd been desperately begging for crumbs in that dressing room when they'd made love, terrified they were falling apart again—needing to know they were okay. How they were once again using sex to solve problems they couldn't fix.

Her heart throbbed. How could she have allowed herself to make the same mistake she'd made the first time around? To think, on some instinctual level, her husband might love her but not be able to admit it?

It was never going to happen even if he did. And she knew, even if she convinced herself that what they had was enough, even if she bought his whole line about them being *more* than love, she'd end up hating him for never offering her what she so desperately wanted. Because she wanted it—she did. The love she'd never had. The love she knew they could have together.

She deserved it. She had always deserved it. She was *worthy* of it. She knew that now. And what hurt the most was her husband was capable of it. He'd loved Lucia once. He just wasn't going to offer it to her.

The ache in her insides grew. She wanted to be the light in Lorenzo's life, his everything as he was becoming to her. As he'd always been to her. This wasn't her sabotaging them, it was *him* sabotaging them.

She took another sip of her coffee. Pulled herself together. Allowing her work to slide wasn't going to make this any easier.

A return email from Juliette Baudelaire sat in her inbox. A short, curt reply.

Not to worry. I found another piece to wear to the luncheon. Given that, I no longer require the bracelet.

Her heart sank. Thousands of dollars of diamonds had gone into that bracelet. But that wasn't even the point—she could resell it. The point was that Juliette knew everyone and loved to talk. Her reputation was going to take a bump for this, she knew it in her bones.

She sat back in her chair. Closed her eyes.

"You okay?" Serina breezed in and hung up her coat.

No, she decided, tears stinging her eyes. She was most definitely not okay. But she wasn't going to let that man take her apart again. Not this time.

"Do you want the good news or the bad?"

Lorenzo eyed his lawyer, his mood vile. "Why don't you start with the bad and work up to the good?"

"The Belmont lawyers called while you were in your

meeting. They want to meet tomorrow in Miami to discuss some final issues."

Lorenzo's fingers curled tight around the toy football he held. Marc Bavaro was going to be the one to finally make him snap. He could feel it.

"What's the good news?"

"The meeting will be at Erasmo Bavaro's place."

He sat forward. "That is good news." But *Miami*...tomorrow?

Cris eyed his scowl. "Please tell me we're saying yes."

"Bene." He blew out a breath. "Make it happen. We need to get this done. But I swear this is the swan song."

His lawyer left. Lorenzo sat back in his chair, his satisfaction at finally moving this game to a place he was comfortable with only slightly improving his foul mood. His volatility had as much to do with his wife's ultimatum as it did with Bavaro's antics. With the fact that she'd thrown that explosive three-word phrase at him, pushed him for things he couldn't give and destroyed the delicate, satisfactory stasis he'd had going on. Backed him into a corner with nowhere left to go.

Flying to Miami tomorrow seemed unwise given the current state of affairs. But what could he do? If he didn't get Erasmo Bavaro on board this deal was as good as dead.

Swinging his feet off his desk, he threw the things he'd need for Miami in his briefcase and headed home to solve his problem. His wife was making herself some hot milk in the kitchen when he walked in.

"How was your day?" he asked, setting his briefcase on the floor. *Reintroducing stasis.*

"Busy." She put down the cup and rubbed her palms against her temples.

"Did you get Juliette's bracelet done?"

She lifted her gaze to his, her face expressionless. "I

lost the commission. She went out and bought something else to wear."

Uh-oh. This did not bode well for the conversation they needed to have. "I'm sorry," he said quietly, "that was wrong of me. But we still need to talk. Work this out."

She shook her head. "*You* need to work this out. I know how I feel."

A twinge of unease spread through him. "What are you saying?"

"I'm saying I can't live without love. I can't stay in this marriage unless you can offer that to me." She shook her head, teeth sinking into her lip. "You have made me face up to my past, Lorenzo. You have made me see how I run from the things that scare me so I won't get hurt. Well, I'm not running now. I *deserve* to be happy. I deserve to have all of you. And if you can't offer that to me, it will break my heart, but I will walk away because you've also helped me realize how strong I am."

His chest clenched. "You're willing to throw everything we have away because I can't say three words?"

Her eyes darkened. "It's more than that and you know it. I've watched you struggle over the past few weeks. I know how hard this is for you. But I can't live with pieces of you. It would break my heart. We would end up hating each other. You know we would."

"No, I do not know that." His fists tightened at his sides. "This is not negotiable, Angelina. You are carrying my child. Our fate was sealed the day that happened."

"No, it wasn't." She shook her head. "You have your heir. We will work that out. But you can't have me. Not like this. I must have been insane to ever agree to that deal we made."

"You aren't walking out on me again." His voice was pure frost. "You know the conditions I attached to this."

"You won't do it." Her eyes were stark in a face gone

white. "The other thing I have learned is that under that armor you wear is the man I met. The man I would have given anything to have. *He* wouldn't let my family suffer. He would not hurt me."

Blood pounded in his ears, a red-hot skewer of rage lancing through him. "Try me, *cara*. Just try me. You think you can leave me and cozy up to *Byron* again with my child inside you? It will never happen. I will drag this divorce out for all eternity."

She stared at him as if she couldn't believe what she was hearing. He couldn't believe what he was saying. But the rage driving him didn't care who or what he hurt.

She didn't flinch. Held his gaze. "Byron and I were over when I realized I was still in love with you and you damn well know it."

He raked a hand through his hair. Struggled to see past his fury. "I have to go to Miami tomorrow. Erasmo Bavaro has agreed to meet with us. We will talk about this when I get back."

"I won't be here." The pain staining her blue eyes nearly tore him in two. "I know who I am, Lorenzo, and I know I can't do this."

She turned on her heel and walked toward the bedroom.

Corrosive anger roped his heart. "Goddammit, Angelina, get back here."

She kept going.

In the center of the red zone, well aware of where it could take him, he downed the rest of the whiskey. He could not afford to go there, not now with the most important deal of his life hanging in the balance. Not ever when his wife was asking more of him than he could ever give.

CHAPTER FOURTEEN

ERASMO BAVARO WAS as cagey as his son Marc and as animated as Diego, a fearsome combination in a silver-haired fox who reminded Lorenzo of his father.

It would have been fascinating to see the two titans face off in their heyday, but on a brilliantly sunny afternoon in Miami, with the Bavaro scion's palatial poolside terrace the backdrop for the negotiations, his focus was on pulling Erasmo into the twenty-first century.

Erasmo, for his part, looked content to stay right where he was. Flanked by his lawyers at the long, olive wood table, coolly dressed in a flamboyant short-sleeved shirt and trousers, he swept a palm over his neatly trimmed, salt-and-pepper goatee and eyed Lorenzo. "Let me tell you a story," he said in a deeply accented voice. "Perhaps it will help you to understand where I'm coming from.

"The night we opened the Belmont in South Beach in 1950, we had the most popular blues singer on the planet, Natalie Constantine, lined up to play. Near the end of her set, Arturo Martinez walked onto the stage and joined her for the last two songs."

Arturo Martinez. The Spanish megastar who had sold more albums in those days than any singer alive.

"They closed out the night in the piano bar. Two legends. Such was the mystique of the Belmont legacy. You could not have paid to be there that night."

"They were great days," Lorenzo acknowledged. "I

wish I had been there that night. But that time has come and gone, Erasmo. It's time for the mantle to be passed on. All good things must come to an end."

"Speaks the man who puts money above meaning." The Bavaro patriarch lifted a brow. "Can I share something with you, Ricci? Money will not give your life meaning when you are my age. Money will not keep you warm at night. Money won't nourish your soul when you've spent fifty years in this business and every boardroom table looks like the rest. *Meaning* will. Your legacy will."

"Speaks a man perhaps lost in his own sentimentality..."

Erasmo dipped his head. "Perhaps. But I would prefer to be remembered as a man who built things rather than tore down the work of others."

The rebuke stung his skin. Lorenzo lifted the glass of potent, exotic rum his host had unearthed from his cellar to his lips and took a sip. It burned a slow path through his insides, but it didn't take the sting out of the old man's words. Nor did the fact that his wife, who'd walked out on him *again*, felt the same way.

Angelina thought he'd sold his soul for his success. Bartered it for an escape from the guilt he refused to acknowledge—the feelings he refused to address. The ironic thing was, in that moment, as the cast of lawyers digressed into legalese he couldn't be bothered to follow, he couldn't remember why this deal had ever been so important to him. Why he was sitting here haggling over a name when the most important thing in his life was back in New York. *Refusing to take his calls.*

And why would she? Regret sat like a stone in his stomach. He'd threatened to withdraw his funding of Carmichael Company if she left...to drag their divorce out for all eternity. Had he really thought that would make her stay?

His insides coiled tight. What the hell was wrong with him? He had no idea what he was doing anymore. Hadn't since Angelina had laid all his truths out for him and challenged him to do the same. Since a phone call in the middle of a meeting in Shanghai had obliterated the life he'd known and had him planning a funeral rather than the family he and Lucia had envisioned.

He rubbed a palm across his forehead, a low throb sitting just below his skin. He'd told Angelina he wasn't capable of loving again. Had meant it. But watching her walk out on him a second time, watching her lay her heart on the line about how she felt about him had done something to him. If his wife, who'd been hurt so many times it was a scar on her soul, could be that courageous, what did that make him? A *coward*?

The tightness in his chest deepened. He'd allowed her to walk away, continued to pretend he didn't feel the things he did for her because then he wouldn't have to face the truth. That he loved her. Had loved her from the first moment he'd laid eyes on her. That he was so afraid of losing someone else, so afraid of losing *her*, so angry at her still for leaving him, he didn't have the guts to put himself out there. To tell her how he felt.

His heart punched through his chest. *Blaming yourself for Lucia's death is easier than making yourself vulnerable again.*

He curled his fingers into his thighs, waiting for the shame, the guilt, to dig its claws into him, to claim him as it always did when he allowed himself to think of that night. But it didn't come. His fear was greater—his fear of losing his wife, the woman who made him whole.

He closed his eyes. What would she think if she knew the true story? That his inability to be present for his wife, to listen to her, the same failings he had brought to his marriage with Angelina, had led to Lucia's death? That *he* was responsible for it?

He finished his drink in a long swig. Set the glass

down. What was clear was that he hadn't fulfilled his end of his bargain with his wife. He'd insisted Angelina be an open book, but he hadn't been with her. He owed her the truth, because if he continued to use his guilt as a crutch, to hide from his emotions, he would lose her anyway. And losing his wife, he realized, wasn't an option.

The lawyers droned on. The sun beat down on his head. Perhaps knowing, *accepting* he should have done things differently and forgiving himself for Lucia's death were two separate things. Maybe he needed to forgive himself for being human in the decisions he'd made…maybe that was something he could live with.

He leaned forward, palms on the table. "We will co-brand the hotels," he interjected, cutting through the din. "'The Ricci South Beach, *formerly a Belmont hotel*.' That's as far as I'm willing to take it."

Cristopher gaped at his about-face. Lorenzo stood up. "You have twenty-four hours to give us a response—after that, the deal is dead."

Marc eyed him. "You're walking out?"

"I'm taking a page out of your father's book. I'm finally getting my priorities straight. You've had a year to do that, Bavaro, I'm giving you another twenty-four hours' grace."

Whether he had that with Angelina after the things he'd said to her remained to be seen.

"Why don't you just take his calls if you're this miserable?"

Angie looked up from her bowl of pasta to find her sister's watchful gaze on her. "Because we both need space. And," she said, dropping the fork in the bowl and pushing it away, "I'm angry at him."

Furious. Lonely. Miserable. But she wasn't about to add fuel to the fire by dragging her sister into this. They were supposed to be having a nice night out at their favorite restaurant, something she desperately needed.

"You know," Abigail said quietly, "Lorenzo called James this afternoon."

She sat up straighter. "*James?* Why?"

"Father is stepping down and making James CEO. Lorenzo's going to come in and work side by side with him to right-side Carmichael Company."

Her jaw dropped. "And I don't know about this why?"

"Apparently it's been in the works for a while, but Father just made the decision this week. According to James, Lorenzo gave Father an ultimatum a few weeks back—step down or he will withdraw his financial support."

"He's good at that," Angie muttered. "Throwing his weight around." She frowned, playing with the straw in her iced tea. "The question is why? He can barely manage his own schedule. How is he going to accommodate this?"

"I don't know," Abigail said softly, her attention on something behind Angie, "but you could ask him. I think your *space* just ran out."

She whipped her head around. Felt the blood drain from her face. Lorenzo, in a silver-gray suit, navy tie and white shirt, stood talking to the hostess. All magnetic, bespoke elegance, the pretty blonde was clearly dazzled by him, her megawatt smile as she pointed to their table blinding.

Angie turned back to her sister, butterflies swarming her stomach. "How did he know I was here?" Her gaze narrowed. "*You* told him."

Abigail sat back in her chair, wineglass in hand. "You just said you're in love with him. Not that that's a news flash. You two need to work things out."

"Traitor," Angie growled. But then her husband was standing beside their table and everything inside her seemed to vibrate with the need to hold him, to have him, she'd missed him so much.

She pressed her lips together. Looked up at him. "What are you doing here?"

He eyed her, his dark stare making her heart thud in her chest. "I've come to get my wife."

Her stomach lurched. "You can't order me around, Lorenzo. I'm done with that."

"It wasn't an order. I'm asking you to come home with me and talk this out."

She sank her teeth into her lip. "Lorenzo—"

"Please." The husky edge to his voice raked her skin. Deepened the ache inside of her to unbearable levels.

She took a deep breath. "I'm not sure it's a good idea."

"You think I don't love you?" he rasped, his gaze holding hers. "What do you think this has all been about, Angelina? Me running after you like a lunatic? Me not being able to forget you? Me acting like a complete jackass? I've been in love with you since the first moment I laid eyes on you. If my behavior hasn't made that clear, I don't know what will."

"He has a point," Abigail said dryly. "As much as I'm enjoying this spectacular grovel, however, there are at least two tabloid reporters in the house tonight. Perhaps you should hear the man out."

Angie barely heard her, she was so utterly gobsmacked by what her husband had just said. At the truth glimmering in his black eyes. Never had she expected to hear him say those three words. Certainly not in a restaurant full of people now staring at them.

She glanced at her sister. Abigail waved her off with an amused lift of her hand. "I'll have the fudge cake while I imagine being a fly on the wall. *Go.*"

Lorenzo captured her fingers in his and dragged her to her feet. Through the crowded restaurant they went, her half running to keep up with his long strides.

The car sat waiting with the valet. Lorenzo tucked her

into the passenger seat, got in and drove home. Angie watched him, head spinning. "What happened in Miami? Did you sign the deal?"

"No. I told Erasmo Bavaro I would cobrand the hotels, that was my final offer, and gave them twenty-four hours to take it or leave it."

"Oh." She frowned. "You said you'd never do that."

"Things change."

"The Bavaros got to you, didn't they?"

"Perhaps. My wife also made it clear she disapproves of my slash-and-burn approach to business."

She eyed him. "Why are you helping James?"

"Because I think Carmichael can be great again, but it needs your brother at the helm. A modern leadership. And," he added, flicking her a glance, "I like the idea of building something again."

"You have no capacity. What if you land Belmont?"

"I will hand it off to the VP I hired last week. It's all part of the plan."

"What plan?"

"To keep you." Quiet words, full of meaning. *Promise.* "It was always about keeping you, Angelina. I just didn't go about it the right way."

Oh. Her heart melted. It was hard to stay angry when he said things like that.

Traffic unusually light, they made it home in minutes. Lorenzo flicked on the lights in the living room, poured them glasses of sparkling water, handed one to Angie and lowered himself into a chair. She curled up in the one opposite him.

"I need to tell you about Lucia," he said quietly. "All of it."

Her heart beat a jagged rhythm. "Lorenzo—"

He held up a hand. "I need to do it."

She sat back, heart in her mouth.

"My trip to Shanghai, the week Lucia died, was an intense trip for me. Three days in and out—nonstop meetings. Lucia wanted to come. I told her no, I wouldn't have any time for her. She was…nervous living in New York. She was from a small village in Italy, she didn't feel safe here. I thought by not taking her with me on that trip, not dragging her through those time zones when we were trying to conceive, she would be better off." His mouth flattened. "I also thought it would help toughen her up. Show her she could do it on her own."

Oh, no. She pressed her fingers to her mouth. The guilt he must feel.

"When the robbers left her alone," he continued, cheekbones standing out like blades, "she called me instead of 911. The call went to my voice mail. I was in a meeting. When I listened to the message, I lost my mind."

Her throat constricted. "No," she whispered. "Lorenzo, no." Tears welled up in her eyes. She got up, closed the distance between them and slid onto his lap. "It wasn't your fault," she murmured, pressing her lips to his cheek. "Tell me you don't think it was your fault."

The soul-deep wounds in his eyes said otherwise. "I should have respected her fears and taken her with me."

She shook her head. "You were trying to make her *stronger*. You were protecting her in your own way. I know that because you've done it with me. You've pushed me when I needed to be pushed, forced me to face my fears. It's how you care."

His dark lashes swept across his cheeks. "I'm not telling you this to inspire your pity, I'm telling you so you understand me. *Us.* It was never about me still loving Lucia, Angelina. It was about me being consumed by guilt. Me not being able to forgive myself for what I'd done. Me never wanting to feel that pain again."

Hot tears ran down her cheeks. She brushed them away,

salt staining her mouth. Finally she understood what drove her husband. Finally she understood *him*. He'd lost the most important thing in his life to a senseless act that could not be explained so he had blamed it on himself instead because, in his mind, he could have prevented it.

She cupped his jaw in her hands. "You have to forgive yourself. You have to accept what happened was beyond your control or you—*we*—will never be whole."

He nodded. "I know that. Watching you walk away from me this week was a wake-up call. I thought I could outrun the past—the guilt. But having to face it or lose you, I realized that wishing I'd made different decisions, acknowledging I've made mistakes, is something apart from forgiveness. That maybe I need to forgive myself for being human. I think it might help me let go."

Her heart stretched with the force of what she felt for him. For the peace she hoped he would find now.

"And then there was you," he said quietly. "Admitting how I felt about you. How angry I still was with you. When you walked away from me the first time, I was just learning to trust, to love again. I *was* in love with you. But I wouldn't admit it—wouldn't allow myself to love you—because I didn't think you were a sure bet. When you left, you proved me right."

Her heart squeezed. "I should never have left. I should have worked through things with you."

He shook his head. "I think it needed to happen. You needed to grow up—to become who you've become. *I* needed to realize who that woman is—to appreciate her. Our timing was off."

Maybe he was right. Maybe it hadn't been their time. Maybe now was.

"Forgive me," he said, pressing his mouth to her temple. "I was a fool to let you walk away a second time... to say those things I didn't mean. If I don't have you, *mi amore,* I am nothing. I am a shell of a man, because you take a part of me with you every time you leave."

Her heart climbed into her throat. "Promise me you will always tell me when you're hurting. Promise me you will always be that open book you talked about and I will."

"Sì," he agreed, lowering his mouth to hers. "No more holding back."

He kissed her then. Passionate and never-ending, it was full of such bone-deep need, such *truth,* it reached inside her and wound its way around her heart, melting the last of the ice. She curled her fingers around the lapels of his jacket and hung on as every bit of the misery of the past week unraveled in the kiss and was swept away.

A sharp nip of her bottom lip brought her back to reality. "That," her husband remarked, "was for ignoring my phone calls this week."

"You deserved it."

"Yes," he agreed throatily, standing and sweeping her up in his arms, "I did. Allow me to demonstrate how very sorry I am."

He carried her through the shadowy penthouse to their bedroom. Dispensing with her dress, he set her on the bed. She watched as he stripped off his clothes, his body showcased to delicious advantage in the close-fitting black hipster briefs he favored.

His eyes turned a smoky black as he stripped them off and joined her on the bed. "You like what you see? Take it, *cara,* I'm all yours."

She straddled his beautiful, muscular body, emotion clogging her throat. "I've missed you," she murmured, leaning over to kiss him. "Nothing is right when I'm not with you. You are my heart, Lorenzo Ricci."

His kiss said the words back. Passionate, perfect, it was everything she knew they were going to be. Because now that they were an open book, now that they had exorcised their last ghost, anything was possible.

Breaking the kiss, she took him inside her slick heat. Gasped when he tilted his hips and filled her with his thick, hard length in a single thrust that stole her breath.

"You can't do it, can you? Let me take control?"

His dark eyes glittered. "You wouldn't have it any other way."

No…she wouldn't. Not in this particular arena.

She let herself drown in his black eyes as he made love to her slowly, languidly, telling her how much he loved her until their breath grew rough and they were both poised on the edge of a release that promised to be spectacular.

"Say it again," she murmured.

"What?"

"That you love me."

His mouth curved. *"Ti amo, angelo mio."*

I love you, my angel.

Her heart wove itself back together. "I love you, too, Lorenzo," she whispered back before he closed his hands around her hips and took her to heaven.

Her first love. Her only love. *Her forever love.*

EPILOGUE

"Papa!"

A squeal of delight from one of her girls was Angie's first hint that her husband had arrived home in time for the Carmichaels' annual winter party, just as he'd promised, after a week's trip to Italy.

Ready for a shower before the party, she slipped on a robe, tied it around her waist and walked to stand in the doorway of the adjoining bedroom. Her husband stood in jeans and a T-shirt, his bag abandoned, a giggling, excited daughter under each arm as their nanny looked on.

Abelie Lucia and Liliana Ines, their four-year-old identical twins, were playing their usual game.

"Lili," said Abelie, pressing a hand to her chest.

Lorenzo gave her a kiss and set her down. *"E, Abelie,"* he said, giving his other daughter a kiss.

The girls collapsed into gales of laughter. *"Mia Abelie,"* her oldest reproved, wrinkling her nose at her father.

"Ah, sì," Lorenzo said, keeping a straight face. "Silly me."

Her heart swelled, too big, it seemed, for her chest. The arrival of their daughters, the love the four of them shared, had changed her husband. The darkness was gone, replaced by a man who embraced the moment. There were still times when she could tell he was remembering, a sadness would come over him that would perhaps never leave him completely, but those times were few and far between.

"Festa?" Liliana said hopefully, turning her big blue eyes on her father.

"No. This party is for big people. But perhaps you can take your gift to bed with you."

Liliana spotted the brightly colored packages Lorenzo had left on the table. *"Regali,"* she crowed.

Lorenzo handed a package to each of them. Her chubby hands moving as fast as she could maneuver them, Liliana ripped open her gift to find a beautiful, dark-haired doll inside that looked exactly like her. Abelie did the same in a more sedate fashion, as was her personality, discovering an identical doll. A deliberate choice, Angie knew, to avoid the inevitable meltdown if one choice was more popular than another.

The girls oohed and aahed over their dolls. Angie observed her eldest's quieter admiration. It had been Angie's suggestion to name Abelie after Lucia. She'd wanted to honor her memory, to honor her husband's memories, to make it clear Lucia would never be forgotten. Lorenzo, in a very emotional acceptance, had agreed.

Abelie, sharp as a tack, noticed a third present on the table, wrapped in a different paper. *"Mamma?"* she asked.

"Sì."

"Can I open it now?"

Her husband turned to face her, a warm glint filling his dark eyes, the one he reserved exclusively for her. He picked up the gift, prowled toward her and bent and kissed her soundly. The girls devolved into another fit of giggles.

Lorenzo's mouth curved as he set her away from him. "Off to the bath," he commanded the girls. "I will come in and give you a kiss good-night when you're done."

"E bambole?" Abelie said.

"And your dolls," he agreed. "You," he said, handing the package to Angie, "put this on and meet me downstairs when you're ready. I need to find your brother before the guests arrive."

He was still giving orders, she noted. But tonight she didn't mind. She was too excited to have him home.

She showered while the girls had their bath, applied a light dusting of makeup in her dressing room and slipped on some naughty lingerie as a "welcome home" present for her husband. Opening his gift, she found a sparkly, beaded dress lying in the tissue, an Italian designer label attached.

Her heart contracted. She slid the dress over her head. The material settled over her curves in a whisper of silk, falling to just above her knee, its fit perfect. Exquisitely crafted, it hugged her body like a second skin, a plunging neckline offering a tantalizing glimpse of cleavage. *A very sexy dress.*

She left her hair loose as it had been that magical night she'd met her husband, slipped on high-heeled sandals and spritzed herself with perfume. After kissing the girls good-night, she made her way down the circular stairway to the main floor, the house ablaze with light and the chatter of hundreds of guests.

The Carmichael winter party, never an occasion to be missed, attracted friends and acquaintances from every corner of the globe. Tonight was no exception. Even the Bavaros were here, the two families having formed a close friendship.

Where before there would have been dread in her veins as she stepped out onto the terrace, a rejection of everything this represented, tonight there was only an allencompassing glow. Her mother was stable and happy. Four years sober, Angie was cautiously optimistic this time her mother would stay healthy. But she'd accepted it was beyond her control. She had her own family now and they were her priority.

She sought out her husband in the thick crowd. It didn't take long because he was exactly where she'd figured he would be—leaning against the bar at the far end of the pool where the band was playing.

Just that little bit aloof, more than a bit untouchable, he looked dazzling in a black tux, his hair slicked back from his face. Her breath caught in her chest. Would she always react to him this way? As if her world had turned on its axis?

She took the last few steps toward him, his dark gaze tracking her. Coming to a stop in front of him, she rested a hand on the bar and looked up into his arresting face. "That's an awfully serious look for a party."

The forbidding line of his mouth softened. "Maybe I'm a serious man."

"Maybe you should stop brooding," she suggested huskily, "and ask me to dance. Unless, of course, you intend on holding up that bar all night."

A sensual glitter entered his gaze. "I think that's an offer I can't refuse, Mrs. Ricci."

Reaching behind him, he produced two glasses of champagne. Glasses in their hands, they took to the dance floor, soaking up a perfect Bahamian night, the scent of a dozen tropical blooms in the air.

Eventually they drifted off into the gardens, majestic palm trees swaying overhead. "I do believe you have dishonorable intentions," she teased when her husband drew back and set her empty glass on the stone wall beside his.

"Certo," he agreed, a heated promise in his eyes. "But first I have something for you."

He slid his hand in his pocket and pulled out a ring. A platinum eternity band set with blazing canary yellow diamonds, it was jaw-droppingly beautiful.

She lifted her gaze to his, heart thumping in her chest. "A circle of fire," her husband murmured, eyes trained on hers. "What we are, Angelina. What you've always been to me. The woman who gave me my life back…the woman who has given me two beautiful daughters who remind me every day what love is."

Her stomach plunged. *Their anniversary!* She opened her mouth to apologize for forgetting, to tell him how crazy it had been with him away, but her husband shook his head, pressed his fingers to her lips.

"I know how you feel. I've always known how you feel. I want *you* to know what you are to me so there can be no doubt as to how I feel." He pressed her palm to his chest. "This is where you are, *mi amore*. Always here."

A lump in her throat grew until it was too big to get any words around it. She stood on tiptoe and kissed him instead. Passionate, reverential, it spoke of a million forevers.

They danced under the stars then, the party forgotten, a brilliant blanket of light their only witness.

Sometimes you caught the elusive corporate raider. Sometimes you even captured his heart.

* * * * *

A DANGEROUSLY
SEXY SECRET

STEFANIE LONDON

To Dad,
for all the important lessons you taught me.
For pushing me to be a good student.
For fostering my creativity.
And for sitting through all my ballet
concerts. I know they were really long.

1

WREN LIVINGSTON COULD MULTITASK, there was no doubt about it. But carrying four bags of groceries while walking up a flight of stairs in a maxi skirt *and* trying to deflect sisterly guilt was pushing it. Even for her.

Add to the mix the fact that her new and insanely hot next-door neighbor was coming down the hallway toward her, and Wren was at her limit. How was one supposed to carry on a normal conversation with all those muscles staring back at you? Impossible.

"Sis?" Debbie whined on the other end of the phone. "Are you even listening to me?"

"Uh-huh." Wren watched as the guy stopped in front of her, his pearly smile gleaming bright against warm brown skin. The black tail of his headphones curved up from an armband sitting snugly over his biceps.

Oh yeah, muscles… Had she mentioned them? He had a lot.

"Can I give you a hand with those bags?" he asked, pulling one bud from his ear.

He must have been about to go for a run, if the gray shorts and navy cotton tank were anything to go on. The fabric hugged a solid chest and caught her eye, drawing her attention up until she set her sights on a sharp jaw, broad nose and sparkling warm brown eyes.

Sweet mother of…

"Oh." She shook her head, cheeks fiery hot as she realized she must have been gaping at him. "No, I'm fine. Very fine. I mean…uhh…thank you."

"You sure?"

"Absolutely sure. One hundred percent." A nervous giggle bubbled up in her throat that she tried to tamp down—and failed. The fizzy sound burst out and she cringed.

Total brain cell destruction in three, two, one…

"Okay, then." His voice was rich and deep, smooth like satin sheets.

He stuck the bud back into his ear and gave her space to shuffle awkwardly past him in the tight hallway. Her shopping bags knocked against the wall and she almost tripped on the sweeping hem of her skirt.

Can you at least stay upright for the next three minutes so you don't embarrass yourself? You're walking like a drunk llama.

She told herself not to turn around and look back at him. But she couldn't resist. Her mouth dried up when her gaze landed on the wide expanse of his shoulders as he jogged down the stairs.

"What was *that* all about?" Debbie asked, and Wren realized her sister was still on the phone. "Since when do you giggle like a little girl?"

"It's nothing." She wedged the phone between her ear and shoulder as she reached the front door of her new apartment. "Nothing at all."

Let's keep it at nothing—you're not here to ogle men.

Her arm ached from carrying all the shopping bags in one hand, the burn in her muscles getting hotter as she fumbled for her keys. Sweat beaded at her hairline. What in the world had possessed her to move into a building with no elevator?

"Didn't sound like nothing."

"Debbie…" Wren sighed as she pushed the door open with a grunt. "It was just my neighbor."

"What's he like?"

Delicious. The word sprang to her mind immediately. The guy from apartment 401 was definitely all that and a bag of chips, as her old boss used to say. So far she hadn't done more than return his friendly hellos and now turn down his offer of help in a most embarrassing way. But she'd be lying if she said he hadn't made an appearance in one—okay, two…at least—dirty dreams.

"He seems nice. Friendly." She let out a silent gasp of relief as she set the bags on the kitchen counter. "Same as everyone else here."

"And where is *here*, exactly?" Debbie's tone was sharp. "You still haven't told me where you're staying."

"I'm in New York."

"New York is a big place. How about you narrow it down to a borough for me?"

Her sister was exactly the kind of person who would show up on her doorstep, wanting to "help" and be part of the action. But Debbie, while she was a great person and the shining star of the Livingston family, was not exactly street smart. Or subtle.

"I don't want anyone else getting involved." She turned and sagged back against the counter, pushing her hair from her eyes.

"*You* shouldn't be involved," her sister huffed.

Maybe. But her best friend, Kylie, had been attacked and she refused to talk about it.

Wren had a strong suspicion the incident had something to do with the gallery where Kylie had been working because anytime Wren mentioned it, Kylie went white as a ghost.

Originally they had both applied for the gallery internship, but only Kylie had been successful in gaining one of the coveted spots. Then, after she returned home, the gallery's owner had called Wren to offer her Kylie's old spot. Seems she'd been next in line.

And just like that, Wren had packed her bags and moved to New York.

"I still can't believe you've gone on this vigilante mission," Debbie continued. "Now *I* have to miss out on seeing my sister because you've once again taken on other people's problems. I can't even send you a goddamn Christmas card."

"It's not even June yet. Christmas is ages away and things will be back to normal by then… I promise." She spoke the words with way more confidence than she felt. "As for Kylie—"

"I'll look after her, I promise." Debbie sighed. "Although I have no idea how I'm supposed to keep dodging her questions about where you've run off to. She knows something's up."

"We stick to the story—I'm away at an art retreat and they have a no-cell-phone policy, so she can't call. But I'll email her when I can. No one else needs to know what I'm doing, got it?"

Debbie grumbled her agreement. They lived in a small town where information had a way of traveling at the speed of light. The only reason she'd revealed more of her plan to Debbie was because her sister had caught her booking a flight to New York after she'd said the retreat was in California.

"If I get in trouble here I don't want to drag anyone else into my problems."

"Don't you mean *Kylie's* problems?"

"Come on, Deb." She sighed. "Kylie is like our sister. I *have* to find out what happened to her. Anyway, my reputation is already ruined at home… What do I have to lose by trying to do something good for a friend?"

"Your reputation is not ruined. A few uptight old biddies think you're a bit wild, so what?"

"They called me a sexual deviant." Her humiliation still burned as brightly as a newly lit flame. "And a blight on their community."

"It's not true. You've helped out so many families at the community center, you've painted faces at the summer fair," Debbie said, and Wren could practically see her sister ticking the items off her perfectly manicured fingers the way she always did when she was mad. "You've made cupcakes for almost every bake sale and your stuff is *always* the first to sell out, you've—"

"Enough." She drew a deep breath and closed her eyes for a moment. Never in her life would she admit how much it hurt that Charity Springs had ostracized her, and hearing her sister point out all she'd done was only making it worse.

She may not be the biggest fan of the small town—or its residents—but it was still her home.

"Debs, please. Can we not rehash this again? I know you're upset with me for leaving and I'm sorry. But I need to do this."

"You 'need' to run around fixing other people's problems, do you? All right, I guess you do." It was as close to acceptance as Wren was going to get, so she'd take it. "What are you supposed to do, spend your days playing spy?"

"I'm working at a gallery and I'm painting. It's not exactly a hard life." She didn't bother to mention the recon activities she was planning, like trying to break into her new boss's email account.

Details. You're doing the right thing by your friend— that's all that matters.

Debbie made a scoffing sound on the other end of the line. "You're so full of shit."

"And you swear way too much for a girl who's going to be an upstanding pillar of society." Wren began to unpack her groceries. Flour for her pizza base, some fresh kale, tomatoes, basil and a delicious-looking knob of buffalo mozzarella.

"Upstanding pillar of society?" Debbie snorted. "Spare me. And I've noticed that your little list of activities doesn't involve screwing your hot neighbor."

Heat crawled up Wren's cheeks. Thank God she'd decided not to video chat with her sister, because she was sure her face would be flaming tomato red right about now. "I never mentioned he was hot."

"That heavy breathing did all the talking for you." Her sister cackled. "Not to mention the fact that you seemed to forget how to string a sentence together as soon as he came near you."

Usually, she didn't engage in her sister's teasing, but right now she was grateful that the conversation had turned away from her secret mission. "Okay, he's good-looking. So what? That's not reason enough for me to sleep with him."

"Isn't it? When was the last time you got laid? And if you tell me that you haven't had sex since you broke up with Christian, so help me…"

For someone who was supposedly a "sexual deviant," she'd actually been quite conservative when it came to sex. There'd been no one in the six months since she'd broken up with her ex—because now all the men in town either thought she was easy or bad news. Neither of which was true.

Sucking on her lower lip, she concentrated on continuing to unpack the groceries. Milk, eggs, butter, vanilla extract.

"Wren?"

A spring-form pan, parchment paper, confectioners' sugar. "Yeah?"

"Really?"

"You said not to tell you if I hadn't…"

"Are you serious?"

"The only guys interested in me now are the ones I don't want." She slammed the box of granola down on the counter harder than necessary. "And I'm not ready to try opening up to anyone else, not after the way Christian humiliated me."

"You're never going to be ready until you take a risk. You have to put yourself out there. Listen to me, I'm a doctor."

Wren gritted her teeth. "First, you don't get to say you're a doctor until you finish med school. Second, why do you care so much about my sex life?"

"Because you're my sister and you deserve to *have* a sex life. You're twenty-six, for crying out loud, not a hundred and six. But if you don't get some action your vagina will dry up like an old prune."

Despite herself, Wren let out a burst of laughter.

"It's a fact. A *medical* fact. Trust me, I'm a doctor." This time Debbie said the words through her own giggles. "Do you want a pruney va—"

"Shut up." Wren shook her head and bundled up the empty plastic bags. "I'm not having sex with the first guy I see just for the sake of it."

"Seriously, you need to stop hiding away because a few people said bad, *untrue* things. You deserve to live a full life. Orgasms included."

"How do you know my neighbor will be good enough to give me orgasms?" Flashes of her dream from last night came back to her—Mr. 401's large hands roaming her body, his full, wide mouth covering her breasts.

Dammit. It wasn't right to fantasize about a guy without knowing his name.

"Judging by the crazy way you were giggling, I think he will." Debbie sounded smug as hell, the evil little thing. "Trust me, you won't regret it. Sex is a very natural and healthy part of life. It's good for your brain and your heart. You're really doing your health a disservice by *not* having sex."

"Is that another medical fact?" She grinned in spite of herself and shook her head. Her sister knew exactly how to push her buttons and get under her skin, but they always looked out for each other. No matter what.

"Yep, I'm sure it's in one of my textbooks. I have to go. I've got a study session planned and the last person there has to buy coffee." She paused. "I miss you, Birdie."

At the sound of her childhood nickname, Wren smiled. "I miss you, too. I'll be home soon. I promise."

"You'd better."

She hung up the phone and steadied herself against

the countertop. Debbie had a point. Her life had been filled with nothing but stress the last few months; maybe it wouldn't be so bad to live a little.

So long as living doesn't involve any promises or commitment. You're done with that crap!

Totally done. She'd trusted her ex, had even flirted with the idea of getting hitched in the late darkness of night when she'd curled up against him. But it turned out that she hadn't really known him at all…and he clearly hadn't known her.

She wouldn't put herself in a position to be ripped apart like that again. But she could still have some fun… right?

Wren drew a knife from the wooden block next to her stove and placed it on her cutting board. She didn't have to make any decisions right now. She would be in New York for at least a month, so she could take her time. Maybe talk to Mr. 401 a little more before she made a move.

But first she had a pizza to make; she wasn't in the habit of doing any serious thinking on an empty stomach.

RHYS GLOVER ROUNDED the last corner of his run, dodging a couple with linked arms as he pounded his feet into the pavement. He loved nothing more than getting fresh air on the weekend, be it running, biking or otherwise. He put long hours into his job—which he wouldn't trade for anything—but it didn't exactly make for an active or healthy lifestyle during the week.

So Saturdays and Sundays were all about getting out of the house. Getting his blood pumping and his heart racing. Getting his sweat on.

*You might be able to do a few of those things indoors
if you had the stones to ask Blondie on a date.*

He shook his head as he slowed to a stop in front of
his walk-up, detouring to collect his mail. Blondie—
aka the smoking-hot fox who'd recently moved into the
apartment across from him—occupied far too much of
his headspace lately. But, try as he might to evict her
image from his mind, the waist-length hair that shimmered like spun gold and those long limbs tempted him
beyond belief. Rhys prided himself on being a man of
solid self-control, but one glance at her and he was as
horny as a teenager.

Chiding himself, he shoved the key into his box. A
small stack of letters sat inside, mostly bills. A bright blue
envelope caught his attention. It bore his stepbrother's
neat, utilitarian print and the childish scrawl of his niece.
A happy face decorated one corner. They insisted on
sending him a real birthday card, even when he told
them he was happy with an email or phone call. A wave
of jealousy ghosted through him.

It wasn't fair to resent his stepbrother, Marc, for the
perfect, happy life he'd been gifted. But it was hard not
to compare. Or compete. They were the same age and
had grown up together as best friends before their parents
had gotten hitched. He'd always envied how easily everything came to Marc—grades, girls, sports. *Everything.*

And now, as adults, Marc still had the edge. He'd
given their parents two grandchildren and he had a beautiful wife whom he adored. Marc often joked that he envied Rhys his bachelor lifestyle, but Rhys didn't believe
it for a second.

Rhys knew part of the reason he felt compelled to
settle down was because it was the one thing Marc had

over him. In their parents' eyes, he'd achieved the dream. Happy wife, two healthy kids…and Rhys was still lagging behind, as always.

But it was hard to have a relationship when he didn't even put himself out there. He was just too busy with work to meet people.

"You don't even know if Blondie's single," he muttered to himself as he started up the stairs.

But she hadn't looked at him the way a woman in a committed relationship would when they'd almost bumped into one another earlier.

The pink blush that had crept into her cheeks had done crazy things to him. The kind of crazy things that were not so easily concealed in a pair of running shorts.

The fourth floor was deserted, and Rhys couldn't stop himself from glancing at number 402 as he walked up to the door of his own apartment. Maybe he should formally introduce himself? It would be the neighborly thing to do.

He glanced down at his sweat-soaked tank and shorts. It might be the neighborly thing to do, but he wasn't exactly going to make a great impression if he knocked on her door smelling like a locker room.

Tomorrow.

Satisfied that he'd committed himself to an action, he pushed open the door to his apartment with his free hand. Toeing off his sneakers, he hung his keys on their designated hook and placed the letters into the inbox he kept on the bureau near his desk. All except the blue envelope, which he tore open as he walked into the living area.

Inside the brightly decorated, homemade card—which looked like an insane craft teacher had thrown up all over it—were messages from his stepbrother and sister-in-law, his eldest niece and a proxy message from the little one. They'd even drawn on a paw print to represent the dog.

He put the card on his entertainment unit, next to his new fancy universal remote—the birthday present he'd gifted himself since his family didn't really get his love of technology. The card looked totally out of place in what Marc jokingly referred to as "the computer nerd's bachelor pad."

By the time he reached the bathroom he was itching to get out of his workout clothes. He pulled off the soaked cotton. A light ache had spread through his muscles, a sign he'd pushed himself hard today and he'd need to spend some time on the foam roller to ease out the knots.

He'd been tighter than usual the last few weeks. Stress, his trainer had said. Lack of stretching, according to the remedial masseuse. Working too hard, his buddies at the security company admonished. But he knew it wasn't any of those things.

Dissatisfaction. A lack of purpose. He'd felt it burrowing slowly under his skin, creating an incurable itch that niggled at him in the quiet portions of his day. In the dead of night. In the dark corners of his dreams.

He shook off the troubling thought and stepped under the running water, sighing as warmth seeped into him. As he lathered up, the scent of soap filled his nostrils. Perhaps it might be a good idea to put himself out there again. After all, his life couldn't be *all* work and no play.

Tomorrow.

The promise rolled around in his mind, and just like that Blondie popped back into his head, soothing all his worries away. God, she was gorgeous. Fair skin and rich golden hair, bright blue eyes. And perky breasts that seemed to often be uninhibited by a bra. This morning he'd noticed the way the pert mounds moved beneath her white tank top, the stiff little peaks of her nipples pressing forward against the fabric.

He was hard as stone just thinking about it. He wondered if those nipples would be golden like the rest of her, or would they be rosy and pink? Would she have a dusting of hair between her legs or smooth, silky skin?

He'd gone way too long without sex and now all the carnal thoughts had piled up like traffic on a highway. But a knocking sound snapped him out of the fog of arousal. He rinsed off the last of the soap suds and shut off the water. Another sharp knock rang through the apartment.

"Hang on!" he called out as he wrapped a soft gray towel around his waist, knotting it to conceal the still-raging erection he was sporting.

His wet feet skidded on the floorboards as he hurried to the door. Who on earth would be dropping by without calling first?

Grasping the knob, he pulled the door open and was greeted with the very object of his fantasies. *Blondie.*

There she was in all her golden glory, long hair tangling around her shoulders and spilling down her body. Eyes wide and blue and bright. It wasn't until he saw the wad of blood-soaked tissue in her hands that he realized something was wrong.

2

"Uh…hi," HE SAID, his eyes darting down to her hands and widening.

Crap. This was really not how Wren had imagined their first conversation would go. Especially not after Debbie had gotten the idea of having sex into her head. But he *was* topless, and boy, oh boy, had her dreams failed to do his body justice. His muscles had muscles of their own, and the gray towel he'd knotted at his waist hid very little. A spark of arousal flared low in her belly.

"You're bleeding," he said, his eyebrows crinkled.

"Oh yes. I, uh…cut myself." A nervous laugh bubbled up in her throat but she pushed it down. No need to do anything else to convince him that she had a screw loose. "I don't have any bandages in my house and I was wondering—"

"Of course. Come in." He held the door and let it swing shut behind her. "Let me grab my first-aid kit."

"Thank you." Only then did the throbbing pain start to push through her giddy state. "I'm sorry I interrupted your shower. I should have thought to buy some bandages at the grocery store today."

But, as usual, she'd gone without a list. Or without any idea of what she needed or wanted to buy. Wren usually let the ingredients inspire her as she shopped—allowing her to make up her dinner menu on the fly—and that meant that important purchases like bandages and anti-septic lotions were often forgotten.

He pulled a small white tin down from the top of his refrigerator and opened it up. The inside was neat and tidy, like a perfect Tetris arrangement of adulthood. Band-Aids, antiseptic wipes, burn lotion, cotton balls and gauze bandages all neatly packed in a way that made her feel slightly inadequate.

"Show me." He held out his hand and she gingerly removed the wadded-up kitchen towel.

Blood immediately pooled in the slice along her palm, trailing along the crease in her skin and rushing toward the edge of her hand. She dabbed at it, but the paper was soaked through.

"Let's get that hand under some running water." He led her to the bathroom sink, her skin sparking at the comforting way he touched her arm. "You've done a number on yourself. Thankfully, it doesn't look too deep. You shouldn't need stitches."

He held her hand under the running tap, the blood washing over her fingers and staining the water pink before it swirled down the drain. In the confines of the small room—which mirrored her own except for the simple gray shower curtain that hung in place of her own chaotic rainbow version—he was incredibly close. The scent of soap on his skin filled her nostrils and made her giddy.

"Are you okay?" he asked as he pulled her hand out

from under the water to inspect the cut. "You're not going to faint, are you?"

"No." She shook her head. Thankfully, she could blame the wooziness on the blood—although the truth was it didn't bother her in the slightest. She'd never been the squeamish sort. "I'm fine."

Mr. 401 disappeared for a moment and returned with the necessary first-aid items. Within moments, she was patched up and almost as good as new.

"Thank you so much, uh…"

"Rhys." He stuck out his hand and she shook it as best she could with her injury.

"Rhys," she repeated, weighing the name in her mouth. It suited him—strong, masculine. Direct. "I'm Wren."

"The pleasure's all mine, Wren."

She inspected the expertly applied bandage. "You've done that before, haven't you?"

"I do a little downhill mountain biking. Cuts and scrapes come with the territory." When he smiled Wren felt like she was staring directly into the sun.

"Well. I'm very grateful you're so prepared."

"You make me sound like a Boy Scout." His honey-brown eyes twinkled.

Judging by the way her mouth had run dry and her heart galloped in her chest, Boy Scout was the last thing she would compare him to. Man Scout wasn't a thing… was it?

"That doesn't seem to fit you," she said, shocking herself with the flirty tone that came out of her mouth. God, if she didn't watch herself she'd be twirling her hair around her finger and batting her eyelashes like some giddy schoolgirl.

Get a grip, Livingston. He's just a man...a hunky, incredibly well-defined, thrilling man.

He chuckled, the low sound rumbling deep as thunder. It made her skin tingle. "What gives you that impression?"

"Boy Scouts don't usually have six-packs, do they?" Her tongue darted out involuntarily to moisten her lips.

What alien had taken over her body?

He didn't seem in the least bit self-conscious of his near-naked state. Wren, on the other hand, might as well have been in her birthday suit for how exposed she felt. Funny, since the naked form appeared often in her artwork...but this didn't compare with brushstrokes on a canvas. He was far too real, far too alight with sexual energy.

His eyes swept over her with a languid slowness, smoothing over her hips and breasts and hair. "No, I guess they don't."

"Can I offer you some dinner?" she blurted out. "I was making pizza when I cut myself and I'd like to thank you for coming to the rescue."

"There's no need to thank me. That's what neighbors are for, right?"

At that moment she kind of hoped neighbors were for wild, hot, no-strings sex. "Please. I'm new and I'd love to have a friend in the building."

"Well, when you put it that way." He grinned and Wren was quite sure her panties were about to melt into a puddle at her feet. "I'd love to. Give me a few minutes to change and I'll come over."

"I'll see you when you're ready." She returned his smile and headed back toward the front door, forcing herself not to bounce up and down with pent-up excitement.

It's just a dinner, you goof. A friendly, neighborly meal between two adults. It doesn't have to lead to orgasms.

But the throbbing between her legs would mark her a liar if she said she wasn't already fantasizing about it. Rhys showed her out, his broad shoulders blocking the door frame as he waited for her to make it back inside her apartment. She risked a glance behind her as she stepped inside and he was still there, the heat in his gaze unmistakable.

A tremor ran through her, excitement and fear mixing in a strange, delicious medley of emotion. The fact that her body was reacting so strongly was a good sign. After what had happened in her hometown, the very thought of sex or nakedness had filled her with guilt and shame.

But now her blood was pumping through her veins hard and fast, her heart fluttering with anticipation. Tonight, she was going to shake off the past and have a little fun.

RHYS CONSIDERED HIMSELF a logical guy. Computers were his world and binary made him feel comfortable. Even the one-two pound of running appealed to his logical side. But right now a little part of him was enjoying the thrill of a situation outside his control.

And things *could* go wrong if he slept with Wren and it didn't work out. They'd have to face each other in the hallway each day, making politely awkward small talk. There'd be guaranteed cringe-worthy moments if either one of them ever brought a date home and the other happened to see. The old Italian lady in 403 was also a huge gossip. Plus, there was a possibility that they wouldn't be compatible in the bedroom.

"Who are you kidding, man?" he muttered to himself as he whipped off his towel and proceeded to get dressed. "There's no way you have chemistry like that without it transferring to the bedroom."

And, if his still-aching erection was anything to go on, his body wholeheartedly agreed. Besides, the only way he'd ever have the chance of finding the right woman was if he actually went on dates. And dinner counted as a date…didn't it?

He pulled a fresh T-shirt over his head and fished out a pair of black boxer briefs from his bedside drawer. By the time he'd added jeans and sneakers to the mix, he'd also decided to take a bottle of wine with him.

When he knocked on her door, a thrill ran through him at the thought of seeing her again. Reality didn't disappoint. She opened the door with a flourish and a tinkling laugh. Long blond waves tumbled over one shoulder, and she'd thrown an apron over her white tank and floor-length flowy skirt.

"Welcome to my humble abode," she said, gesturing with a pair of tongs like a grand magician. "It's a little sparse at the moment. But I can assure you my pizza will make up for it."

"I have no doubt." He stepped in and took in the surroundings, placing the wine down on the kitchen counter as she grabbed two glasses.

She hadn't been kidding about it being sparse. Other than a small table with two chairs, a battered couch and an overturned cardboard box acting as a coffee table, the room was empty. He'd expected to at least see boxes with her belongings dotted around, but there wasn't a single one in sight.

"It's very…minimalist," Wren said. She poured the wine and handed him a glass, holding her own out so they could clink them together.

The wine was good, not too sweet and not too dry. The flavor danced on his tongue, and he wondered what it would taste like on her lips. Her tongue. The fantasy rushed up, tracking along his muscles until his whole body felt coiled and tight.

This is what happens when you leave it too long between drinks.

"I'm not sure how long I'll be staying," she said. "So I didn't want to waste money on getting lots of furniture."

Disappointment stabbed at him, but he brushed the feeling aside. There was no sense worrying about the future of their relationship when they hadn't even had one meal together. "Not sure if you're a fan of New York yet?"

"It's more that I'm not a fan of long-term decisions."

He cleared his throat. "Where did you move from?"

"Somewhere you've probably never heard of." She stuck the tongs in a large silver bowl filled with a colorful salad. "I'm a small-town girl."

"Living in a lonely world?" he quipped.

She grinned. "I appreciate a man who knows his Journey lyrics. Sadly, my life is far less fabulous than the song would have you believe."

"Is that why you moved to New York?" He leaned against the counter and inhaled the aromas of their dinner. Fresh basil, melting cheese, a hint of something spicy.

"I'm here for work." Her answer was carefully worded. Guarded. "But it's not a permanent position, which suits me fine."

Message received, loud and clear.

But he still wanted to get to know her better, even with her line in the sand. Perhaps "not permanent" was exactly what he needed right now. No pressure, no expectations. Like a dry run for reentering the dating world.

He could always come back to his life plan later.

"Are you a New York native?" she asked.

"I moved from Connecticut a few years ago. I've always wanted to live here, enjoy the bright lights and all that."

"Do you like it?" She whisked the salad dressing in a bowl, then plucked a teaspoon from a drawer to do a taste test.

"I do. Especially when I have such interesting neighbors."

She smiled, her cheeks flushing a vibrant shade of rose pink. "You mean clumsy neighbors who can't figure out how to slice an avocado without hurting themselves?"

"Same, same."

She moved about the kitchen with ease, her long skirt swirling around her feet with each dance-like step. There was an airiness to her, a whimsy that was so different from the serious women he was usually attracted to. She bent to open the oven and heat wafted up into the air, carrying with it the scent of her cooking.

"That smells incredible." His mouth was already watering, and he'd had some of the best pizza in all of New York. "Don't tell me you're a professional chef."

"No, just an amateur one. But I did make the base from scratch." She slid on an oven mitt and pulled out the tray containing their dinner. "I really enjoy cooking. It relaxes me…well, when I'm not cutting myself."

"Tell me that doesn't happen too often."

"Thankfully it *is* a rare occurrence." She placed the tray down on the stove and Rhys could see she was relying on her uninjured hand to hold the weight.

"Do you need a hand slicing it up?"

"No, I'll be fine. If you could take the wine to the table, that would be great."

Moments later they were seated, steaming slices of pizza resting on large white plates in front of them. But the way Wren looked at him made him hungry for something else. A sensual smile curved on her lips.

"Eat up," she said, gesturing with her hands. "It's best when it's hot."

"I like it hot," he said, picking up the slice and blowing at the steam shimmering off the pizza's surface.

"I can see that."

"Are you flirting with me?" He bit into the pizza and moaned as the hot, cheesy goodness hit his tongue.

"What if I was?" She took a bite of her slice and flicked her tongue out to catch a stray droplet of sauce. "Are you open to a little neighborly flirting?"

She folded both of her feet under her so that she sat cross-legged on top of the chair, tangling the frothy layers of her skirt around her legs. Realizing that she was still wearing her apron, she reached behind herself and untied it. As she pulled the apron over her head, her tank top rode up, revealing a slice of lightly tanned skin and smooth, flat belly.

She scrambled to tug the fabric back down, her cheeks flushing, but Rhys carried on the conversation, pretending he hadn't almost choked on his pizza. "Flirting is fine by me. In fact, I've been looking for someone to practice my flirting skills on."

"Is that so?" She reached for her wine. "Are you a little rusty?"

"That's for you to judge."

"Go on, hit me with your best pickup line." Her eyes sparkled and a smile twitched on her lips.

This was about to go downhill. Fast. Pickup lines weren't really his style. In fact, he excelled at meeting women in unconventional ways…like having them turn up at his apartment, bleeding.

He shook his head, laughing, as he took another bite out of his pizza. "I prefer a more casual approach."

She planted her fists on her waist and flapped her elbows up and down. "Buck, buck, buck."

"You did *not* just call me chicken." Damn, the girl had sass.

"Let me hear your line, then." She grinned.

"Oh, you're on." He reached his arms above his head, making a show of stretching his neck from side to side. Her eyes skated over him, wide and stormy. "I don't have a library card, but do you mind if I check you out?"

"No!" She roared, throwing her head back and letting out a burst of laughter that was belly deep and totally disarming. Totally and richly at odds with the rest of her dainty, fairylike appearance. "That's terrible."

"Are you a fruit, because honeydew you know how fine you look right now?"

She gasped. "I didn't think it could get worse—"

"Are you a parking ticket? 'Cause you've got *fine* written all over you."

"Please." She held up a hand, her shoulders heaving as laughter spilled out of her. The sound warmed him from the inside out. "Stop."

"Your body is sixty-five percent water and I'm thirsty."

He pretended to brush the dirt off his shoulders. "I could go all night."

"Okay, okay. You win." She clapped her hands together and bowed. "You are the king of the worst pickup lines I have ever had the misfortune of hearing."

"Don't say I didn't warn you."

"Fair. I promise to listen to you next time." She drained the rest of her wine and immediately topped them both up. "I'm curious now. How do you usually pick up women?"

"I'm a bit out of practice." He figured honesty was the best policy. Besides, the last thing he wanted to do was talk about the sad state of his love life right now.

"Me, too." She nodded to herself. "Looks like we're in the same boat."

Over the course of the next hour they finished the whole pizza and made a start on another bottle of wine. A delicious and languid feeling spread through him, loosening his limbs and his tongue. Maybe it was her incredible cooking, the good drink or some combination, but he couldn't remember the last time he'd felt as connected to another person as he did with Wren.

She unwound her legs and untangled her skirt, stretching her arms back and thrusting her breasts forward. His mouth watered as the fabric stretched, making it sheer enough that he could see the shadow of her nipples through the fabric.

Nope, that woman did not need to wear a bra at all.

"THANKS FOR SHARING the pizza with me," she said, trying to sound casual. "I get a little excited when I cook and I always end up with way too much."

"I'm open to helping you deal with any leftovers that

might come up." Rhys flashed another pearly white smile and Wren wondered how many times that smile had drawn women to him. "But let me at least do the dishes."

"No way. You saved me from bleeding all over the building, trying to find bandages." She held up a hand. "Dinner was my treat. The dishes can wait."

"Well, thank you. It was delicious. You sure you're really not a chef?"

"No, I'm an artist." The words slipped out and brought with them an immediate sense of guilt. "Well, what I mean to say is that I work in a gallery."

"That's not what you said." His dark eyes scanned her face, curiosity obviously piqued. "You called yourself an artist."

Shit. She'd been so desperate to have that title for so many years that clearly the idea still floated around in her brain like a piece of flotsam waiting to trip her up. Being an artist was no longer her dream. And after she finished using her art as a cover to find out what happened to Kylie, it would be out of her life for good.

"I dabble," she said eventually, waving a hand as if to dismiss the idea.

"What sort of art?"

She swallowed against the lump in her throat. "Painting."

"I'm always fascinated by artists. I look at a painting and have no clue how the inspiration would have come to them, or how they would even know where to start." He shook his head in wonderment and it was like a knife twisting in her chest.

Years of her life had been devoted to the inspiration that had clogged her head. More years had been spent perfecting her technique, channeling her passion. Years that were now a total waste.

"What do you do?" she asked, desperate to steer the conversation away from the part of her life she wanted to leave behind.

"I'm in IT for a security company. It's like getting to solve a giant puzzle every day." He laughed. "Nerdy but true."

"People keep telling me that nerds will rule the world one day, if they don't already."

"I guess you could say that." Darkness flickered across his face before the smile returned, bringing a cheeky glint to his eye. "I don't suppose you want to show me any of your paintings? If they're half as good as your pizza, I'm betting you'll be the next Picasso."

"I don't know about that," she said, knotting her hands in her lap.

"About being Picasso or about showing me your work?"

Part of her balked at the idea of showing him her art—of showing *anyone* her art—but his face was totally earnest. His interest in her work appeared genuine, and besides, what harm could it do?

This is New York, not some tiny hick town that thinks a woman's body is a product of the devil.

"I'm no Picasso, let's be clear about that." She pushed up from her chair and motioned for him to follow. "Come on, my work space is through here."

Rhys's presence filled the air around her as they walked, his steps mirroring her own. He said nothing as she pushed open the door to her bedroom. Her mattress rested on the floor since she hadn't bought a bed frame yet. The quilt she'd been using as her duvet was draped over it, creating a white puddle of fabric around the edges of the mattress.

Early evening light filtered into the room, highlighting the stack of canvases that she'd leaned against the wall. She'd brought ten in total. Eight complete and two works in progress—though she hadn't touched a brush to them in over six months.

The canvases had been a requirement for the portfolio portion of her interview at Ainslie Ave, the gallery where she now worked as an assistant and acted as a mentee slash intern to Sean Ainslie himself.

"These are just experiments," she said, reaching for the first two in the stack. One was a vivid fall landscape and the other depicted a young student hunched over a writing desk. She'd modelled the girl on her sister, painting her long blond locks in wild swirling strokes, mimicking the fury of the student's pen scratching across paper. "They're nothing special."

"Do you really think that?" His eyes never left the paintings. They darted and scanned as though he was committing the images to memory. She watched for some sign of judgment, but he simply stared at the paintings in a way that felt fiercely intimate.

And terrifying.

"This one was from my abstract phase," she said, brushing off his question. The third canvas was a garden, but to the untrained eye the angular swipes of green paint could be anything at all.

A swamp monster, perhaps.

"And this one was a gift for my mom."

Her mother had a thing for roses and her garden back home was filled with them. Wren had painted her a small canvas for their guest room. It showed a single American Beauty bloom, just like the flower that had won her mother first place in the county fair a few years back. It'd hung on the wall until Wren had sneaked it out one night after "the incident." Nobody seemed to have noticed its absence.

"You're very talented," Rhys said, his gaze finally traveling back to her. "You've been blessed with some creative hands."

"I'm sure my parents would rather I'd been blessed with a head for numbers." The words came out stinging with truth. "My sister is going to be a doctor, so by comparison art is probably not the job they would have chosen for me."

"But you're working in a gallery, too?"

Wren dropped down onto the floor and sat cross-legged. After a moment, Rhys followed her. The rest of her canvases sat against the wall, facing away from them like a group of children who'd been sent to the naughty corner.

"Yeah, I'm an assistant for an artist who has his own gallery. I organize his appointments and manage his calendar. I also greet people who come to meet him at the gallery." She toyed with the end of her long silk skirt, twisting the fabric around on itself. "Then I get to paint in his studio and he gives me critiques and tips. Plus, I learn about how the gallery is run and get to watch him with potential buyers. Stuff like that."

"And you think you're not an artist," Rhys scoffed.

Con artist, maybe.

"It sounds weird to call myself that." She shrugged. "I guess it's a leftover doubt from my family always nagging me to get a real job and work in an office. Like you."

"Working in an office does not mean you've made it

in life." He leaned back on his forearms and surveyed the room. "Trust me."

His large form was so appealing laid out that way, a dessert for her eyes. All that sculpted muscle and sexual magnetism made her body thrum. And here he was, on her floor right in front of her. A gift for the taking.

Debs's words floated around in her head: *You won't regret it. Sex is a very natural and healthy part of life.*

She'd tried to enjoy sex with Christian, but it had been very repetitive. Her ex had only ever wanted to be on top and had complained when Wren had suggested they try other things. It was something he'd thrown back in her face when he'd discovered her secret paintings.

But something deep down told her that Rhys would be different. That *being* with Rhys would be different.

"You're looking at me very intently, Wren." His lips wrapped around her name in the most delicious way.

"I am." Tension built inside her, filling her chest and stealing her breath. "Is that a problem?"

"No problem. I was only wondering if you're planning on making a move."

Was she? Shit. She'd told herself she had time to get to know him before she acted on her attraction, and then she'd cut herself. Now they were here. And she desperately wanted to find out if her theories about him were true.

"If you're not…" His brown eyes were lit with fire. "I will."

Please. Please, please, please.

She opened her mouth to respond when a crash shattered the quiet, halting her words. The stack of paintings behind Rhys had slipped, put out of balance by her removing the heavier ones that had been holding them in place.

"I'll get them." She scrambled to her feet in an attempt to prevent him from getting there first, but she accidentally leaned on her injured hand.

"It's fine, I've got it." He reached for the paintings, his frame stilling suddenly.

Wren's face filled with heat. She didn't need to guess which painting he'd discovered.

"Wow." The word was so filled with shock that it made her stomach twist into a knot. "This is…"

"I wasn't going to show you that one." She walked over to the pile and started replacing them against the wall, flames licking her cheeks.

He held the painting in his hand—the one that had been the cause of her troubles back home and, most ironically, the one she secretly thought of as her best. It was of a woman, her legs open and her head thrown back in ecstasy. Eyes closed. Lips slack.

The shades of pink and red and brown blended together, raw and earthy. It was intensely sexual, so much so that Wren wasn't sure how she'd painted it. At the time her brush had moved as if of its own accord. The painting wasn't hers; it belonged to someone else. To some*thing* else.

"Please give it to me." She held out her hand, hating the way her voice trembled when it should have sounded cool and unaffected. But those were two things that her tender heart had never been able to master.

She was *always* affected by what other people thought.

"Please," she demanded, this time louder.

Rhys handed her the painting, a strange look on his face. It wasn't outright disgust, as had been Christian's expression. But she couldn't handle even the mildest form of judgment right now. Not about this.

The only reason she'd even brought the damn thing with her was because Kylie had mentioned that Sean Ainslie had a thing for nude portraits.

Now the damn thing was humiliating her again.

"I think you should go," she said, fighting back the wave of shame as memories assaulted her.

You're depraved, Christian had said when he'd discovered this painting along with the twelve others in the collection. All nudes, all women. *You're a sexual deviant and you're using me as a cover.*

It wasn't true. She had simply been fascinated by the idea of female sexuality. Enamored by it from an artistic standpoint…not that anyone in her damned hometown would understand that. All they had seen were things that should be hidden away.

"Wren," he started. "There's nothing to be ashamed of."

"I'm not ashamed," she lied. "I would just prefer it if you left now. Please."

He hovered for a moment, his eyes, which had darkened to almost black, flicking between her and the canvas that she held tight to her chest. Protecting herself or the painting, she wasn't sure.

"For what it's worth, I think your paintings are incredible," he said, shoving his hands into his pockets. "Thanks again for dinner."

"You're welcome." Her voice was a whisper as he walked out of the room, leaving her alone to ponder why the fates had decided yet again to use her art to humiliate her.

"Maybe you should take a hint," she muttered to herself as she placed the remaining paintings back where they belonged. "Listen to your parents and get a real job."

She would. Just as soon as she figured out what had happened to Kylie, she would head home and enter the real world.

3

WREN SAT BEHIND the sleek chrome-and-marble desk that crowned the entrance to the Ainslie Ave gallery. Her boss was expecting a potential client for a private viewing, so he was locked away in his studio preparing, which left her with a few precious moments of solitude to do some digging.

Hopefully, the chance to snoop would not only yield some valuable information but also help her to keep her mind off Rhys. And how he probably thought she was a nut job after the way she'd ordered him out of her apartment last night.

She cringed. The whole evening had been going so well. They'd had a great rapport and she'd gotten definite vibes of interest from him. Heated glances, an invitation to make a move. Then she'd blown it.

"Rookie move, Livingston," she muttered to herself as she clicked out of Sean's calendar. "You don't think before you act."

It was a criticism that had been handed to her over and over by her parents. Most of the time it followed, "Why can't you be more responsible, like your sister?" Wren had never been too good at plotting out her moves before she made them. Often guided by impulse, she'd landed herself in hot water on a few occasions and had earned herself a bit of a reputation—unfairly, in her opinion—for being a wild girl.

She wasn't wild. Irresponsible, perhaps. Spontaneous, definitely. But certainly not wild in the sense that they meant it back home.

Not that anyone believed her.

Shaking off the well-worn thoughts, she forced herself to focus on the task at hand. Her self-loathing could wait. She'd been working here for exactly three weeks now and all her preliminary searches had turned up zilch. Well, unless you counted a snarky online review of an exhibition Sean had run two years ago…which she didn't.

Sliding down from her stool, she padded quietly across the showroom floor. The place was silent save for the swish of her skirt against the polished boards. The other two interns, with whom she shared reception duties and a cramped studio space, were painting today. She'd gotten to know them quite well in the last few weeks—thanks to the assistance of her amazing chocolate brownies—although she could tell both girls believed Sean Ainslie was a god among men.

The paintings in the showroom had been switched around this morning after Sean's conversation with the client. He'd since selected a shortlist of works that he thought would suit the client's needs. The rest of the paintings were locked away in some specially designed climate-controlled room to which Wren had not yet gained access.

Sean Ainslie came from money; she knew that for sure. His wealth wasn't due to his art, although he'd had moderate success with a collection of paintings depicting the burned-out carcass of the iconic New York yellow cab. Yet the paintings he had ready for viewing were entirely different in feel and style.

Wren studied a smaller canvas, which showed an ice-cream cone melting in the sun. The painting had a slight cubism feel to it, the shapes on the waffle cone exaggerated and angular. Sharp. The vibrant colors seemed at odds with Sean's darker, grittier pieces.

"Why were you drawn to that one?" Sean's voice echoed against the high ceilings and bounced around, causing Wren to jump.

"It's different from your other works." Wren pressed a hand to her chest and felt her heart beat wildly beneath her skin. Sean unnerved her, especially his ability to sneak up on her out of nowhere. "I was wondering what inspired it."

"I used to visit Coney Island with my grandfather when I was a kid." He came up behind her and stood close. Too close. "Everything about that place was so... plastic. It felt unreal to me, even back then. Like it was something I'd made up in my head instead of being a real place."

The scent of stale cigarette on his breath made Wren's stomach churn. She tried to subtly put some distance between them by pretending to look more closely at the painting. "I've never been there."

"Don't bother. It's a cesspool."

"Right." She nodded.

"Have you got the coffee on?"

"Yes." Taking the opportunity, she stepped away from him and returned to her post at the front of the showroom. "I've also put out the croissants. Mr. Wagner should be here in five minutes. Would you like me to stay in the room in case you need anything?"

Please say no, please say no, please say no.

Sean's thin lips pressed into a line as he considered her question. The scar on his left cheek seemed to twitch as the muscle behind it moved. "No, leave Mr. Wagner to me. The last thing I want is him getting distracted by a beautiful young woman."

Wren forced her expression to stay neutral, despite her lip wanting to curl at the sleazy way he was looking at her. "Very well."

"Feel free to get some work done in the studio, but don't go home. I'll need you to clean up once Mr. Wagner has gone."

"Of course."

She retreated before Sean could make any more requests…or comments about her appearance. He seemed to do that on a daily basis. Wren certainly wasn't averse to compliments, but her skin always seemed to crawl whenever he was around.

The other interns—a blonde named Aimee and a girl with a Southern accent named Lola—were painting in relative silence in the studio. Their stations were crowded with paints and tools, like chaotic rainbows of creativity. Her section, in stark comparison, was spotlessly clean.

If only her mother could see that for once she had the cleanest workstation in the room.

Sadly, this wasn't due to a newfound love of tidiness… but more because her Muse had refused to show up. She'd taken on more reception duties to avoid her creative block, but Sean would expect her to produce something eventually. After all, she should be having the time of her life with an opportunity so many other artists would kill for.

Supposedly, anyway.

"Looks like it's just you and me, old friend." Wren stood in front of the canvas, which was mostly blank except for an angry-looking smudge in one corner. She laughed to herself in the quiet room, the sound rough and insincere. "And with friends like these, who needs enemies?"

Neither Aimee nor Lola glanced in her direction. But before Wren had a chance to pick up a brush, the sound of talking floated down from the showroom. Sean's client had arrived, which meant he would be occupied for some time. That gave her a window of opportunity to check out the storage room and some of the other rooms at the back of the gallery where she didn't normally go.

Tiptoeing out into the corridor, she listened to make sure that no one was coming her way. The storage room was at the very end of the building—which had once been a mechanic's workshop that had lain abandoned for several years until Sean had purchased it. The storage room had been tacked on to the structure and fitted with a keypad to limit entry. Wren hadn't yet been able to come up with an excuse that would allow her to request access from Sean.

She stared helplessly at the blinking keypad. It seemed strange to lock up a storage room so tightly. Even if it housed valuable paintings, why were the interns kept out? It didn't make sense. Wren had worked in a small gallery a few towns over from Charity Springs. Sure, small towns were different from the Big Smoke, but she'd always had access to the gallery's stock.

What had she been thinking turning up here without

a plan? For the first time in three weeks, Wren felt the stupidity of her decision weigh on her. A naive part of her had assumed it would be easy to show up here, figure out what had happened and run back home, evidence in hand. Ready to reassure her friend that she would have justice, after all.

"That's because you don't think before you act," she muttered to herself. Again.

"Wren?" A female voice caught her attention. "Are you free? I have a question."

Wren spun to find Aimee peering out of the studio, her fair brows wrinkled. "What's wrong, Aimee?"

"I need to put a note into the shared calendar about my day off this week and I couldn't get in. Then I tried to reset the password and now I've locked us all out." She threw her hands up in the air. "I don't know why computers hate me so much."

Wren tried not to roll her eyes. In the three weeks she'd been working at Ainslie Ave, Aimee had managed to lock herself out of the computer system at least four times. Clumsy fingers, she'd claimed, but Wren found that hard to believe considering the delicate and intricate portraits she painted.

"Can you help me?" the other woman pleaded. "I don't want to disturb Sean again. He got very frustrated last time."

"Sure." Wren headed back into the studio and took a seat on the stool in front of the old laptop that served as their shared work computer.

Within minutes she'd located the problem—Aimee had made a spelling error when she'd created her new password, which explained why she hadn't been able to use it to log in after the reset.

"Okay, that should do it." Wren clicked over to their email program. "I've reset it again and tested that it works. I'll leave a note on the desktop with the password this time so you don't forget it."

"Thanks." Aimee had the decency to look mildly sheepish.

Wren was about to move away from the computer when she noticed something strange about the email inbox. A ton of unread emails had banked up from contacts she'd never seen before. Normally, the inbox the three women shared was filled with general requests from the website's contact form. There might be the occasional email requesting information or dates of shows, but otherwise they didn't get many direct emails from clients.

"Are you logged in to Sean's email account?" Wren asked, looking up suddenly.

Aimee cringed. "Yes, but please don't tell him. I needed to, uh...delete an email." She fiddled with the end of her paint-splattered tank top, the chipped pink nail polish on her fingers glinting like shards of broken glass in the afternoon sun that streamed in from a large window beside them.

"How did you get into his account?" Wren could hardly believe Aimee was the password-cracking type.

"He keeps it written down." She averted her gaze and spoke softly so that Lola couldn't hear them. "Please don't say anything."

Wren knew for a fact that his passwords weren't written down anywhere in the studio...after all, she'd looked. Which meant that Aimee had been places that Wren hadn't, and from the expression on her face she wasn't too comfortable sharing that information.

"I won't, but I don't think it's a good idea to be logging in to his email account from our shared computer. You might get someone in trouble," she admonished, feeling immediately hypocritical because she knew exactly how she was going to exploit this opportunity.

"You're right," Aimee said, knotting her hands in front of her. "I'm sorry. I don't want to get anyone in trouble."

"I won't say anything." Wren turned the laptop back to herself. "And I'll log out so I can check on the shared inbox and make sure we haven't missed anything. You'd better get back to your painting in case he comes in."

"Thank you."

Perhaps it made Wren a horrible person to be admonishing Aimee while planning to use her lapse in judgment to scan through Sean's emails. But Wren had learned a thing or two about morals in the last six months—they were not as black-and-white as she'd been led to believe. For example, in Christian's mind it had been perfectly okay for him to make up stories about her because he felt she was a bad person for hiding her "depravity."

Besides, she wasn't hurting Aimee. She was simply making use of a happy accident to help her friend.

There was nothing suspicious in his emails. Time for plan B. Her nails clicked quietly against the keys of the laptop as she searched for the passcode to the storage room. Nothing. But she did manage to find his birthday, address and home phone number, which gave her something to work with. Wren wasn't a master spy by any stretch, but she *had* sat in on an internet security session at the community center back home during one of her volunteering stints. At the time she'd thought it was boring as hell, but some of the stats had stuck with her. Like how the majority of people use their birthdays as pin codes for ATMs and online banking. Perhaps that extended to locked rooms, as well.

Taking a second to check that no one was watching her, she logged out of Sean's email and pocketed the note she'd scribbled with his details. Tonight, after everyone had left, she'd "accidentally" forget to set the alarm so she could come back and have a crack at the storage room lock without leaving a trail.

RHYS WASN'T THE kind of guy who ever had trouble sleeping. He pushed his body hard at the gym and he pushed his mind hard at work each day. Those things combined meant he was usually out the moment his head hit the pillow.

But not for the last three nights.

Stifling a yawn, he rubbed at his eyes and reached for the coffee on his desk. The nighttime hours had been ticking past slowly while Rhys's eyes remained open in the darkness. All he could picture were flashes of Wren and her painting. Of the sexual energy mixed with her embarrassment.

He hadn't seen hide nor hair of her since that night... but that didn't dull the vivid memory.

The painting had taken him aback. Not because he thought there was anything wrong with it—far from it. But he'd been shocked by how strongly his body had reacted to the desire and curiosity and abandonment in her work. Art was not his thing—numbers and data were. But she'd invoked a kind of visceral reaction that was totally foreign.

And then she'd kicked him out.

He wasn't sure what to make of it. But one thing he

did know for certain was that he wanted to see her again, despite understanding that she wasn't planning to stay.

"Boss?" Quinn Dellinger poked her head into his office, her mass of dyed pink hair almost blindingly bright under the office lighting. "You got a sec?"

"Sure, sure." He motioned for her to take a seat as he shoved thoughts of Wren from his mind. Work was his priority right now, not women. Not one woman, no matter how tempting. "What's going on?"

Quinn's chunky combat boots clomped on the floor. For a woman so petite she made a lot of noise. "I've been assigned a case but I need to do a site visit and none of the other guys are free to come with me."

As a newly appointed junior security consultant, Quinn wasn't yet cleared to do site visits on her own. She had another few months of shadowing the more experienced consultants before that could happen.

"I'm ready," she added. "I can do it. I just need you to sign off."

"You're familiar with the policy, Quinn. Three months of supervision before you can fly solo."

Her button nose wrinkled, causing the clear stud there to glint in the afternoon sunlight. "And it's worth upsetting the client for some stupid policy?"

"It's not a stupid policy. We have it for a reason."

He didn't need to repeat the story; *everyone* at Cobalt & Dane Security was well aware of what had happened when they'd sent a rookie in alone. One bad incident was all it took to make sure that new security consultants had the proper training and supervision so that they didn't lose anyone else.

"I know how capable you are, Quinn. I wouldn't have promoted you if I didn't believe in your skills." Rhys reached for his coffee and swigged, praying the caffeine would soon work its magic. "But that doesn't mean I'm going to bend the rules for you."

She rolled her eyes but a smile twitched on her lips. "You *never* bend the rules. For anything."

"Tough but fair, you know the drill," he said.

"Yeah, yeah." She folded her arms across the front of her black skull-and-crossbones T-shirt. "So what should we do about the client, then? He said he wants us there today but everyone else is busy."

"I thought Owen was in the office today."

She shook her head. "He got an emergency call out to that private client we signed—the crazy stockbroker guy. He's paranoid. I told Owen as much."

"It comes with the territory. Doesn't mean we can ignore the client's needs." Rhys tapped his fingers against the surface of his desk. "And Jin is still out sick?"

"Yep. Aiden's around but he's scheduled to do a visit to the data warehouse with Logan." Quinn's cheeks colored slightly despite the neutral expression on her face. She and Aiden had only told the team they were dating a few weeks back, and every time his name came up in conversation she blushed like a schoolgirl.

Rhys thought it was cute, but Quinn would probably throw something at him for saying so. "Okay, well, I guess it'll have to be me, then."

Perhaps a trip away from the office would do him good. He'd been staring at the same email for the last ten minutes and his lack of progress was starting to grate on his nerves. Fresh air and something to focus on might help him to get into the zone again.

"You never do site visits." Quinn cocked her head. "Ever."

"You seem to think I never do a lot of things."

God, did everyone really believe he was that dull? Sure, he liked to follow the rules. He was a "by the book" kind of guy. What was so bad about that?

She shrugged, seemingly unaware of the questions her words had stirred. "Whatever works. I'd rather get out there today and keep this guy onside. He sounds like a bit of a control freak."

"Let's keep our insults about the client to a minimum, shall we?" Rhys pushed up from his chair and stuck his phone into his back pocket.

"Sure thing, boss. Whatever you say." Quinn grinned at him as they fell into step.

After a quick pause at her desk so she could collect her things and confirm with the client that they would now be coming to complete the site visit, they were off.

"This will be fun. We haven't had an excursion together in ages." Quinn had a spring in her step as they walked through the office.

"That's because you're annoying."

He didn't mean it, but he and Quinn had that kind of relationship. There were no filters, no walking on eggshells. She was one of the first people he'd hired when he'd started as IT manager four years ago. They'd developed a deep mutual respect. She was whip smart and loyal to the bone, two qualities that were sorely lacking in the world.

"*I'm* annoying?" She pressed her hand to her chest and he noticed a small, heart-shaped ring on her finger. "Those are mighty words coming from Mr. Spreadsheet himself."

He ignored the dig. "What's with the ring? I've never seen you wear anything that didn't have a skull on it."

Her cheeks turned hot pink. "It was a gift."

"Are you engaged?"

"No." She laughed as if that were a ridiculous notion, but her voice sounded tight and a little strange. "It's just a ring."

"A ring from your boyfriend." He nudged her with his elbow and she immediately swatted him. "Hey, I'm not judging. I'm happy you've found someone who puts up with you."

"He's man enough to handle me." Her expression turned serious as they entered the elevator. "I know you two didn't get off on the right foot, but he's it for me. I love him."

Rhys had been forced to hire Aiden because he was friends with the boss, Logan Dane. Given Rhys's feelings about hard work and the need to prove oneself, it hadn't been a great start to their working relationship.

"You're getting all mushy on me, Dellinger," he joked.

"It's true. He's a good guy, Rhys. I want you to respect him."

Rhys didn't point out that respect had to be earned instead of given out like candy. But Quinn was practically family to him, so he would keep his feelings to himself and take the high road. He *always* took the high road.

"I do respect him. He's on my team now so I'll treat him the same as I treat any other employee."

She grinned. "Tough, but fair."

"That's my motto."

"I appreciate it." She laid a hand on his arm, the pink stone in her ring glimmering. "Honestly."

He cleared his throat. "For what it's worth, you deserve to be happy."

"So do you, boss. Why don't you ever seem to have any ladies hanging around?"

Probably because Rhys kept his work life and his love life totally separate. He'd never believed in mixing the two, though he accepted that not everyone agreed with him on that.

But that didn't mean he could avoid the little stabs of envy he got watching his friends pair up and find happiness. Maybe it was old-fashioned, but he wanted that stability. He wanted a woman to come home to, wake up next to. To make him feel like he was valued. Needed.

"This is not appropriate conversation for a manager and his employee," he said, reminding himself that the goal right now was to have fun with a woman and *not* worry about the future.

"Stick-in-the-mud," she grumbled.

She might be right, but right now Rhys didn't have anything that he wanted to share. Especially not with being so occupied by Wren and her painting. His whole body hummed as she drifted back into his mind. There was no way he'd be able to forget what he'd seen, so he'd just have to stage a meeting with her to clear the air. And maybe fulfill a few fantasies...

4

"YOU'RE AVOIDING SOMETHING, WREN." Sean Ainslie's voice cut into Wren's thought process.

Her brush hovered over the same patch of blank canvas that she'd been attempting to start work on for the last half hour.

"Avoiding something?" She put the brush down onto her workstation and looked up. "What makes you say that?"

His eyes swept over the lackluster canvas. A few strokes of color decorated one of the bottom corners but it was clear she had no direction. She hadn't sketched anything out, hadn't planned what the painting would look like. Hell, she couldn't even legitimately claim that she was too swept away by her Muse to do any of the preparatory work.

She had nothing, and as a result, the painting *was* nothing.

Oh, it's something all right. It's a hot freaking mess, is what it is.

"I saw so much inspiration in your portfolio, Wren. So much…" His hands fluttered in the air in front of him.

"Passion. Creativity. Your paintings were bold and vibrant. This…" His hands dropped down to his sides. "I don't know what this is. Do you?"

"I'm a little blocked," she admitted.

Every time she tried to touch the paintbrush to the canvas she pictured Rhys's expression when he'd looked at *that* painting. The memory filled her with a strange mélange of excitement and shame, anticipation and disgust. Part of her wished that she'd let him stay. If for nothing more than to see where they would have ended up. Visions of his deep brown skin and warm eyes filled her mind.

"Just paint whatever pops into your head right now." Sean touched her shoulder and she jumped, startled as she reached for her brush almost involuntarily. "Whatever image is in your mind now, paint it. I want you to get over this hurdle, Wren."

Biting down on her lip she shut her eyes and let the memory of Rhys gazing at the painting wash over her. His full lips, the wicked way they'd parted as his eyes had widened. The slight flare of his nostrils.

She started mixing paint as she let her mind wander. His pupils had grown as he'd looked at her canvas, his breath stalling in his throat. Her life had contained few moments as electric as that, as intensely intimate and vulnerable. Wasn't that the purpose of art? Laying yourself bare?

Being open and receptive?

But that's how she'd been hurt before. With her heart so open and unprotected, it was ripe for the picking. Her fingers tightened around her brush as she stopped midstroke. The faint sketch of a man's face—the high points of his cheeks, the rough contours of his lips and the strong angle of his jaw—filled the canvas.

People can only hurt you when you let them. So don't give them the opportunity.

Her hand hovered again, the moment lost like steam into air. Fear had crept back in and chased inspiration away. Sighing, she threw the brush down into the palette, flicking sienna paint across the carefully mixed palette of earthy flesh tones.

It was useless. *She* was useless.

Sean opened his mouth to say something but they were interrupted when Lola poked her head into the room. "Sean? I've got the security people from Cobalt & Dane here to see you."

"Tell them I'll be out momentarily," he said. As Lola disappeared he turned back to Wren. "I want to see a complete painting next week. The whole point of you being here is to work on improving your art. I can't help you with that if you don't produce anything."

"I understand."

"If you're not able to do that I'll have to find another intern. It's not fair for you to take a valuable position in my program if you're not going to do the work. There are plenty of other artists who would eagerly step into your place."

The words stung but she kept her face neutral. "I'll do better, I promise."

When Sean left the room, Aimee turned from her station and offered a sympathetic smile. "It's not easy to be creative on demand, is it?"

The genuine empathy caused moisture to rush to Wren's eyes, but she blinked the tears away. She wasn't the kind of girl to let her pain show; she locked it all away where no one could see how much she allowed other people's words to cut her.

"No," she admitted. "It's not."

"You just have to give yourself permission to be crap," Aimee said.

"That flies in the face of every piece of advice I've ever received." Wren frowned at her canvas as she picked up her brush.

Her whole life she'd told herself she needed to be incredible, that she needed to be "the best." That's why it'd hurt so bad when Kylie had initially been chosen over her to gain a place in Ainslie's internship.

If she couldn't be the best, then her parents would never consider her art as anything but a hobby. But if her talent was honed and she pushed herself hard, they might believe in her.

Giving herself permission to be crap was laughable.

"Hear me out." Aimee put her brush down and flicked her long blond ponytail over one shoulder. "I can almost guarantee you're psyching yourself out of this painting. You keep thinking that no matter what you do it'll never be enough, right?"

"Well, not exactly…"

"But close enough?"

Wren huffed. "Maybe."

"So give yourself permission to paint something no matter how crappy it is. Better at this point to have a crappy painting than no painting at all." She folded her arms over her apron and smiled with an air of smugness. "Trust me, it'll get the creativity flowing again."

Maybe she had a point. If Wren failed Sean's ultimatum, it would put a swift end to her mission. Better to give him a mediocre product rather than a blank canvas.

He might kick her out of the internship anyway, but she could still have a chance. Whereas if she continued on the path she was on, she'd *definitely* be out.

Wren sucked in a breath and touched her brush to a shade of burnt orange. Perhaps painting Rhys would help get him out of her head. Then she could kill two birds with one painting.

RHYS FOUND HIMSELF tuning out as the client went on a diatribe about how underappreciated artists were. Judging by Quinn's glazed-over eyes, she was struggling to pay attention, as well.

"Why don't we talk through the security incidents you mentioned over the phone, Mr. Ainslie?" Quinn suggested tactfully. "You said there was some unauthorized access to your storage room…?"

"Right." Sean Ainslie narrowed his dark brows and interlaced his fingers. "I have a storage room where I keep all the paintings that aren't on display. They're very valuable, you see."

"Of course." Quinn nodded, one hand fiddling with the pink ends of her braid. "What alerted you to the break-in?"

"The thief didn't actually get into the room. The incorrect pin code was entered three times and I have my system set up to alert me when that happens. I had to reset it the following day. I questioned the staff here but no one has owned up to it."

"So was anything stolen?"

"No. Nothing. But I think the culprit may try again, so I'd like to take some preventative measures. I've been a customer of Cobalt & Dane for quite a few years now, but I've never had an incident this severe before."

"I assume you'll be happy to give us access to your security-camera footage," Rhys said.

Sean looked sheepish for a moment. "There isn't any."

"You don't have security cameras?" Rhys resisted the urge to raise a brow. "Or the footage isn't accessible?"

"There are no cameras."

Rhys's suspicions were instantly roused. What kind of person would store a bunch of valuable paintings in a room with a high-tech locking system and then not have security cameras? It didn't make sense.

"Hasn't someone from Cobalt & Dane advised you that a monitoring system for the gallery would be a good idea?"

"I don't like the idea of having cameras on my employees," he explained. "I trust these girls, and the idea of having cameras on them felt a bit *1984*."

Quinn cast a glance to Rhys, which confirmed that she also wasn't buying his story. "Okay," she said slowly. "You also mentioned an email breach…?"

"I was looking for an email in my inbox the other day but I found it in the deleted folder. I definitely didn't delete it. I think someone has been accessing my emails, as well."

"Quinn can have a look through the email security logs and see if there's any strange activity," Rhys said. "Do you have any idea what this person might be after?"

"Not a clue." Sean shook his head, but there was a guardedness to his expression that didn't seem to match his words. The guy was hiding something; Rhys was sure of it. "All my paintings are valuable, but there isn't one that's worth significantly more than the others."

"Try to think if there's anything in particular a thief might want. It might not be a painting. It could be information. We strongly recommend that you install cameras. It will be hard for us to assist you in keeping this place secure if there isn't anything for us to monitor. In the meantime, it might be worthwhile for us to have a chat with your employees. I understand you've already talked to them, but it would be good for us to go over anything that they might have seen or heard."

"Of course." Sean motioned for them to follow him back out into the gallery.

"You can take the lead in talking to the staff," Rhys said to Quinn as their footsteps echoed through the spacious gallery showroom. "If you get stuck I'll jump in."

"Great." Quinn nodded, lowering her voice as they let Sean walk ahead. "We should debrief when we get back to the office."

"Agreed."

After spending a few minutes with a dark-haired woman named Lola, who appeared genuinely shocked that anything was amiss, they headed past Sean's office to the studio.

"My other two interns are in here," Sean said as he rounded a corner into an airy space lit with streaming natural sunlight. "Aimee and Wren, this is Rhys and Quinn. They're here to ask a few questions and I expect you both to give them whatever they need."

Rhys's chest clenched when he caught sight of Wren, her golden-blond hair piled messily on top of her head and a streak of dark orange paint on her cheek contrasting against her fair skin.

What a coincidence.

Her blue eyes widened in mild panic as her lips formed an O shape. No sound came out.

"I need to make a phone call," Sean said. "I trust you two will be fine to talk with the girls?"

"Quinn, why don't you talk with Aimee in one of the other rooms and I'll stay in here with Wren," Rhys said, his voice smooth and unflustered. He knew exactly how to sound in charge—the product of years of faking it until he made it.

"Sure thing, boss." Quinn introduced herself to the other intern and they left him alone with Wren a minute later. An easel and canvas partially obscured his view of her.

"Well, this is quite a surprise," Rhys said, keeping his distance. The last thing he wanted to do was spook her, especially given how their last encounter had ended.

"You're telling me," she said, her hands knotting in front of her. She wore a long flowing dress colored with swirls of pale blue and purple. The thin straps left plenty of skin visible. A simple silver chain held a piece of roughly cut blue stone just below her bust. "What are you doing here?"

"We're looking into a few security concerns for your boss."

"Oh?" Her tone and expression gave nothing away.

"There was a failed attempt to access the storage room as well as suspected email hacking." He leaned against the wall and folded his arms across his chest.

"I don't know anything about that." The response was too automatic. Defensive.

"That's okay. We're going to be taking some preventative measure to ensure it doesn't happen again." He inched closer and noticed her body tense up. "Is it okay if we talk? I can bring Quinn in, if that would make you more comfortable."

"No, that's fine."

"What are you working on?" He thought he'd start with something easy, something nonthreatening. But the second he took a step forward she visibly pulled back, her body language screaming at him not to come closer.

Maybe he'd misread the situation when they had had dinner together.

"It's no good."

"I've seen your work, Wren. I'm sure it's incredible." God, who had treated her so badly that she thought so lowly of herself? Of her work?

"You seem to have a lot of blind faith in my abilities," she said, her hands wringing in her lap.

"Well, I'm no expert but I know what I like." He inched closer.

"It's not finished," she said with a note of resignation. Her eyes lowered to her lap and he peered around the edge of the canvas.

The image struck him. It wasn't more than a collection of rough strokes, lacking the depth and shading that she'd no doubt add later on. But the image was unmistakable. He recognized his own deep brown eyes and broad nose, the warm tone of his skin and the heavy shadow along his jaw.

Words eluded him.

"You weren't supposed to see this," she said, pushing up from her stool.

"That's the second time you've said that to me." He tore his eyes away from his own image.

"I don't know which one was more embarrassing," she admitted, folding her arms across her chest. "But in any case, you're not here to discuss my work. So ask me what you need to ask me."

"Have you noticed anything strange going on in the studio? Any people hanging around that seem suspicious?"

She shook her head. "No, I don't think so."

"Any odd phone calls?"

"Not that I can recall."

"Have either of the other girls been acting strange? Asking questions about the storage room or security?"

Her delicate shoulders lifted into a shrug. "Well, they wouldn't ask me those questions because I don't have any more access than they do. We all share an email account and work out of this room, and we take turns at the front desk and help Sean organize his schedule."

"So no one is in charge?"

"Just Sean. There's no hierarchy among us interns."

Wren had a good poker face, he'd give her that. He couldn't be sure if she was telling the truth or hiding something, since her initial defensiveness seemed mostly related to the painting.

Excitement stirred inside him. Imagining her sitting at this very stool, her mind on him as she swept her brush over the canvas, caused a tight ache in his chest. Why would she choose him?

Drawing a deep breath, he shoved the questions aside. Right now he was on company time, so those curiosities would have to wait until later. He dug a card out of his jacket pocket. "Here's my number. If you see anything out of the ordinary, give me a call."

"Sure." She took the card and turned it over in her hands. "I'll do that."

Silence hung in the air but he couldn't tear himself away from her. Not yet. Not when she'd been the ghost in his mind for the last few days. The faint sound of

Quinn's voice floated into the room. She was still questioning the other intern.

"I haven't seen you around much." He jammed his hands into the pockets of his suit pants.

Her lips lifted into a rueful smile. "That's because I've been avoiding you."

"Honest. I like that."

"Well, cat's out of the bag now, isn't it? You're a smart man. I wouldn't try to pull one over on you." Her fingers toyed with her necklace, causing the blue stone to shift and catch the light. It was roughly cut, raw and natural in its beauty. Like her.

"I felt like we had unfinished business after the other night," he said. That was putting it mildly.

"That's what I've been avoiding."

So maybe he *hadn't* misread the signals. "Why?"

"I had a rough time back home and I came here to get away from it all. I'm still…wounded," she said carefully, her eyes focused on the window that looked out into the alley behind the building. "I don't want to get hurt again."

"I guess it's a good thing I'm not planning on hurting anyone. Well, other than the bad guys."

"Of course." A smile crossed her lips but it didn't quite come up to her eyes. "Very noble of you."

He cleared his throat. "If you feel like company tonight, I have a very comfortable couch and I'm not a terrible cook, if I do say so myself."

It was probably wrong for him to engage with her outside the boundaries of the job, but hell, they were neighbors. This conversation could have happened anywhere. And besides, this was Quinn's assignment, and other than supervising her site visits, she'd be doing the investigative portion. So it wasn't like there was a con-flict of interest.

Wren's hesitation thickened the air around them. "A comfortable couch?"

"Yeah, that thing people sit on while they watch TV? It's long and has cushions—"

She swatted him and laughed. "I know what a couch is."

"So come and hang out on mine. We'll eat, have a drink… We don't have to address the unfinished busi-ness if you don't want."

The furrow of her fair brows tugged at his heart. "Why are you being so nice to me?"

"You don't know anyone in the city, as you said the other night." He shrugged. "I thought you might like the company."

"Another noble gesture."

"And my apartment is fully furnished, so there's that."

She tried to purse her lips but a grin broke through. "Are you judging the state of my apartment, Rhys?"

"Not at all."

"I'm going for the bohemian-chic look," she said un-convincingly. "It's all the rage."

"Is it?"

Her tinkling laugh echoed against the high, white ceil-ings and the sound barreled through him. Damn, that sound could put him on cloud nine. "No idea. I'm just making things up as I go."

"That's all any of us can do."

At that moment Quinn stuck her head into the room. "Ready to go, boss?"

He stepped away from Wren, suddenly aware of how they'd gravitated toward one another. The space had shrunk between them until her shoulder was mere inches from his. She seemed to have that effect on him.

"Yes, let's make a move. I'll meet you out front," he said. When Quinn retreated, he turned back to Wren. "If you decide to come over, I usually have dinner around seven."

He actually had dinner precisely at seven every night, but he suspected that would sound a little type A if he said it aloud.

"I'll keep that in mind." She rolled her bottom lip between her teeth and a light flush crept over her cheeks.

As he walked out of the studio, he forced himself to keep his eyes forward. If she came over, great. If not, well, he wouldn't push it. But his body was already coiled tight with the thought that she might want to pick up where they'd left off.

He'd just have to be careful to keep a clear demarcation between his work and his extracurricular activities. But it wouldn't be an issue—he had no reason to suspect Wren was involved in the security breach. She had her own paintings—what could she possibly need with Sean Ainslie's?

5

WREN HAD BEEN on edge ever since Rhys had shown up at work. Not just because he'd appeared as if the images in her head had come to life, but because he was there hunting for things *she'd* done. Naively, she'd assumed that when her attempt to get into the storage room had failed her boss would be none the wiser.

Wrong. Now he'd hired a security company to come in and investigate, which would no doubt throttle her ability to play detective.

So why was she standing at Rhys's door, her hand poised to knock?

"Because you're a glutton for punishment, that's why," she muttered. "You don't know when to back away."

Her logical side—she *did* have one, though it was the runt of the litter—said it would be better to keep in contact with Rhys so she could stay abreast of his company's investigation. Her emotional side thought that sounded manipulative, and she supposed it was. But the fact that Sean had involved a security firm meant he was extremely serious about protecting his privacy, and that made her even more suspicious of him.

So she'd have to forcibly ignore her guilt about lying to Rhys. She didn't like being dishonest, but she wasn't about to give up on finding justice for Kylie.

"You're doing it for her." She stared at the gold-plated numbers on Rhys's door for a moment longer before she knocked. "Kylie would do the same for you."

Footsteps sounded inside and then Rhys swung the door open. Wren's knees almost buckled at the dazzling smile he gifted her. Paired with the fitted black T-shirt that stretched across his broad chest and the half apron accentuating his trim waist, it was a killer combination.

"Couldn't resist my offer?" He held the door open and motioned for her to enter.

"I couldn't resist the offer of a comfy couch. I think mine was home to a family of raccoons before I got here."

"If that's what brought you here, I'll take it."

Wren had been in Rhys's apartment before, but she'd been more focused on her bleeding hand and his half-naked state the last time she was here. Now she had the opportunity to take in his space.

It was tidy to a fault, not a single cushion out of order. Next to the big-screen TV, he'd hung a shelf that was lined with books arranged by height. A set of hand weights rested in a rack near the window. They, too, were arranged by size. On top of the solid coffee table was a fancy-looking remote.

"You may be the tidiest person I have ever met," she said, gazing around the apartment and feeling slightly inadequate. "Seriously, I want to fling some paint across your floor just to mess things up."

"A clean space is a clean mind," Rhys replied as he headed back to the kitchen. "I can't think if there's too much clutter. Besides, it doesn't take much effort to keep something clean. I have a system in place."

"A system?"

"Yeah, a routine, you might call it."

"Stop. This conversation is becoming way too adult for me." She leaned against the kitchen counter as he gathered up a handful of chopped onions and tossed them into a pan on the stove.

"I guess I shouldn't tell you about my cleaning routine spreadsheet, then?" Laughter rumbled in his chest at her widened eyes. "I'm kidding, I'm kidding."

"I get the impression you're one of those people who's totally in control at all times." She watched as he added green peppers to the frying pan and stirred them with a wooden spoon.

"No one is in control of life at all times." He thought for a second. "But I do try to keep a firm hand on things."

I wouldn't mind if he kept a firm hand on me.

Wren stifled a smile as she watched Rhys work the kitchen like a pro. He had his back to her, granting her a secret moment to openly admire his ass. The man wore a pair of jeans like nobody's business.

Why had she come here? To torture herself, apparently.

A deep ache built within her. It had been so long since she'd had sex, and with the stress of her fleeing her hometown and getting herself installed at Ainslie Ave, she hadn't made much time for self-appreciation, either. Her hands twitched with the desire to knead the firm muscles beneath his jeans. She could almost imagine how it would feel to clutch that ass as he plunged deep inside her.

"Wren?"

"Huh?" Her cheeks were as hot as an open flame.

"I asked if you're allergic to anything? I should have checked before I decided what to cook."

"Oh no, I'm healthy as an ox." Physically, anyway. Emotionally...not so much. "I'll eat pretty much anything. When you're raised in a tiny town, you don't always get a lot of choice."

"I'm sure small-town living has its perks." Rhys cracked a few eggs into a bowl and whisked them with a fork. "Not that I would ever consider leaving the city."

"Why's that?"

"I like being able to keep busy."

"And *I* like the anonymity of the city." She watched his deft hands making their dinner as gracefully as if he were conducting a symphony. You could tell a lot by watching people use their hands—and it was clear he knew *exactly* how to use his. "It's so freeing to be able to leave the house without people gossiping about your every move."

"That happen a lot to you at home?"

"Oh yeah. It's kind of like being famous without any of the perks."

"Sounds awful."

"It truly is." She sighed. "The worst thing is that people don't hesitate to make things up."

"Why let the truth get in the way of a good story, right?" He shook his head. "I really don't get why people thrive on gossip. There's so many more interesting things out there in the world."

"Couldn't agree more."

Within minutes Rhys had put two perfectly formed vegetable omelets onto pristine white plates. The scent of garlic, cheese and eggs made Wren's mouth water. She realized then that she'd barely eaten all day. Too busy worrying about the fate of her internship…and the possibility of what might happen if she saw Rhys again.

Time to find out.

"So, do you have any idea who might be behind the security issues at the gallery?" They took their seats at a small table with two chairs. The space was cozy and her knees brushed against his.

"Not yet. Today was just a preliminary meeting. Quinn will be running the investigation, so she'll most likely be back to ask more questions and help Sean set up a proper security system."

"A proper security system?" The omelet seemed to stick in her throat. There went her hopes of trying to break into the storage room again.

She'd found out during her first week that he didn't have any security cameras when she'd asked if there was a backup procedure for the camera tapes. She'd dodged suspicion with a false story about her duties at the community center back home, and he'd told her that he didn't believe in keeping an eye on his staff in that way.

"Yeah, I can't believe he doesn't have a proper security monitoring system in place already. If his paintings are worth that much, it seems crazy not to have cameras."

Wren chewed slowly. She was positive Sean had the money for security cameras. Which meant he chose not to have them because he didn't want footage of the inside of his gallery. All the more reason to suspect he was doing something illegal or, at the very least, unethical.

"Well, it doesn't matter anyway," Rhys said. "We'll find whoever did this. And if they've committed a crime, we'll hand them over to the police."

Had she committed a crime? Did going through someone's emails count as an offense?

All the more reason for her not to say anything to Rhys. She couldn't risk getting fired and possibly fined—or, God forbid, arrested—just for the sake of a romantic fling.

"That does seem crazy. Well, I hope you find whoever is doing these things." Guilt twinged in her gut, but she reminded herself why she was here—to help her friend. The usually confident and bubbly Kylie had come home a shell of her former self, and she deserved payback. "This omelet is incredible, by the way. Thanks for cooking."

He reached for the bottle of wine and topped up her glass. "I'm just being neighborly and returning the favor."

"You patched me up when I cut myself—that debt was already paid."

"Maybe I just wanted to see you again."

The sound of their silverware clicking and scraping filled Wren's pause. "I'm surprised, given what happened. I shouldn't have kicked you out like that. It was rude."

"That night *has* been on my mind." He sipped his wine and Wren watched him, transfixed, as the muscles in his throat worked as he swallowed. Everything about him was so strong, so sure. So powerful and yet controlled. Restrained. "I've thought about it a lot."

"You've thought about that night or just my painting?"

"All of it. I wasn't lying when I said I was going to make a move, Wren."

The confident way he spoke told her he wasn't used to being rejected. And who would say no to him? Not only was he hotter than Hades, but the man was an utter gentleman. A rare combination in her experience.

"You can tell me to stop being pushy," he added with a sly grin. "It's a bad habit, I know. I can be single-minded like that."

Grateful for the opportunity to delay addressing her attraction to him, she reached for her wine. "You're driven. That's not a bad thing."

"*Driven* sounds much better. Mom jokes I was born with a life plan in my hand."

"I bet she's very proud of you."

RHYS TRIED NOT to grimace at Wren's kind—and no doubt well-intended—words. If only it were true. His mother *was* proud of him; she just happened to prefer expressing that pride from a distance.

"My family is complicated," he said eventually.

"Aren't all families?" She shot him an empathetic look. "I don't think 'unconditional love' is as cut-and-dried as people would like to believe."

"Or as equally handed out."

"I'm the sister of an aspiring doctor. I get it." Her head bobbed slowly. "Who's the golden child, brother or sister?"

"Stepbrother."

"Ouch."

"I can't hate the guy. We've been best friends since we were in elementary school. It was like one of those kids' movies. His parents were divorced and my mother was a widow." Part of him felt disloyal for spilling his family drama to Wren. He loved his family. But in the short space of time he'd known Wren he'd become comfortable around her. He trusted her. "When my mom married his dad I thought it was the best thing that could have happened. But it got difficult as the years went on."

She tucked her feet up under her and cradled the wineglass in both hands. Her cascading golden hair and long, flowing skirt made her look like a goddess who'd stepped off a canvas.

"Why did things change?"

"We got older. I started to understand the way the world worked." He kneaded at the knots in the back of his neck. "You see, my dad was black but my mom's white. And my stepfather and stepbrother are white, as well. Which meant I spent a lot of time being asked if I was adopted."

"That would be awful," she said quietly.

"Yeah, it's tough enough being mixed. You feel like you don't truly belong in either camp. And I wasn't really bullied at school, but I was always on the fringe of things. Nothing I did ever got me into the inner circle of any group." He rubbed his palms against his thighs. "What made it worse was that my mom only saw my dad when she looked at me. So after a while it seemed as if she stopped looking."

He'd never said that aloud to anyone before, never admitted that his mother had all but ignored his presence for a portion of his life. And the older he got, the worse it had become.

When he looked back at old photos of his dad, he could see why. Despite the difference in the depth of their skin color, he had his father's full lips and strong jaw. He had the same intense eyes and heavy brows. The same strong cheekbones and slightly too-big ears. Ears made for listening, his mother had called them once.

It dawned on him then that this was why Wren's painting had made such an impact on him. It wasn't just that she'd been thinking about him, it was that she'd been *looking* at him. Acknowledging him.

In her head he was real and present and alive.

"I ended up moving to the city so I didn't have to

keep haunting her like that," he said, shutting out his revelation.

"You moved because you were haunting someone and I moved because I was *being* haunted. Can't win, can we?" she asked with a shake of her head.

"The reason you're haunted, does it have something to do with the painting I saw?" He cleared his throat. "The one of the naked woman."

"My problem was about the paintings," she said with an emphasis on the *s*. "I have a series of them. And, yeah, that's part of the reason I left. My town wasn't quite ready for something so 'shocking' as the naked body."

"I guess some of those towns can be quite conservative."

"Oh, I knew that. It's the whole reason I never showed the paintings to anyone except a few people I trusted in the art community. But my ex found them and…he got pretty mad."

"Why the hell would he be mad about a couple of paintings?"

"He thought I was going to cause a scandal." She laughed, but the sound was hollow. Humorless. "He had grand plans to be a district attorney one day and eventually make a move into politics. He told me he couldn't be with someone who was going to ruin his career with sinful, disgusting activities."

Rhys's chest clenched. The pain in her voice was palpable. "Your ex is an idiot."

"It wouldn't have been so bad if he'd just dumped me and moved on. But oh no, Christian thought *he'd* been wronged, and he wanted to take me down a couple of pegs. Teach me a lesson." Her jaw tightened. "He took photos of the paintings and showed them to people in town to make sure there was no chance any of my 'filthy secrets' could come back to bite him. I could never be the kind of woman he wanted by his side, but he also didn't want anyone else to have me…so he made sure I was 'damaged goods' as far as the town was concerned."

Rhys blinked. "Are you serious?"

"I wish I wasn't. But that tells you a lot about our relationship," she snorted.

"And people really thought a few nude paintings were that bad?"

"I didn't really have the chance to tell my side of the story. Christian went to a few loud voices in the community and the rumors were all over town before I had the chance to do anything about it. He said he felt it was his 'duty' to make sure I wasn't working with any children while I was creating pornographic material."

"I don't even know what to say." Rhys shook his head, trying to quash the anger that had bubbled up in him. "That's ridiculous."

"Anyway, enough of my sob story." A smile tugged at her lips. "It's all in the past, and I'm here now."

But for how long? The question hung at the edge of his mind.

Why can't you stop planning the future for once and live in the now? Live in the now with her.

"I'm glad you're here," he said.

Her dazzling smile kindled warmth in his chest. "And I'm glad you didn't let me bleed out in the hallway."

"My first-aid skills are good, but I've got other skills that are better than that."

"You're a fabulous cook, too."

Hunger gnawed at him. "That's not what I meant."

Her pupils dilated, the black centers eating away at

the rim of blue around them. Her chest rose and fell rapidly, causing her breasts to press against the thin tank top and reveal the faint shadow of her nipples. Her hand fluttered at her collarbone, toying with a thin necklace.

She intoxicated him. The very sight of her was so addictive that he was already desperate for a taste, as though he knew just how delicious she would be.

"I'll do the dishes," she said, standing and reaching for his plate. As she leaned over he could see that her blush extended down her neck and across her chest, coloring her skin with a rosy hue. "It's only fair since you cooked."

She stacked the plates in her arms and headed off in the direction of his kitchen. Draining the rest of the wine in his glass, he gave her a moment. Wren was skittish and now he understood the reason for that. She'd been hurt— run out of her hometown by a vindictive, selfish bastard.

But he *also* knew when a woman was attracted to him—and Wren's face hid nothing.

Collecting the glasses and the half-empty bottle of wine, he followed her. In the small space, he could feel the heat radiating around them. Neither had said a word, but the air held a sizzling tension. Anticipation raced through his veins.

"Please, stop helping," she said as she collected the dirty saucepan and wooden spoon from the stove. "Let me do it."

She brushed past him, her bare arm sweeping against his. The subtle touch sent shock waves through him, flipping the on switch to his entire nervous system. It caught the on switch to his cock as well, which stood to full attention, straining against the fly of his jeans.

Holy hell. He couldn't seem to control himself around

her. Turning as though he were about to rinse the wine-glasses in the sink, he adjusted himself.

"It's no trouble." He flipped the taps on, but the water gushed out far stronger than he'd expected and it sprayed him all down his front.

"Oh no!" She clamped a hand over her mouth. "The taps here have a mind of their own. I swear they're haunted by evil water ghosts."

She reached for the dish towel and wadded it up in her hand, pressing it straight to the wet patch on his stomach, dabbing up and down.

If he'd thought he was hard before, he was like marble now.

Her hand drifted over him, hovering at his waist as her eyes caught on the totally noticeable bulge in his jeans. Cheeks flaming, she sucked on her bottom lip and drew her hand back as if burned. Shit, she probably thought he was some sex-crazed freak.

"Wren, I'm sor—"

"You'll need to lose it." Her eyes came up to meet his like two smoldering sapphires.

"Huh?"

"The T-shirt." She flicked her hand in his direction. "A dish towel won't fix that. It has to come off."

He hesitated for a moment but the lust in her eyes urged him on. Curling his fingers under the hem of the now-soaked cotton shirt, he peeled it up and over his head. Cool air swept over his skin, tightening his nipples and making him hyperaware of every inch of his body.

"The jeans, too," she said, keeping her face straight. "They're soaked."

He glanced down and saw a small dark patch where

the denim had absorbed the water. They were hardly soaked. "You sure about that?"

"Let me help you." She stepped forward and reached for the buckle on his belt.

Her fingertips grazed his bare skin and he had to stifle a moan. He might have started the fire, but she was fanning the flames.

6

WASN'T SHE SUPPOSED to be keeping her distance? At the very least she should be drawing boundaries, given he was the guy who could get her in a world of trouble right now.

Then why did you come here? You knew where this would go. He won't leave your head until you do something about it.

Her fingers trembled as they wrapped around the sturdy leather of his belt, grazing the hard ridge pressing against his fly. His hips jerked as she released the buckle.

"Christ, Wren." He uttered her name so low she almost didn't hear it. But he only took a second before he grabbed her hips and pinned her against the kitchen counter. "I thought I was going to be the one to make a move."

"So move," she said, taunting him softly.

A gasp escaped her lips as he nudged his leg between hers, his thigh applying just the right amount of pressure to the needy ache there.

"Yes." The word slipped from her lips and Wren felt

her last remaining ounce of restraint disappear into the ether.

What did Debbie say—you've got to use it before you lose it?

Maybe it was stupid to get entangled with Rhys. No, it was *definitely* stupid. And not only that, it was irresponsible and selfish. She was keeping secrets from this man who'd been nothing but kind to her. Even after she'd spilled out all the pain of what had happened to her back home.

Stupid, stupid, stupid.

But right now her brain wasn't the one in the driver's seat. So there would be no obeying the speed limit, no following the rules. Her body had taken over, and it wanted to make up for lost time.

"How do you feel about dessert?" she asked.

Hard granite dug into her lower back as his hips held her fast. "What do you have in mind?"

"Let's skip whatever you had planned and go straight to bed."

"Health conscious. I like it." His hot breath whispered across her skin as his full lips grazed her cheek.

"Yes, *exactly* what I was going for." She rolled her eyes, her laugh breaking off into a moan as he nipped at her earlobe. "Do you have to be such an adult about everything?"

"I'm thinking some very adult things right now."

Her hands drifted up his chest, tracing each ridge of muscle one by one. "Oh yeah?"

"Super adult. It would make my spreadsheet look like child's play."

Laughter bubbled up in Wren's chest as she placed a finger over his lips. "Okay, enough dirty talk."

Mercifully, he brushed her hand aside and finally captured her mouth. The soft glide of his tongue against hers left her weak at the knees. He tasted of wine and heaven. Boy, oh boy, could he kiss.

This was A-grade, five-gold-stars, Nobel Prize levels of kissing.

His hands were at her waist, then her rib cage, then her breasts. Kneading. Squeezing. Flicking.

"Oh!" Her head jerked back as he pinched her nipple through the thin layer of her tank. It felt as though a volt of electricity had shot straight through her.

"Is that a good 'oh'?" He chuckled against the side of her neck as he nipped at the sensitive skin there. Each bite was soothed with a swipe of his tongue in a maddening pattern. Nip. Swipe. Nip. Swipe.

"That's a 'don't stop if you know what's good for you' oh," she said, lolling her head back as his fingers hooked under the strap of her tank and pulled it down, exposing her breast to his hands.

His palm circled her, only stopping to allow his thumb to take over. And then his mouth… Oh, dear God. His mouth. He drew her nipple between his teeth, holding it gently there while he flicked his tongue against her, drawing out every soul-deep pleasure sound she could possible make.

Shamelessly, she rubbed against him. It had been so long since she'd felt this good, strung tighter than a wire and ready to snap. His other hand fisted in her skirt, trying to get at her through all the layers of fabric.

"Dammit," he growled against her breast. "This skirt is ridiculous."

"It's not ridiculous."

"It is." He stood back and watched, his dark eyes almost totally black as they drank her in. "No, it's criminal. Hiding those legs away should be illegal."

Laughing, she made a show of swinging her hips like an exotic dancer. "Well, I do *not* want to get arrested."

"Ditch the skirt."

A sharp sound pierced the air as she drew the zipper down, and in an instant the fabric puddled at her feet. The heel of his palm found her center, grinding a series of slow, intense circles against her sex. Her clit ached, desperate for friction and release.

"Yes," she gasped, running her hands around the back of his head as he suckled her breast. His hair was so short there was nothing for her to grab on to, but that didn't stop her from trying.

His mouth came back up to hers as his hand shifted, a finger breaching the edge of her panties to softly stroke the seam of her sex. He'd be able to feel just how wet she was, how insanely aroused and excited. But she didn't care—couldn't care. Not while he was pushing her so close to an orgasm she knew would shatter her completely.

"Rhys...uh!" The words dissolved on her tongue as he kissed her, the tip of his finger pressing against her entrance.

"Are you ready?" His words were rough, sharp. Like gravel. "Are you ready to feel my fingers inside you?"

"Please, please." She couldn't string any more words together, so she looped her arms around his neck and pressed her lips to his ear. "Yes."

The second he slid a finger inside her she thought she'd break. Her internal muscles clenched around him immediately, trying to draw him all the way in. But he held on to his control, sliding in and out slowly. Easing her into it. Stretching her.

She ground her hips against his hand and moaned, cursing under her breath. Then he shifted, curling his finger at just the right angle, rubbing the little bundle of nerves deep inside her and that was it. Game over.

"Oh. My. God." Her body shook and she tumbled, wave after wave of pleasure crashing over her. Filling her. Drowning her.

He held her there until it subsided. Until her heart slowed and her breath came in longer beats. Until she was able to stand on her own. Only then did he withdraw his hand and kiss her trembling lips.

"See. So much better than spreadsheets," she said with a shaky laugh.

"Couldn't agree more." A chuckle rumbled deep in his chest and he bundled her up in his arms, the hard length of his arousal pressing into her belly.

Almost immediately her hunger returned. At full force.

Her fingertips grazed him, feeling the strength of him through the cotton of his boxer briefs. She wasn't done yet, not by a long shot. Finding the slit in his underwear, she snaked her hand in and wrapped her fingers around him. He was hot against her palm, thick and heavy. *Very* thick.

She swallowed. She hadn't been with many men during her somewhat lackluster sex life. And *none* of them had felt like Rhys. The sheer virility of him thrilled her. Smoothing her hand up and down, she squeezed tentatively and was rewarded with a low, ragged groan.

Then she remembered. *Condoms.*

They hadn't exactly been high up on her shopping list

when she'd fled to New York, so she hoped he would be better prepared. She didn't want to stop now; she didn't know if she had the strength to walk away without experiencing that long, hard length inside her.

"Shall we move this party to the bedroom?" he said as his lips brushed the shell of her ear.

"I'm hoping you're prepared."

"If you're talking about protection, of course. I didn't want to be presumptuous but…" He grinned.

"You *are* a Boy Scout. I knew it."

He grabbed her hand and led her toward his bedroom. "Come on. If I don't have you now I'm going to burst."

"Is that a fact?"

She couldn't deny how good his attraction made her feel. It smoothed over her, filling in the cracks and dents and chips in her confidence. It restored her. Made her believe that she was a sexy, young woman who could start over. Start fresh.

"One hundred percent." He drew her to him by the waist, his large hands skating around to her lower back and pressing her against him.

"Not a hundred and ten?" she teased.

"There is no more than a hundred percent."

Her calves hit the edge of his bed as he backed her up. Drawing his eyes away only for a moment, he yanked open the top drawer of his bedside table and rummaged around until he produced a foil packet. Then he tossed it onto the bed and returned to her.

"Now we're prepared," she said, her palms running up and down her thighs. Unsure where to start.

"More." The word came out so strangled, so forced that it fueled her on.

She slipped her hands between her legs to brush against her drenched panties. "Like this?"

"Hell. Yes."

She whipped the tank over her head and turned, tipping forward from her waist so that her hands landed on the bed and her ass waved high in the air. A guttural groan came from behind her, and a moment later he was pressed against her. Rough hands held her in place as he rubbed the hard length of his cock against her ass.

"Holy shit, Wren. You're incredible." His fingers hooked into the waistband of her panties and pulled them over her ass and down her legs. "Stay there and let me look."

Her whole body clenched as cool air drifted across her sex. She'd never done anything like this before. Sex with her previous boyfriends had been bland as cardboard. But she hadn't known anything else. This, however, seemed natural. Clearly, she'd been missing out.

Then she felt his cock press against her inner thigh, smudging moisture against her. A second later the sound of foil tearing broke through their heavy breathing, and Wren turned to face him, watching him roll the condom down his length.

"We'll go slow, okay?" His palm cupped her face and she kissed his hand.

"Yes, please." She reached out to touch him, her fingers skating over the swollen head of his cock.

He eased her back against the bed and used his strong thighs to part her softer ones. The contrast of his warm, brown skin against her fairness sucked the breath out of her lungs. He was so beautiful. So confident and capable and strong.

Yet there was a gentleness to him, a level of care that she wasn't used to.

Closing her eyes, she breathed in the surroundings. The scent of sex, the unique male aroma mingling with clean laundry, a hint of cologne. She wanted to absorb it all.

"You still with me, Wren?" His lips brushed over her jaw and down her neck.

"All the way." Her fingers raked down his back as he shifted forward, the head of his cock pressing against her opening.

"Tell me how it feels, okay?" His hand cupped her breast, and he rolled a nipple between his thumb and forefinger.

"Amazing." The word dissolved into a cry as he pushed inside her, filling her. Taking her.

She sucked in a breath and let it out slowly, willing her body to relax into it. As he started moving, all the blood in her body rushed south and she melted against him. Each stroke pushed her higher and higher, his hips bumping her as he built up speed.

He rained kisses down over her. "You feel so good wrapped around me like that."

"Wrapped around you?" A wicked smile curved on her mouth and she lifted her hips, anchoring her legs around his waist. Urging him to go deeper. Drawing him in.

"Wren!" His hips jerked and he pumped into her, the rhythm frantic as they chased pleasure.

The muscles in his arms corded as he thrust, and she gripped him, digging her nails into his skin. Marking him as hers. Her name fell from his lips as he shuddered inside her.

The silence washed over her as they lay there, tangled

in one another, and a deep calm claimed her. Maybe her sister had been right all along. Sex was just what she needed to feel in charge of her life again.

RHYS HOVERED IN that fuzzy stage between sleep and wakefulness as sunlight breached the gaps in his blinds.

Last night had been everything he'd wanted. He and Wren had shared a physical connection that could only be described as electric. Together, their bodies just... worked.

After a steamy shower together, they'd tumbled back into bed and slept soundly until he'd reached for her in the middle of the night. In the darkness everything was new; he'd learned her body all over again. Mapped it with his hands and his tongue. Explored every inch of her until sleep had claimed them once more.

His muscles ached as he stretched, his hand gravitating toward her as if that instinct had already been ground into his subconscious. But his palm connected with a flat surface. Blinking, he pushed up to a sitting position and surveyed the room.

No Wren.

"You have to wake up to reality at some point," he said to himself.

They hadn't exactly made any promises to one another last night—it had been raw and unbridled. Spontaneous. Without expectation.

In other words, the total opposite to how he did everything in his life.

He rolled out of bed and padded into the kitchen. The rush of early morning traffic greeted him from the open window, highlighting the quietness of his apartment. Still no Wren. Disappointment curled low in his gut.

He'd been hoping to wake up with her and perhaps extend their night of passion into the morning. Before he had the chance to decide how to handle her stealthy exit, his work ringtone cut through the silence and he grabbed the phone from the coffee table.

"Rhys?" Quinn's excited voice made him cringe. "I'm glad you're already up."

He looked at the screen. It wasn't even seven thirty, and Quinn was notoriously *not* a morning person. "How much coffee have you had?"

"Not much," she said in a way that told him she was well and truly caffeinated. "When do you think you'll be in?"

His gaze swept over the empty apartment. It wasn't as if he had anything to hang around for given that Wren had vanished. "I'll be leaving in a few minutes. Why?"

"I couldn't sleep last night, so I was doing some digging on Sean Ainslie and his employees. I found some interesting stuff."

If this were any other job he would have told Quinn to run with the information and only come to him when she got stuck—managing the tech side of security for Cobalt & Dane kept him too busy to be involved in every single assignment. But he wanted to keep an eye on the situation in case things became dangerous. It wasn't too long ago that a seemingly ordinary information security job had resulted in Quinn being cornered alone by a person connected to their client.

He didn't want anything to happen that might put Quinn—or Wren—in the crosshairs.

"Keep digging," he said, heading back into his bedroom. "I'll find you when I get in and you can bring me up to speed."

By the time Rhys made it into the office, Quinn was almost bouncing off the walls. She sat at one of the senior security consultant's desks and was talking a hundred miles a minute.

"You'll have to cut her off, Rhys," Owen said, laughter crinkling his eyes. "If she consumes any more sugar and caffeine she'll launch into outer space."

"I haven't had *that* much," Quinn protested, her smile bright and slightly too wide.

"Her eyeballs are vibrating."

Rhys shook his head. "You have to take better care of yourself. Coffee is no substitute for sleep."

Owen snorted. "Have you seen what she drinks? You can't call that coffee. It's basically a liquefied energy bar."

"Come on." Rhys tilted his head toward the boardroom. "Let's go through what you found."

"I invited Owen to sit in," Quinn said as the three of them headed to the empty room. "He's got capacity at the moment, so he can accompany me on the site visits rather than taking up more of your time."

They all took a seat at the large boardroom-style table. The room was often set up as a "war room" for big assignments and strategy planning.

"Are you sure you've got capacity, Owen?" Rhys leaned back in his chair and kept his tone even. "I don't want to take you away from any other assignments that Logan has you working on."

The senior consultants all reported straight up to Logan Dane, so there was no way Rhys could tell Owen *not* to assist Quinn with the case, especially if he'd been directed to lend a hand by the big boss.

But that didn't mean he would let go of the assignment completely, either. Not while Wren could be at risk.

"I'm more than happy to help out," Owen replied with an easygoing shrug. "Quinn told me there are some tech security elements, which is out of my realm, but I understand there could be some physical security elements, as well. She mentioned a possible break-in attempt."

The technology and information security stuff fell squarely in Rhys's territory thanks to the years he'd spent helping banks protect their information. But Owen was a former police officer and had come from a background that made security a key component of his life. A personal obsession, one might say. Between Quinn and Rhys's tech smarts and Owen's robust experience, they made the perfect team.

Whatever was going on at Ainslie Ave, they would figure it out quickly and quietly.

"There was a failed attempt to access a locked storage room, but the owner of the gallery couldn't find any signs of a break-in to the gallery itself," Rhys said.

Owen nodded. "So we're looking at the possibility of an inside job."

"It *is* possible." Quinn flipped open her laptop. "But the gallery owner himself is behaving strangely. He's got this expensive security system for the one storage room and an alarm system for the building. Yet he has *no* security cameras inside the gallery. It's possible someone who's not a staff member got inside without setting off any alarms, but we have zero proof because there's no footage."

"So what did you find last night?" Rhys asked, eager to move the conversation along. He drummed his fingers against the top of the desk.

"I was digging around to see if the client has had a falling-out with anyone, or has any shady connections that might point to who's behind the break-in attempt. Sean Ainslie comes from a very wealthy family. Old money. His father was also a judge, and he retired a few years ago, so I wondered if he might have enemies."

"Okay," Rhys said. "And?"

"That's not what I found." She held up her hand when he huffed with impatience. "The website has profiles for all the interns that he currently has working for them: Lola, Wren and Aimee."

"So what?"

"Well, the old profiles of the past employees are still saved in the back end of the gallery's website. I compiled all the head shots." Quinn turned her laptop around so Owen and Rhys could see the screen. "Do you detect a common theme?"

Fifteen young female faces stared back at him. Wren's fair skin and blue eyes immediately captured his attention. In the photo, she was laughing. Her eyes shone like they had last night when he'd taken her to bed.

Memories flooded him, his body instantly recalling the feeling of her hands on his chest. Cupping his face. His ass as he thrust into her.

"Boss?" Quinn waved a hand in front of him. "I said, 'Do you detect a common theme?'"

"They're all young women." He shrugged. "What's your point?"

"*Attractive* young women," Owen added. "Are you thinking that he might have become involved with his interns?"

Quinn nodded. "It's very possible. Especially since

I found photos of him with a few of these women at industry events."

Rhys's stomach churned at the thought of Sean hitting on Wren. "Go on."

"One news article references a huge fight he had with a Marguerite Bernard. It said that his gallery was hosting a show for another local artist but the night ended abruptly when the couple had a huge screaming match and he kicked everyone out. According to her website she started working at a different gallery a few months later."

"It could just be a lover's quarrel," Rhys said.

"I wouldn't have thought much of it until I saw this." She reached around the computer and brought up another picture.

It was a picture of a woman. Swelling had almost closed her eye over completely and an eggplant-colored bruise mottled her fair complexion. The skin appeared to be split across her cheekbone.

"Shit," Owen muttered, shaking his head in disgust.

Rhys grunted in agreement and clenched his fists.

"This is Marguerite Bernard," Quinn continued. "This picture was posted on her Instagram page two days after the incident at the gallery. The caption says, 'He will get away with this. His father will protect him and I won't have the chance for justice. Remember, control is not love.' There are a bunch of hashtags under it, as well. She doesn't reference Sean by name, but the timing certainly fits."

Fighting back the sick feeling in his stomach, Rhys tried to focus on the job at hand. Now, with even more reason to be worried for Wren's safety, he needed to ensure that they handled this situation accordingly. Knowing Quinn's background and recent experience, she might want to jump in and blame Ainslie. But they had to tread carefully, refrain from doing anything that might spook him until they had more information.

Which meant Rhys needed to play devil's advocate.

"I understand this is very disturbing," he said. "But I still don't see what this has to do with the potential break-ins. Do you think Marguerite might have done it?"

"Not necessarily, but I've looked into a few of the other women who've worked for Ainslie, and a number didn't stay at the gallery very long." She closed the lid on her laptop. "I'm going to reach out to them and ask if they experienced anything shady about Ainslie's practices."

"You seem to be treating him like a suspect rather than a client," Rhys warned.

Her head bobbed. "I have a funny feeling about this guy. Something doesn't seem right, but point taken. I'll be discreet."

"I thought Quinn and I might head over to the gallery later today so I can suss this guy out," Owen added. "Can't hurt to get another set of eyes on him, right?"

"Of course." Rhys nodded. "I want to be kept fully updated on this assignment. Okay, Quinn?"

"Are you worried that I won't be able to handle it?" Her eyes narrowed at him.

He drew a deep breath. Quinn's insecurities had certainly improved since she'd started dating Aiden, but her journey to confidence wasn't one that would happen overnight. Just as her defensive shield still popped up from time to time.

"Did I say that?"

"No," she admitted.

"I've met with the client. Therefore, my name is stamped on this, and I don't take that lightly." He turned to Owen. "Quinn will run with this assignment and you can provide guidance and mentoring as appropriate."

Owen nodded. "Got it."

Rhys stood. "Good. I expect an update tomorrow morning."

In the meantime, he would have to stay occupied so he didn't drive himself crazy over Wren. No easy task, since her beautiful face appeared the second his brain wasn't fully engaged on a task.

It's just a fling. She's already made it clear that she's not going to stay, and the sooner you believe that, the saner you'll be.

Unfortunately for Rhys, knowing she was leaving didn't necessarily mean he could avoid wanting her to stay.

7

THE LAST FEW days had been a whirlwind for Wren. She'd felt guilty ever since leaving Rhys's apartment at the crack of dawn on Tuesday morning. Now it was Friday and she hadn't seen him all week. Maybe she should have stayed. Morning-after etiquette wasn't exactly her forte, and she'd wanted to save him the trouble of having to kick her out. Or, rather, saving herself the humiliation of *being* kicked out.

Watching his beautiful sleeping form had stirred some uneasy emotions inside her. She was supposed to be in New York to figure out what'd happened to her friend. *Not* to be picking up devastatingly attractive men and using them to broaden her sexual horizons.

But Rhys wasn't just that. The way he'd made her feel…hell, it was soul-soothing. Healing. It was about the sex and yet it wasn't.

Which made her guilt over lying to him so much stronger. Not to mention that she'd yet to make any progress at the gallery.

"You'll bury yourself with all those thoughts," she muttered to herself as she lugged her canvas up the last flight of stairs to her apartment. The messy interpretation of Rhys's face stared at her as she trudged.

At least the dust storm of feelings had the benefit of spurring her into action. She'd decided to take cupcakes to Aimee in the hopes a little "girl time" would butter the woman up and Wren could ask about her relationship with Sean. Turned out buttercream frosting was as good as truth serum.

Aimee must have been looking for a sounding board, because she'd let the information fly as soon as they were alone in the gallery's kitchenette. She'd fought with Sean recently; he'd gotten a little rough. The bruise on Aimee's upper arm was hidden by a floaty top, but there was no denying the distinct finger-shaped marks.

Had Kylie fallen prey to Sean's charms, as well? Wren would never have thought her friend would be the type to get involved with her boss. But there were similarities that Wren couldn't ignore and she already suspected Sean was to blame for Kylie's black eye and fractured bones.

Wren wondered if the email Aimee had tried to delete contained proof of Sean's abuse. Or of their relationship? But when she'd had tried to get back into Sean's email to see what else she could dig up, it looked as though he'd changed the password. After a few failed attempts to get in, she'd reluctantly stopped, afraid that if the password had to be reset he would get suspicious again.

It was yet another day where she'd gone home empty-handed.

From the depths of her bag her phone started to ring. "Dammit," Wren cursed under her breath.

She paused at the top of the staircase, leaning the canvas against the wall while she dug her phone out. "Hello?"

"Big sis!"

"Why do you always seem to call when I'm carrying stuff up stairs?" Wren tucked the phone between her ear and her shoulder. "That's some talent you've got."

"I aim to annoy," Debbie said cheerfully. "How's things? Banged your neighbor yet?"

A strangled noise halfway between laughing and choking came out of Wren's mouth. "What?"

"I take that as a confirmation. Go, you." Her sister laughed. "I hope my pep talk helped things along."

Wren rolled her eyes as she shuffled awkwardly down the corridor with the canvas and her bag. "My sex life has nothing to do with you and that's how it should be."

"Whatever works. Was it amazing? Was *he* amazing?"

"It was and he was, if you must know. Not that it's any of your business." She unlocked her front door and carried the canvas to her empty easel. Staring into her version of Rhys's big warm eyes sent a flutter through her stomach.

"I'm happy for you. Now we don't have to worry about the prune—"

"If you finish that sentence I'm going to come home and throttle you," Wren threatened. "And don't start again with the 'I'm a doctor' BS."

"You're so mean."

"No, I'm setting boundaries. It's a healthy thing to do. You should try it sometime."

Debbie huffed. "Well, I guess I won't bother telling you the real reason I called, then."

Her sister could be a little melodramatic sometimes. Crocodile tears had been her best weapon as a child, her ability to wrap their parents around her little finger far surpassing Wren's natural openness. Part of her used to resent Debbie's way of doing things, but now Wren saw honesty as something to be wary of. Something to be used wisely. Like a currency.

"Spill," she demanded, wandering into the kitchen and flicking on her coffee machine.

"I checked in on Kylie today." Suddenly Debbie's tone was heavier, burdened with emotion.

"How is she?"

"Not good. She's lost a lot of weight." And that was saying something since Kylie was already on the thin side. "She said that someone called her today asking about her work at the gallery."

"Did she say who it was?" Could it have been Rhys? It surely wouldn't take him too long to connect Kylie to Wren. Their hometown was small enough that it would be easy to assume they were acquaintances, at the very least. Perhaps Sean had said something.

"Some girl. Kylie was so flustered by the call that she didn't think to get her name." Debbie sighed.

It must have been Quinn. "Right."

"She was seriously shaken up. They were asking about whether or not she had a relationship with the gallery owner."

"Why would they want to know that?"

"I have no idea."

Wren rubbed her hand over her face. "Did Kylie catch where they were calling from? Was it the police?"

"No. A security company, I think she said."

Definitely Quinn.

Debbie paused. "Tell me you're safe, Birdie."

The concern in her sister's voice made a crushing weight land on Wren's chest. "I'm fine, I promise."

"Kylie was asking about you again. I told her you

were probably being brainwashed on your 'art retreat' into some tree-hugging, plant-eating hippie as we speak."

She could practically hear her sister rolling her eyes. "Good."

"In all seriousness, though, you should come home soon. I'm doing my best, but she's closer to you and I don't think she's telling me everything about what happened."

"I'll email her. But I don't have any results yet, so I can't come home."

"What exactly do you think you're going to find? This seems like a wild freaking goose chase."

Wren swallowed and reached for a mug from the rack next to the sink. The floral design had a chunk taken out of it from when she'd accidentally knocked it over while cooking dinner one night. Her fingertip traced the imperfection.

"I don't know," she admitted. "But there's something up with this Ainslie guy. I can just…feel it. He's doing something bad, and I'd bet my last ten dollars that what happened to Kylie wasn't a first."

"Please be careful."

"I'm *fine*, Debs. Cross my heart." She poured her coffee and hoped that the false confidence in her voice was enough to placate her sister.

"Okay. I'll leave you alone, but I'm calling again in a few days and I don't want you to give me this 'I need boundaries' bullshit. I'm your sister and I will find you so I can whip your ass, if necessary."

"You're getting all Liam Neeson on me," Wren teased. "Are you going to threaten me with your 'very particular set of skills'?"

"Damn straight I am. Now swear to me you'll check in more often?"

"I solemnly swear to check in more often." She smiled in spite of herself. "Hand on heart."

They finished the call a moment later after Debs gave her another "pep talk" about her sex life. The woman couldn't seem to go one phone call without bringing it up. She was twenty-three, though. So perhaps being at college meant she had sex on the brain.

"*You* have sex on the brain," she said to herself with a shake of her head.

The last few days had been a giant waste of time. Instead of being able to concentrate on her work, her head had been full of Rhys. Not just because the sex had been amazing, but because she'd felt amazing afterward.

With Christian, sex had been like a field of land mines. Sometimes she'd navigated it safely, sometimes not. It was impossible to tell what would set him off—it might be that she suggested something he considered "dirty" or that her body didn't respond the way he'd expected.

He was a product of his uptight, guilt-focused upbringing. His messed-up views on sex—and now, with space from him, she *knew* they were messed up—had caused her a lot of angst. Which often made it hard for her to fully enjoy sex. And that meant she often couldn't relax during the act itself.

But Rhys was different. With him she was free to be herself. For the first time in her life she felt sexy and beautiful. Amazing as the orgasms were, it wasn't the most important part. It was laying in his arms afterward, feeling safe and secure and wanted. Not feeling judged.

A tiny voice in the back of her mind niggled at her. *Why stop at one night?*

She wasn't going to be in New York for too long, so that meant there was no risk of anything long-term. No risk of him getting the idea that he had some claim or control over her.

But there was the slight problem of the fact that he was the one person she *should* keep at a distance. Her desire for him battled with her desire to get revenge for her friend. He was the one person who could put a stop to her helping Kylie. And she wasn't yet sure she could trust him to keep her secret and not hand her over to the police.

Then you'll just have to keep your lips shut and talk with your body. It's about time you took what you wanted without worrying about anyone else—you're done with that!

BY THREE O'CLOCK Rhys was driving himself to distraction. With Quinn out of the office and working on the Ainslie Ave assignment, he felt disconnected from his job. He wanted to know what was going on—but checking in too often would only lead to trouble. Either Quinn would get suspicious, or she would think he doubted her.

Neither of which he wanted.

But knowing that didn't help him focus on work. After rearranging his already-neat drawers, wiping down his desk and alphabetizing his books, he'd had enough. Now he was jogging upstairs to his apartment, craving a run. His nervous energy had to be burned off.

Ever since Monday night his body had been wired. Electrified. Buzzing.

As he bounded up the last few steps, he caught sight of Wren's door. His feet carried him toward it without his brain having a chance to react. This had been his game the last few days, wanting to see her but resisting.

His willpower slowly wearing down until now it was merely a whisper.

Maybe he should check if she was home, just in case.

"Just in case what?" he muttered to himself. "She'll probably be at work, anyway."

At that moment—like some kind of sign from the heavens—music started to play inside her apartment. It floated through the door, tempting him.

You should check in and ask about Ainslie. You know, because of the assignment.

His brain had conveniently pushed aside the fact that Quinn would have already asked those questions. But right now he was clutching at straws for an excuse to see Wren that didn't have anything to do with the fact that she'd left in the middle of the night.

He raised his hand to the door and knocked twice. When she opened it, Rhys wondered if he'd accidentally found a secret gate to heaven. The scent of chocolate wafted out and Wren stood there looking like a vision. She had on a white tank top, her long legs exposed by a pair of tiny denim shorts. Her hair was held back with a red head scarf.

A dark streak marred her cheekbone. "Uh, hi," she said, a flush immediately creeping across her skin.

"You have a little something..." He reached out and swiped at the mark. "Chocolate or paint?"

"Chocolate. I'm baking brownies." Her eyes glimmered. "Would you like to come in?"

"Sure. I had a few questions for you about the gallery, if that's okay?"

"Of course." Was it his imagination or did her eyes dim at the mention of her work? "That shouldn't stop me from serving up some dessert, should it?"

"Hell, no."

She held the door open for him and he stepped inside. The kitchen was a disaster zone; there were mixing bowls and wooden spoons piled up in the sink. A bag of sugar had tipped over and spilled fine crystals onto the countertop. Packets of ingredients littered the bench. As Rhys followed her to the source of the glorious scent, something crunched beneath his shoe.

A walnut.

"Sorry for the state of the kitchen," she said with a nervous laugh. "I'm a messy cook. But I promise the taste will be worth it."

He toyed with the idea of sharing his process for "cleaning as you go" that kept his kitchen near spotless while he cooked. But the words halted in his mouth as Wren bent over to open the oven. His mouth watered, and it wasn't from the intensified scent of chocolate brownies.

The sight of her shapely ass being thrust high in the air as she tipped forward, red oven mitts on her hands, damn near fried his brain cells.

"It's fine," he managed to get out as she straightened up and placed the baked goods onto a wooden cutting block. "I would say 'me, too' but you'd see right through that."

"You're right." She laughed. "I wouldn't believe it for a second. I bet your kitchen is cleaner after you've finished cooking than mine is before I've started."

"I'm going to plead the Fifth on that one," he said.

"You know, getting messy isn't always a bad thing," she said as she dipped the knife into the center.

Gooey melted chocolate clung to the blade. She swiped her fingertip along it, gathering up the excess batter before popping it into her mouth. Watching her lips wrap around her finger sent a bolt of lust through him.

Damn, she could make even the simplest things look tempting as sin.

"You had some questions for me?" she asked, her lip twitching with a cheeky smile.

"I do. Did you end up meeting with Quinn or anyone else from Cobalt & Dane in the last few days?"

She shook her head as she sliced up the brownies. "No, I believe they came in on Tuesday but I only worked half a day. I think Aimee and Lola spoke with them. And then I was supposed to be painting this afternoon but I couldn't seem to focus, so I brought the canvas home with me. You know, change of scenery and all that."

"So you started baking?"

"It's my favorite method of procrastination." Her delicate hands moved deftly and a few seconds later she pushed a plate toward him.

"Are you still working on my portrait?" He forked a generous piece of the dessert into his mouth and moaned at the perfectly rich, sweet taste.

It had been a hell of a long time since he'd eaten anything this decadent—his diet was designed for optimum nutrition, and that didn't allow for a lot of sweet treats other than the occasional glass of wine.

But Wren's baking was as tempting as she was.

"I am. But I'm feeling a little stuck with it," she admitted. "Sean said if I don't get him a complete painting soon he's going to boot me out of the program."

"That's harsh."

"I understand his point—there are plenty of people who would love to have my spot. But sometimes the creativity just won't come." She sighed. "Anyway, you didn't come here to listen to my woes."

"I could sit for you," he said. "So you can paint me."

"You want to be my model?"

"If it would help. I mean, I can sit and ask the questions I need to ask and you can paint." He cleared his throat. "You know, two birds, one stone and all that. It'll be more efficient that way."

God, he sounded like an idiot. What was it about Wren that got him all tangled up? As if she wouldn't see "more efficient" as a thinly veiled ploy for him to hang around longer.

"That might just be what I need." She abandoned her half-eaten brownie. "What's your modeling experience?"

"Zip."

She grabbed a chair and positioned it in front of her canvas. "Really? I'm surprised."

"Why?"

"You'd make a good model, I think. My life-drawing class would have loved you."

"You've done life drawing?" He settled into the chair and tried to get comfortable.

"Yeah. I had to drive to one of the bigger cities near my hometown to take the classes in secret." The click-clack sound of her setting up her brushes filled the pause in their conversation. "That kind of thing is frowned upon where I come from, given the naked body is *so* sinful." She rolled her eyes.

"Personally, I'm a fan of the naked body."

Memories of their night together flickered in his mind, but he tamped them down. He was here to find out what was going on at the gallery and to make sure that Sean Ainslie was keeping his hands to himself.

Yeah, right, keep telling yourself that.

"So, about the gallery," he started.

"Hmm?" Her eyes looked past the canvas, darting over him as if she were analyzing him down to his bones. Breaking his face up into components and committing them to memory.

"Has Sean Ainslie ever hit on you?"

That question seemed to throw her off-kilter. "No, why?"

"Quinn had a hunch that perhaps he was getting involved with his interns."

"Is that such a bad thing?" She frowned as she turned back to the canvas.

"Not necessarily. But we think he may have assaulted one of his interns previously. Some information points to them being an item."

She stilled on the other side of the canvas. Part of her was hidden, but he could see her hand hovering in front of her. Motionless. "Which intern?"

"A woman named Marguerite. Do you know her?"

"No." She adjusted her bandanna. "But he *is* seeing one of the current interns."

Hmm, so Quinn might have been on the money, after all. "Who?"

"Aimee." Her eyes remained on the canvas.

He made a mental note to check in with Quinn and find out whether she'd come up with that same information. "How do you know that?"

When she dragged her gaze up, guilt painted her features. "I don't want to get anyone in trouble."

"You won't. We're just trying to understand what's going on."

"Aimee told me."

He nodded. "Okay."

"I thought this was supposed to be about a security incident." Her light brows crinkled. "I mean, what does one have to do with the other?"

"We're looking for a motive. If he's abused one of his employees in the past, there's a chance she or someone she knows has targeted him for revenge purposes. I get how they might not seem connected, but we have to consider all angles. And Sean couldn't give us any information on who he suspected might be trying to break into the gallery, so we have to start somewhere."

"If he really has abused his staff, would you blame them for acting out against him?"

"No, but my personal feelings on the situation don't matter. Our job is to make sure we find out who's been breaking into the gallery and into Sean's emails." He paused for a moment. "If there's evidence that he's been hurting his employees, then of course we'll do the right thing and hand that over to the police. But that doesn't absolve me from my responsibilities to protect his company. I'm not taking one side over the other."

She nodded, her expression guarded. "Have you considered the possibility that perhaps it was a crime of opportunity? Well…an almost crime of opportunity?"

"Yes, but that doesn't explain why this person managed to get into the gallery without tripping the alarm but couldn't get into the storage room."

She resumed painting, her movement slow and gentle behind the canvas. "No, I guess it doesn't. But I can tell you one thing, I am *not* romantically involved with Sean Ainslie. I may not be perfect, but I'm a one-man kind of woman."

One man. *Him.*

"Is that so?" Lord help him, but hearing those words made him feel all kinds of satisfied. "The bed was a lot emptier the other morning than I would have liked."

"Maybe you imagined the whole thing," she said softly.

"I don't think so, Wren. You know I'm not the creative type. I could never have dreamed up something that spectacular."

She bit down on her lip as she painted. "You might not be creative but you *are* good with your hands."

"So why the ninja exit in the middle of the night?"

"I didn't want the morning to be awkward."

He chuckled. "It would have been many things, but awkward isn't one of them."

"How can you be sure?" Her voice sounded so small, so vulnerable.

Hidden by the canvas, she continued to paint. Something told him paintings were her shield, a way for her to express herself that didn't require words.

"Because I had an amazing time and I was hoping it might continue. I think we work well together and there's nothing awkward about that."

"But we're so different." She put down her brush and stepped out from behind the easel. "You're the perfect specimen of adulthood and I'm…not."

"I was hoping after all we'd shared that my maturity wouldn't be the thing you focused on." He pushed up from his chair and walked over to her.

"It's not, but you're so perfect at everything." She laughed. "It's kind of intimidating."

"I'm *not* perfect at everything."

Her arms folded across her chest, propping up her bust so that his eyes were drawn there. The white tank top was splattered with paint. "Oh yeah? Tell me something you're bad at."

"Relaxing." He held up a hand when she rolled her eyes. "Hear me out. I go crazy on the weekends if I don't have anything to do. Since I met you, I've actually had a meal without working while I was eating."

"I'm not sure that counts."

"Okay." The challenge was most definitely accepted. "I suck at keeping plants alive, I can't make out the difference between expensive wine and cheap wine. I'm an embarrassingly terrible poker player and I was told once by an ex that I give really painful massages."

Wren laughed. "I don't know which of those is my favorite."

"I've never given a massage to anyone since that conversation. It's my secret shame."

"I don't believe it for a second." She reached out for his hand and rubbed her thumb over the center of his palm. "Your hands were good to me the other night."

The small touch sent excitement rocketing through him. All Wren had to do was get close and his body lit up like a fireworks display. Normally, he was able to keep his attraction to women contained, controlled. But with Wren, everything he normally held dear seemed to fly out the window.

"I'm happy to hear it," he said.

"Want to see how the painting is going?" she asked, her voice soft and low.

Knowing how cagey Wren had been about showing him her paintings the night they'd first had dinner together, this show of trust warmed him. "Definitely."

She slipped her fingers between his and tugged him

closer to the easel. "It's nowhere near finished. But having you here really helped me to get in the zone."

"Must be my type A personality rubbing off on you."

"Maybe."

From the first version he'd seen, this was leaps and bounds ahead. The lines were filled in; his eyes seemed dark and intense. She'd shaped his mouth to have an almost imperceptible lift at their corners, like they were sharing a private joke as she painted.

"It's incredible," he said. "You're incredible."

Viewing himself through her eyes, he wasn't invisible. He wasn't second best. He wasn't the boy who'd struggled to belong. She saw him for who he really was. He couldn't let that go, no matter how much his sensible side told him to walk away from this woman.

She wasn't planning to stay, so falling for her was a bad idea. He'd be setting himself up for disappointment. But that was before they'd started to explore the chemistry between them.

What if she had a reason to stay?

8

WREN MIGHT BE the impulsive type, but even she could see that getting involved with Rhys was a dumb idea.

His security company was making headway with their investigation. They'd already figured out that Sean was crossing the line with his employees—how much longer would it take before Rhys figured out her reason for being at the gallery?

My personal feelings on the situation don't matter.

His words danced in her head. It was clear that once he found out the truth, he'd still think her in the wrong, even with her good intentions. Which meant it was one thing to indulge in a night of passion, but it was quite another to go back for seconds.

But that was the problem with Rhys—she couldn't get enough. She couldn't keep her distance. She didn't *want* to.

"We have something here," he said. "I'm not sure what it is, but I can't ignore it."

"You know I'm not going to be staying after my internship is over," she said, as though it might shake her brain into action. How could she explore these burgeoning feelings for him while at the same time lying to him? She couldn't.

But sex was something she could keep separate from her emotions. If she drew a line between the two, maybe she could have it all.

"Is that set in stone?" He searched her face, his own expression unreadable.

"I have to get back to my family," she said. "Besides, if I stayed I would inevitably make your life messy and disorganized."

He pulled her against him, his large hands cupping her face and tilting her up to him. "Maybe you can teach me to be messy while you're here."

Relief swam through her. She couldn't promise anything, nor could she allow herself to get emotionally entangled with him. But that didn't mean she was ready to give up the incredible feeling of his hands on her.

"You couldn't handle it," she teased.

The graze of his lips across her jaw sent a shiver racing down her spine. "Try me, Wren. I dare you."

"You dare me, huh? I don't back down from dares."

"I was hoping you'd say that." His mouth captured hers for one blissful second. One all-consuming, earth-shattering moment.

It was wrong, she knew that. Wrong to kiss him while she was keeping secrets from him, wrong to allow him to touch her even though their goals were in direct competition. But her body overrode her sensibilities.

"You're on," she said, pulling away.

She ordered him to sit as she went into the kitchen.

The man had no idea what he'd started. Anyone from her hometown would know not to dare her unless they expected to suffer the consequences. Once, in high school, she'd gotten herself suspended for letting a duck loose in the library on Kylie's challenge.

Grinning to herself, she pulled a jar of chocolate sauce from the cupboard and found a small paint brush. The sauce had been intended to go with the brownies, but now she had a much better use for it.

"Should I be nervous?" Rhys asked in a way that sounded anything but.

"No, but you might want to take your top off." She sauntered back to where he sat, being sure to swing her hips.

"Is that what I think it is?" He eyed the sauce and divested himself of his T-shirt.

"We're going to have a little painting lesson," she said, ignoring his question.

With languid slowness, she drew down the zipper on her shorts. She was urged on by the catch in Rhys's breath as she shimmed out of the denim. It would be so easy to become addicted to the way he reacted to her, as though she were the sexiest thing he'd ever laid eyes on.

Under his heated gaze, she might be able to believe it.

"Ready to get messy?" she asked with a grin.

"You'd better not be teasing," he growled. "If we're going to do this, I want to do it properly."

"Of course you do." She set the tub of chocolate sauce down and dipped the brush into it. "Mr. Perfect doesn't do things by halves, does he?"

"No, he doesn't."

The brush dripped with sticky, chocolaty goodness. "Last chance to back out."

"Not a fucking chance, Wren." His eyes met hers, his pupils wide and his breathing ragged.

She climbed into his lap, sauce in one hand and her

brush in the other. The hard ridge of his erection pressed against the inside of her bare leg and she made sure to wriggle enough to elicit a groan from him.

Power surged through her body. She'd never felt like this before, so in control and fiercely sexy. It made her whole body pulse with desire.

"You're all mine now," she whispered as she streaked the chocolate across his chest. "All dirty and all mine."

Another streak followed, and this time she chased the brush with her tongue, catching a flat, dark nipple between her lips. A low, guttural sound emanated from within him as he ground up against her, his hands flying to her hips.

"You like that?" she teased.

The brush peppered his skin with sticky marks, her tongue smudging and swirling the chocolate around. She used her teeth, her lips and her hands to mark him. To claim him.

"Don't think you're the only one who gets to have fun," he said, thrusting his hands into her hair as he pulled her in for a searing, chocolaty kiss.

Her lips were sticky with sauce and it melded perfectly with the taste of him. "I'm the artist here."

His hands were under her tank top, her breasts spilling into his palm. With a rough flick of his thumb, her sex clenched so tight that her breath stuttered. She pressed against him to alleviate the pressure, but it only made her want him more.

"Damn," he muttered as he kissed his way down her neck, almost knocking the jar out of her hand. "We need to get you naked."

"My hands are full. You'll have to help me out."

She'd expected him to pull the fabric over her head,

but instead he grabbed the tank top at the neckline and ripped the whole thing open. The sound of cotton tearing pulled a shocked laugh from her, which dissolved into a heady groan as his mouth came down to her chest.

"Yes," he breathed, snaking one hand around her waist as he sat back and raked his eyes over her.

Dipping the brush into the sauce again, she let the chocolate drizzle over her now-exposed chest. Anything to make him put his mouth on her again.

"You're going to have us both covered in this stuff," he said before dipping his head.

"That's the plan."

Her head rolled back as he took one nipple between his lips, alternating between sucking and flicking his tongue over the sensitive bud. The moment he used his teeth on her—so gentle and yet not quite—her eyes fluttered shut.

His arm around her waist, strong and sure, kept her from melting to the ground. She wasn't sure if she could come from simply having his mouth on her breast, but the pleasure spiking hard and fast inside her said it was indeed a possibility. Her whole body tensed and ached for him; it responded to his every touch as though he'd been doing it for years. As though he'd written her instruction manual.

"You taste so good," he moaned between her breasts, nuzzling them and nipping at the tender flesh there. "And not just from the chocolate."

The spot between her legs throbbed, and she rocked against him, the friction making stars dance before her eyes. She needed him inside her. Soon.

"There's somewhere else I want to taste." He looked up, his eyes black with arousal.

Feeling bold, she got a little more sauce onto the brush

and carefully placed the jar on the ground. "Your turn to be Picasso."

With a wicked grin, he took the brush from her and stood, supporting her weight with one arm. The torn tank slipped down her shoulders, and she shrugged it off. Thank god she hadn't bothered with a bra.

"I can't do my best work in this cramped position," he said. "I want to be able to see all of you."

Before she could figure out where he was taking her, he'd placed her softly down on the kitchen table. His gentleness totally belied the rough edge in his voice and the raw excitement on his face.

Tucking a finger into the waistband of her panties, he dragged them down her legs.

STANDING IN FRONT of Wren, her body laid out like a feast, he felt as mighty as a god. There was something about her responsiveness that filled him with heady, primal power. With her, he could do anything. Be anything.

Right now he wanted to be the man to bring her pleasure.

"Ready for a taste of your own medicine?" he asked, pushing her legs apart with his hand.

Her teeth dented her lower lip and she nodded. "Yes."

Dragging the brush from her belly button down to the bare patch of skin at the apex of her thighs, he forced himself to move slowly. This wasn't something that could—or should—be rushed. He would draw her pleasure out, string her along as much as willpower would allow.

The streak of dark chocolate against her white skin was striking and erotic. He circled the brush lower, creating a swirl over the lips of her sex. When he stroked her clit with the brush, she gasped and arched her back. Her slim fingers curled around the edge of the table, and it was all he could do not to guide them to his steel-hard cock.

Patience. He would have his turn soon, but not before he tasted her.

The brush caressed her skin as he painted her, concentrating on the bundle of nerves between her legs. A low, throaty moan was his reward.

"Please, Rhys," she gasped. "Oh God, please."

"I thought art was supposed to take time," he teased. "You can't rush a masterpiece."

Her hips bucked as he applied more pressure, her lashes fluttering. He'd never seen a more beautiful sight.

"This masterpiece is about to combust," she said through gritted teeth.

A chuckle rumbled deep in his chest. "I'd better take care of that."

At the first swipe of his tongue she let out a low, keening moan. He took his time, cleaning her up with his tongue until there wasn't a trace of the chocolate sauce left. His lips peppered her with soft kisses as he worked his way around her, avoiding the one spot where she wanted him most.

She grasped his head, seeking to control his movements. "Please, Rhys. I'm dying."

"No, you're not." He nuzzled her. "I'll look after you."

Running his hands up and down her thighs, he parted her with his thumbs. She was swollen with desire, her body totally primed and ready for him. The sight made all the blood in his body rush south, leaving him light-headed in the best way possible.

"I need to come," she whimpered.

Her pleas turned into a low groan of surrender as he drew her clit between his lips, focusing on that one sensitive spot until the shudders started. Her thigh trembled against his cheek and her breath quickened. When the moment of her release hit, her nails dug into his shoulders and she cried out his name.

He'd never forget how it sounded on her lips.

Gathering her up in his arms, he carried her to the bathroom. Her arms wound around his neck as if out of instinct. "Where are you taking me?"

"You've had your fun. Now I'm going to clean us up," he said, pressing a kiss to her forehead.

"See, I knew you couldn't handle being messy."

"I don't think you'll be complaining once we get started."

Her bathroom was the same as the one in his apartment, at least when it came to the layout and fittings. But instead of his fluffy gray towels hanging from the rack, she had threadbare versions in an almost psychedelic pink-and-green print. The top of her sink was dotted with several tubes of lip gloss, a hairbrush and a bottle of perfume. A pair of hot-pink panties sat in one corner on the floor.

"Don't judge me," she grumbled as he set her down, shoving the panties to one side with her foot.

"No judgment. Why don't you get the water running and I'll get out of these pants?"

Her eyes sparkled. "Good idea."

She stepped into the shower and turned on the tap. Water ran down her body and she jumped up and down on the spot while it warmed up. The cold spray made her nipples pink and stiff.

For a moment all he could do was stare. As steam

started to billow up, she tilted her head back and let the spray of water slide down her. It mixed with the chocolate on her chest and ran down her body, washing away the evidence of their messy interlude.

"You're supposed to be stripping," she said, pointing to his jeans. "Come on, I've shown you mine."

His cock was straining hard against the fly of his jeans, and he gave in to the desire for some friction there. Rubbing the heel of his palm up and down the hard length, he watched as Wren's eyes widened. He loosened his belt and unzipped the denim, letting it drop to his feet. As he pushed down his boxer briefs, he felt her eyes on him.

They were hungry eyes. Excited eyes. The kind of eyes that made him feel alive.

"Like what you see?" he asked as she drank him in.

Her head bobbed. "Yeah."

He kicked the discarded clothing to one side and joined her in the shower. The warm water loosened muscles he hadn't realized were bunched up. He'd been coiled like a spring waiting to have his moment with her.

"You don't have to stop at looking," he said, cornering her against the tiled wall.

"That might get messy," she warned.

"I'm coming around to your way of doing things." He bent his head to hers and claimed her in a scorching kiss. "I can handle a little mess with you."

There was no hesitation when she reached for him, her fingers wrapping around his cock as though they belonged there. She squeezed him and ran her hand up and down, twisting her wrist slightly. Feeling him. Learning him.

"Is that good?" she asked, her voice breathy.

"Hell yeah." He reached for her free hand and guided her to cup his balls. "This feels good, too."

Her curiosity was like a drug and her touch moved from tentative to bold. Stoking harder, she rubbed the tip of him between her legs.

"Jesus, Wren. What are you doing to me?"

"Something right by the sound of it."

He jerked into her grip, his hips bucking of their own accord. There was only one way this could end, and that end would be pretty damn sudden if he didn't take back control. "Tell me you bought some protection."

"Oops."

"Wren," he growled. If they had to stop now the frustration may kill him.

"It's okay." She pressed a finger to his lips. "Let me take care of it."

She sank to her knees, her hands running down over his stomach to his thighs. Bracing herself against him, she dropped her head to the tip of his cock. Her tongue darted out to taste him. Test him.

It was sweet, sweet torture.

She guided his hand to her hair, and he threaded his fingers through the now wet strands. When she sank her mouth onto him, he groaned and the sound vibrated within the confines of the shower. There was nothing more erotic than watching himself slide in and out of her pink lips. Or the way she wrapped her fingers around him, working him slowly to orgasm.

She drew back, releasing him from her mouth. "You taste good."

"You feel good." He rested his head against the tiles, relishing the consistent stroke of her hand. "Those lips are incredible."

"Just my lips?" Her tongue swirled around the sensitive crown of his cock.

"That, too." The words were strangled by his pleasure. "Everything, Wren. So. Damn. Good."

She guided him back into her mouth and hummed in response. The vibrations almost sent him over the edge, and he fisted his hand in her hair. She scraped her teeth gently along the underside of his cock, ratcheting up the sensation.

"Wren." His hips jerked as she sank down farther, taking him as far as she could.

A tight ache balled up inside him as she sucked, and she flicked her tongue over the sensitive head until his thighs twitched. Release washed over him. He let her name fall from his lips over and over and over as he emptied himself inside her.

A moment later she was wrapped up in his arms, and they stayed there until the water turned cold and goose bumps broke out on her skin. It would have been easy to stay there forever.

Why do you always have to leap to forever? She's spelled it out for you already. She's not going to stay.

But he shoved the thoughts aside, wanting his worries to disappear like the water down her drain. He couldn't let go of the idea that their bond went far beyond mind-bending pleasure and into something more emotional. More real. All he had to do was convince her to give them a shot.

9

AFTER THEIR SHOWER, Rhys took Wren to his place. They didn't want to fall victim to a lack of condoms again, and it wasn't long before they wound up on his bed in a tangled heap of limbs. She'd lost count of the number of times he'd made her body soar.

It was a new experience for her, this contentment and trust that she had with Rhys. Sure, he teased her about her messy, disorganized lifestyle—and she gave it back to him—but that kind of teasing had an inherent sense of familiarity. In fact, she felt more at home in his arms than she ever had in Charity Springs.

It would be hard to say goodbye to him, but she couldn't forget about the people who needed her back home.

With her cheek pressed against his rib cage, the slow rhythm of his breathing soothed her. Her fingertips gently traced the dark trail of hair that ran from his belly button to underneath the white bedsheet. Even after what they'd done, he was still semi-hard, his length tenting the sheet.

"Go on, I don't bite," he said, his voice husky. "You can touch me."

"I thought you were sleeping." She tilted her face up

to his and kissed him. His tongue moved against hers with a lazy confidence that made her whole body tingle.

"Hard to sleep with a beautiful girl getting handsy with me."

"I can stop."

He brushed her hair back from her forehead. "Don't you dare."

But just then her stomach grumbled. Outside, the sun had started to dip and rich gold beams of light filtered through her blinds.

"I forgot to have lunch today," she said. "I guess brownies and chocolate sauce don't make for a very good meal replacement."

"Want to order in?"

A happy bubble expanded in her chest. "It's like you can read my mind."

"Let me get it." He pushed up from the bed and pulled the sheet over her.

Within the hour they were curled up on his couch, eating Chinese food.

"I can't believe you don't like fried rice," she said, tucking into her chow mein. "And don't even get me started on the tofu."

"My body is a finely tuned athletic machine," he said, but he couldn't keep a straight face. "I've never had as many empty calories as I did this afternoon."

"Those calories were one hundred percent delicious and worth it."

"Agreed." He dug around in the container with his chopsticks. "But I do take nutrition seriously."

"You take *everything* seriously."

"It's a product of my upbringing, I guess." He popped a piece of chicken into his mouth and chewed.

At the mention of his past, his face hardened. The warmth in his eyes dulled and small tension lines formed at the corners of his mouth.

"How so?"

"I guess I thought that if I became the perfect son then my mother would love me again," he said. "I studied my ass off. I ate whatever crazy green shit she put on my plate. I never talked back, never broke a rule."

Her heart bled for him. She knew how hard it was to be the "other" child, to always be second place. Only her relegation to the back of the line was because of her disappointing lack of focus, rather than grief. Still, the reason didn't matter so much as the outcome. She understood his pain.

"I even quit basketball," he continued, staring straight ahead, his face rigid. "I would have given up anything."

"But it didn't work?"

"No. I was too much my father for her to ever see me as a separate person. And when I told her that I wanted to go into the police force, she flipped." He snorted. "I don't know why she was so worried. It wasn't like she even seemed to enjoy my presence half the time."

"Why didn't she want you to become a police officer?"

"That's how my dad died. He crashed his car while chasing a guy who was fleeing the scene of a drug bust." He looked at her, and some of the warmth crept back into his eyes. "He was a complete hero. I wanted to be just like him."

"But your mom thought it was too risky?"

"Yeah. Nothing I could say would make her change her mind. Eventually she said if I chose to live that kind of life then she'd have nothing to do with me." Pain streaked across his face but it was gone as quickly as it had appeared. "So I went to college and studied technology instead."

"That's sad that you didn't get to pursue your dream." She put her food aside and scooted along the couch to be close to him. She couldn't ease his pain but she wanted to try, nonetheless. "I'm sure your father would be proud of you, even if you didn't follow in his footsteps."

"I'd like to think that." He fished out the last piece of chicken from his dinner and placed the empty container on the coffee table. "And I'm happy with my career now. I'm doing what I'm meant to be doing. I'm good at my job and it's the one area of my life where I can score a touchdown or two."

His self-deprecating smile tore her heart into pieces. It wasn't only that she'd come to respect Rhys deeply. He was kindhearted, giving and—despite his slight obsession with tidiness—wonderfully accepting of who she was.

Would he be so accepting if he knew why you were here? Not likely.

"I'm not sure what *you* would call it, but I'm certain we scored a touchdown before," she said, swallowing back her guilt.

She wanted to trust him, wanted it deep down to her bones because she sensed he was different. That he wouldn't turn on her like Christian had. But this wasn't only her secret. It was Kylie's, too. And knowing that Rhys was such a stand-up guy meant there was a chance he would turn her in, even if he didn't want to. And that would end all hope of finding out what had really happened to Kylie.

"Good team effort," he replied with a grin as he

draped an arm around her shoulder. "And it was definitely two touchdowns."

"Not that you're counting."

"I like knowing you're satisfied." His voice was deep and growly against her ear. "I don't want you to go home with the feeling that I left you hanging."

"No chance of that. And I do appreciate it." She rested her head against his shoulder and relaxed into him. "My ex wasn't really the giving type."

"Is that why he's an ex?"

"No." Her hands instinctively curled into fists like they always did when she thought about what Christian had done to her.

The worst part of his betrayal was that she'd been stupid enough to allow it to happen. She'd been totally blind to his flaws until it was too late. Christian's deluded sense of self-righteousness and self-importance had jumped up and bit her in the ass.

"Our sex life wasn't the reason we broke up, but it certainly wasn't a positive part of our relationship," she said, shoving aside her bitterness. "Too many guilty feelings."

"Guilty feelings?" Rhys raised a dark brow. "Why the hell would you feel guilty for having sex?"

She shook her head. "The people in our town are conservative, and they have a pretty screwed-up view of women and sex. Apparently, we should do it to keep our men happy but we shouldn't enjoy it too much."

"I don't even know what to say to that." He shook his head. "That's messed up."

"Yeah, it is." She bobbed her head.

"I'm surprised you want to go back to that."

"There are people there I care about. My sister is there. My best friend...she needs me."

"That might be so, but what do *you* need?"

She blinked. "What do you mean?"

"It's not a trick question." He chuckled. "If you didn't have to worry about anyone else, what would you do?"

Wren sucked on her bottom lip and grappled for an answer. It shouldn't be so hard to come up with a "perfect life scenario," but for some reason she found herself tongue-tied. Perhaps it was because part of her had given up on the idea of being an artist…but without that she was no longer sure of who she was.

"How about living on a remote island with magical Wi-Fi and an endless supply of brownies?" she said with a glib shrug.

"I'm not buying that."

"Honestly, I don't know what I want right now." She nestled her head into his shoulder again and breathed in the faint scent of soap on his skin. "All I know is that after the internship I have to go back home."

"Because your friend needs you? Surely she would understand that you've got to live your own life."

"Something bad happened to her."

The truth hovered on her tongue, but she couldn't bring herself to ruin the perfect bubble of comfort that surrounded her and Rhys. For the first time in months she was happy and wanted.

As soon as I have something on Sean, she promised herself. *Then I'll come clean.*

If she came to Rhys with proof, it would soften the blow and help to show him that she hadn't intended to deceive him. Only to help her friend.

"She's not doing great." Wren swallowed against the emotion rising up her throat. "She's lost all the joy in her life and she's not eating. I'm afraid for her, and she doesn't have anyone else."

"That's very noble of you." His fingertips traced circles on her bare arm. "But she'll get over this rough patch, and you have to put yourself first at some point."

"Yeah, I know." If only she could figure out what putting herself first actually meant.

"I'm happy to help you forget about home for a while longer." He traced the gentle circles lower and lower until he'd found the sensitive skin of her inner thigh. His touch held promises of pleasure to come.

"I'm happy to let you."

His fingers brushed higher, skating under the edge of her shorts and grazing her panties. "Does that mean you won't sneak out on me tonight?"

"Presumptuous," she teased. "Who said I was staying the night?"

The pressure of his touch intensified as he slipped a finger beneath her panties. A moan escaped her lips before she could stop it. Damn Rhys and his talented hands. She had no chance of hiding how she felt *or* what she wanted.

"You're free to go at any time." He let out a cocky chuckle as she arched against his hand.

"I guess I could stay awhile." Her eyes clamped shut as he found her sweet spot. "Since you're being so persuasive."

"Glad to see my plan is working."

Wren's mind went blank as he eased her back on the couch. For now, she wanted to lose herself in his touch. She could deal with her conflicted feelings tomorrow.

BY THE TIME Monday rolled around, Wren had yet to find clarity on her situation. She'd disentangled herself from Rhys on Saturday morning, intending to leave, but then he'd kissed her and somehow they'd ended up having breakfast together.

She'd made a point of leaving before lunch, because she needed space to think. But by Sunday she was craving him again and she'd knocked on his door with an offer of dinner and a movie. They'd made love on his couch, their bodies working so perfectly together that Wren almost forget why she'd come to New York.

Wren dragged herself out of her reverie as voices floated down the gallery hall. Lola's soft Southern twang was instantly recognizable, as was a harsher New York accent. As they came closer, Wren caught snatches of their conversation.

"Sean will be with you shortly, but if you want to have a chat with Wren, she's in here." Lola appeared in the doorway to the studio with two people. "Wren, you remember Quinn Dellinger from Cobalt & Dane? And this is her colleague, Owen Fletcher. They're supervising the installation of the new cameras today."

She left her station to shake their hands. "Hello."

Quinn's sharp hazel eyes darted around the room. "We wanted to give you a heads-up to watch out for our guys. They'll have ladders and wires all over the place, so step carefully. We don't want anyone getting injured."

Could this mean the storage room would be open? Maybe this was her opportunity to see what was inside. Wren forced her expression to remain neutral. "Thanks."

At that moment Sean poked his head into the room. "I trust you have something to work on," he said to her, his cold stare making her step back instinctively.

"Yes, I do."

She'd realized at some point over the weekend that giving Ainslie a painting with Rhys's face probably wasn't the smartest move. Apart from the obvious risk of Sean recognizing Rhys and wondering why Wren had chosen to paint him, there was something preventing her from parting with it. It wasn't yet finished, but her Muse had reappeared. She'd even found herself thinking about new paintings and wanting to reach for her brushes. There was that itch in her fingertips, creative desire slowly igniting inside her like a flame resurrected from the very last ember.

But that left her with a problem. Sean's ultimatum. She needed a painting and she needed it quickly. So Wren had gone back to her passion and painted a woman. Her sister.

"Good, because you owe me a painting this week and I don't want you to bother the team while they're working."

"I understand, I'm working on something new for you."

Over the next hour, Wren forced herself to work quickly while the Cobalt & Dane team started the installation. A technician, accompanied by Owen, was installing a camera right outside the studio. Wren used the opportunity to excuse herself under the guise of going to the restroom.

Instead, Wren inched along the hallway toward the storage room. Quinn was in there, talking to someone. Was it Sean? She was sure he'd mentioned having an appointment today. This could be her one and only chance to get inside.

She could only hear Quinn's side of the conversation; she must be on the phone. Wren gathered her long skirt in one hand to stop it from brushing along the floor as she tiptoed along.

"The installation is going well," Quinn said. "We're fitting the last group of cameras, but we'll have to configure the software because the client has a few custom-izations. Yeah…" Pause. "Well, I *could* come on my own if you would sign off on this damn training."

She must be talking to Rhys. Wren flattened her back to the wall just outside the storage room and strained to hear if anyone else was inside.

Nothing.

Sucking in a breath, she moved closer and leaned for-ward to take a peek into the room. At that moment Sean Ainslie came out, a dark expression on his face.

"Are you looking for me, Wren? I thought you had work to keep you busy." He folded his arms across his chest. He was a lot more built than she'd first guessed. His fitted T-shirt exposed a gym-honed body. But in-stead of all that physical power appealing to her, it made her feel ill.

"I, uh…yes, actually. I wanted guidance on my paint-ing," she lied. "I realize you're busy but I had a burst of inspiration and I would really appreciate your expertise."

"You know the rules about the storage room, Wren," he said, but his expression had lost its edge.

"I'm sorry, I didn't even think…"

"It's fine. Let's take a look at this painting."

Nodding, Wren stifled a sigh of relief. She'd weaseled her way out of trouble this time…but she may not get a second chance. Perhaps Rhys would be able to access the cameras to check inside. She made a mental note to suss out whether he would do that once the installation was complete.

REALITY HAD BURST the happy bubble that was Rhys's weekend. Monday had flown past in a blur of meetings and he hadn't left the office until 9:00 p.m. Tempted as he'd been to call Wren on his way home, he didn't want her to get the impression that she was a booty call…as much as her booty had *definitely* been on his mind.

The next day, he was sitting at his desk, wondering where his Tuesday had gotten to when Quinn and Owen arrived to give an update on Ainslie Ave.

"How'd the installation go?" he asked, dragging his focus back to work.

"Good." Quinn took a seat on the other side of Rhys's desk. "We're currently working through the customization requirements for the monitoring system."

"Has anything else come up?"

Owen raked a hand through his blond hair. "I managed to speak with the interns after we finished up for the day. They all seemed a little cagey about answering questions, particularly where Sean was involved."

"So no confirmation that he's sleeping with any of them?" Rhys remembered Wren's admission about Aimee.

"Not a thing."

Interesting. Either Aimee had lied to Quinn or she'd lied to Wren.

What if Wren lied to you?

He shoved the thought aside immediately. What reason would Wren have to lie to him? If something really was going on between Sean Ainslie and Aimee, perhaps the other woman had a reason for keeping it quiet. A reason she wouldn't feel comfortable sharing with a security company.

"I had some luck with the gallery's ex-employees, though," Quinn said.

After a few minutes detailing her calls to several former Ainslie Ave employees, she got to the one that she was most excited about. "I spoke with a woman named

Kylie Samuels. She worked at the gallery until six months ago when she returned to her home in Charity Springs, Idaho."

The name of the town rang a bell, but Rhys couldn't place where he'd heard it before. "What's the significance of that?"

"Well, I did some research and it barely has seven hundred residents." She paused as if for dramatic effect. "And guess who *also* happens to come from Charity Springs? Wren Livingston."

Rhys tried not to let the surprise show on his face. Why wouldn't she have mentioned that someone from her hometown had also worked for Ainslie Ave? Perhaps it hadn't occurred to her. Or maybe she didn't know this Kylie Samuels. Though that *did* seem unlikely for a town of such a small size.

"Any signs they're connected to one another?" he asked.

"I assumed you wouldn't be satisfied with circumstantial evidence," Quinn replied with a smile that made her look like the cat who'd got the cream. "They both attended the local high school and I found a picture of them from a fund-raising event."

She pulled up the photo on her laptop. It seemed to be several years old and showed two girls with their arms wrapped around one another's shoulders. Wren's ear-to-ear grin struck something in his chest. She looked so much more at ease in this picture, so free and innocent. Her hair was shorter and her face was painted with big blue flowers, making her resemble some kind of fairy or nymph.

"That's Wren Livingston," Owen said, pointing with his pen. He was oblivious to the fact that Rhys knew her face intimately, and now her body, as well. "And this is Kylie Samuels."

They could have been sisters. Kylie had blond hair, too, though it was a few shades darker than Wren's. And she was smaller. Skinny rather than slender. They wore the same breezy smiles and crazy face paint.

"What did Kylie have to say?" Rhys asked.

"She really didn't want to talk to me," Quinn said. "But I managed to get out of her that she ended the internship early because of a clash with Ainslie. She said it was something to do with her paintings, but when I pressed her she clammed up."

"Did you ask her about whether or not she was friends with Wren?"

Quinn huffed. "Barely. The second I mentioned Wren's name, Kylie said something about having an appointment and then she hung up on me. I've been trying to call her back since late last week to get more information, but she won't take my calls."

For the first time Rhys felt guilty for skirting the lines of appropriateness by sleeping with Wren. Up till now, it hadn't bothered him too much because he'd seen no reason why she would be involved in the security breaches. But this information about her friend shed some new light on the situation. It created a link where there hadn't been one previously.

Was it possible that she'd been lying to him this whole time?

"Keep chasing the ex-employees," Rhys said. "See what else you can dig up. But we have to continue servicing Ainslie as a client."

Rhys called an end to the meeting but asked Owen to stay behind. As much as he trusted Quinn, she had a fiery personality, and once she decided that she didn't like someone, her mind was hard to change. He needed a more balanced opinion.

"I want your take on this," he said, running a hand over his closely cropped hair. "I get something seems off about this guy, but surely he wouldn't have called us in if he had something to hide."

"I have seen stranger things in this line of work," Owen replied with a wry smile. "There's definitely something going on. He seemed resistant to the cameras, and I'm not buying the line about him not wanting to monitor his staff."

"Me, either."

"The external security is also pretty strong. He's got a monitored system that they set every night, which notifies him if there are multiple unsuccessful attempts on the pin code at either the front door or the entrance in the loading dock. If the alarm is tripped, then it notifies our call center and we dispatch someone to check it out. But…" Owen paused, rubbing a hand along his jaw. "There were no external security cameras until yesterday. Not even for the loading area behind the gallery. That's strange."

"How did things go with the tech side of things?"

"Quinn is handling that, since that's more her forte than mine. She's still making her way through the email logs, but it does look like someone used Ainslie's log-in on the interns' terminal in the studio."

"Is it possible Ainslie needed to access his email while he was in that room?"

"Sure, it's definitely possible. But we're going to correlate the log-in time stamp with activity on his account to see if anything strange is going on."

"Okay, I want an update as soon as possible."

"You're getting quite involved in this case," Owen commented. "I thought you were supposed to be the big-picture guy."

He was. Rhys's role didn't require him to get involved in individual assignments beyond the initial approach and ensuring his staff were keeping to schedule. And since the tech security part of the Cobalt & Dane business was growing quickly, he really didn't have time to dive deep into the details. Senior security consultants—like Owen—were the ones managing such things.

It occurred to him that maybe Owen thought he was overstepping.

Rhys cleared his throat. "This is the first assignment that Quinn is leading and I want to make sure she's fully supported."

The lie was sour in his mouth. This wasn't like him at all; normally he was Mr. By The Book. Now he was keeping things from his team and had possibly crossed a line with Wren.

He'd speak to her tonight, get them both on the same page. He couldn't break any more rules now that there was a chance she was involved.

10

WREN NARROWED HER eyes at the half-done canvas in front of her. It had started out a mess but the vision was finally beginning to come through. Her deadline to deliver a painting to Sean was drawing near and she finally felt confident that she'd have something to hand in.

Wren softened Debbie's blond hair with a fan brush. She stroked the painting as if combing the hair, merging some of the brassier tones into the pale, light-reflecting sections until the color looked seamless and natural.

She lost herself in the image until her phone buzzed. Kylie's face flashed up on the screen like a ghost arriving to haunt her. It was the third time she'd called today.

"Aren't you going to get that?" Aimee asked as she turned away from her canvas. "Or are you avoiding someone?"

"I'm not avoiding anyone," Wren replied. "I'm simply trying to find the right moment to talk."

It wasn't untrue. Wren had to keep up the ruse with her friend that she was on an art retreat that restricted mobile phone usage. That meant she would call Kylie back at the time they'd agreed on over email.

Why would she be calling early? Maybe the security company called her again.

"I hate cell phones," Aimee said. "People just expect you to drop everything to take a call and if you don't message back quick enough...watch out."

She was still wearing longer sleeves but she appeared to have forgiven Sean, if the goo-goo eyes she'd given him that morning were anything to go on.

"How's the arm?" Wren asked as she continued working on Debbie's hair.

"Oh fine, it's nothing too bad. I, uh... I overreacted the other day." Her voice sounded cheerful on the surface, but there was something hollow beneath it. A false confidence that Wren knew all too well.

Her voice had been the same when she'd covered up for Christian with Debbie or her other friends. It was the sound of backpedaling.

"You didn't overreact." Wren looked up.

"It was an accident."

"Bruises like that *aren't* an accident."

Aimee refocused on her painting. "I don't want you to get involved."

"Then why did you tell me about it? If he's hurting you—"

"He's not." She swiped her hands through her long gold hair. "I don't know. I was having a rough day... It's nothing."

"It's *not* nothing."

At that moment footsteps cut through the quiet of the gallery and Sean walked in, a small canvas tucked under one arm. "What's going on?"

"Just working," Wren replied, keeping her face as neutral as possible. Her body seemed to tense whenever he was around.

Aimee's eyes had dropped to floor. Something about the way she avoided his gaze didn't feel right to Wren. Aimee's bottom lip was drawn tight between her teeth. Sean whispered something in her ear and she nodded, her expression blank.

"Enough talking," Sean said to them both. "If you're in need of *more* work, the kitchen could use a clean."

As he walked away Wren caught a glimpse of the canvas he was carrying. The bold streaks of orange and teal seemed familiar, but her mind couldn't place where she'd seen it. Before she could get a closer look, he was gone.

"Please don't ask me about it again," Aimee said with a heavy sigh. "Okay? It's none of your business."

She walked out of the room, leaving Wren alone with her thoughts. When her phone started buzzing, Kylie's smiling face flashing up again, she answered it.

"Hey. Sorry I couldn't answer before, I—"

"Don't you dare tell me that you're at an art retreat, Wren. Just don't." Kylie's anger radiated through the phone line. "I know you're at Ainslie Ave."

Shit. "I can explain—"

"What the hell were you thinking? I got out of there for a reason. Now you're on some secret vigilante mission and you refuse to take my calls." She sighed. "I had to find out from some damn security company who called me to check on Sean, and then when you wouldn't answer your phone…"

It's official, you're the worst friend in the world.

Standing up as quietly as she could, she tiptoed to the front of the gallery and slipped outside. "I'm sorry, I never wanted you to worry."

"How could I not? You don't know what an evil piece of shit Sean Ainslie is." Her voice wavered. "He's a monster, Wren. You need to come home. Now."

"I can't."

"Why not? What on earth do you think you're going to do?"

"I'm trying to figure out what he did to you, since you won't tell me. Then I'm going to get proof of it so we can go to the police."

"The police? Oh, Wren." Kylie let out a bitter laugh. "There is no proof. Ever wondered why there are no security cameras in that place and yet he keeps a giant room all locked up? That's because he doesn't want to leave any evidence."

"What did he do to you?"

"Apart from shattering an eye socket and fracturing my wrist?" The sound suddenly became muffled and Wren thought she could hear a faint sob.

"Just tell me. We can fix this."

"There is no 'we.' You're there, being stupid and acting without thinking—as usual—and I'm here. Broken and worrying about my best friend."

Wren winced at the sting of her friend's words. "What happened to you?"

"Please don't make me talk about it."

"Why? If he's done something so bad, shouldn't he be punished?"

"It's not worth it." Her words were strained, and Wren felt awful for putting her through this. But if she didn't push, Sean would keep hurting people. Like Aimee.

Kylie likely wasn't the first victim, and she sure as hell wasn't the last. Wren owed it to them both to put a stop to Ainslie's behavior.

She opened her mouth to argue, but the sight of a tall figure walking toward the gallery halted her speech. Late-afternoon light made Rhys's skin look even warmer and more touchable. His crisp white shirt revealed a V of skin at his neck and the sleeves were rolled back to expose strong forearms.

"We need to talk," he said.

WREN'S BLUE EYES WIDENED. For a moment she was silent. "Let's chat later," she said into the phone and ended the call. "I wasn't expecting to see you here today, Rhys. Is this official security business?"

"It is. Can you take a minute to talk?"

Her eyes darted to the door. "I was supposed to be starting my shift on the front desk in a few minutes."

"We can talk there."

A crease formed between her brows. "Sean doesn't like it if we're sitting around talking."

"He hired Cobalt & Dane to look into his security issues, so I'm sure he'll make an exception." He hated to be a hard-ass, but it would drive him crazy if he didn't get to the bottom of Wren's involvement with Sean Ainslie. "Shall we?"

She nodded and motioned for him to follow her inside. "Sure."

Today she wore a blue skirt that clung to the sweet curve of her hips and ass, accentuating her long lines. A paint-splattered apron sat over a white T-shirt that showed a hint of creamy skin without revealing too much.

But his mind could fill in the gaps. He knew how soft her shoulders were and how perfectly the swell of her breasts and the gentle indent at her waist filled his palms.

Stop it. This is business, and you're not laying a finger on her until you learn the truth.

"So, what can I help you with?" she asked as she removed her apron and stashed it away in a cupboard behind the desk.

"Do you know a Kylie Samuels?"

As the color drained from her face, Rhys realized he'd made a terrible mistake. Perhaps she was a lot better at hiding things than he'd given her credit for. Judging by her expression, Kylie Samuels was more than a simple acquaintance.

"Can we not talk about this here?" Her hands twisted in her lap.

"This is work, isn't it?"

"Please." Her eyes darted to the hallway that led to Ainslie's office. "I'll tell you everything, but I can't do it here."

Ice trickled through his veins at the hushed tone of her voice. He knew fear when he saw it. But he barricaded his sympathy deep inside. "What are you scared of?"

"There's more to Sean than he's letting on. Something bad is going on here, Rhys." She drew a deep breath. "And I'm scared I've screwed things up with you."

Why would she think she'd screwed things up with him if she'd simply forgotten to mention that someone she knew had worked here? It was an admission of guilt if he'd ever heard one.

"Please let me explain myself. Tonight—I'll make dinner," she said with a hopeful smile.

"Maybe we should go out." The farther away they were from any flat surfaces the safer it would be, since it was clear his self-control seemed to vanish around her.

He scribbled the address of a quiet diner not too far

from their walk-up. They'd be able to get a booth away from prying eyes and he wouldn't be tempted to let his body do the thinking for him if they were in a public place.

"Do you need to speak to Sean while you're here?" she asked. "I can call him out, if you'd like."

"No. Quinn and Owen will run Sean through the new monitoring system later. We've also got an update for him with the log-in reports."

"Find anything interesting?" she asked.

"I can't discuss that with you."

"Of course, I was just kidding," she said, but her eyes were suddenly guarded. Closed off.

In other words, message received.

He had to draw a line in the sand with her until he knew exactly where they stood. It had been wrong to assume Wren wasn't involved from the beginning. Naive, even. But that didn't mean he had to continue down that path. A mistake could be corrected at any point, and that's exactly what he would do now.

11

RHYS ARRIVED AT the diner early and procured them a booth. He'd been antsy all afternoon, unable to concentrate on the work he'd brought home. Unable to think about anything but how his carefree connection with Wren had become a career hazard. A potential liability.

Of course, he could be overacting. There might be a perfectly reasonable excuse for her not mentioning her friend's involvement with the gallery. Perhaps they'd drifted apart and were no longer friends. Or maybe she'd really believed that it wasn't worth bringing up.

Nothing wrong with being optimistic, but the rose-colored glasses are coming off now. Your number one priority is to get the facts.

The moment Wren walked into the diner heads turned in her direction. She was still in the fitted blue pencil skirt, but she'd swapped the T-shirt out for a black lace-trimmed camisole. The effect was mouthwatering. Appreciative eyes swept over Wren from all directions and Rhys found himself fighting back the urge to claim her with a kiss.

Facts first. Your lips don't go near her until you have what you need.

"Hi," she said almost shyly as she slipped into the seat across from him. A few wavy strands of blond hair had escaped her ponytail and framed her face.

In the intimate space of the booth, his senses were heightened. The accidental brush of her knee against his almost undid his resolve to keep his hands to himself.

"This is a cute place," she said. "I hope their burgers are good, I'm starving."

"This isn't a date, Wren."

Her lips pursed. "I know that, but thanks for making yourself clear. I'm still ordering food, though."

"I want to make sure we're on the same page," he said, signaling to a server. "This is work, nothing else."

"Got you loud and clear, Captain," she replied with more than a hint of sarcasm. "I bet you keep your employees on the straight and narrow."

"What's that supposed to mean?"

Her eyes remained on the menu. "You're a bit of a hard-ass when you're in work mode."

"Tough but fair, that's my motto."

"Yes, well, I'm sure that's fine at the office." She paused as the server took their orders. "But I'm not your employee."

He resisted the urge to ask her how she classified their relationship. It wasn't information that would help him right now. "So tell me how you know Kylie Samuels."

"Gee, you're not wasting any time, are you? Straight down to business." She poured water into both their glasses, her hands shaking ever so slightly. "She's an old friend. We grew up together."

"And you were aware that she'd interned for a brief period under Sean Ainslie?"

"Yes."

Wren's entire demeanor had changed—normally, she had this relaxed, fluidity to her movement. Now she appeared stiff and jerky. She wore an expression on her face that was so closed off, she may as well have been wearing a bag over her head.

"Do you know why she finished up her internship early?"

Her hands knotted in her lap. "Not exactly."

"I thought you were friends. It seems odd that she gave up an opportunity and returned home but didn't tell you why...and now you're here doing the exact same internship."

"She refused to explain why she came back. She wouldn't talk about it at all..." Her gaze was riveted on an imperfection in the table.

"Why do I feel like there's a 'but' coming?"

"When she came home, she was all beat up." Wren picked at the chipped laminate, her lips curling in anger. "She had a black eye, a busted eye socket, a broken wrist and bruises on her arms. Someone had really worked her over."

Rhys's stomach churned as he remembered the photos of Marguerite Bernard's swollen face. "But she wouldn't say who did it?"

"No. But it didn't take much to put two and two together. Anytime I mentioned the internship she either burst into tears or started yelling at me to keep quiet." When Wren finally looked up, Rhys saw a fire blazing in her eyes that was totally foreign. "I asked her if she'd gone to the police and she said no, because there was no proof."

"Is that why you're here?" The pieces of the puzzle started to click into place and Rhys didn't like the final image that was coming together.

"Yes."

"How did you get the internship?"

"Kylie and I had applied at the same time, but she got the job and I didn't." Her cheeks colored but she reset her shoulders. "Sean approached me after Kylie dropped out, and I thought it was the perfect opportunity to find out what had happened to her."

"Were you the one who tripped the security alert for the storage room?"

She looked him square in the eye, chin tilted slightly. "Yes."

"Have you accessed Sean Ainslie's emails by using his log-in credentials?"

Sucking on her lower lip, Wren appeared utterly torn. Her brows crinkled and she bounced her leg in an agitated rhythm beneath the table.

"I want you to be honest with me," he said.

"Yes. I accessed Sean's emails."

Shit. How on earth would he be able to explain that he'd been sleeping with the very person he'd been hired to catch? That he'd been too stupid and too naive to suspect her because she had an angelic face?

"Say something, Rhys," she said.

"Were you spending time with me because you wanted inside information?"

Wren felt the sting of his question down to the very marrow of her bones. "No, of course not."

Rhys sat like a hard, immovable lump of stone on the other side of the table. When the server arrived with their food a few minutes later, the young man looked awkwardly from one to the other. The tension must have been billowing from their table.

She'd just admitted to accessing her boss's email without authorization. To the guy with the black-and-white morals. There was a high chance that her reasoning wouldn't matter, that he wouldn't listen to her plea.

But the truth was she'd grown to trust Rhys, and it was clear she wasn't getting very far on her own. Obviously it would have been better to obtain proof before involving him, but the fact of the matter was that he was *already* involved.

She'd involved him the second they slept together.

And she didn't want to lie anymore, not now that they were more than neighbors.

All she could do was hope that he was the good man she believed him to be. That he'd be able to look past her indiscretion to the bigger problem—Sean Ainslie.

"Did you know who I was when you moved into your apartment?"

"No," she said, glancing at the burger she now had no appetite for. "You being my neighbor is a coincidence."

His deep brown eyes were coldly assessing. "Did you sleep with me to make me trust you?"

A lump formed in her throat. "How could you even ask me that?"

"There's so much you haven't told me, I want to be sure."

"I'm a painter, not an actress." She pushed her fries around with a fork. "I can't fake feelings any more than I can fake orgasms."

It hadn't sounded all that dangerous in her head but the moment she'd said the words aloud her stomach pitched. Feelings. What on earth did that mean and why the hell had she clued him in?

He appeared as baffled by her admission as she was. "You do realize that you've admitted to lying to me and now you're claiming to have feelings for me?"

"It's complicated," she muttered.

"I'd say it's more than complicated."

"You know what? Maybe it isn't. *Maybe* it's incredibly simple." Frustration roiled within her, but she couldn't take it out on him. *She*'d done wrong, here. But if she could make him see it was all with good intention, he might help her. "I get that I've screwed up. I'm sorry for not being totally honest with you. I'm sorry that I let us cross a line knowing it could make things hard for your job. But I am *not* sorry that I'm here trying to get some justice for my best friend."

"What did you think was going to happen, Wren?" He rubbed at the back of his neck, a crease forming between his dark brows. "That you would come here and play spy like you're in a goddamn Hollywood movie? That you would magically find this evidence on your own and wrap everything up with a neat little bow?"

She tamped down the urge to argue with him. She *needed* him, needed to regain his trust. "Maybe."

"If Sean did assault your friend, what did you think he would do to you?" His voice was getting harder, louder. "What if he hurt you the same way? What if you weren't as lucky as your friend?"

That's when she saw it. *His* feelings…for her. He was angry and terrified. For her.

"I'm smart, Rhys. I know how to play him."

"I don't want to insult your intelligence, Wren, but what you've done is pretty damn stupid." His fists clenched. "And dangerous…and possibly illegal."

Cold fear dripped down her spine. "What happens now?"

"I don't know." His fingers dug deeper into the muscles of his neck. "But I do know you're not going near Sean Ainslie until we figure it out."

"I have to go to work. It'll tip him off if I don't. And I have to keep an eye out for Aimee."

"Why?"

"She had bruises on her arm." Wren popped a fry into her mouth and tried to force herself to eat, but it tasted like nothing. "Finger-shaped bruises. She said Sean had gotten rough with her, but when I tried to talk to her about it again today she clammed up and said she overreacted."

He shook his head, the disgust evident on his face. "Did she say what caused him to get angry?"

"Not really. She said they were arguing about a painting. He wasn't happy with what she'd done. Artistic differences, I guess."

"That doesn't seem like a reason for him to get physical."

"Do you think men who hurt women have their brains wired properly?"

He grunted. "Point taken."

"I'm convinced he's hiding something in the storage room." She gave up eating and instead pushed her food around on her plate. "That's got to be the reason he freaked out and called your company when I tried to get in. He's meticulous about making sure no one gets inside."

"How so?"

"He gave me this big spiel on my first day about how it's full of valuable paintings and that when we're setting up for a showing, only he is allowed to get the paintings out. I wasn't sure what to make of it at first—I mean, a lot of artists are eccentric and private, but he flipped out when he thought Lola was trying to get inside one day when she was mopping the floors."

"Have you ever seen him go into the room?"

"No, he must wait until we're all gone for the day. Or maybe he does it early in the morning."

"Do you think he has any paintings that are worth a lot of money?"

Wren shrugged. "I honestly don't know. I don't think he sells as many paintings as he'd like people to believe. His style is…eclectic. But not in a good way."

"What do you mean?"

"There's no common thread or general theme. A lot of artists will experiment and try new things, but in Sean's work, I can't even see an attempt to build upon a particular style or technique."

"What's he like as a teacher?"

"Pushy, talks a lot of shit that doesn't mean anything."

"What about the other girls?"

"They eat it up." Wren shook her head. "They're young and grateful that someone has given them an opportunity in an industry that's so competitive. They believe he can turn them into wunderkinds."

"That's not the case?"

"Not from what I've seen. But maybe I'm just jaded and that's affecting my view."

Wren had worked with several different art teachers over the years. They'd all given her different advice that often clashed and contradicted. Art, she'd come to realize, was like cutting out a part of your soul and showing it to the world. It hurt when people rejected what you'd made because they were, in essence, rejecting you.

And the closer you got to painting something from deep within, the more likely you were to end up bleeding.

"Why do you say you're jaded?" He looked genuinely confused.

"I'm not exactly the poster child for a successful career in the arts." She leaned back against the booth and pushed her mostly untouched plate away. "I've had more success painting faces at county fairs than I have painting on a canvas."

"You're not giving yourself enough credit."

"I am. I have to take some responsibility for what I painted and where it landed me."

She'd spent many nights wondering why she'd left the paintings in a place Christian could easily find them. Why she'd thought it a good idea to paint such provocative things in the first place. Only they weren't provocative, not really.

"How did you come to paint naked women?" Rhys asked, finally tucking into his meal.

"It happened by mistake, at first." Wren smiled at the memory. "I was planning on a series of portraits of female farmers. I put up an ad on a rural community forum saying I was looking for models and I found Cassie. When she came to my house I had a chair set up for her and she just…stripped."

"Without you asking?" A smile tugged at Rhys's full lips.

"Yep, without any warning at all. I was totally gob smacked, but I didn't know what to say…so, I painted her." Wren tentatively reached for her plate and found her appetite returning. "She had this big scar that ran up the side of her leg from a farming accident. When she tried to hide it, I asked her if she would mind me painting it. By the time we were finished she said it was the first time she'd ever felt beautiful with her scar showing. She'd never had the courage to show it to anyone and that's why she'd applied to be my model."

"To get it over with?"

"Yeah. That's when I knew what I was supposed to be painting. These women of all shapes and sizes would come to me and I would paint them as I saw them. Without their barriers or their masks or their shields. Just them and their natural beauty… Like how I painted you."

"You didn't know anything about me then," he said.

"Don't you ever meet someone and have a connection with them that defies logic? Like you see their truth." The irony of her words wasn't lost on her, but she wanted Rhys to understand how she felt. "I could tell you were a good person. I don't meet a lot of people like that."

"And I don't have the connection with anyone else that I have with you…" Silence settled over the table. Rhys looked perplexed.

"But?"

"But that doesn't mean I can ignore what you've told me tonight."

Wren wanted to reassure him that she wasn't an evil person. Sure, she seemed to make bad decision after bad decision…but it was all with good intention. That had to count for something, right?

"How long do you think Sean will keep hurting women if we don't intervene?"

"We don't have any proof he's doing that."

Her heart sank. Could he really turn a blind eye to Sean's behavior? They *didn't* have proof, sure. But Wren was certain they could find it if they worked together. At the very least they could get one of Sean's victims to speak up—and maybe if one person confessed the others would follow.

"Are you going to turn me in?" she asked.

"I need to think on it, Wren. I'm in a really difficult situation here." He seemed genuinely conflicted, and that made her feel even worse.

"But you agree that Sean is up to something, right? I know I'm not an angel, but I'm trying to figure out what's going on so he doesn't hurt anyone else." She reached for his hand across the table. His skin was warm, soft, but he didn't embrace her. Didn't give her anything back. "Please, Rhys. Give me a little more time. I'll try to get Kylie and Aimee to talk. I'm on your side."

"My side?" He pulled his hand away from her grip. "You do realize who hired me in the first place, right? My side is supposed to be *Sean's* side…which is most definitely not where you are."

"But you're investigating him, aren't you? That's why someone from your company called Kylie to ask questions. If you were just helping Sean with his security, you wouldn't be snooping around and talking to ex-employees."

"We're doing what we were hired to do, which is find out who's been trying to get access to Sean's information and why." He pulled his wallet out of his pocket and tossed a few bills onto the table. "And now I know."

"So that's it?" Wren pushed up from the table and followed him out of the diner and into the parking lot. "You don't care that he might be beating these women?"

Rhys whirled around suddenly and she almost face-planted into his chest. "That's the reason I haven't made up my mind on how I'm going to handle this yet."

So it had nothing to do with her. The realization stung, but then she'd known from the beginning that Rhys had a very strong moral code.

Shoving her pain aside, she steeled herself. "I want him to pay for what he did to my friend and I want to make sure it doesn't happen to Aimee, either. *Or* the next unsuspecting woman he hires."

"I want that, too," he said.

"Then let me help. I'll get the girls to talk, I'll keep an eye on Sean at the gallery and I can call you if anything suspicious is going on." She wrapped her arms around herself, praying that he would give her this chance. "Please."

"Fine. I'll keep this under wraps for a couple of days, but you have to promise me you won't do anything stupid."

"Don't you mean, anything *else* stupid?"

"I mean it, Wren." His features were hard; his eyes gave nothing away. "I don't want you to be the next person he hurts. I want to figure this out, but it's not worth risking your safety. You call me the *second* anything shady happens, okay?"

"I promise."

For a man who'd sworn that he wasn't protecting her, he seemed very set on making sure she kept out of harm's way.

As she stood in the parking lot of the diner, watching Rhys get into his car, she vowed that she would fix things with him. If only she could find evidence that Sean was the bad guy here, then maybe he'd forgive her for lying.

12

WREN DIALED KYLIE'S number as she walked home. It would do her good to stretch her legs before the sun went down; fresh air always seemed to create space in her mind when she felt jumbled up.

"Are you going to hang up on me again?" Kylie asked.

"I'm sorry about earlier. I had to deal with something." She rubbed at her temple while Kylie's anger simmered on the other end of the line. "And I'm sorry I've been keeping you in the dark."

"Then come home."

Wren sighed. "I can't."

"I don't understand why you're doing this."

"Because I want to help you, Ky. And this bastard shouldn't be allowed to hurt anyone else." The balmy evening breeze whispered along her bare arms. It was a beautiful night, far too serene and peaceful for her to be arguing with her best friend. "Can't you see that?"

"If you were really interested in what's best for me then you would have consulted me first instead of running off there behind my back. You're doing this for *you*."

The words were like a slap across the face. "How on earth is this for me?"

"You needed something to focus on after Christian screwed you over. You needed some kind of problem to solve, just like you *always* do when your own life isn't going according to plan." Kylie sighed. "I love you, Wren. You're the sister I never had, but don't delude yourself that this is all about helping me."

"What was I supposed to do, sit by and watch while you broke down? While he's getting away with it?"

"You could have stayed with me. You could have done what Debbie is doing. But instead, you ran away because it suited your situation."

"I wanted to help you," Wren said, swallowing the lump in her throat.

"I'm getting help…with a therapist. I'm working through what happened with a professional, Wren. You being in New York and trying to force me to talk about it *isn't* helping. It's stressing me out." Kylie's voice wavered. "Please come home."

For a moment Wren considered it. But what about Aimee? What about the next girl or the one after that?

She held her breath, debating how much to say. "There's another girl…he's hurting her, too."

The silenced seemed to stretch out for an eternity. Only the steady sound of Wren's footsteps against the pavement told her that time hadn't stopped completely. There was a faint, muffled sound on the other end of the line. Kylie was crying.

"I'm sorry, Ky." She wanted so badly to press for more details—anything that might help to gather proof against Ainslie. But her friend's tears halted her words. "I promise I'll come home as soon as I can."

"I have to go," Kylie said, her voice rough and edgy. "Maybe don't call me for a few days, okay? I need to stop thinking about this, and talking to you while you're there…"

Wren's stomach sank. "If that's what you want."

"You know what I want. I won't feel better until you're far away from him." She sniffed. "Just think about coming home. Hell, don't come home if you don't want. Go somewhere else. *Anywhere* else."

"I'll call you next week."

"Why don't I call you…when I'm ready."

Wren blinked back the first prickle of tears. "Okay."

She ended the call and brushed the back of her hand against a tear that had dropped onto her cheek as she walked up the path to her building. The sky had turned dark and the temperature had dropped. Goose bumps rippled across her skin.

How was it possible that she'd screwed up so badly while having the best intentions? Rhys was angry at her. Kylie was angry at her. Debbie…well, her sister wasn't angry but she resented Wren leaving her behind.

Wren trudged up the stairs of the walk-up, her mind swirling like a tornado. She tried to shake off the bad feeling that had settled into her bones. Rhys was right; what she'd done was stupid and naive. She hadn't helped Kylie; in fact, she seemed to have made things worse.

But Aimee still needs your help. She's still in danger. If you don't stand up to Sean, who knows what might happen to her?

As she walked to her front door, her gaze snagged on Rhys's apartment. She was tempted to knock, but it was probably best to give him time to cool down. After all, she'd dropped a pretty big bombshell on him tonight.

Wren walked into her apartment and had been inside for all of five minutes when a knock on the door made her heart leap into her throat. Had Rhys decided to come to her? The thought filled her with warmth.

She rushed to the door and opened it, the smile dying on her lips when she saw that her visitor wasn't Rhys. It was Sean.

"I hope you don't mind me showing up on your doorstep," he said, sounding decidedly uncaring. "I want to clear up this tension between us."

Wren swallowed down her instinct to slam the door in his face. "What do you mean?"

"You're not being honest with me. A true artist doesn't bottle his or her feelings up, Wren. That's why you're having issues with your paintings. You're suppressed." He swayed and planted a hand on the door frame, leaning in. "You have no idea how to tap into your true self."

The scent of stale whiskey invaded her nostrils. "Have you been drinking?"

"So what if I have?" He stepped forward and pushed her back into her apartment, slamming the door shut behind him. "Are you judging me? I should have known after I hired that twit Kylie that everyone from your hick fucking town was a purist prude."

"I told you, Kylie and I have nothing to do with one another," she lied, warning bells ringing in her ears. "And I still don't understand why you're here."

"'I still don't understand why you're here,'" he mimicked in a high-pitched voice. "Who's the boss, Wren?"

"You are." She forced herself to breathe slow and even.

"Are you sure you believe that? Because I'm getting a strong vibe of insubordination from you." He raked a hand through his long, dark hair and a chunky gold ring glinted on his right hand. It looked like the kind of ring that could do a hell of a lot of damage if it connected to bone.

Like shattering an eye socket, perhaps?

"I want…I want what's best for our working relationship," she stammered. "I value my position at the studio and if I've done something—"

"Bullshit," he spat. "You know *exactly* what you've done."

Her mind spun. Was he referring to her getting into his email? Setting off the alarm on the storage room? Had he discovered the truth about her and Kylie?

"Spare me the deer-in-headlights look, Wren." He rolled his eyes. "I know you've been talking to Aimee about me."

Damn. "I just wanted to make sure she was okay."

"It's none of your business." His voice escalated, taking on the shrill edge of a person about to lose their shit. "You ought to be careful, being so nosy. I might think you were the one trying to hack into my account and delete my emails if you weren't so stupid and obvious."

Wren said a silent thank-you for small mercies. For as long as Sean didn't suspect her, she could talk her way out of her supposed indiscretion.

"You're right," she said, hanging her head. "I shouldn't have talked to her about it."

For a moment she thought she'd appeased him. He glanced around her apartment as if he'd forgotten why he was there. But then his eyes landed on something behind her and a dark shadow rolled across his face.

"What is *that*?" he thundered.

"What?" Wren whirled around and cursed under her breath when she saw what he was looking at.

The portrait of Rhys.

"Why are you painting someone from the security company?"

"I don't know what you're talking about," she said quickly, but the words were breathless and hurried. "It's just a man."

She was about to turn when pain burned at her scalp. Sean fisted his hands in her hair and dragged her toward the painting.

"Explain yourself," he said into her ear. The words were a mere whisper, and yet it frightened her more than if he'd yelled. "Tell me why the fuck you have a painting of Rhys Glover in your apartment."

RHYS STOPPED HIS car at a red light. He'd driven block after block, hoping that the answer to his problems might be around the next corner. But a good half an hour after he'd left Wren at the diner, he was still at a loss.

Why the hell hadn't he seen this coming?

Anger at himself roiled with frustration at Wren. She was so...idealistic. And impulsive.

And spontaneous and sexy and so damn beautiful.

"You're a glutton for punishment," he muttered to his reflection in the rearview mirror.

He drove home deep in thought. But no matter how hard he tried, the solution wouldn't come. There wasn't a magic bullet. No matter which way he turned he was doing wrong by someone.

Pissed as he was that she'd lied to him, he understood her reasons and admired her fierce loyalty to her friend. What he would have given to have someone stick up for him like that when he was growing up...

Still, Logan would flip if he found out that Rhys had

gotten involved with a suspect. While security consultants might not be held to the same standard as police officers or other law agents, his boss *was* ex-military. And he ran a tight ship.

Rhys parked his car and headed up to his apartment. Maybe he should cut things off at the pass by telling Wren he couldn't see her again. It would draw a line between them, a line not to be crossed until this thing with Sean Ainslie was over.

But then what? The *only* reason she was in New York was to snoop around the gallery. Once that was tied up she'd be headed back home. He pounded his feet into the stairs as if it might expel the frustration from his body.

It wasn't worth risking his job for something temporary, no matter how much he enjoyed her company, both in *and* out of the bedroom. Perhaps it made him a boring rule-follower, but that's how he wanted to live his life. It's how he'd *always* lived his life.

And when has following the rules gotten you what you want?

Shaking off the doubt, he climbed the last few stairs to their shared floor. Cooling things off with Wren was necessary right now. At least until he had a plan for the Ainslie Ave assignment.

Rhys crossed the narrow hallway to her front door and lifted his hand to knock. Raised voices halted him and he pressed his ear to the door. It was hard to make out specific words but he could detect a man's voice, deep and forceful. A second later there was a whimpering sound and then silence.

It might be nothing. But given Wren's involvement with a man suspected of beating women, he couldn't risk ignoring his instincts. He strained to hear through the door, but everything had gone quiet.

"Shit," he muttered under his breath.

A muffled sob broke the silence, and the sound speared through Rhys's heart. Wren wasn't the kind of person to cry at anything small, but he also didn't want to bust into her apartment and interrupt something personal.

He hesitated until he heard something that sounded like "please, stop." The arguing started up again, but Wren's voice was drowned out by the deep timbre of a man.

A man who sounded a lot like Sean Ainslie.

Shit.

Rhys tested the handle, knowing that the doors didn't automatically lock when they closed. He hoped Wren's landlord hadn't installed any additional security like he had.

The handle eased down and he let out a small sigh of relief. Now all he had to do was get himself into the room and convince Sean to back down. This was well out of the realm of his training at Cobalt & Dane—he was the guy who could crack firewalls and follow a digital trail. He didn't rescue people.

The door opened soundlessly and he saw that Sean had a fistful of Wren's hair. They were facing a painting, *his* painting.

"Please," Wren pleaded. "You're hurting me."

"You need to come clean," Sean growled. "Don't make me force it out of you."

"Sean Ainslie," Rhys thundered. "You let her go right fucking now."

"Let me guess, it must be her partner in crime." Sean turned around, Wren's hair still in his fist.

"We know what you've been doing," Rhys said, stepping forward. His whole body was charged with furious energy.

Rhys wasn't a violent guy by any means—he'd always described himself as a lover, not a fighter. But all Sean could see was that Rhys had a good half a foot and at least twenty-five pounds over him. Not to mention the sight of him hurting Wren was enough to make Rhys want to Hulk smash Ainslie's face.

"You don't know shit and neither does she."

Wren's blue eyes were wide and she winced as he jerked her head. "Let me go."

"In fact," Sean continued, "I'll wager that your boss will be pretty pissed to hear that you're involved with your client's employee. That's poor form, Rhys. You're fucking her, aren't you?"

"If you don't let her go, I'll make it so that you can't use that hand ever again." He sucked in a breath, his fists shaking at his sides. "And then I'm going to make sure she presses charges for assault. I'm confident there are other women who would have a similar story to share."

Tension vibrated in the air as Sean stayed silent, his grip tight at Wren's scalp. Her head was bent to lessen the strain, but the redness around her eyes and blotchiness on her cheeks told him all he needed to know. He was going to nail Sean Ainslie to the wall. But he'd do it *his* way...by the book.

"Fine." Sean released Wren and she gasped in relief as she stumbled backward, her hands going to her head. Sean walked right up to Rhys, cocky as ever, and tapped him on the chest. "I'll still be putting a call into your boss. It's Logan, isn't it? I've met him before. Nice guy,

I'm sure he'll be keen to hear about his company's dead-weight."

"Rhys." Wren's voice was low and warning. "Let him leave."

But he couldn't let Sean go, not that easily. He thumped a hand down on the other man's shoulder and leaned in. "There's a special place in hell for men who hurt women. I will personally ensure that you end up there."

Sean laughed and knocked Rhys's hand away. "We'll see. You remember that my father is a judge, right?"

"*Was* a judge," Rhys said through gritted teeth.

"Still got the connections." Sean winked and left them alone in the apartment.

"Don't you dare go after him," Wren said, wrapping her arms around herself. Her slender frame started to shake. "I don't want you doing anything that might come back to hurt you. Although it sounds like you already have."

"It'll be fine."

"Will it?" She went to the front door and turned the lock. "He said he was going to call your boss."

"He doesn't have proof of anything."

But Rhys had no idea how Logan would take it *or* if he would believe Sean. Either way, there would be some explaining to do. Clients didn't usually accuse the consultants of sleeping with their staff and compromising an investigation.

"I'm so sorry I've dragged you into this," she said, her brows furrowed.

"This is my job. I was already involved." He closed the distance between them and reached out to touch her face. "I heard shouting coming from your apartment and..."

"Thank you," she whispered. "He showed up and bullied his way in. He was angry that I'd been talking to Aimee about him—"

"Shit, Wren." He squeezed his eyes shut. "This isn't a game. I don't want to imagine what might have happened if I hadn't been on my way over. He could've really hurt you."

"I know, I know. But he mentioned something about deleted emails. Can Quinn find it? I know Aimee deleted something from his email account, but there might also be proof that he's got something shady going on."

"We have proof. He came here tonight to threaten you."

"And what am I going to tell the police? That he pulled my hair?"

"It's assault, Wren."

"What he did to the other girls was assault." She sighed and pulled his hand to her cheek. "Maybe we can get Aimee and Kylie to press charges, and the other girls, too—"

"You need to let it go, let Cobalt & Dane handle it. I don't want you going back to the gallery." Rhys sighed. "Though after he calls Logan we will probably no longer be employed by Ainslie Ave."

"But you've got access to the security cameras, right?"

"Not if he terminates his contract with us." He held up his hand when Wren opened her mouth to argue. "But that's a problem for tomorrow."

Right now, he wanted to wrap himself up in her. The fear he'd experienced tonight had worn him down. His mind whirred with the what-ifs—what if he hadn't heard the commotion from her apartment? What if he hadn't decided to go to her in the first place? What if Logan fired him and then she left, anyway?

"You look so upset," she said softly.

"I'm not upset. I'm relieved you're safe, I'm worried about tomorrow and I'm frustrated at myself for handling things badly." He pulled her toward him. "But things are what they are—nothing we can do to change the past."

"You're right." She nodded, pressing her cheek against his chest.

He wrapped his arms around her small shoulders and let himself hold her tight. He allowed his body to enjoy the way she fitted against him, let her touch feed the gnawing ache inside him. No matter how he tried to erase his desire with logic and rules, he felt good with her. He felt…satisfied.

That didn't happen often, if ever. His life was a constant climb, chasing one thing after another. Trying to be better. Trying to be more. Trying to be worthy. But with her, all that restlessness fell away.

"Do you want something to eat?" she asked, tilting her face up to his. "Maybe some dessert?"

"Dessert is the last thing on my mind, Wren."

"Then what is on your mind?"

Tomorrow was going to be a shit show. When Sean called Logan, he could lose his job. At the very least he'd be in Logan's bad books, and that was not a place anyone wanted to be.

Screw it. He'd already fucked things up royally; he may as well enjoy tonight before it all came crashing down.

"You," he said, leaning down to brush his lips against hers. "Just you."

13

WREN SIGHED AS he peppered kisses along her jaw. His breath was heavier now, his muscular arms tightening around her. Only they didn't feel restricting, they felt like her safe place. They felt like protection. Instinct took over and she leaned forward, her tongue brushing the skin on his neck. When she drew back and looked up at him, her heart was in her mouth.

The buckle of his belt and the hard length of his erection dug into her belly. His mouth found hers, hot and desperate and open. His hands thrust up into her hair and he tilted her head back, kissing her deeply. Entirely. The world tilted around them.

"I want you, Wren, and I can't seem to stop wanting you."

He was torn; she could hear it in his voice. He was a good man, a principled man, and she'd come along and dragged him into her craziness. But she couldn't stay away from him, either. "Please," she breathed. "Don't stop."

Suddenly her back was against the wall, though she'd scarcely been aware of moving. He hoisted her skirt up, bunching the fabric at her waist with one hand, and wrenched her leg over his hip. The fly of his pants rubbed at her aching sex. She wished she'd gone commando; there was too much of a barrier between them.

His mouth was at her neck, lips sucking and tongue flicking and teeth scraping. He kissed along her jaw and found her mouth again. The faint stubble on his face lightly scratched her cheek and she knew tomorrow there would be subtle marks all over her. Marks that would make her body burn with the memory of tonight.

His hand found the hem of her top and slipped underneath it, palming her breast so slowly she thought she might explode with desperation. She reached for his belt buckle and struggled to loosen it.

"Is this a security belt?" she panted, gasping as his deft fingers found her nipple through the thin lace of her bra. Mercifully, his belt gave way.

His throaty laugh rolled over her skin, sending a shiver down her spine. "Got to protect the goods."

"You're always so cautious," she teased. "So careful."

"I don't want to be careful now." He paused his assault on her senses and rested his forehead against her. Her hand stilled at his waist.

"Why?"

His eyes were endless and deep, the warm brown gaze almost turning her to liquid on the spot. That stare could do a lot of damage; it could make her trust again. Make her feel like maybe it was okay to be her crazy, impulsive self.

"Because I know this is wrong. I should be trying to think about how I'm going to save my job…" His hands cupped her face, the pads of his thumbs brushing her cheekbones. "But I don't care."

"You should care." She closed her eyes. "Your job is important."

"Yes, it is. But nothing I do tonight will change the course of what's going to happen." His lips pressed to hers. "And right now all I want is to hold you and be as deep inside you as I can."

The words made her whole body tense in anticipation. "I want that, too."

Without warning, he picked her up and carried her to her bedroom. She locked her mouth over his, the force of her kiss almost bringing them both to the ground as they walked into the dark room. Her hand groped for the light, but he was moving too fast.

"You really need a bed frame," he groaned as he knelt down, still cradling her in his arms. She felt his muscles flex as he moved, the sheer strength of him stoking the fire inside her.

"At least mattresses don't squeak."

As he laid her down, their legs tangled. Without light all she could do was feel. Already her hands seemed to know his body, seemed to understand how to touch him.

She found the bulge of his cock trapped behind wool trousers and she cupped him. Even with the barrier, heat radiated from him. She used her other hand to bring his head down to hers. The easy slide of his tongue between her lips was almost enough to make her come on the spot.

Her fingers found his zipper and she drew it down, her mind focused on nothing but getting the hard length of him in her greedy grasp. Twisting so she could get her hands down the front of his boxer briefs, she drew him out.

"That's what I want," she whispered. He was hard as rock, pulsing and sensitive.

He swore under his breath as she thumbed the head of him, spreading a drop of precum around.

"Christ," he hissed. "You'd better slow that down."

She squeezed. "Or what?"

His lips were at her ear, his breath hot on her skin. "Or I'll have to flip you over right now and make sure I at least get inside you before I come."

An involuntary whimper escaped her. "That sounds pretty good to me."

Her eyes were slowly adjusting to the dark, and the outline of him had formed against the city lights filtering in through her blinds. The streetlights winked. Between the darkness and the reassuring weight of him pressing her into the mattress, she didn't want to move. Ever.

This was it, she realized. This was what it was like to feel loved. To feel protected and cherished. To feel wanted.

Even after all she'd done, he'd been there when she needed him.

Her chest clenched as the thought replayed over and over in her head, like a needle catching on a scratched record.

She resisted the idea—this wasn't love. It was lust, mutual attraction. Affection, perhaps, but not love.

You get that out of your head right now.

Refocusing, she worked her hand up and down Rhys's cock. His moans urged her on. The way he thrust his hips forward to meet her momentum should be enough for her. His body should be enough.

He's a great guy, but he only did what he felt was right. It's about his morals, not about you.

Then why did she want more from him?

"Stop it," he growled and she jumped, her mind automatically connecting his words with her thoughts before she realized that he couldn't know what she was thinking. "You're too damn good at that."

He brushed her hand aside and crawled down her body. His hands were on her legs, shoving the fabric of her skirt up her thighs, his lips blazing a trail from her knee to her hip. Not a second was wasted; this wasn't about teasing or about drawing out the inevitable.

He was impatient and she loved it.

"You need to stop wearing panties," he said as he yanked at the waistband of her underwear.

"Yes, sir." She lifted her hips and he undressed her roughly, without finesse.

But then his mouth pressed against her sex and all the tension in her body evaporated. His full lips worked her like he'd studied her for years. As if he knew the exact pressure, the exact speed with which to propel her into nirvana.

"God, Rhys." She reached for his head.

The steady flick of his tongue over her clit was maddening. A tremor started in her thighs as she fought to hang on, fought to make it last more than a few seconds. But he was too good for that, and soon she was flying over the edge, her hips rocking against his face while she took everything he offered her.

He had crawled up beside her before she'd even realized that he'd moved. "I love the sound you make when I'm between your legs."

"I make a sound?" She honestly could have been doing the Macarena for all she knew. When he touched her, her mind became a blank slate.

"It's like a kitten trying to growl." He was already undressing her, tugging her tank top over her head. "Sexy *and* sweet."

"I'm glad you enjoy it."

"I could listen to that sound all day."

She pushed her skirt down and wriggled until she was able to kick it off into the dark room. "I wish I could let you be down there all day, but I don't think my body could handle it."

"I'm game if you are." The sound of fabric rustling cut through the quiet, and soon he was naked and on top of her.

The hairs on his legs brushed her sensitive skin as he nudged his thigh between hers. Her teeth clamped down onto her lower lip as he guided her hand back to him.

"Oh, so *now* you want it," she teased, relishing the weight of him in her palm.

"I want it like nothing else." He shifted, easing her legs apart. "I want you wrapped around me, Wren. I want to feel how tight you are."

She fumbled around for the condoms she'd finally remembered to pick up from the store. Her fingers brushed the foil packets and she handed one over to him. The sound of foil tearing sent pleasure rushing through her like a drug.

It made everything slow down and speed up at the same time. Lolling her head against the mattress, she waited as he sheathed himself. It was sweet torture. A second later, the fat head of his cock pressed at her entrance. They hovered there, feeding off each other's anticipation. Then he plunged into her.

As he moved inside her, she wrapped her legs around

him and clung to him. His face pressed against her neck and she cupped his head, holding him to her as though it were the end.

It most likely was. In the morning he would realize he'd made a mistake, and soon she would be going home. Blinking back tears, she pressed her lips to his cheek, urging him on with soft whispers.

With a final thrust, his whole body shook. There was no air between them; there was nothing that would force them apart. Except tomorrow.

RHYS PACED UP and down in front of Logan's office. He hadn't even made it into the Cobalt & Dane headquarters before he'd been summoned with a terse email. This was it. All his hard work fighting to get people to believe in him, to believe in his talents, would be over.

Never before had he felt so conflicted. He was angry— at himself rather than at Wren. How could he have not suspected her? Was a pretty face all it took to throw him off his game?

But that was the problem, Wren wasn't just a pretty face, and that was *exactly* why he'd wanted to get close to her. She was inspiring, refreshing. She made his blood pump harder. Her spontaneity called to him, which was odd. It should have bothered him how she never planned anything or how she never spent time worrying about sensible things like buying a bed frame or throwing her underwear into a clothes hamper. She probably didn't even own a clothes hamper.

It certainly bothered him that she'd put herself into a potentially dangerous situation for something that wasn't her problem.

Yet he was breaking the rules for her. Something that went totally against his nature.

It's because you know she's right. Sean Ainslie has proved what he'll do to get his own way, and you have a responsibility to make sure you listen to the facts.

But the fact was, Wren had done the wrong thing by trying to dig into Sean's business. Still, he could rationalize his decision to keep quiet because she hadn't stolen anything and her attempt to access Sean's storage room had failed. Therefore, her indiscretions were minor. He just had to make sure they stayed that way.

You'd better hope to hell she took your advice to steer clear of the gallery.

He shook his head. If he'd been able to take the day off to make sure she didn't leave her apartment, he would have.

He pushed down the worry and tried to prepare himself for the beat down he was about to get. For a brief second he'd toyed with the idea of lying, but he'd dismissed it just as quickly. Tough but fair, that was his motto. And he hadn't gotten that way by being dishonest.

"He'll see you now," Logan's assistant said.

Rhys pushed open the door and walked in with his head held high. Sure, he'd made a mistake but he was still the same person, still the same guy who prided himself on following the rules and doing the right thing.

"What the fuck went down last night?" Logan raked a hand through his longish hair. "Sean Ainslie called me at the ass crack of dawn to say that you physically threatened him."

"Did he tell you that I threatened him *after* he attacked one of his staff members?" Rhys braced his hands on the back of a chair facing Logan's desk.

The room was bright and airy, thanks to a window that overlooked Manhattan. Yet no amount of sunlight could make this room feel warm and inviting. Logan had an air of authority that chilled even the warmest space.

"He said that he'd gone to meet one of his employees to talk about a work issue and that you barged into her apartment and threatened to break his hands." Logan shook his head. "For starters, what were you doing at her apartment after-hours?"

"She lives in the same building as I do—her apartment is the one across the hall from mine. I heard yelling."

"So you know this woman...?" He looked down at his notes. "Wren Livingston."

"She was new to my building. We'd met a few times in passing before we started investigating Ainslie's complaint." He left out the bit where she'd showed him her erotic paintings. "But I didn't know she worked for Ainslie until the day that Quinn and I went to the gallery."

"Did you make a note of it in your report?"

"No."

His brows furrowed. "Why not?"

"I didn't think she was involved."

"You mean to tell me that you immediately ruled out the employee of a client with a security breach even though the signs pointed to it being an inside job?" Logan rubbed a hand over his face and exhaled. "Why would you do that?"

"She didn't appear to have any motive."

"And you determined that how?"

This was where things got messy, because he'd determined it based on gut instinct, which wouldn't fly with Logan. Hell, if one of Rhys's employees had come to him with the same story, it wouldn't have flown with him, either.

"She didn't appear to have the skills to break into Ainslie's account."

"Because lurking in someone else's email requires a lot of technical skill, does it?" Logan held up a hand. "That's bullshit and you know it. I want you to be straight with me, Glover. Because I can tell something is going on here and I will *not* be kept in the dark."

Rhys drew in a long, deep breath. "Quinn and I came across information that indicated Sean Ainslie was assaulting his employees. Wren Livingston was able to corroborate this information for us, and then, last night, I saw it for myself. He came to her apartment and physically assaulted her. If I hadn't overheard them fighting, she'd be in much worse shape than she is currently."

"How did evidence of assault come up in the course of a routine security monitoring job?" Logan dropped down into his seat, his expression guarded but his tone no longer filled with ice.

Rhys ran Logan through everything they'd found—from the digging Quinn had done into Ainslie's ex-employees to the conversations between Wren and Aimee.

"But," Rhys continued, "what tipped us off first was that he had a monitored security service for the building and some heavy-duty protection on his storage room, but no cameras."

"According to his file, we installed the alarm system for the building about eight years ago." Logan leaned forward and looked at his laptop screen. "The security room was done five years ago. Since then we've only had the odd incident response call and two site visits for equipment maintenance. Nothing in here about security cameras."

"Don't you think it's odd to go to all that trouble with the outside of the building and for one room, but not to put cameras inside the place?"

"That is unusual," Logan said with a slow nod of his head. "But it's not our job to investigate our clients. They hire us for a purpose and we fulfill that purpose. This is a service job, Rhys. We're not the FBI."

"Is Ainslie still a client?"

Logan sighed. "I told him to take a few days to calm down and that I'd talk to you about what happened last night. In the meantime, I have promised him that you won't be going anywhere near him *or* Ainslie Ave."

"So you don't think we should intervene if people are being hurt?"

"I didn't say that." He motioned for Rhys to take a seat. That was Logan's way of saying that he was willing to listen. "But I need you to be honest with me. Are you emotionally invested in this girl?"

The question came out of nowhere. Rhys had been prepared to be asked if he was sleeping with Wren, if he felt she'd used sex to manipulate him. If he understood that getting physical with the employee of a client was wrong.

But not this.

"Answer the question, Glover."

It had started out physical. It was *still* physical. But last night had taken things to a whole new level, an emotional level. He'd slept with his arms around her, fearful that something might happen if he let her go. Even if that meant spending the night on her shitty mattress on the ground and waking up feeling like his spine had been turned into a pretzel.

It wasn't just that he was worried for her safety… He didn't want her to go home to Idaho. Realization ebbed through him like a drug. This wasn't just about seeing where things might go. He *knew* where they would go; he knew they would work together.

They would be happy.

"Yes," he said, the word making him feel relieved and yet more burdened. "I'm emotionally invested."

"Wrong answer." Logan stretched his neck from side to side. "If we're potentially going to breach our service contract, I want to be damn sure we're doing it for the right reason. And your heart is *not* the right reason."

"Is that your way of saying you believe me about Ainslie?"

"I do. He's always seemed like a cagey son of a bitch, but no one ever put two and two together before you and your team." He drummed his fingers against the desktop, his expression still unreadable. Logan had a hell of a poker face. "But that doesn't mean I'm stupid enough to keep you on this assignment. You'll hand it over to Owen and he'll run with it from now on. Quinn can support him and you can observe, but that's it."

Okay, so at least he wasn't getting fired.

"What about Wren?" He knew it looked bad to even ask, but there was no way in hell he was letting anything happen to her. Pride be damned.

"We'll keep eyes on Ainslie while this all goes down."

"Thank you."

"You're not off the hook, Rhys. Be thankful you still have a job, but I'll expect you to work your ass off to get back in my good books."

A few weeks ago those words would have ended him. But now, knowing that he was doing something for a higher purpose than just furthering himself and his career, he could take it. For Wren, he could endure a lot worse.

14

Wren sat in a meeting room at the front of the Cobalt & Dane offices, staring at a wall clock. Each time the second hand moved, it made a ticking sound that was starting to drive her insane. She didn't need a reminder that the minutes were slowly melting away.

Rhys had left her apartment in the wee hours of the morning, claiming he needed to be at work as early as possible. After he'd left, she'd tossed and turned, unable to sleep for worrying about how badly she'd messed up his life.

"Wren, thanks for coming down," Quinn said as she walked into the room, with Rhys in tow. "Sorry to drag you in here without much notice."

Relief eased through her chest. At least he hadn't been fired. "It's fine."

Rhys nodded at her but didn't say anything. The line between his eyes told her he'd had a rough morning.

"So Rhys has updated me on what's been going on with Sean, including that he came to your apartment last night. Is that correct?"

Quinn made notes as Wren relayed what'd happened,

leaving out the part about Rhys staying over...just in case that information wasn't widely known.

"We're going to monitor the gallery through the security cameras that we've set up." Quinn tapped her pen against the edge of the table. "Now, if you have any contact with either Lola or Aimee, please don't mention this. We don't want to spook Sean."

"Of course."

"We're breaking our contract with him by doing this," Rhys said. "So it's really important that we keep this activity quiet."

A lump formed in her throat. "I understand. I promise I won't say anything."

"We'll monitor the cameras for a couple of days and see if Sean accesses the storage room. I understand you think he's hiding something in there?" Quinn said, watching her with hawk-like eyes.

"That's right, but I have no idea what."

"I didn't see anything but paintings when I was in there. I made sure to look thoroughly, too, because I suspected the same thing," she said. "It was literally just dozens of paintings. Some very strange ones, too."

"Oh?" Wren tried to listen to Quinn while pretending that she wasn't slowly driving herself crazy trying to figure out what Rhys was thinking.

"Yeah, some weird paintings with vegetables that had faces," Quinn said with a shake of her head.

"Like an angry carrot with a pitchfork?" Wren asked, her blood suddenly running cold.

"Yeah." Quinn glanced up sharply.

"And a screaming pumpkin?" She knew the painting exactly—right down to the brushes that had created the strange and haunting image.

"Yes."

"They're meant to represent the plight of farmers in today's society and the issues around agricultural decline," she said, echoing the words she'd heard once before, when the idea of the collection had been conceived.

"Are you very familiar with all of Sean's paintings?"

"He didn't paint them. My friend Kylie did."

The pieces of the puzzle started to fall into place. Why Sean was so secretive about the storage room. Why Kylie had refused to let Wren come into her studio after she'd returned from New York. Why the Ainslie Ave shows seemed to be weirdly eclectic and lacking in direction.

Because none of them were Sean's paintings.

"Why would he have her paintings if she's no longer working at the gallery? Would she have sold them to him?" Quinn asked.

"He's stealing them," she said, her heartbeat kicking up a notch. "I saw him carrying a painting the other day that seemed familiar, but I couldn't place it at the time. I remember now. It looked a lot like one that Aimee was finishing up when I first started at the gallery."

"Can you prove it?" Rhys asked, his hands bunching into fists on top of the table.

"I'm sure I have a picture of Kylie while she was painting the pumpkin. She'd started working on it before she left for New York, and I told her I wanted a picture before she got famous." The image was clear in her mind—her friend standing at the canvas, wearing her pink apron as she always did when she painted. The idea was fresh, weird. She had been sure it would get her noticed in the art world.

It had. But she'd been noticed by the wrong person.

"I did think it was strange how Sean seemed to only

hire young women from small towns," Wren added. "None of us have the fancy education that most galleries require for our work. Kylie thought that meant he was looking for pure talent. The kind of rawness and honesty that some of those rich students don't have. But what he really wanted were girls who were desperate and far away from home."

How stupid had she been to come here? How stupid had she been not to stop Kylie from coming?

"I guess he figures it's a low-risk scam since none of the gallery's customers are likely to recognize the paintings of an unknown artist. And if he traumatizes the true artists, they're too scared and ashamed to say anything. But he takes the precaution of hiding the paintings in this locked room in case one of the interns happens to recognize the paintings…as I did. I told him that Kylie and I were no longer friends because I didn't want him to suspect my reason for accepting the internship, but I guess he was worried I'd see one of her paintings there."

"If we can get footage from the storage room of her paintings, that might be enough to charge him with theft," Quinn said, her face intensely serious.

Rhys shook his head. "His father was a judge. We need something concrete or else it won't stick."

Rhys was right; his father would no doubt do everything in his power to get Sean off the hook. They needed an admission from Sean on *why* he'd done what he'd done. Something he couldn't wriggle away from.

The reason she'd never seen him working on a painting himself was because he had no talent. So he stole it from others, hoping to find his golden goose.

An idea sprang to Wren's mind.

"I'll get him to confess," she said.

Rhys shook his head vehemently. "You're not going anywhere near Sean Ainslie."

"Hear me out." She held up a hand. "You can put a wire on me or give me a recording advice. I'll confront him at the gallery and get him to say that he's been stealing the paintings and abusing these women."

"No fucking way."

"Hang on," Quinn interjected. "Shouldn't we at least run this past Owen? It might be our best bet at making sure we nail this guy once and for all."

Rhys looked as though he were about to explode. She hadn't ever seen him so furious, not even last night when he'd confronted Sean. Normally he was cool, calm and collected. Ever the guy in control of his environment. But now a muscle in his jaw twitched, and his arms were folded tightly across his chest.

"Can you give us a minute?" he said to Quinn.

"Sure thing." She got up and left the room, closing the glass door with a soft click.

Neither one of them said anything at first, and Wren had to stop herself from wrenching the clock off the wall and stomping on it until that damn ticking stopped.

"You're not going in there," he said, his voice brittle. "It's too risky."

"What happens if I don't? He'll get away with it. Then he'll find another girl and do the same thing all over again. It's not right."

"I won't risk your safety for this, Wren. No way in hell."

"You're not the one risking my safety. *I* am. It's my decision to make, not yours."

"You're so…impulsive." He threw his hands up in the air. "Have you thought this through at all? What if he attacks you like he did last night? What if something goes wrong?"

"I understand there are risks, but I'm willing to take them." She drew a steadying breath. "I want to help."

He rubbed his hands over his face, his dark brows knitted together. "Think about yourself for once, Wren. Put *yourself* first. You don't have to always be looking out for other people."

"What else am I going to do?"

Since she'd come to New York, her life had been a crazy ride. But she'd felt so…free. Being with Rhys had allowed her to be comfortable in her skin, to enjoy sex, to not be ashamed of what she wanted to paint. Not only that, she'd finally been able to pick up her brushes again without being paralyzed by fear. She'd painted again because of him.

But Sean Ainslie's crimes would hang over her head unless she made sure he got his due.

"Maybe do what most people do. Get a job, find something you're passionate about…some*one* you're passionate about."

"Maybe I'm not like most people."

Part of her wanted to buy into the fantasy that she could stay in New York. Stay with Rhys. But that wasn't going to happen.

She owed it to Kylie to finally be a good friend by doing something that would actually help her heal. What she should have done in the first place—be there for her. In person.

Her friend had been right. Wren had run away because it suited her, because she'd wanted distance from her own problems. But now she knew that she had the strength to stand up to the bullies and the liars. If she stood up to

Sean and helped to put him away, then she could face the people of Charity Springs. She could return home to the people that needed her, like Kylie and Debbie.

She could be the person who'd done something good, for once.

"Then what are you going to do after this is all done?" he asked.

"I'm going home."

THE WORDS CUT right into him. Silly him, assuming she'd consider staying in New York.

Staying with *him*.

After last night he thought things might be different between them. He'd shown her that he believed her, that he listened to her. Cared about her. But apparently that didn't count for anything.

"You're going back there?" He ran a hand over his head, trying to tamp down the anger that was rearing up within him. "To that hick town where the people call you a sexual deviant?"

"It's my home, Rhys." She blinked at him, her brows furrowed. "I never said I was planning to make a life here."

"You ran away from that place because of how they treated you, and all of a sudden you're feeling the pull of loyalty." He shook his head. "I thought you hated that place."

"I'm angry about what happened to me, of course, but my family is there. Kylie is there... She needs me."

"What do *you* need, Wren?" He stood, shoving back his chair so hard it almost toppled over. "Because it's hard for me to tell whether or not you care about your future. You seem to base all of your actions on other people."

"No, I don't." Her face reddened in a way that told him she knew damn well he was right.

"No? You came here to find justice for your friend. You're now offering to put yourself at risk to get Sean Ainslie to confess." He ticked the items off his fingers. "And let's not forget how you buttered me up to make sure I wouldn't turn you in."

"That is *not* true." Her face looked as though it might crumple, but instead she stood and drew in a deep breath.

"Isn't it? Because from my standpoint, it seems like everything you've done is to serve someone else. You don't live your own life."

"I do. I spent time with you because I *cared* about you."

Cared. Past tense.

Because now she didn't need anything from him. The realization that she'd used him was like a slap across the face.

"You don't get to say that to me." The frustration tumbled out of him unbidden. "Not after you've screwed my reputation only to throw it back in my face by putting yourself in danger."

The hurt that streaked across her face wrenched like a knife in his chest. "I didn't force you to sleep with me."

"My record here has been one hundred percent clean. I have been a model employee until this. And now my reputation is on the line, and for what?"

She'd let him believe she wasn't involved when she was and, worse than that, she'd let him believe that he meant something to her. That he was important and real and visible.

"I'm sorry, okay?" She threw her hands up in the air. "It was selfish, I know that. But I wanted to help my friend and…I liked you. You were the first guy who's ever made me feel like I'm not useless and wrong. If I could change things, I would."

"Well, you can't. I'll have to earn back Logan's trust, and he's not the kind of guy who dishes it out easily."

"What do you want me to say?" she said, wrapping her arms around herself.

I want you to tell me I mean something to you.

"If you don't know what I want from you, then it's clear you don't actually care for me at all."

She looked so small and vulnerable, and his instincts urged him to bundle her up in his arms. But he couldn't touch her again, not now that he knew how little he'd meant to her. The thought of staying with him hadn't even crossed her mind.

"Are you trying to hurt my feelings?" she asked, her voice coated in frustration.

"This isn't about feelings. It's about actions."

She shook her head and sucked on her cheek, though he could still see the tremble in her lip. "Have you ever thought that maybe life isn't all black-and-white? You can't just spreadsheet everything out and use a formula to make a decision."

"Do you think that's what I did last night?" Damn it, she had a way of dragging him out of his logical mind-set into dangerous emotional territory. "Do you think I came to your apartment because a formula told me so?"

She blinked. "Well—"

"No, I came to your apartment because I couldn't stand the idea of not clearing the air between us. When I saw Sean there…" Why was he even bothering? "You know what? It doesn't matter. You've made up your mind."

"I never meant to hurt you."

"Just promise me one thing," he said. "At some point in your life, you'll start basing your decisions on what *you* want instead of hiding behind everyone else's needs."

15

WREN FELT AS if the air had been sucked from her lungs. He made her sound so…weak.

But the truth was, she couldn't stay in New York. She had no job, no purpose. When she wasn't on a mission for someone else she had no direction. What was she supposed to do? Sit around all day working on paintings that would never sell while slowly dying from the fear that Rhys would one day realize she was talentless? That she wasn't going anywhere in life?

He was a go-getter. A person totally in control of his life, of his career. He would be successful in whatever he chose to do.

"Is it so bad that I want to do right by the people in my life?" She asked, hoisting her bag over one shoulder. "That I want to help people?"

"Help yourself, Wren. One day you'll be grateful you did."

"I told you from the start that I wasn't going to be here for long. I was never planning to stay."

He nodded, the expression on his face impossible to read. He was shutting her out; she could tell from the way he looked at her, almost as if she was invisible. Like he was looking *through* her.

It hurt far more than she was prepared for.

"I'll send Quinn back in," he said. "She'll take you through what needs to happen next."

As he walked out of the meeting room and disappeared into the office, Wren blinked away tears. Perhaps it was for the best. She'd potentially damaged his career, lied to him and misled him… Why would he want anything to do with her after that?

You're doing the right thing. You're taking care of the people you care about.

But didn't she care about Rhys? Spending last night in his arms had made her feel so complete. So whole.

At that moment her phone started to vibrate and Kylie's face flashed up on the screen like a sign.

"Hey," she answered.

"Wren, I felt so bad about what I said last night." Kylie's voice was tight, her stress evident. "I'm sorry I told you not to call. I'm just… I'm messed up right now."

"It's fine. I shouldn't have pushed you," she said. "Anyway, I've almost wrapped things up here."

"Does that mean you're coming home soon?" The desperation in her friend's voice made a lump lodge in her throat.

"Your wish is my command."

"You don't know how happy that makes me. I miss you *so* much." She paused. "Are you okay? You sound upset."

"I'm fine. I'm just worried about one of the other interns," she said. It was the partial truth. Kylie didn't need the burden of Wren's relationship woes on her shoulders.

"Sean has been roughing her up and I think he's taken her paintings, too. He's got this whole scam on rotation."

"Shit. You figured that out, huh? I was too ashamed to admit that he convinced me to trust him. He was just so charming and nice, he said I had talent…"

"Kylie, you are *not* at fault for what happened to you. He took advantage of your trusting nature and he chose to abuse you. That is not on you." She paced the office. "I wish you'd talked to me about it…but I understand why you didn't."

"He made me feel like no one would believe me. Did you know his dad is a judge? He said even if I decided to report him nothing would happen because his father had gotten him off before."

"Son of a bitch," she muttered, shaking her head. She wasn't going to tell Kylie of her plans to help rope Sean into confessing; Kylie would only try to talk her out of it. "How's everything at home? Are you settling back in?"

"Yeah, I guess. I'm still really sore, but Debbie has been wonderful. She keeps visiting and bringing board games over to distract me. Last Saturday she skipped going out with her friends so we could have a movie night."

Wren said a silent thank-you to her sister. "She's got a big heart."

"So do you, Wren. Though I would have preferred you to be more like Debs and play games with me instead of going off on a vigilante mission."

"I don't want anyone else to go through what you went through."

"Me, neither." Kylie sighed. "But maybe I'm selfish and I just want my best friend to be here with me. It's much safer."

"We'll get him, Ky. I don't give a shit if his father is a judge, we're going to get proof of what he's doing." She swallowed. "He has your paintings, too, doesn't he?"

There was a sniffle on the other end of the line. "I should have said something to you about that, but he said he'd make me pay if I told anyone. I didn't even tell the therapist because I'm afraid he'll find me."

"He won't find you, Ky. I'm coming home to look after you."

"He said I owed him. That they were payment." Her voice sounded far away.

"We'll get them back, okay? I promise."

Rhys might be right about her always doing things for other people, but that was just who she was. Since it was clear he didn't understand that about her, it was probably best that she was heading back home.

A FEW DAYS later they were poised to make their final move on Sean Ainslie. Rhys had almost bitten his nails down to the quick. Technically, he wasn't supposed to be part of the team overseeing the surveillance of Wren's entry to Ainslie Ave. But he'd talked Owen into allowing him to observe in case anything went wrong from a technical standpoint.

Owen knew it was a bullshit excuse, but he hadn't argued. So long as Rhys didn't intervene in any way, he was free to observe.

They'd decided not to involve the police at this stage because it was unclear how deep of an influence Sean's father had. A corrupt judge would have many connections, and they didn't want to risk someone tipping him off. They just had to hope that Sean was cocky and stupid enough not to suspect Wren was taping him.

If he was going to bet on the reliability of anyone being stupid, it would be Sean Ainslie.

"She'll be okay, Rhys. I promise." Quinn placed a reassuring hand on his arm as they watched the screens capturing the footage from the gallery. "She's feisty. I appreciate that."

"I don't," he muttered, pretending to check his emails on his phone to avoid Quinn's raised brows.

"Bullshit, you love feisty women. How on earth would we be friends if you didn't?"

"You're my employee."

She rolled her eyes. "Next time you need help with a firewall, I'll remind you of this conversation."

"I told her not to do this." His stomach churned as the speakers wired to her mic crackled to life.

"Looks like she hasn't taken that advice."

He grunted. "It wasn't advice."

"What was it supposed to be? A command? I'm surprised she didn't tell you to shove it."

"I was looking out for her."

"No." She shook her head. "You're trying to instruct her how to live her life. Those are two different things."

"Are you saying I'm bossy?"

Quinn studiously tapped away at her laptop, making sure the recording function was set up for the Ainslie Ave cameras. "That would be putting it mildly."

"Gee, thanks."

"We're not friends, remember? I don't have to be nice to you."

God, he was really not in the mood for bantering with Quinn today. "I'm going to fire you one of these days."

She snorted. "I can see why she dumped your ass."

His head snapped up. "What the hell is that supposed to mean?"

How had she figured out that he and Wren were together? Nothing connected him to her except the conversation he'd had with Logan, and he was pretty sure his boss wasn't about to spread that information around.

"Logan said there were some complications in you working on this case. I get the impression you're not supposed to be here today."

He grunted in response.

"And I took the fact that you even knew her name to mean something was going on between you two." When he raised a brow she continued, "Normally you only care about the numbers. It's all stats and KPIs and closure rates. You never take an interest in the people side of things."

"You make me sound like a dictator."

"I get it, the numbers are an important part of your job. But there was mad tension in that meeting room when we were setting this whole thing up. Wasn't difficult to put two and two together."

He sighed and leaned back in his chair, turning away from Quinn's sharp, analytical gaze. "Doesn't matter now, anyway. As you said, she dumped my ass."

"Because you were a prick."

"That a fact or just an educated guess?" he said sarcastically.

"I'm gonna plead the Fifth on that one." She tucked her feet up under her so she was perched on the chair like some kind of punk Buddha. "So, you got in trouble, huh?"

"Dammit, Quinn. Are you trying to piss me off?"

"No." She held her hands up, but a smile tugged at the

corners of her lips. "Not at all. I'm kind of impressed actually. I've never seen you break the rules. Well, except for that one time where you accidentally put recycling into the regular trash can."

"Shut up."

"Seriously. You *never* push the boundaries. She's got to be one hell of a woman to tempt you to the dark side of employee misconduct."

Their argument was cut short when Owen called for a quick powwow over the speakers. He was near the gallery with Wren, making sure she was appropriately wired up. They had Jin, another senior security consultant, inside the gallery posing as a potential client in case things got nasty. Two more security consultants were positioned outside, ready to storm in if Jin or Wren needed backup.

But the layers of contingency didn't put Rhys at ease. He felt sick to his stomach that she was going to be walking in there to face that son of a bitch. But no amount of logical reasoning had been able to talk Quinn and Owen out of this plan. The thing was, if it had been anyone else in her place, he wouldn't have batted an eyelid.

Ainslie needed to be taken down and this *was* the best way to do it.

"Have you told her you care about her?" Quinn asked once Owen had stopped speaking.

"No," he admitted. Why would he when it was clear she never had any intention of staying? Nothing he'd done had changed that…so why cut himself open in front of her?

"No?" Quinn raised a brow. "Why not?"

"It's none of your business."

"You've been miserable ever since she offered to do this. I *know* what that feels like, trust me."

"Wren and I are not the same as you and your lover-boy."

"Maybe not. But you care about her and I haven't seen you care about many people. I have to wonder why that is."

"I made the right decision," he said, ignoring her comment. "It was tough but—"

"Yeah, yeah. Tough but fair. I'm familiar with the motto." She smiled and let the snarky expression drop. "Look, I'm not trying to tell you what to do. But, from one friend to another, maybe think about what that motto means. Tough doesn't necessarily mean you have to push people away."

"I know that."

But it was hard *not* to push people away, or at the very least keep them at a distance. It was easier not to get involved, not to risk anything. Still, Wren had managed to sneak past his barriers without him even noticing.

Pain wrenched in his chest. Why hadn't he tried harder to stop her? She didn't have the training for this. She was driven totally by her emotions and impulses, which meant she hadn't considered the consequences.

If something happened to her today...

She could get hurt and she'd have no idea how he felt; she'd have no idea that he loved her.

He sat stock-still as the truth burned through him. He loved her. It wasn't a shock; the feelings had been brewing for a while. But this was the first time he'd admitted to himself just how deep those feelings went.

What if he'd realized too late?

His gut twisted in response. Quinn was right; he'd tried to command Wren to live her life according to what *he* wanted. Instead of offering support like a decent person would do, he'd been a bossy asshole.

He made a promise then and there, as he watched Wren appear on the security-camera screen, that he would tell her he loved her when this was all over. No matter what, he would tell her.

16

WREN'S HANDS TREMBLED as she approached the gallery's front door. For all the bravado she'd mustered up when she'd decided to volunteer, not much of it had stuck around for the grand finale. She forced herself to think of Kylie and Aimee, how scared they must have been when they realized they were being played. That the man they'd fallen for was nothing more than a thief and an abuser.

She had to be brave for them.

Part of her had hoped that Rhys would be here to support her. The other part of her had been terrified that he'd show up and all her resolve would melt away. Last night she'd lain awake, tossing and turning with nerves, her stomach tied up in knots. The reality that soon she'd be leaving New York had washed over her, and instead of making her feel relieved, it made her want to cry.

She shoved the thoughts aside as she reached for the gallery door. Slowly, she drew in a steadying breath, and pushed.

The little bell above the door tinkled as she stepped inside, her head held high. This was it. All she had to do was get Sean to confess his crimes. It shouldn't be hard; he loved talking about himself. And now she had the leverage she needed to get him to confess the truth.

"Wren." Lola blinked from behind the reception desk. "What are you doing here? I thought you'd gone home to your family?"

A family emergency, that's what she'd told Lola to keep her in the dark. They couldn't risk any hint of the operation leaking to Sean. Not after the head of Cobalt & Dane had been forced to go to Sean Ainslie personally to make sure they were still employed by the gallery. Without the contract, they couldn't access the cameras.

"I need to speak with Sean," Wren said, hoping to hell her tone didn't reveal her nerves.

"He's just about to meet with a buyer." Lola nodded toward an attractive dark-haired man in a fitted black suit who was wandering around the gallery, looking at the paintings.

Wren recognized him as Jin, one of Owen and Quinn's colleagues. He was her safety net. The guy who was going to make sure she got out in one piece if Ainslie lost his shit.

"It's urgent," Wren replied.

"Gee, you guys don't make it easy for me," she said, shaking her head. "I can't believe you and Aimee both quit at the same damn time."

Aimee had quit? That news sounded too good to be true.

Lola picked up the phone and dialed the extension for Sean's office. Wren could hear his peevish tone even standing a foot away.

He won't get to treat anyone else like shit for much longer…

When he strode into the gallery, he ignored Wren and

walked straight over to Jin, hand outstretched. Then he motioned for Wren to follow him down the hall. Her heart leaped into her throat. Of course he wouldn't want to have the conversation out in the open—but how would Jin keep an eye on her if he took her out back?

"What the fuck do you want?" he asked. "If you've come here for your shitty canvas, I've thrown it out. Probably for the best. I'm not sure you have any talent."

"Then why did you hire me?" she asked, folding her arms across her chest carefully, so as not to obstruct the mic taped just inside of her blouse.

The tiny thing barely looked powerful enough to capture the voice of the person wearing it, but Owen had assured her that so long as she stood within a few feet of Sean it would record his voice, too.

"Because I liked looking at your ass," Sean replied with a cocky grin. "Too bad you haven't got anything of value from the waist up."

"Oh, so it wasn't to steal my paintings and pass them off as your own like you did with all the other girls who've worked here?"

Surprise streaked across his face but it was gone almost as quickly as it appeared. "You have no idea what you're talking about."

"Yes, actually, I do. I know everything, Sean. I know that you hire young girls from small towns because they're vulnerable and eager to please. I know that you steal their paintings and beat them up if they try to stop you. I know that you're a thief and a liar and you deserve to be put in jail."

His eyes darted around behind her. They were still in the hallway, but right at the back of the gallery. Jin wouldn't be able to hear what they were saying, but Owen would be communicating with him via an earpiece. She just had to trust that they were good at their jobs.

"And how are you so sure of all of this, Wren? Sounds like a great story to me. Maybe you should have been a writer instead of a painter."

"I've been in touch with your former employees. I spoke with Kylie and Marguerite. I've been speaking with Aimee."

At the mention of Aimee's name, a fire lit in his eyes and his mouth flattened into a thin line. "Bullshit."

"They told me that you keep the paintings in your storage room and you cover up their signatures and replace them with your own." Neither of them had said that directly, but it was an educated guess...one that was on the money if his thunderous expression was anything to go on. "Why do you do it? Is it because you have no talent of your own?"

His hand reached out so quickly she didn't have the chance to back away, and he caught her arm between his fingers. As he squeezed, pain shot through her.

"You're playing with fire, Wren. I know you're not smart, but let me spell it out for you." He leaned in so close that his breath heated her skin. Her stomach pitched violently but she managed to hold herself together. "You have nothing on me, you will *never* have anything on me and even if you did, I'm untouchable."

Wren felt a flutter of panic in her chest. Sean still hadn't given her anything incriminating. She needed to push him harder, get him to confess.

"No one is untouchable," she said. "It doesn't matter if your father is a judge. He can't save you from everything. How would he feel if he knew his son was an abusive bastard who preyed on young women? Don't you think he'd be disappointed in you?"

His fingers bore down on her, making her skin burn.

"You think he doesn't know?" Sean laughed. "I went to him after I messed Marguerite's face up just in case that mouthy bitch decided to go to the cops. Dear old Dad had a word with her and she didn't make a peep."

"So your father threatened some poor girl just to help you cover up what a piece of shit you are? I guess the apple doesn't fall far from the tree." She tried to pull her arm away but he held tight. So tight that the blood supply to her hand was being cut off. "What did you do with her paintings? Because it's not like you've made it big yet. Guess your plans aren't working out too well."

"I sold them," he said with a sneer. "Made fuck all, too. Guess she wasn't as talented as she thought."

"Or maybe you just haven't got a good eye. If you did, you would have been able to paint something decent yourself by now."

"Hardly," he snarled. "I'm scraping the bottom of the barrel with you worthless country girls. But I've found my golden ticket with Aimee."

Wren tried to shove him, her fear and anger bubbling over. But she was half his size. "You leave her alone."

"Maybe I'll work her over extra good tonight, just for you."

Tears pricked her eyes. "Please leave her alone."

"She's got what it takes, and I'm going to sell those paintings for all I can get."

"She'll leave you," Wren said, blinking through her blurry vision. "She'll realize she doesn't have to take this shit from you and she'll leave."

"No, she won't. I've got her locked up now and I'm

throwing away the key." The grin on his face was bordering on manic. "I made sure to do that after you got into her ear last time. So you can blame yourself for that one."

A sob wrenched out of her. "You're a monster."

"It's just business. Her paintings are going to make me rich."

At that moment footsteps sounded beside them and Sean released Wren so quickly her knees buckled and she dropped to the ground. Her arm throbbed as the blood started moving through it again.

"What the fu—"

"Keep your hands to yourself."

Wren looked up to see Jin pointing a gun straight at Ainslie. He stood over her, giving her a chance to stand up and scoot behind him.

"You okay, Wren?" Jin asked.

She nodded and Sean fumed at the both of them. "Get the fuck off my property. Now."

"You realize you've just admitted to holding someone against their will?" Jin said. "I thought you were despicable, but that takes the cake."

"We have to find her," Wren said, wrapping her arms around herself.

"We will. But first we're going to wait here until the NYPD arrives."

RHYS PACED THE length of his apartment, waiting for the Cobalt & Dane team to wrap up with Wren across the hall. Tonight they'd be putting her up in a hotel to make sure that she was safe—just in case Sean's father managed to get him out of holding.

Watching her go toe-to-toe with Sean had been one of the toughest things he'd ever done in his life. All he'd wanted to do was go to her, to step in front of her and protect her from that asshole. He'd wanted to dry the tears that had rolled down her cheeks once she'd finally gotten out of the gallery. Anything to make her feel better. Anything to make up for acting like a jerk when she'd volunteered to help take that bastard down.

All he could do now was hope that she'd hear him out when he told her how he felt.

After Ainslie had admitted to kidnapping Aimee, things had moved swiftly. Owen had called the police. Jin had an old buddy from his days with the NYPD who worked in the special victim's unit. They'd jumped on the case and had thankfully found Aimee within hours.

She'd seemed unharmed, but they'd admitted her to the hospital, anyway. She was in good hands now. As for Sean, he'd been taken into custody and would likely be charged with a slew of things, including kidnapping and assault.

Voices floated in from the hallway and Rhys recognized the calming tones of one of the counselors Cobalt & Dane regularly contracted. When the sounds faded to silence, he made his way to the front door. Owen had promised Rhys he could escort Wren to the hotel so long as he called the office as soon as Wren was checked in. He wasn't used to being micromanaged, but nothing could upset him now.

Sean was in custody. Wren was safe.

He walked over to Wren's apartment and knocked. This was it, confession time. When she swung the door open, he was greeted with a sight that almost tore his heart in two. Wren's face was swollen and puffy, and her cheeks were mottled with patches of pink and red.

"Don't stare at me like that," she said, dropping her

eyes to the floor. "I know I look hideous. I'm an ugly crier."

"You couldn't be ugly if you tried, Wren." He reached out and brushed his thumb along her cheek. "On the inside or the outside."

She held the door open for him, her eyes avoiding his. The second he stepped into her apartment he saw the small collection of boxes in the spot where her couch used to be. They were haphazardly stacked and didn't appear to be labeled.

"Heading home so soon?" he asked, fighting back the hurt that trickled through him like a toxin.

"Kylie is coming to get me tomorrow. Owen said they'd need me to come back at some point to testify against Sean, but I could go and be with my family for now." She drew her bottom lip between her teeth.

The careful speech he'd planned—and practiced—seemed to evaporate on the spot. He wanted to be with her more than anything, but facing her rejection was tearing him apart. Suddenly he felt like that desperate kid he'd always been, the one who'd craved his mother's attention. Who'd tried—and failed—to fit in with his new family. Who'd just wanted to be accepted.

"Are you taking me to the hotel?" She wrapped her arms around herself.

"Yeah." He nodded. "But, uh…I wanted to talk to you about something first."

"Sure. I haven't got anywhere for us to sit, though." She looked around. "And everything is all packed up so I can't make us coffee."

"I don't need any of that." He ran a hand over his hair and willed himself not to chicken out. "I wanted to apologize for the other day. I shouldn't have said the things I did."

"It's okay. I know I jump into some things headfirst." A smile tugged at her lips. "You can add 'impulsive' to my list of undesirable traits along with messy and clumsy."

"Wren, nothing about you is undesirable. The truth is, I was scared shitless about you going in there today. But more than that…" His mouth was suddenly drier than desert air. "I was lashing out because I was hurt. I was hoping you'd want to stay with me, and when you said you were going home I threw it back in your face."

"The things you said weren't exactly false. I *do* hide behind other people's problems." Her head bobbed. "I realized that today. I've spent so long 'not being good enough' that I felt like I needed to do things for people so they would like me."

"People like you for who you are, Wren. Not what you do for them."

"I understand that now. Kylie and Debbie will love me no matter what, and my parents still love me even though I might not be the successful child."

"What about *me*?" he asked, taking a step forward.

"What about you?" Her face tilted up, eyes wide.

The moment he reached for her hands he remembered all the things he wanted to say. "Do you know that I'll love you no matter what? Do you know that I'll do anything to be with you, Wren? I can't let you go without laying it out."

"You love me?"

"I do." He pulled her closer and she curled into him, her head resting against his chest. "You make me feel…

real. When you painted me, I was floored. No one has ever looked at me like that before."

"What do you mean?"

"Like they weren't trying to figure something out. When I was growing up, a lot of people would compare me to Marc or Mom. They didn't understand how I belonged, if I was adopted. If I was black or white. And then Mom didn't really look at me at all." He paused.

"I just painted what I saw."

"I like seeing myself through your eyes."

"Did you just compliment yourself?" She raised a brow and he laughed.

"I guess I did."

"Good. It's about time." Her fingers traced the buttons on his shirt. "You're so hard on yourself, it must be exhausting."

"It really is."

As he cradled her, the silk of her hair was soft under his palm. He was braced for her rejection, but painful as it would be, he knew he'd never forgive himself if he hadn't told her the truth.

"I can't figure out why someone like you would love someone like me," she said quietly. "I don't bring anything to the table. I barely function as an adult."

"You *are* an adult. Look at what you've done today— you do a lot of good, Wren. You're fearless. The world needs more people as strong as you."

"I don't care what the world needs, Rhys. I only care what you need."

"You." Rhys slid his hands up her neck and tangled them into her hair. "I need to wake up to your beautiful face every morning and see you looking at me like I matter. Like *we* matter."

"You're not going to change your mind?"

"No way. I've never needed anything more." His lips came down to hers, soft at first and then hungry. Desperate.

"I was going to come and see you before I went to the hotel."

"Really?" He brushed a strand of hair from her forehead. "What was your plan?"

"Silly, I don't do plans." She pressed her lips to his chest. "I had no idea what I was going to say. I just knew that I couldn't leave without asking whether you regretted the way we ended things. Because I did. I regret it so much."

"You don't have to regret it." He lowered his forehead to hers. "Stay."

"Okay," she breathed.

"Okay?" He never would have believed that such a benign word would one day cause the best change in his life.

"But first I need to go home and make sure Kylie and my family are okay after everything that's happened. Then I'll pack up my things and tell them that I'm moving here to be with the man I love."

"All right, but I'm coming with you."

"Deal." A laugh bubbled up in her throat. "What am I going to do for work when I'm back in New York? What about our living arrangements?"

"Listen to you with all those adult questions," he teased, bringing his mouth down to hers. "I must be rubbing off on you."

"Don't expect me to start a spreadsheet anytime soon." She screwed up her nose.

"So you love me, huh?"

Wren's eyes sparkled. "I do. You're the most kind-hearted, sexy, honest man I've ever met."

"Sexy, huh?" He wrapped his lips around her earlobe, heat surging through him when she moaned. "I like the sound of that."

"Well, we *do* have a hotel room at our disposal tonight." She grinned. "I'm assuming they have a bed frame, too."

"Oh, and here I was getting used to sleeping on the ground." He chuckled.

"Really?"

"No. It was awful."

She wrapped her arms around him and laughed. "See, didn't I say you were honest?"

Epilogue

Six months later

WREN TWISTED HER hands in front of her. Seeing her paintings up on a wall—knowing soon there would be people standing here, eyeing them critically—filled her with a strange mix of emotions. The art show was showcasing work from ten artists in total, all former employees—and victims—of Sean Ainslie.

When she'd headed back to Charity Springs with Rhys in tow, Wren had needed something positive to keep her busy. She had her man by her side, which had made her feel like the luckiest girl in the world, but she knew deep down that there was one more thing she could do to help Kylie and the other women who'd been hurt by Sean.

She straightened Rhys's portrait. It'd felt right to include it in the show; after all, it was the painting that had brought her back to art. That had made her want to be creative again. Without that painting she might have given up altogether.

But it wasn't really the painting that had healed her wounds. It was him. His hands, his mouth, his arms.

His love.

She'd wanted to do the same for the other women. So, she'd come up with the idea of the show to support Sean's victims, and hopefully to stop them from giving up their passion. To allow them to claim what was rightfully theirs.

Kylie and Debbie had taken on the tasks of organizing a space and getting the word out. Wren had rounded up the other artists. A few had declined, determined to keep that part of their lives in the past. Which she definitely understood. But eight had said yes, with three more agreeing to come along and support the cause. Wren had decided to ask for a small donation upon entry, with the proceeds to be given to a local charity for abused women.

"Everything looks amazing, Birdie," Debbie said, her hand slipping into Wren's. "This was such a wonderful idea."

"I hope it goes well. I don't want to let these girls down."

"You won't. Just the fact that you're doing this means so much to them, and it means the world to Kylie." Debbie rested her head on Wren's shoulder. "I know Mom and Dad don't always see why your art is important, but I do. You have a good soul and the way you share that is through your paintings. I'm so proud of you."

"Thank you." Wren pulled Debbie into a hug.

"Careful!" She touched a hand to her hair, laughing. "Do you know how much I paid for this blowout? Damn, Brooklyn is expensive. I have no idea how you're going to be able to afford to live here."

"I don't get blowouts at fancy salons, for one." She drew a breath, the nerves prickling along her limbs, filling her with buzzing energy. "And I got lucky—a local community center hired me based on all the volunteer work I'd done back home. They're not paying me a fortune, but it's something."

"I don't want to hear that you're living on baked beans and toast, okay?"

"So now you're my nutritionist as well as my doctor?" She nudged her sister in the ribs.

Having the support of her sister had made the move a lot easier. As for her parents...well, they loved her in spite of her impulsiveness, and that was all that mattered.

She glanced over to where Rhys stood talking to one of the other artists. He looked so handsome tonight in his dark suit and crisp white shirt. It made his brown skin gleam and his eyes sparkle. If they weren't at such an important event, she'd be dragging him out back so she could show him just how sexy he was. Just how much she loved him.

The word made a lump form in her throat. For an artist, the idea of love shouldn't be so scary, especially not when she'd survived having her work and reputation ripped apart by a whole town.

But it was utterly terrifying in the best way possible.

Earlier, she'd rounded up everyone involved in the show and they'd toasted with champagne to a successful evening. To triumph over horrible people and to never letting your dreams die. Seeing them all—especially Kylie—with smiles on their faces, nervously chatting and swapping stories about their art, warmed Wren.

Aimee hadn't been able to make it; she wasn't out of the woods physically or emotionally enough to face the past. But she'd sent her love in the form of a huge bunch of flowers and a promise that they would talk soon.

It was also great to see just how different everyone's

styles were. Kylie had her vegetables; Marguerite had the most beautiful garden landscapes. There were Fauvist birds, abstract flowers, Pop Art portraits. Then there were Wren's nudes, alongside Rhys's handsome face.

From a distance Wren could see the monochrome style of her paintings—all earth and flesh tones. It had taken her a long time to cultivate a theme for her work, to get comfortable in the voice with which she painted. But the people viewing her work seemed to be enjoying it.

"I can't believe you put my ugly mug up there with all those beautiful women." Rhys's voice ran down the length of her spine, making her shiver.

"I happen to think it's quite an attractive mug," she replied, turning to face him. "I wouldn't have painted it otherwise."

This close, she could easily breathe in the smell of soap and a bare hint of cologne on his skin. She'd come to crave that smell because it was uniquely him.

"This is an incredible thing that you've done, Wren. You've taken something ugly and transformed it into a thing of beauty."

"I know it won't change what happened to these women, I know that they'll always be affected by what he did to them. But if this helps them find the strength to keep going, then…that's a good thing, right?"

"Yeah, it's a good thing."

The sound of conversation and clinking glasses filled the air. The gallery was getting full, and all Wren wanted was to have Rhys all to herself. They had a hotel room close to the gallery for the night, a treat that he'd insisted on.

"I regret ever giving you a hard time for looking out

for other people," he said, his hand linking with hers. "You have such a kind soul. I really love that about you."

"Really? I thought you loved me for my brownies." She sipped her champagne and looked up at him, a smile tugging on the corner of her lips.

"Well, that too. Kindness and brownies, it's a good combination." He grinned. "In fact, it's such a good combination that I want to make sure it's part of my life forever."

"I'm not going anywhere..." Wren turned to give Rhys a playful shove when she noticed he'd dropped to one knee.

He held a box out to her, the plush velvet insert cradling a single, sparkling diamond that captured every color of the rainbow in its fractured light. "Wren Livingston, you're the best person I know. Your kindness and messiness is unsurpassable. I could not think of anything I want more than to spend the rest of my life living in your colorful, chaotic world."

"You do?"

All eyes in the gallery were now on her, the anticipation palpable in the air. Given Rhys's fear of rejection, his proposal was sweet on so many levels.

"One hundred percent."

"Not a hundred and ten?" She couldn't stop herself from laughing.

"There is no more than one hundred percent." He took the ring from the box and reached for her hand. The band was a perfect fit. "Will you marry me, Wren?"

"Yes," she breathed, and the whole room erupted in applause. As he stood, he swept her up into his arms and brought his lips down to hers.

"I guess I should have asked if you'd keep making me brownies for the rest of my life," he said as he pulled back.

"Too late. Bargaining time is over." She wrapped her arms around his neck. "You'll just have to take me as I am."

"That's all I've ever wanted."

* * * * *

LET'S TALK
Romance

For exclusive extracts, competitions and special offers, find us online:

- facebook.com/millsandboon
- @MillsandBoon
- @MillsandBoonUK

Get in touch on 01413 063232

For all the latest titles coming soon, visit
millsandboon.co.uk/nextmonth